SONGS MY MOTHER TAUGHT ME

SONGS
MY MOTHER
TAUGHT
ME

A NOVEL

HELEN WINSLOW BLACK

FOUR ELK PRESS
Buena Vista, Colorado

Four Elk
Press

ISBN (paperback): 979-8-9904180-0-4
ISBN (ebook): 979-8-9904180-1-1

Library of Congress Control Number: 2024913340

Cover and interior book design:
Olivia M. Hammerman (Indigo: Editing, Design, and More)

My thanks to Betsy Thorpe. —H.B.

to my mother, her mother, my daughters

"Somewhere in the heart of experience there is an
order and a coherence which we might surprise
if we were attentive enough, loving enough,
or patient enough. Will there be time?"

—Lawrence Durrell, *Justine*

"We say of some things that they can't be forgiven,
or that we will never forgive ourselves. But we do—
we do it all the time."

—Alice Munro, *Dear Life*

Contents

Part One

The Real Marriage

Chapter 1

The Kindness of Strangers

NATHAN CLIMBED EAGERLY INTO THE STROLLER WHEN WE got to the Baltimore airport. He'd just turned three, but I was six months pregnant, and the stroller would make the walk easier. He checked to make sure his stuffed puppy was in his backpack, then zipped it up and settled back. The tiny backpack was new: red, white, and blue, with shiny stars along the sides. We'd bought it a few days before in preparation for the trip. He'd picked it out himself. And that was when I'd said it. "You get to go on a big plane to see Daddy Larry," I said, "and Smooshy can come in your new backpack!"

I'd told him more than once, sprinkling it into our daily chatter, always in the same words, never failing to add, "A nice lady named Leeza will go with you!" But of course he really didn't understand. The names were meaningless. I was sure of that. He had no idea what was going to happen—that's what I'd said to my husband this morning when I saw dawn's early light fingering through the bedroom shutters. "He has no idea," I said, staring at the ceiling. "No idea."

John rolled over, hooked an arm around my waist, and pulled me in. "He'll get through," he said. "Kids are resilient. He'll get through it. And then he'll be home." He put a warm hand on my growing belly.

Home. The sun brushed a gleam on the brass handles of my grandmother's oak dresser and warmed the walls to a beautiful ocean blue. The color I'd painted it when we moved in.

"Do you want me to go with you?" he asked.

In our ocean bedroom, we were a little raft in calm seas, and he was my anchor. I knew what a real marriage was like now, because I'd had the other kind, with Larry. With Larry, it had always and only been about what I could do for him. I was an object of utility. That might sound like an exaggeration, but it wasn't. Hard as it was for me to believe, I'd gotten myself roped into that kind of relationship. My sister once mused to me, "Even people with high IQs can be stupid" and then rushed on to say, "Not you, of course. I don't mean you," but she did. Kind of. I knew now: Real marriage was about reciprocity. And John and I were there for each other.

And sometimes just knowing that was enough.

I put my hand on top of his. "I can do it," I said. "You have to go to work. This is my job. I'll be okay."

"Then don't forget to take your cell phone. Call me if you need to." I'd had that flip phone for almost a year and was supposed to keep it in my purse for safety reasons when I went out, as all my friends did, but it mostly sat on the kitchen counter.

"I promise," I said.

"I mean it," he said. He turned my chin so that our eyes met and tapped my belly with each word. "Call. Me."

Now I trudged through the terminal, pushing Nathan past clusters of people all in unaccountably high spirits: here, high school kids in matching team jackets, goofing with one another while trying to ignore their hovering parents; there, a family group with shiny balloons and a "Welcome Home" sign. Everyone was here for a happy occasion, it seemed—everyone but me. And the gate areas were so jammed, I could barely make my way through. I wiped a sheen of sweat off my forehead. Even at train stations, I thought irritably, you had to be a ticketed traveler to get to the platform. Why couldn't they do the same at airports? I was trying to meet someone I'd never even met, for heaven's sake. I felt in my purse for the envelope. Yes, there it was. The snapshot Larry had mailed me of his fiancée. I pulled it out for another look. Would I find this person, this Leeza, in such a crowd?

Suddenly I did. Down the terminal, there she was, leaning against a pillar with her arms crossed. I recognized her from a distance; you couldn't miss that hair. Beneath those aggressively peroxided spikes, I could see her snap her gum, likely to keep the embers of internal hostility smoldering in a controlled fashion. The woman was a real clothes horse: skintight jeans, a peacoat with an upturned collar, and an expensive leather bag strapped across her chest. Knee-high platform boots—I hated platform boots. But the worst part of the getup was the toy plane dangling from the fingers of one hand.

There she was, the girlfriend, free to flit across the friendly skies with her groovy messenger bag and a wallet amply lined by Larry for purchases of lattes, fashion magazines, and sparkly new toys with which to entice young children not her own. And here I was, Larry's ex, sweating, dressed in what amounted to a circus tent with armholes, awkwardly lumbering along with the stroller, as it grimly dawned on me that I was sending my child three thousand miles on a plane with a complete stranger who chewed gum like a cud.

I took a sharp turn into the restroom.

A long, frosted glass window tempered the fluorescent lighting with a welcome natural glow. Sanctuary. I set my bag down on the wide marble window ledge and unfolded the changing table from the wall.

A woman at the sink with dripping hands tipped her head at the dispenser. "That one's empty," she barked to the custodial worker entering behind me, who replied, "I just do the bins," then turned to me and shrugged.

I smiled back. I'd taken her for my own age, but on second glance recalculated: She had the open countenance of a teenager. With difficulty, I lifted Nathan onto the table. He'd been toilet-trained for three months, but I'd put him in pull-ups for the long trip to be safe. He didn't need changing, but I was stalling. The day had come, and my heart was pounding.

It had been eight months since I'd flown into this airport to begin afresh, to start married life for real. John had moved to Maryland ahead of me, during which time he'd acclimated to his new job at Harkin Guaranty's Baltimore office. Once he knew the lay of the land, he put in an offer on a home in a nearby development coveted by junior executives as an affordable place to start a family in the upscale Cross Keys area. Wedged onto the site of a demolished school, the neighborhood of traditional brick row houses put in its place had luxurious updates—central air, three bathrooms instead of one—and circled a green space with its own playground. John could have sold me on a canvas platform tent, I was so happy to start our life together. It was going to be a new life, happily distant from Nathan's father, who was uninterested in his child and would conveniently fade into the wings.

Or so I'd hoped.

My former husband had perfected torture-by-legal-system to a fine art. Larry dragged out our divorce proceedings for two years, and then, when finally forced into court, refused point-blank to agree to the visitation plan recommended by the court-ordered psychologist. Or indeed any visitation plan. The judge had no idea what to do with a father who lived two thousand miles away from his toddler son. So finally, because she wanted to go home to dinner, she kicked the can down the road, issuing a final divorce and a temporary visitation plan—four nights a month in Tulsa.

And then, shortly thereafter, I remarried and moved to Baltimore.

Larry, who may have been crazy but wasn't dumb, immediately filed an emergency motion demanding I send two-year-old Nathan round-trip to Seattle for two weeks each month like an express package. Emotional blackmail! I hired a lawyer, and she bludgeoned him down to one week but got no traction on the location. The best she could do was persuade him to put off this cross-country travel until after Nathan's third birthday. Until then, the one-week visitation would be in Baltimore. Which he never exercised for all those months. Because he couldn't be bothered to get on a plane.

Even now, I reflected. He'd sent his lackey.

The cleaner was waiting for me to finish. As soon as I latched the changing table back into the wall, there she was, maneuvering the cart into the corner with the precision of one for whom imaginary lines were very important. Then she saw me struggling to lift Nathan up to the sink.

"No, no! There's a stepstool." She looked under the counter, and her face creased with concern. "There's always a stepstool here, but it's gone. I can pick him up if you want. I work here," she said, showing me the laminated card clipped to her belt loop.

Nathan never knew a stranger and raised his arms immediately when she bent down to pick him up. I leaned over and pumped his soap.

She shifted him on her knee. "Lotsa suds! Gotta do a good job for Mommy!" CHARM CUSTODIAL was stitched on the pocket of her polo shirt, and underneath, Violet.

"Violet—what a pretty name! Say thank you to Violet," I instructed.

"Ba!" Nathan said, as she slid him down.

Slowly I rummaged in my purse, slowly I reapplied lipstick. I wanted to stay in here with Violet. I felt safe with Violet. She radiated good will, whereas I could see even from a distance that Leeza was prickly. I watched Violet put on latex gloves, lift the round top off a pebble-textured waste can, and show it to Nathan.

"Look! A metal doughnut!" she said, then turned to me. "Not really. I was just making a joke for him."

She put it back and reached into one of the narrow receptacles slotted beneath the towel dispensers. "Now, these ones, only paper towels s'posed to go in these. But people put *everything* in 'em." She fished out a soda can and held it up triumphantly. "See? I have to take care of it." She put the can into one of the hampers hanging from the cart, then stuffed a sports section from *The Sun* into a different one. "They're getting new bins in the summer, out there. Paper in one, cans in another, different colors, so you know which is which. Don't know if they can do that in the bathrooms, though. Ain't might be enough room."

"That will make your job easier, won't it?"

"No, *ma'am*. You can't never make people do the right thing all the time, even when you spell it out. They just don't notice, or don't care. I'll still have to make sure of things." She stripped off her gloves. "You can't never count on people doing the right thing. I'll still be in charge. That's what they told me," she said proudly, lining up her cart again and taxiing into a neat three-point turn. "I'm in charge."

I carefully pulled a comb through Nathan's downy hair and then my own and refastened my ponytail. Things were simpler for Violet, not because she was doing simple things, or simpler things than I had to do, but because she was sure she was right. Well, I thought I was right too; I *knew* I was right. That this whole thing was wrong. But I wasn't in charge.

The minute we had achieved jurisdiction in Maryland, we tried to get the temporary visit location changed back to Baltimore; Nathan would be three soon, and the dreaded cross-country travel was looming. But the judge didn't bite. Instead, he scolded us for filing an emergency motion just because the mother regretted agreeing, for a brief time, to seven nights of cross-country travel, and she needed to cooperate, because what that child *really* needed was not a series of piecemeal, temporary motions but to have a finalized, permanent plan. Which was already set on his docket, so stop wasting his time, because he'd rather do the whole thing at once, and soon.

Soon, I thought. I knew what that meant. The mills of justice, like those of God, ground slowly. "Soon" was a very elastic term in the law, and "soon" where tiny children were concerned was always "too late." As witness. I buckled Nathan back in the stroller, pushed it out, and trudged closer: Gate 16, 18, 20...

Leeza caught sight of me, and I could see the tumblers spin, then lock into place: *evil bitch ex-wife.*

I shored up beside her and smiled gamely. She ignored me and focused all her sparkling attention on Nathan, kneeling down to introduce herself and present the toy, on which, of course, his eyes were riveted.

As she straightened up, the klieg lights switched off bank by bank, and by the time we were eye level, her face was shuttered, although a trace of a sneer played about her lips. "I know you're having some difficulty with the transition. I hope you understand it will be best for him if you embrace this with a positive attitude."

You arrogant bitch, I wanted to hiss. Instead, I stuck out my hand. "Pleased to meet you."

For a brief second, this unmanned her. She took just my fingers, gave them a little shake, and forced a smile.

"Look, Mama!" Nathan had discovered the pilot in his toy could be taken in and out like a peg. I made admiring noises and released him from the stroller, then showed Leeza the supplies zippered into his tiny new backpack.

She patted her messenger bag. "We won't need any of that. I came fully equipped."

"This is where we keep Smooshy," I went on, opening the front pocket. "He'll need Smooshy. He's very important. Don't lose him."

"I *do* understand security objects." She handed the little floppy puppy to Nathan, then crouched down again. "Nathan, can I meet Smooshy?"

Smooshy was duly deposited into Leeza's hands. She handled the stuffed toy gently and made a show of conversing with it. Nathan smiled. I tried to remind myself that, despite the pixie-cut-meets-electric-socket hairstyle, this woman was on the verge of earning a master's in psychology and had, by all accounts, capably raised a son herself, who was nine. This boy would probably be a better companion for Nathan than Larry, who during his single visit to Tulsa, back when, had shown he hadn't a clue what to do with a toddler. My son would be in safe hands, and for that I should be grateful.

Smooshy's ears flopped from side to side. *Nathan! Do I get to come on the airplane with you?*

Nathan nodded vigorously and reached for the puppy, but she evaded his grasp.

So is it time to say bye-bye to Mama now?

He frowned, then stuffed Smooshy back in the pocket, zipped it up laboriously, and pushed it at me. "Pack-pack."

"Why don't I take that?" Leeza said.

Nathan grabbed my leg.

"Let me get him a little treat at the news shop," I suggested, handing her the bag and peeling his fingers off my knee. Leeza pressed her lips together in a thinly veiled concession of defeat and sat down with pack-pack while I carried Nathan to the concourse shop.

Why was my outgoing toddler not cottoning to this woman? Was he picking up on my jangled nerves? I slid him down and held him by the hand as he picked out his own snack. Someone touched my elbow, and I turned around to see an elderly woman in a formal suit that made me break out in a sweat just to think about being covered in wool on such a hot day.

"Aren't you on that plane to Seattle?" she said kindly. "You'll be boarding soon, dear. They're going to start the extra time soon, and it looks like you might need it." She patted Nathan's head. "It never works to rush the little ones, does it?" She smiled, and he beamed at her, holding up his bag of chips.

Back at the gate, Leeza was prepared. She knelt down and showed him a photograph. "Look at this! This is Daddy. We're going to visit him. Remember Daddy?"

He shook his head. "Home. Daddy's home."

He meant John, of course. How would he know who Larry was? He'd never lived with him and hadn't lain eyes on him for an entire year, which was 33.33 percent of his whole lifetime. From this perspective, flying him across the country for a week verged on the cruel. But there was nothing we could do about it.

"Home," Nathan said again.

Leeza and I exchanged glances. We were now united in but one goal: making a very small child as comfortable as possible in an impossible situation. Reluctantly, I took the photo.

"Look, Nathan. Look, Puddin'. Daddy Larry! Remember I showed you the other pictures of Daddy Larry? You get to have the fun *plane* ride with Leeza now and visit Daddy Larry. I'll see you when you get back! Look!" I pointed out the window. "There's your plane."

"Okay," he said matter-of-factly.

"'Daddy Larry'? You really shouldn't do that." Leeza shook her head. "You should call him Daddy. He needs to learn. It's not healthy."

"There's what should be and what works." I drew a breath. Quickly, before I lost my nerve and changed my mind, I opened my wallet and took out two pieces of folded-up paper, worn almost to illegibility and falling apart at the creases. My old restraining order, detailing the abuse. "I have something. You probably don't want to see it, but I feel like I should show it to you."

She took it with two fingers, as though it might be radioactive, unfolded it, and emitted a small gasp.

Nathan, chip in hand, looked from her to me and back again.

Leeza's eyes narrowed, and her upper lip rolled in disgust. "I shouldn't have talked to you," she hissed. "He *told* me not to talk to you. He *warned* me."

A sari-clad woman nearby with a baby in her arms was staring at us. I wanted to be in her world, over there. Not mine. She looked so calm and elegant, while here I stood, making a public scene. I felt sick to my stomach.

"I needed to show you," I stammered. "I mean, I can't *not* have done it."

"He *said* you'd try something. It's a pack of lies," she blared, while the woman pulled her other child close to her knee, a boy a little bit older than Nathan who had been shyly watching him play. "You're obviously a very sick person. I've kept myself from saying anything like that, but I'm telling you now. I want you to know that I'm not going to let that impact the way I deal with Nathan. At all." She folded the paper back up, ripped it in half, then in half again. "I can't imagine anything more inappropriate at this moment. And, under the circumstances, I think it's a very good thing for Nathan to develop a bonding relationship with his Other Parent."

She took his hand and marched to the end of the boarding line, thrusting the paper scraps into the waste can on her way.

Crimson faced, I followed and sank down on the bench of turquoise vinyl seats. What was I thinking? Did I think she was going to say, "Thank you! I see the light!" No. Of course not. But I didn't think she'd throw a public hissy fit.

Suddenly, I felt it all over again: the blows to my head while I held Nathan, inches above his fragile infant skull; the forced sex to prove that *he* wasn't being inconvenienced, that *he* was more important, while I held the baby in my arms. He hated the baby, but now the baby had to be flown across the country like an expensive parcel, just because he could make that happen. Because he was the father. He was important. He had rights. I'd wanted someone else in that household to know about Larry's past behaviors and be watchful. He'd be all alone with that baby, three thousand miles away from me. Leeza was the only one who would stand between them, and I'd just made her hate me even more than she already did, which was quite a feat. Clearly, this was not the best of all possible worlds.

I scooted along the row to keep pace as they shuffled forward in line, behind the Hindu family. Nathan was now on his hands and knees, executing loop the loops with the plane as they moved along. Nathan fed the pilot in between dive-bombs, which meant offering him a chip and then putting it in his own mouth. Each time he looked over, I smiled and gave a little wave, then scooted down a seat.

We'd reached the podium. The flight attendant held out her hand, and a frown appeared on Leeza's face as she realized the boarding passes were not in her hand. She flipped open her messenger bag, looked down, then up, down again, clapped her hands on her back pockets, and then, swiftly, fixing me with a glance of pure hatred, she dumped the bag at my feet and dashed back to the waste can, where, unfortunately, everyone else about to board had just thrown their messy garbage. She peered in, then—failing in an attempt to remove the lid, one of Violet's "doughnuts"—she stuck a manicured hand into the circular opening and went fishing until she found what she was looking for.

She laid the boarding passes on the seat beside me, opposite the podium, and attempted to wipe grease and ketchup off with a tissue. I offered an antibacterial hand wipe; she took it without making eye contact. Then she gathered herself, straightened up, and extended the torn and sodden remains of the boarding passes to the attendant, who took them reluctantly between thumb and forefinger.

I smiled and waved kissy fingers bye-bye as Leeza towed Nathan through the door. He swiveled around twice more on the jet bridge, and I was ready each time, holding the folded-up stroller and blowing kisses, while a hot flash slowly crept up my Judas neck and down my Judas arms. He disappeared from view.

I went to the restroom and threw up three snack chips, then scooped water from the sink to rinse my mouth. The room now felt cold, not soothing and safe. Nathan's third birthday had seemed so far away when we'd made this agreement! In his living memory, my son had never spent a single night away from me. I felt for the cell phone in my purse, a touchstone, and then went back to the gate. I couldn't leave yet. Nathan might be looking out his plane window, trying to see me. I sat down by the window and tucked the stroller under my feet.

"So you're not on that flight?"

It was the woman from the concession stand. She dipped her head conversationally at the window. Her jacket was draped over her shoulders, and she was knitting.

"No," I said. "Not me. Just my little boy."

The needles halted. "By himself? Isn't he too young for that?"

"Not by himself." I belted my hands and smoothed them over my dress, until they were firmly anchored beneath my belly.

Outside, the suitcases were loaded and the conveyor pulled away, but I could still count four workers, engaged in whatever task came next on the list. They were wearing reflective vests and ear protectors.

"Not by himself," I repeated. "He's with someone," I added needlessly, then folded my lips in.

The needles resumed. "You're wise to wait. I always wait until the plane takes off. You never know."

"What do you mean?"

"I remember once, a few years ago, my daughter got on and I left, and then they made everyone get off again. I can't remember why. Needed to repair something? She had to sit in the airport for five more hours. All by herself. We could have stayed together. Had dinner. She lives in Seattle, moved there about twelve years ago. I always come with her to the airport. She tells me not to, but she's my one and only, and I wanted to see her off."

Her pearls matched her ivory blouse. She'd dressed up for the trip to the airport; Baltimore really *was* Charm City. I shifted toward her, glad for conversation.

"What does she do in Seattle?"

"She works for FEMA. Started out a long time ago in D.C. She's the deputy administrator for Region Ten in Seattle. Deputy administrator." She inclined her head toward me, smiling. "Hard to let her go…She's my one and only. We lost her brother in Vietnam. But it was a good move for her."

Outside the window, the carts and trucks were driving away, and a flagger stepped briskly out while two others removed the wheel chocks.

"She's been asking me since her daddy died to move out there, but I don't know. Maybe I will. Maybe it makes sense. I'd said no, but now I'm starting to feel a little lonely."

She gazed out the window. The hands clasping the knitting needles were the boniest I'd ever seen, a stark landscape of ridges and valleys, completely devoid of fat, as though life had worn it all away, leaving her skin the thinnest of cloaks over vein-embroidered spatulate bones. They gave away an age one would never have guessed from her eyes and thus formed the true and graven map of her life, into which was etched every path she'd ever walked: every diaper, every dish, every diploma, every folded flag.

I looked at the back of my own hand, then made a fist and squeezed. I could see the tendon flexing in my wrist. "Maybe you should," I said. "Move."

The plane backed out, executing a glacial three-point turn into the taxiway. I felt a punch to the gut, and my eyes welled.

She turned to me. "When I say goodbye to my daughter, we say a little prayer together. Would you like to know what it is?"

I nodded mutely.

She set her knitting aside and moved into the empty seat between us. I closed my eyes and folded my hands, and she put hers over mine. "*May the Lord bless you and keep you,*" she prayed. "*May the Lord make His light to shine upon you. May the Lord watch over all your goings out and comings in, until we meet again.*" Her hands were fragile and weightless as a dandelion puff, yet warm and full of strength. That a father could be so cruel, and strangers be so kind. How grateful I was for the kindness of strangers.

"Amen," I whispered. "Amen," I said, and opened my eyes. The plane was gone.

Chapter 2

Leaving Tulsa

I DROVE MY VERY PREGNANT SELF HOME FROM THE airport alone, thinking: This was *not* how things were supposed to turn out. Almost a year before, I'd left Tulsa accompanied by a cloud of butterflies, and I'd taken that for a good sign, in the nature of a blessing. Confirmation that I was taking the high road, the path of determination, courage, and optimism.

But this? That jet bridge corridor did not look like the high road to me, and that there would be such a turn of events had not even remotely occurred to me when John had taken the Baltimore job offer. On the contrary, I'd rejoiced that it meant we wouldn't have to live in the same city as Larry. I'd taken it, I recalled bitterly, as a good sign. But watching confusion dawn on my son's little face as Leeza towed him down the that carpeted tunnel, I felt utterly helpless. More helpless than I'd ever felt before and more responsible for his pain. Was I a good mother? Was I doing something wrong? And now I had dragged a new husband into this protracted mess. Not that John was complaining. That's one of the things I'd always liked about him—John was incredibly calm. He probably had the lowest blood pressure of any lawyer I knew. My sister, Karen, was always touting self-help books to me that encouraged viewing difficulties as opportunities. But that kind of optimism wasn't working for me now. All I could think was: What am I doing wrong?

THE YEAR BEFORE, MY DIVORCE had been finalized at last, and I was moving. It hadn't been a snap decision; the realization had grown on me as I plowed through two years of divorce proceedings while finishing law school and caring for my baby son, and the realization was this: Tulsa was not my home. My future lay elsewhere.

Where was I headed? Chicago might have been the logical choice, but I didn't want to be *that* close to family. I had to strike out on my own, find my footing without having to worry about scrutiny from my mother. My sister, Karen, and I got along just fine. We'd always been close. As children we were blond, blue-eyed birds of a feather: I wore her clothes, had her teachers, got her grades, and even chose her musical instrument—the cello. I looked up to her in every way, and there had never been any competition between us. We were both entirely too good-natured for that. I was actually *excited* about hand-me-downs; every spring, every fall, my own little personal store of gently worn clothing, surreptitiously coveted all year long, would appear magically on my bed one day in neatly folded piles. I didn't have a store-bought dress of my own until I had a growth spurt at age twelve and drew eye level to Karen. From then on, we each had to have our own clothes.

But my mother was another matter. She did not treat us the same. Admittedly, I'd been a bit more of a handful than Karen as a child and maybe even more than my active little brother, because he, of course, was not expected to be demure. I was more unkempt—bobby pins flying out of my hair, knee socks falling down—and more talkative, too: I was always asking questions. I always wanted to know *what* and *how* and *why*. Why does Grandma grow tomatoes when she can buy them at the store?

What's a limerick? Is a penguin a fish or an animal? How do bridges stay up? Why do you iron the sleeves first? Why is the sky blue? My father was very patient with these questions and sometimes drew me pictures to explain. My mother, less so, but admittedly she bore the brunt of it. She complained about my *why, why, why* to my father until one day he took her by the shoulders and gave her the impish grin she could never resist, planted a big kiss on her mouth, and said, "Congratulations! Looks like we've got another Wellesley philosophy major in the making!"

For some reason, this shut her up.

Altogether, I'd had a happy childhood, almost annoyingly placid, under the roof of two people who loved each other very much. In adolescence, I did get used to being taller than my sister, but when I grew exactly as tall as my mother—we even had identical voices; her friends mistook us on the phone—I felt the chill of a new, critical scrutiny whenever I was around her. I was confused because it was directed only at me. When my sister came home from college, I asked her about this, and Karen agreed. "She gets on your case more," she said. "But I think it's because you're younger, so she worries more." She hesitated. "And—you're more *like* her."

Thinking back on that long-ago remark of my sister's, I realized that it wasn't too much of an exaggeration to say the last time I'd truly felt approval from my mother was when I'd graduated. From Wellesley. As a philosophy major.

After that, she seemed critical of my life choices, her oblique remarks delivered with the air of reasonable objectivity befitting a philosophy major. And now, though well over thirty and a law school grad, I was still fighting this covert battle. This was why I picked Minneapolis as my destination, which was a whole lot closer than Tulsa and far less expensive than the Windy City. Shouldering the rent on a nice apartment would be difficult on my own, though, with day care costs so high. So I sold my friend

Max on moving with me. It wasn't a hard sell; I knew he was ready to leave the South. He wanted to see more of America, and I needed an apartment mate, so we were joining forces to accomplish tandem goals, with no romance between us to complicate matters. I was declaring a moratorium on romance. Given the way I'd disastrously torpedoed my relationship with John, it was imperative.

At graduation, my classmates maintained the polite fiction that I was headed to Seattle to join my husband, who'd moved ahead of me due to a job offer. But the next day, John came over to say goodbye on his way out of town. He wanted to show me his new car, he said, but we both knew that was a pretext. After I'd admired it, I told him the truth of my plans: I was staying in Tulsa, renting an apartment, and filing for divorce.

He'd looked at me in delight and relief and wrapped me in a hug. "Kim, you're doing the right thing," he'd said. "The right thing for yourself and for Nathan." Though I was tall, I fit well beneath his chin; with my head against his chest, I heard his voice through my bones. He let go then and grinned down at me. He had wonderful dimples and a cleft in his chin I could hardly resist. "I won't say I'm sorry, though," he went on. And then he kissed me. A kiss that lasted me for over a year, a kiss that had been, I later and regretfully supposed, the highlight of our relationship, because when he'd finally flown back to Tulsa to visit me after a year of long-distance dating, I'd felt compelled, on that last wonderful day, to confess my active sex life.

I had three interviews lined up in Minneapolis. And I did have some funds: I'd achieved a small property settlement on the bungalow Larry had sold out from under me and was allowed to keep my car, which I'd promptly sold. Larry had picked out that car; it belonged to my old life. I'd buy a new one in Minnesota. But as for immediate income, there was little. Larry's monthly child support during the two years of pendency had been based on minimum wage only, because his finances were so nebulous. The final award was doubled, which sounded nice until I realized double $62 was only $124 a month. There was, of course, no spousal support; I'd waived that after Larry's lawyer threatened to request it of *me*, since—cue the tiny violins—he was now a full-time student while I was working full-time as a lawyer. I needed a good job, and I needed it fast, because I did not want to ask my mother for handouts.

The truck was Max's brilliant idea after I'd stopped by his apartment to fret about how much a rental would cost. He tromped across the street to the Borden Milk lot to negotiate with the manager, a balding, ponytailed bag of bones who was convinced that Max was mentally impaired because of his Austrian accent and paint-splattered clothing, which allowed Max, in a creative feat of reverse engineering, to drive the deal of the century on one of their old, decommissioned vehicles.

Max had promised to do a good cleanup job on the van, but when he arrived on moving day, I saw he'd exceeded expectations. The whole front of the snub-nosed Divco, from the hood to the skinny bumper, over the fat fenders and across the doors, was paved with ceramic tile remnants, huge colorful fake gemstones— where had he found those?—and studded with other scavenged artifacts: a family of brass cogwheels in graduated sizes. A tire gauge. Mirrored sunglass lenses, a few compact discs with rainbow shimmer, some bike reflectors, the spatulate blade of a cake knife. On top of the rearview mirror on the passenger side, he'd mounted a little girl's bicycle bell, complete with pink and purple streamers. This glittering encrustation ended at the cab. From there back, the van was creamy vanilla: a truck with a split personality, a truck with hidden depths, a truck with artistic balance, a crackerjack truck with a surprise in the box. I paced around the truck, smiling, while Max leaned against the door, studiously blowing smoke rings up into the cottonwood branches.

As a child, I organized and categorized, made lists, questioned the whys and wherefores. In college, I chose what I considered the most fascinating and challenging major of all, philosophy; after that, I embraced the whole immense systemization of human conduct called the law, with an impressive wardrobe of highlighters and color-coded notecards, which I stowed in file folders labeled in large and small caps, the font we used for law journal footnotes. CON LAW. TORTS. CONTRACTS. This perennial search for knowledge had always sprung from joy, not anxiety—until I had a bit of a real-world setback, namely, marrying a man who turned abusive as soon as I got pregnant. At that point, my urgent foundational query became, first: How did this happen? and then, How can I keep it from happening again? The questions were urgent, and I'd applied myself. Of course, it had taken time, but I'd figured it all out, I'd thought, and recovered confidence in my decision-making abilities, as well. All that remained was restoring my faith in human nature.

And I could do that in a truck like this.

In this cheerful pimped-up Divco, I could remember what Immanuel Kant had persuaded me in our imaginary conversation as I'd sat alone, trapped in divorce hell, in the Tulsa County Courthouse two months earlier: the Categorical Imperative really did exist, and goodness was our shared human bedrock. I could travel forward with that firm and optimistic compass, which would guide me to my true north, to the best of all possible worlds.

The hood ornament was a ten-inch aluminum Winged Victory at figurehead angle. I reached out and touched her head. She didn't wobble. Max blew out a plume of smoke and gave me a *V* sign. "This is for your journey." He arced his other hand across an imaginary horizon, the cigarette leaving a tiny vapor trail. "This is you. In your little American tennis skirt. Soaring into the future."

Soaring into the future. I liked that. My legal training, with its statutes, rules, and procedures, discouraged me from simply following my nose. But my precedents were bad, so I'd thrown them out. I wasn't living in the world of hypotheticals anymore. I was out there in the world of action, naked in the breeze: quitting my job, taking my baby, and driving off in a clunker of a milk van decorated like a child's music box with an Austrian painter so foot-loose and fancy-free that the entirety of his personal belongings fit into one backpack. This undertaking was on the order of what you might call a course correction and actually, when compared to other corrections—marrying a psychopath, for example, or having scantily protected sex with a stranger—a totally innocuous one. Even healthy. And a side benefit was that when I stood next to Max, I felt very conventional, which was secretly comforting. When all was said and done, I really was a refugee from plaid.

I turned in my apartment keys and negotiated an immediate walk-through with Bitter Depressed Office Manager so she couldn't scam me in absentia, and then we left, Max at the wheel. I sat with my chin in my hand, watching the line of cottonwoods standing sentinel along the Arkansas River. Here was where I used to take my runs, through the seasons. There was the pay phone I'd used to call the domestic violence crisis line. And there was the place Larry had sneered, "You look woebegone," after hitting me in the face at home, afterward insisting we take a walk with the baby. So he could pretend. Lip service—that was all Larry had ever paid to family life. A river ran through it. Wherever I turned in Tulsa, the river was always there, trapping me in an invisible current of past mistakes below the deceptively placid surface. A river ran through it, and that's why I had to leave.

Max turned off Riverside Drive at Thirty-First Street.

But couldn't you say that your whole life is like a river? It starts as a tiny rivulet high up in the mountains, clean and pure, and grows bigger as it cascades down, widening and deepening as it travels across the plain. Each time you step into its waters, you're farther downstream, and the current is faster. There's more to contend with. So it behooves you to deal with things head-on. Because if the river is your life, you take it with you wherever you go. You can't leave it.

The only way past something is through it.

At the next stoplight, I scanned the Quiktrip parking lot for the skinny cowboy who'd walked up to my open window that night while I waited for my one-night stand to buy condoms. *Jesus has your answer,* he'd said. I always looked for him when I drove by and had spotted him a few times, but we'd never spoken again. I still kept the card he'd given me in my wallet. Romans 12:12: *Be joyful in hope, patient in affliction, faithful in prayer.*

"Let's top off the gas," I suggested. "I didn't have any breakfast. I need a redneck mocha."

In the store, I added two packets of Swiss Miss to my paper cup of slightly stale but piping-hot coffee, while the cashier stood with his back to me watching Max top off the gas. When I went up to the register, I noticed the cashier had one of those substantial loops of chain hanging out of his front pocket, the kind that implied impressive responsibilities, like those of a jail warder.

"That all for you?" he said, ducking down a fraction of an inch to avoid the faded advertising panel hanging above his head, touting a now-defunct cigarette brand. Who would buy cartons retail, I wondered, when they could get them tax-free at the smoke shops in Indian Territory?

I handed him my money and asked shyly, "There's a guy that hangs out here sometimes? A cowboy in a pearl-button shirt…"

He rested an arm on the top of the register. "Hands out them Bible verses. Yeah. I know him. Ever' once in a while he actually comes in and buys something." He opened his right hand, shook the coins for an accurate count, then closed it, rotated his wrist, and stabbed at the keys with a fat forefinger. The economy of motion verged on the poetic. His other arm was still draped over the register, perhaps to keep him from toppling over from the exertion.

"Ha'n't seen him around in a while." He offered me the receipt, and when I shook my head, he crumpled it and did a miniature overhand toss into a wastebasket I couldn't see.

I pulled a small packet of chips off the snack rack, and he poked at the register again. "Sixter-three cents."

I dug out another dollar bill, creasing and folding it lengthwise. Suddenly it seemed mission critical to see the cowboy in the pearl-button shirt one more time. I wanted to thank him for his message, tell him I'd taken his advice to heart. That while it might have looked at that moment like it was too late for me, it really wasn't.

I rested my hand on the pocked linoleum counter. "Do you think...if he comes in, you could tell him I said hi? Tell him I got my head straight. Tell him thank you."

With thumb and forefinger, he took hold of the dollar bill, extracted it delicately, and smoothed it on the counter. Spreading his hands wide, he rocked back, then forward, with a thoughtful expression on his face like an auto mechanic on the verge of diagnosing engine failure.

"Well. Like I said. I ha'n't seen him in a while."

The counter's aluminum edge strip was grimy. Beneath it, fat stacks of newspaper bulged out from a recessed shelf, their headlines concealed.

"But you know..." he went on, in a softer voice.

I looked up.

"You know," he repeated, "I will just do that," he said firmly, nodding a promise.

Back in the truck, I handed a squealing Nathan the bag of chips. At two years old, he recognized forbidden fruit when he saw it. He settled back in his cow-print booster seat, professionally installed by a certified mechanic, and munched away. I took a sip of my scalding mocha, then reached out the window to finger the streamers on the bicycle bell on the rearview mirror. I felt a sense of relief and suddenly realized the reason I wanted to see the cowboy in the pearl-button shirt was that I needed to tell him what I hadn't been able to say to John after admitting I'd cheated. I needed to say it out loud: I'd changed. If John had closed off further dialogue in that regard—well, that was his loss. The message had been tugging at me, so I'd done what I could. And now the tug was gone. I nodded at Max in the mirror, and he started the engine. I was ready for our last stop.

But when it actually came down to leaving my best friend, Dana, I couldn't budge.

We stood there, Dana and I, in her front yard, and my feet took root. All I could do was stand there, clinging for dear life to my best friend since arriving in Tulsa five years before. I couldn't let go. It was the longest hug in the world.

"You're not getting rid of me anytime soon," Dana crooned as we rocked back and forth. "*Soon* as you get where you're going, I'm coming to visit. Pick a nice place. A nice place to visit."

My legs started to shake.

And then, over her shoulder, I saw a butterfly. It wafted over the yuccas bordering the side yard, pulling one and then another behind it on an invisible thread, weaving between the topmost branches of the big-leaf magnolia tree. I loosened my grip. We all stood watching, open-mouthed and breathless, as a whole dancing wave broke over the roof and washed past, dipping through the open yard and lifting above the row of maples across the street, down, then up again. A river of butterflies, flowing from the south, carving its way through the air: my ancestors, stepping in to help me. They marshaled their forces as a legion of butterflies and streamed around me at the moment of departure to carry me over that painful threshold on a tide of beauty.

"The Monarch migration!" Dana cried as the soft tide flowed over our heads, and in that moment my whole rib cage lifted with a deep breath that unlocked my throat and allowed me to exhale, to say it. I turned back to Dana, pressed my cheek to hers, and whispered in her ear, "Goodbye." Then I climbed into the truck. And while she waved with one hand clapped to her mouth—exactly like my mother at the train station the day I'd left for college—we drove off on the road to Tahlequah in a perfect storm of butterflies.

Chapter 3

The Phone Call

Thirty-six hours later, we were sitting in a booth at the Top of the Town Café in Springfield, Illinois, waiting for our hamburgers. My new cell phone sounded off, and it startled me. My fellow associates at Prentice Schroeder had encouraged me to get one before I went on a cross-country road trip—it was now considered a necessity, not a luxury. Heads swiveled at this evidence of state-of-the-art in the rural Midwest. Blushing, I scrabbled in my purse to answer it.

"John!" I exclaimed when I heard his voice.

Max's head snapped up. He'd been drawing pictures on the back of his placemat for Nathan, who took advantage of this opportunity to make a grab for the pencil.

Even though our long-distance romance had died on the vine, we'd moved on to a new footing—or was it returned to an old one?—after an appropriate interval, and had careful, friendly conversations once in a while. But this? My jaw dropped.

"John!" I bolted outside and lifted the phone to my ear again. "What did you just say?"

"Marry me."

There was a phone booth in front of the café. I walked over, stepped in, and pushed the accordion door shut. My knees felt weak, and I braced myself against the wall.

"John. You broke *up* with me. We're not even dating. Why are you saying this all of a sudden? Are you just jealous that I'm taking a three-day road trip to Chicago with my attractive platonic friend?"

"He's not attractive. And he's a loser."

"He is not! Don't say that."

"Okay then. He's not a loser. He's just not marriage material."

I sighed and poked at the chrome flipper on the coin return slot. I'd given up trying to disabuse modern men of the antiquated notion that women viewed the opposite sex exclusively through the lens of potential matrimony.

Into my prolonged silence, he said, "Kim, since I moved out here, I've tried to date other people. But I don't even want to. It's been nine months, and I can't stop thinking about you. You're all I want! I love you so much. I just want us to be together."

I cleared a small circle on the smudged glass with a finger. I was allowing his voice to come back to me, its warmth and gentle humor. I'd abandoned the cherished hope that John and I might end up together; I was simply moving on and forward with my life. After all, according to the philosopher Leibniz, we lived in the best of all possible worlds, so there should be nothing to regret. But...if I were to be honest with myself, philosophy hadn't been completely working for me here.

"Listen," John said, "I'm calling from Seattle. I just signed a full-time offer. I'm not doing outside contractor work in Portland anymore. I widened my search. It's a good firm. They're taking me on as a senior associate. Partner track. It's what we wanted, remember? This is what we talked about. We can afford it now. You can stay home with Nathan. So...will you marry me?"

The stoplight at the corner turned green, but the cars on both sides hesitated, waiting politely for general consensus before moving forward.

"Kim. Say something. Say anything. You're making me nervous."

In the back of my mind, music began to well, softly: a simple, unison string line, ending in a dissonant chord and delicate harp glissando. Then the words came: *You've been a fool / And so have I...*Bernstein. The lead-in to the final chorus of *Candide.* I'd told him about it at that August picnic, how I'd just seen it, how the final chorus made me think of him: *We'll build our house and chop our wood / And make our garden grow...*because he'd spoken of wanting a garden. And he'd said yes, a home and a family and a garden. He'd tend the garden and I'd raise the children; I wanted to stay home until the youngest went to kindergarten, and he said that was exactly what he wanted too.

Now I could remember: The air had been singing. The very molecules of the air, singing at a pitch and in a harmony only the two of us could hear. And now they were again. This truth was fundamentally more important than the size of any paycheck. Maybe the cowboy in the pearl-button shirt had been right. God was forgiving; the universe was forgiving. Second chances did exist.

Some women got proposals over candlelit dinners, or on the beach at sunset, or during a hike in the woods. Some got proposals on bended knee, or delivered with engagement rings hidden in flower bouquets. I got one long-distance in a defunct phone booth on the corner of Fifth and Main in Springfield, Illinois, wearing the same T-shirt my toddler had spilled orange soda on that morning.

"Did I just screw it up?" he asked. "I screwed it up. I should have just called to ask for a date, instead. Oh God, why did I do that? Listen, let's just have a date. Let's please just get back together and see how it goes. Please. I've waited a long time! Longer won't matter." He paused. "Remember how long I waited for you?"

I nodded. "Six hundred forty-two days." That's how long it took to accomplish the divorce, to get to that moment when I stepped out of the courthouse onto a magical dusting of snow, and the beauty of the unforeseen lay before me.

"I guess for a long time I was afraid you *would* ask me and then that you wouldn't," I said. "Either way, I was afraid. But I'm past all that. I'm not afraid anymore."

The beauty of the unforeseen: I'd chosen to consider it that way, as a happy and hopeful prospect, and perhaps that was why, when it truly did happen, the unforeseen, as it was happening now, it would also be truly beautiful. The music returned, faint but growing. I pushed open the door of the phone booth. Above a mass of late-spring foliage, the Sangamon County Courthouse dome was shining gold in the sun against a pale blue sky. Something stirred and lifted in that blue distance. It fluttered closer, flying past the gold-tipped dome and wafting over the leafy crowns of trees at the same time it traveled up inside me, to arrive fully unfurled on the palm of my hand at the precise moment it emerged from my throat: "Yes."

A solid yes, obvious, no choice at all—except that it was, actually. A choice. Which was the way it had to be for it to work.

"So what do we do now?" I asked.

"Go to Chicago," he said. "Don't unload the truck. I'll come out, we'll get a license, get married, and then we'll drive together to Seattle."

"I don't think you've seen the truck yet. Also, it doesn't belong to me. It belongs to Max. What about Max?"

"Well, he's not coming with us! We're not setting up a commune here."

"Very funny," I said, then sighed. "None of this sounds very romantic. John, I'm tired of being unconventional. I don't want to get married without a wedding. I did that before, and I think it was a bad sign. I want a proper wedding with a dress."

"So go buy a dress."

We made a few brief plans, and then I went back into the café. I sat down again and rubbed my forehead.

Max looked at me. "What's up?"

"I'm getting married."

"Yes," he nodded. "I know. I thought so." He turned the place mat around. In the top corner was a tiny sketch of me in three-quarter profile standing just outside the phone booth. My face was lifted, and I had one hand held up, palm open, gently cupped as though in offering. "You never looked more beautiful." He turned it back around. Head down, he added more shading with tiny hash marks, then fleshed out the phone booth a little more.

When I'd gotten pregnant by mistake, Max was the one I turned to; he was the only one I told. We both knew I wasn't serious about the likely father. His response was immediate: *Do you want to get married? I will marry you. I can be the father.* A gallant gesture but also an absurd one. Max was solid. We were close. But I wasn't going to marry a friend just to save face. My miscarriage a few weeks later rendered the whole point moot.

The waitress emerged from the kitchen balancing our three plates, the door rocking behind her with a succession of loud *whaps* that gentled until the door was still. My life had taken a ninety-degree turn in less than the time it took for three burgers to arrive at the Top of the Town Cafe. Max finished the drawing, signed it, and pushed it over.

"You remember what I told you?" He leaned forward earnestly, folding his hands on the table. "What I thought? When I met you? 'If I ever marry any woman, that will be the one.'"

I nodded.

"You realize you have now consigned me to lifelong bachelorhood."

I touched the edge of the place mat and exhaled softly. "Can I still be your muse?"

He reached out and touched my cheek. "You will always be my muse." There was still paint on his hands, though we'd been driving for three days. He always had paint on his hands.

The waitress was hovering. She dealt out the plates. "Can I get you anything else?"

I looked up, suddenly unable to process this simple question. I busied myself folding the place mat with the Lincolnland map facing out, Max's sketch protected on the inside. "You know," I said, "I think I've got just about everything I need right now," and a sob caught in my throat.

The waitress glared at Max. "What did you *say* to her? What did you do?"

"Nothing!" He took the ever-ready cigarette from behind his ear, fingered it, then tucked it back. "She just got engaged."

She stared at us each in turn while Nathan jammed french fries into his mouth.

Max wagged his hand. "Not to me. To someone else," he said, pulling a small wad of paper napkins out of the dispenser for me.

I wiped my eyes as the waitress readjusted her apron, softening around the edges, aware now that she'd stepped into the shoals of a small interpersonal sea much different from the one she'd imagined. Max beamed up at her and tapped the advertising slogan on the plastic dispenser.

"'See America First!'" he declared. "I certainly am."

Chapter 4

Member of the Wedding

A SCANT THREE WEEKS LATER, JOHN AND I WERE MARRIED at Elmwood, the large, turn-of-the-century Wisconsin lake house that had been our extended family's summer home for decades. The property didn't belong to us anymore; my mother and her siblings had sold it to a Minnesota company as a corporate retreat a scant six months ago, which I maintained would make it view our request to marry there with sympathy. My mother strenuously disagreed, but I was equally strong-willed. I picked up the phone myself and exercised the negotiation skills I'd honed in law school. Ensign Insurance did ultimately agree, which I took as a good omen. We could only use the grounds and not the house, but that didn't matter. All I wanted was the chance to be back in this magical place and share it with John. To get married there, just as Karen and Frank had done two years before.

It was a relatives-only affair, which translated to my large extended family, plus the addition of the mysterious Claudette, John's birth mother, who'd surprisingly accepted the invitation I'd persuaded him was proper to make. We'd get married on the dock and then have cake and champagne on the old grass tennis court. It would be a small wedding but with all the components: a dress, flowers, even music, courtesy of my brother-in-law, Frank

Massey, a professional French horn player who'd put together a pickup brass quintet. A small wedding, but a real one, and that was exactly how it should be. Because this was the real marriage.

On the day of the wedding, Uncle Will pulled his camper to the far side of the circle drive at a tasteful distance from the action. Karen had cleverly kitted it out as a mobile bride's room, all the way down to the ice bucket of tiny designer bottled waters. There, I dressed, with the help of Cassie, my brother's fiancée. Out the window, I could see Karen patrolling the area to ward off unauthorized visitors, with her young son, Sammy, by her side. Sammy was wearing a leash, cleverly disguised as a fanny pack with a cord attached, the end of which was wrapped around his very pregnant mother's wrist. He was working hard to master the technique of pushing a tennis ball with a stick along the shallow cement gutter of the grass court.

Clad in blueberry lace-over-satin and flat heels, Karen followed him gracefully without missing a beat of her conversation with Claudette. Claudette trailed along, jabbing the air occasionally for emphasis with a hand curled around an as-yet-unlit cigarette, which set the armload of bracelets on her bony wrist ajingle. The fragility she exuded from within her portrait collar might have been explained by the fact she'd recently been widowed by her second husband, a retired aluminum can company executive whose fatal stroke while yachting in the Mediterranean on their tenth-anniversary trip had allowed her to endow a chair in his memory at the New York Philharmonic.

I'd heard the whole story of John's non-relationship with his mother on the drive to the Milwaukee airport to pick her up. Claudette had run off to New Mexico during the Summer of Love to sit at the feet of a second-rate painter with Russian émigré cachet and a magnetic personality; it was probably as close to becoming a flower child as a nice girl from the Main Line with a degree in art history from Swarthmore could muster. When the father of the child she'd contributed to the commune at New Buffalo unexpectedly dropped dead of a heart attack at the age of thirty-five, the whole adventure suddenly palled. She packed up her broomstick skirts and Indian jewelry and returned to Wayne, leaving the baby with his paternal grandparents. Her parents were relieved. The father of the child was not another social register dropout, but a local electrician much older than she; they'd tried to entice their daughter back by threatening to cut her off but had been unable due to the complexity of the family's financial structure. They bankrolled an art gallery for her, and Claudette was low-hanging fruit for older execs casting about for a young second wife. After six months, Claudette was successfully in the arms of a more presentable man.

The ride back from the airport with this woman had hardly even been awkward, despite the fact that it was only the fourth time she'd lain eyes on John since he was a baby. The most recent had been his graduation from Stanford, where she'd scolded him roundly for not remaining there for law school and then left without offering to help pay for it. He had college debt, and with his part-Navajo heritage, he'd had a full scholarship dangled in front of him at Tulsa. That institution had apparently been beneath her notice. John hadn't even wanted to invite her to the wedding, but I said it was only proper; when she accepted, we were both surprised. He said with a shrug, "I guess she just wants to look you over." I realized he was right when I saw the naked relief on her face as we drove into Elmwood and then met the family. She'd just wanted to make sure she wasn't acquiring a pesky, impecunious relative. It was a small bonus when she discovered my sister was a professional cellist, and from that moment on, fearing the cultural desert that must be southern Wisconsin, she'd fastened on to my sister like a limpet.

Right now, as they passed close to the van, I could hear Karen and Claudette discussing the fate of the symphony orchestra in America.

"You're so right," Claudette was saying. "Board members have to be experienced professionals. They have a fiduciary obligation. It doesn't matter if it's a nonprofit. There's too much at stake." She turned as I stepped out of the camper. "Don't you look lovely," she gushed, reaching out with a manicured index finger to touch the butterfly lace. "*Such* a beautiful veil," then turned her head to exhale a plume of smoke while holding the cigarette hand dramatically aloft.

I gave her a tight-lipped smile, but I got the Karen look, which in this instance translated to *Be gracious,* so manners compelled me to do a polite twirl and tell the story behind the veil. Cassie and I had unearthed the wide length of antique ivory lace at a bridal consignment shop in Rogers Park. "What a find. This must have just arrived. I haven't even seen it yet," the clerk said, running her hand over the ladybugs, grasshoppers, and butterflies scattered among the more traditional floral motifs. Aunt Thea had taken the lace and whipped up an elbow-length, two-tiered veil attached to a plain circlet.

"Truly heirloom," Claudette exclaimed. "You'll have to save this for a daughter."

"I think I'll take a little walk to clear my head before the ceremony," I murmured, which was code for *This is not someone I have any interest in bonding with on my wedding day.*

"That's fine," Karen replied sunnily. "You have plenty of time," which was code for *I'll take one for the team here.*

Claudette dropped her cigarette and ground it into the lawn with a heel. "Stay clear of the underbrush!" she warned, unnecessarily; my ivory satin dress was tea-length.

I escaped past the van to the asphalt drive leading through dense woods to the front gate and the main road. Sunlight filtered through the high tent of elm and hickory, then the lacy understory of ironwood, and dappled the ferns on the ground. I took a deep breath of loamy air. Two years ago, when Karen had gotten married here, I'd been a brand-new mother shamefully concealing my impending divorce from my relatives. Today, I was undergoing a correction, and I now viewed the extended chain of lifelong marriages in my family as a happy resource.

Before my divorce, I'd dreamed of my grandmother, who'd died long ago. She'd taken my hand and led me down this drive all the way to the gate; she'd been about to show me something hidden there, but then I'd woken up. Maybe that's why I was taking this walk right now, I reflected. I wasn't just following my sister's footsteps; I was following my grandmother's, trying to find what she'd been about to share with me in the only way she could, in dreams.

A candy-red convertible eased up alongside me. I recognized the caretaker of the house. "I'm taking a little walk," I explained. "Just to the gate and back. To clear my head."

"Aha! Good to hear. No second thoughts then." He palmed the steering wheel and smiled.

"I thought you were supposed to stay on-site the whole time we're here and make sure we're not up to anything nefarious? Wasn't that a stipulation of our being here?" One among several: We were neither employees nor lessees, but guests; we were not making any payment for use of the property; and said use was limited to the grounds with the exception of the restroom in the barn. The house was off-limits.

"I don't care about Legal." He looked left, then right. "They're not here, are they? They're not looking over my shoulder. Heck, I would've let you inside, no problem. There wasn't anything on the schedule. But folks showed up this morning unexpectedly, and they all had sticks up their asses. A show-up without notice, and they won't even tell me if they're staying overnight. Now I've been sent out on a pointless errand. Give me an outdoor wedding anytime!"

He drove off with a backward wave.

I arrived at the entrance, put one hand on the cement pillar, and tried to wiggle the gate. The hinges wouldn't budge. It hadn't been closed in a long time, perhaps never, and was now bound in place by vegetation. A red-winged blackbird flew out of the woods and scudded across the street to the Bloodgood farm, which was in the first stage of transition to a housing development: stubby rolling fields staked out with wide curving streets, some of them already paved, and median planters sporting spindly linden trees. I turned and looked back down our drive, carving a narrow tunnel through the primordial-looking woodland that buffered our rambling relic from the forces of progress. I was standing exactly where my grandmother had led me. In the dream, we'd arrived right here, at the edge of the property, but then I'd woken up and missed the ending. I didn't discover her gift then, and it was fanciful to think I'd find it now. Maybe there was nothing there. But perhaps that was her gift, that was what she wanted me to see: that I could do it by myself. That I already had within me what I needed to go beyond the evergreens. I was trying to go back to Square One yet again, and this time I would be successful. Square One was not just about going back to my own roots, I realized, to the roots of my ancestors, but to the roots of the earth itself. I stood quite still, savoring the connection and realizing that although we didn't own it anymore, we'd sold this property to an owner who wanted to preserve and not develop it. These woods would not be lost.

I adjusted my veil and started back, walking carefully down the middle of the drive. On both sides, mayapple and wild ginger crept over fallen branches, covering them with new life as they rotted and returned to loam. The woods thinned to spindly hawthorn, the light increased; there was a rampant fringe of blackberry, bordered by a looping necklace of Uncle Will's daylilies, and then I was out in the open again, walking toward the house, on the crest of the hill above the lake.

I blinked in the sun. A slight figure was floating toward me—my late grandmother, coming to meet me in her favorite pale blue bouclé suit with the big cloth-covered buttons, her hair wrapped around her head in a cornsilk braid. I breathed her in.

"I'm so glad you're here," I said. "I've been thinking about you."

Of course I'm here. What a lovely veil. She lifted an edge with her finger, a gentle touch that washed Claudette's away. *From a distance it looks very traditional, but when you get up close, you see how truly different it is.* Then she opened a little box, and in it I saw the mother-of-pearl bracelet I already wore. I felt her touch on my wrist. *I wanted to give this to you. Here's your "something old." I gave Karen the coral one, but I'm sure you'll trade them around.*

My mother had said the same thing earlier, in exactly the same words.

"Will you come with me?" I asked.

Always, she said. *Always.* She touched the bracelet again gently. *It goes perfectly,* she murmured, then drifted away.

I opened my eyes.

Karen stood there, smiling at me as I fingered the mother-of-pearl bracelet. She put her hand on my wrist. "It goes perfectly," she said. She handed me my bouquet, then waved to her husband, part of the brass quintet perched down on the bluff above the dock. They began the prelude. She gave me a final check, then put her hands on my shoulders. "Just know," she said, "you're doing it right this time around."

AFTER THE CEREMONY, THE QUINTET struck up the "Prince of Wales March." John took my arm, and we left our beaming witnesses behind, walking the length of the dock back to shore and up the limestone steps to the lawn. Frank caught my eye, lifted his French horn a few inches, and gave me a three-fingered wave. I blew him a kiss, and we continued on until we reached the hilltop, where we stood breathless under the cedars beside the house. I looked up at John, so handsome in his suit, full of energy, high color in his cheeks. I put my hand on his lapel.

"Welcome to the family," I said.

"I can't believe we actually made it," he said. "We actually got to here." He covered my hand with his, then suddenly, with a grin, took it and towed me toward the house, up onto the porch, where a boxcar-sized mass of lilacs in full bloom screened us from the clutch of family members coming up from the dock, ascending the steps, and unfurling onto the sloping lawn.

"We're not supposed to be here," I whispered urgently.

"Just for a minute. We need to escape the madding crowd." He opened the screen door, then tried the heavy main door and found it unlocked. He pulled me into the front hall. I opened my mouth to protest again but stopped: the wool carpet beneath my feet, the Art Nouveau grandfather clock, the smell of dust suffused with creosote—everything was the same, even the bookcase, still filled with the same books. Everything was the same, except for the velvet curtain across the wide dining room doorway, tugged closed on its fat wooden rod. We'd always left it open.

"*Now* I can get a proper kiss from the bride," John said, and executed a dip that made my veil fall off.

Suddenly the curtain swept back, revealing a man dressed in a checked shirt and jeans with a very surprised expression on his face.

"What the—" he exclaimed, and turned back to the paper-littered table behind him, where five other people, in similar expensive casual wear, sat frozen as though in a tableau: *Weekend Work Conference.*

A woman broke the spell by flipping her laptop shut. Then she stuck her hand into the jute satchel at her feet and pulled out a pack of cigarettes.

"You can't *smoke* inside this house!" I exclaimed. "It's a tinderbox. It's over a hundred years old."

She looked up with a pinched expression.

"It's against the rules," I added lamely, picking up my veil.

"Rules," she echoed, taking off her readers to scrutinize me more clearly.

John stepped forward. "I'm sorry, we didn't mean to disturb you. But—Mr. Freeman? I recognize you from the paper. We've been following your case at the office. *Gianelli v. Harkin Guaranty*, 6–3, and Stevens resisted the urge to write a concurrence. Congratulations on that. Really solid. Significant case for employment underwriting." He turned to me. "Really helpful guideline for ADA risk management. Disability rights are going to be *very* important in the next decade."

Why was he babbling?

"And you are?" The man stepped forward. He had a florid face, a close-cropped beard, and the brisk manner of someone used to sizing things up quickly.

"John. John Halvorsen."

"Pleased to meet you. And congratulations." He smiled, retaining his grip on John's hand. "And…who is 'we'?"

"Dunwoody Scudder Ellis. In Seattle. I just started there…" He trailed off with a puzzled expression and turned to me. "I thought you said Ensign owned this property."

I tucked my bouquet under my arm, then quickly took it out again so as not to crush the flowers, and, embarrassed, stuttered something in which "interfering" was the only intelligible word. We'd broken the terms of the contract. But Freeman, suddenly smooth and twinkling, waved all that away.

"No apologies necessary, Mrs. Halvorsen. Elmwood is a wonderful setting for business conferences. I know Ensign is grateful to your family for this resource," he went on, repeatedly glancing at the woman still holding the unlit cigarette, who I realized must be the CEO of Ensign. "We'd all like to express our appreciation in some way. May we put you up at the Pfister in Milwaukee for the weekend? Would you accept that as a gift from us?"

Would we *not!* We nodded mutely.

"How 'bout the bride rejoins her family while we take a minute to discuss the arrangements," Mr. Freeman said jovially. He unlatched the screen door and held it open. "I know I can rely on your discretion, Mrs. Halvorsen."

"Of course," I squeaked, ducking out, as the screen snapped shut behind me.

After Cassie had gotten us in formation beneath the cedars for a photo, and after Karen had finger-brushed my hair and settled my veil, John reappeared. He took his place at my side and flashed a business card. "That was the CEO of Harkin Guaranty. In case you didn't catch that." He flicked it over to show the handwriting on the back.

I adjusted his boutonniere. "What was *he* doing here? That whole thing was really weird. I could tell it was an important meeting because they all had *cell phones* sitting on the table. So we barged in, but so what? We're not corporate spies. I don't like being made to feel like an intruder in my own home."

"It's *not* your own home," John pointed out. "Anymore. And… they know we're not corporate spies. Further than that, my lips are sealed." He grinned. "All *you* need to know is that I just signed an NDA that's gonna get us a lake-view king suite at the Pfister. *And* he asked for my résumé. He said they were always on the lookout for new talent. HR is going to call me on Tuesday morning. So there."

"But you already have a job! In Seattle!"

"Stick with me, kid. We're going places." He slicked back his hair. "Yep. Cell phones. Guess it's time to get me one o' them."

"They're very handy," I said. "For example, if I hadn't gotten me one o' them, you'd have had to telephone-propose while I stood in my mother's kitchen with her breathing down my neck."

"Which could really have affected the space-time continuum," he added soberly, then grinned down at me. I could never resist those dimples and leaned up for a quick peck on the lips.

"Hey, you two! Give us that kiss again," Cassie called, but Nathan was clamoring at my feet, so I hoisted him up on my hip, where he played with my veil while we obliged.

Chapter 5

Home Base

"DANNY'S WAITING!" NATHAN CRIED, STRAPPING ON HIS fisherman sandals. Danny, who lived in the row house opposite ours, was Nathan's new best friend, and Jessie, his mother, was mine. Nathan shot out onto the deck when I unlatched the screen door.

"Playground song!" I called, and he halted, then clumped down the steps one at a time, holding each slat along the way, as we sang.

Hold the railing
Hold the railing
Fetch the wagon and stand by the gate!

The gate of song and verse opened onto the commons, a long, elliptical green space holding many attractions: picnic tables, open areas for sports or walking dogs, and especially, the tot lot. Over the fence I could see Jessie installing Danny's baby sister in a pink playpen, where, dressed entirely in pink, she was almost completely camouflaged. The picnic table under the old oak was our Home Base, so named because we'd heard it had been behind home plate on the ball field of the demolished school.

Nathan reached the bottom of the steps and raced down the brick path. It was mortised with grass that threaded down the narrow backyard, a retro-luxe detail that made these rowhouses appealing. You could run a push mower right over it, which inspired John's sliding-scale mowing nomenclature: "Williamsburg" meant freshly done, while "Tulsa" meant overdue. The lawn looked very Williamsburg today, I thought, making my way to the end of the yard, where the sunflowers Jessie had helped me plant along the back fence were now six feet tall.

Nathan put Smooshy into his little red wagon and cried out, "Sunflowers, Mama! The sunflowers are *big!*" He threw both hands up over his head.

"That's right! But remember, they need to be *this* big." I lifted my arms up to the sky. "*Way* high."

"Way high! *Then* baby will come!"

"That's right. *Then* baby will come."

I opened the gate, and he barreled toward the tot lot, the wagon jouncing behind him. "Baby will come! Baby will come!" he screeched.

My friend Suzanne looked up, startled, then turned back and inserted another tiny spoonful of butternut squash into her baby's mouth. "Damn. You had me thinking I was going to win the pool."

"That's an infraction," Jessie said. "A dollar in the bunco jar for you, Suzanne. You can't make her laugh after thirty-five weeks; she'll wet her pants."

This was why I'd clicked so quickly with Jessie's group of four stay-at-home moms. Besides having children in the same age bracket, which was an indispensable requirement, we all had a good sense of humor—also indispensable these days for young moms swimming against the current and staying home with the kids. Our ringleader, Mardie, called us twenty-first-century renegades.

I sat down heavily. "Anyway, sunflowers aren't tall enough."

"Another Reuben from Jimmy's?"

I unrolled the top of the waxed white bag that John had driven from the office to deliver. "I'm not sharing."

"I was the same with pistachio ice cream," Sita volunteered. "Just you wait. After this baby, you won't be able to look a Reuben in the face ever again."

Jessie turned from the playpen, where she'd been slathering sunblock on Meghan, otherwise known as Miss Pink. "How's Nathan doing? Did he sleep through the night?"

"Yes, finally. Day Four and I think he's getting better," I said. Nathan had taken three cross-country trips so far, and I'd learned the readjustment period was about as long as the trip itself. "He's sleeping through, in the crib with the rail down. Next week I'll try putting him down in his twin bed."

"Next week. And then it's not long before he has to leave again," Sita said sadly, hugging her knees. They all murmured reassurances. My new mom group was horrified at Nathan's travel schedule, and it was to them as much as to my pediatrician that I'd turned for advice when Nathan had reverted to needing pull-ups again in the daytime, and diapers at night. And the nursing. Their advice had been the same as my doctor's: "Don't worry about it." If he needed to snuggle at my breast for ninety seconds before nodding off, it was what he needed. He needed the routine, the security. Because, as Jessie had said, he'd lost his home base.

Mardie splashed into our midst with a picnic blanket and her two children, in matching shorts and jelly sandals. If we were a team, she was our captain; she'd lived here the longest and had the oldest child, a little girl who had obtained the unimaginably mature age of five and was now whining with hunger. Mardie jammed a straw into a juice box and handed it over, then swiftly unwrapped grilled cheese sandwiches cut into triangles.

"Oh my gosh, this girl's exhausted! Can you say overstimulation? Three hours of day camp for her probably feels like what the first day on the floor of the New York Stock Exchange would be for us."

She added celery sticks and a handful of potato chips to each plate, and then came the cries from the other children: "Anna has chips! Bella has chips! I want some!"

"I thought we were banning potato chips," Suzanne said primly.

"Oh, sorry!" Mardie peeled the lid off her yogurt. "Well, eat those first, kids. We don't want to cause a riot," she ordered, pointing with her spoon, then looked up at us. "What?" she protested. "C'mon, they're *organic!*"

The children finished eating and scrambled away to the play equipment, all but the daughter who'd fallen asleep on Mardie's lap, still holding a potato chip, which Mardie removed and popped into her own mouth. "I'm glad we're doing this now, before she starts kindergarten. That'll be five mornings a week, not three. I can see we're going to need a long on-ramp."

"They're talking about all-day kindergarten next year," Suzanne said. "Not this coming year, I mean. *Next* next year."

We all looked to Mardie. She wiped her mouth and pronounced: "Fate worse than death."

"I think it's only if you pay for it, though," Suzanne hastened to clarify.

"Why should I pay for my kid to take a nap at school when I can do that in my own home for free? My God, it's the only time I can go to the bathroom."

"It's a good option if you want to go back to work," Sita pointed out.

"I don't *want* to go back to work," Mardie said. "I'm working *way* too hard to go back to work. I'm too tired to go back to work." Mardie had been a paralegal. She liked to tease me: *Who wants to be a lawyer? Paralegals get good pay and none of the responsibilities.*

"I do," said Suzanne. "I'd like to go back part time. My mom said she'd take care of Joey. But my boss didn't want to hear it. He said, 'Wait until you're *really* ready.'"

"That's insulting," Mardie said.

"I guess I can understand his point of view," Suzanne said. "There's plenty of dental hygienists around willing to work full time, and that's easier to manage."

Sita broke in. "My cousin on Long Island just got a new pediatrician, and it's two of them. Two female doctors and they're each having their first baby, and the clinic is letting them job share. So each gets to work part time, but my cousin is guaranteed that she's always going to see one or the other of them."

"Now, that's creative."

We turned around on the picnic bench to face the action on the play equipment, Mardie swiveling gently on her blanket so as not to disturb her sleeping daughter. Both swing sets were full, the one for babies and the one for toddlers. A knot of small children was busily scooping bark chips around the base of the empty hexagonal jungle gym, and two children were attempting the long, low-set monkey bars, their mothers following along.

"I can't believe you want a hot sandwich in this weather," Mardie ribbed in quiet tones, as I munched doggedly on the second half of my Reuben.

"You gave your kids grilled cheese," I pointed out.

"They were *cold*."

"I'm jealous," Sita said. "*My* husband never delivered lunch to me when I was pregnant."

"That's because he works downtown. The Nuthouse is only five minutes away." The Nuthouse was our name for Harkin Guaranty, located on the remainder of a large country estate that, over the years, had been slowly engulfed by metropolitan Baltimore, except for 140 picturesque scenic acres on a wooded eminence that contained the original mansion. It had seen life as a sanatorium in the teens and twenties before its transformation into a corporate campus.

Sita said she had a feeling that John would deliver me lunch no matter how far his office was; he was just that kind of guy. And

Mardie said he ought to write a book called *The Care and Feeding of Your Pregnant Wife*, that she'd give it to Matt as a hint.

"Does Matt still want to make the move up?" That's what we called trading up to a four-bedroom single-family in the older, established neighborhoods east of York Road or the newer subdivisions out Loch Raven way.

"He's just saying that. I told him I wanted another baby, and he said if we had a third we'd have to move because we'd need a bigger house and I'd have to go back to work. But I priced out the daycare and went through the math with him. I wouldn't net enough for that to make sense. Putting kids in bunk beds for a while is just fine. So he'll have to come up with a new argument."

"Don't leave!" Jessie cried.

"I don't want to leave. But at some point, when you stop being a baby incubator, you're going to have to move up if you have more than two kids. You'll just need the room. But I'd put it off as long as I could. I love this neighborhood."

"Me too," I said.

"There's no harm in hanging on. Values are only going to go up." Sita's husband was interning in anesthesiology at Hopkins and was the only one of us who viewed Baltimore as temporary, despite the fact she'd lain out for beautiful custom drapes, which made her house our preferred location for Mom's Night. "Anyway, who needs a big yard? We've got this—" She spread out her arms at precisely the moment we all saw a tiny girl determinedly climbing the jungle gym, a seven-foot geodesic dome of galvanized pipe. The smallest children never attempted this, instead contenting themselves with climbing in and out of the hive openings at the bottom.

"Who's *with* her?" Mardie said. "She can't be more than two. My gosh, look at her scoot!"

The little girl clambered all the way to the circular opening at the top. She sat there for a moment, legs dangling, looking around in surprise, unsure of what to do next, then slipped off her perch and fell through. We all jumped up, but it was Jessie who outstripped us all, diving in to scoop her off the ground before she even had a chance to react. She threw us a thumbs-up sign.

Suzanne stood with both hands clapped to her head. "She could have cracked her skull on those bars."

"Or broken an arm."

"Thank God she dropped straight as a bullet."

We flocked around Jessie, who had by now extricated herself from the structure and was jiggling the child on her hip. "My, aren't you a good climber!" She turned in a circle. "Let's find Mommy! Where's Mommy?"

The child put her head on Jessie's shoulder and pointed at two women with a golden retriever on a leash, who were walking, then trotting with concern, along the green.

Mardie stalked toward them waving her arms like a demented windmill.

"What the *fuck* do you think you're doing?" she cried. "How can you turn your back on your *kid*? We don't *do* that here. Your kid is more important than your gossipfest and your fucking *dog*." We caught up to her, and I put a restraining hand on her arm, but she shook me off. "You think because there are so many of us here, we're all babysitting *your* kid for you?"

The mother gulped back a sob, took her child, and beat a hasty retreat.

Jessie sat down at the picnic table and spread ten fingers across her forehead as though trying to hold her brains in place. "My own child's life flashed before my eyes."

I patted her on the back. "This is just one of those moments when you have to say all's well that ends well," I offered.

"And people tease *me* for bringing out a playpen," she went on. "I'm *always* going to be bringing out a playpen. I'm going to be bringing out a playpen when she's, like, twelve years old," she said, and we both laughed.

In the sandbox, our oblivious sons were working with great industry, filling plastic buckets, turning them upside down, and smoothing them with a spatula all in accordance with some ambitious master plan inscrutable to all but themselves.

"I don't want to go back to work," Jessie said. "But I shouldn't complain. It's easy for me. Aviation has great benefits. I have a four-day week."

"I'm jealous. Fingers crossed that that kind of flexibility spreads to law firms by the time this little one is in kindergarten." I patted my belly.

"We'll give it time. Luckily, you have a few years to go before then." She sighed, gesturing at the playground, the swings, our sons in the sandbox. "I don't want this to be over. But it's time. We decided I'd take five months. That's more than most moms. They just get three. Working moms, I mean." She slung an arm around my shoulder. "We're *all* working moms."

"You can say that again," I said, as a wail pierced the air and we rose to meet the challenge of a dispute over the all-important spatula.

Chapter 6

The Same River Twice

"How's my beautiful wife?" John called, dropping his briefcase at the foot of the stairs. I turned sideways from the stove for our swing dip, modified to keep me as vertical as possible, and ran my finger across his brow. His forehead was beaded with sweat, and the front of his dress shirt clung to his chest; all this had happened in the few seconds it had taken him to sprint to the air-conditioned house from the front curb, where he'd parked his air-conditioned car. I went back to prodding meatballs with a fork in one saucepan and stirring tomato sauce in another. One of the things I enjoyed most about being a stay-at-home mom was cooking, especially for such an appreciative audience. John couldn't cook at all, and I often teased him that he was an utter throwback to an earlier generation. He'd joke back, "Yes, clearly I married you not because you're a hot sexy babe but just for your cooking," after which we'd usually end up in bed. Except lately—I was two weeks from my due date and supremely uncomfortable.

And having bizarre food cravings that John graciously accommodated, such as spaghetti and meatballs during a ninety-plus-degree heat wave. He pulled out a handkerchief and mopped his forehead. "Ah, of course. Exactly! Actually, I was hoping for roast beef and Yorkshire pudding."

I threatened him with the fork. "I can do that tomorrow."

He ducked out of reach back into the living room, hung his jacket over the newel post, and called, "I'm looking forward to that gazpacho in December."

At five a.m. my eyes flew open: a contraction! I timed them for an hour before waking John, who couldn't contain his excitement. He got Nathan up and dressed, while I took the phone and stood on the back deck. I dialed Jessie. I knew she'd be up.

"Look out the door," I said.

Across the commons, I saw her step out her kitchen door in her bathrobe, phone in one hand, a blanket-wrapped bundle on her shoulder. I gave her two thumbs up. "I'll send Hank over to get Nathan," she said. "Suzanne's going to win the pool, but I'll forgive you."

We arrived at the tenth-floor maternity ward in advance of the midwife and were checked in by a nurse who was a woman of unusually few words for someone in a people profession.

"Who? Oh, yeah. *Her*. She called." A clipboard materialized on the counter. "Dad, maybe you can fill this out, okay?" She turned to the nurse beside her. "Let's get her up on the board. Just leave attending blank and put *her* in underneath."

Her young colleague froze in the act of uncapping her marker. "No attending?" She had a wispy ponytail and a tiny teddy bear pinned over her name tag.

"She's that Nancy," the older nurse replied. "The RN in solo practice." She looked at me dourly and added, "It would just be the on-call if there's a problem." Was this a way to treat a woman in labor? I thought. I already had a tinge of regret that we were doing a hospital birth, and this wasn't helping. Nathan had been born at home, which was my preference, and Larry had evinced no concern one way or the other. He'd been a detached participant, to put it mildly, and it was only happenstance that he was in Tulsa when I went into labor. John, however, had concerns. This was the first time around for him, and he was nervous. I wanted to honor that. I didn't want to push him.

Two hours later, after multiple hands of gin rummy that proved unsuccessful in distracting me from the medical paraphernalia beeping and blipping beside me, a couple of other nurses I hadn't seen before poked their heads in and asked how I was doing.

I looked up from my hand and smiled politely. "Fine. As well as a woman in labor can be doing." When she left, I turned to John. "My, but they have a lot of help around here."

John sprang up and closed the door, but no sooner had he done that than Wispy Ponytail reappeared, slowly pushing it all the way to the wall with her fingertips as she whispered in gentle admonition, "Sorry, kids, but we have to keep this open. How're you doing, Mommy?"

"Okay, but it's like Grand Central Station around here."

"Sorry about that," said Ponytail. "I think I know what that's about. It's up on the board, you see."

"What's up on the board?"

"No anesthesia. That you're refusing anesthesia. They've never seen a childbirth without anesthesia before."

"Should we charge admission?" John asked.

She *heh-heh'ed* softly and padded out.

Sometime later, the midwife, Nancy, came in. She checked me silently, stripped off her gloves, and told me what I already knew, that my contractions had stopped. "Don't worry, Dad," she added, seeing John's face. "This happens. Everything's fine with Baby. Go home and relax. Let me know when the fun starts again, and we'll all come back."

IT WAS QUIET AND DARK when I woke up. I was on top of the bed, still dressed, with a blanket over me; John was under the covers. What time was it? This would never end. I was a failure.

I levered myself up off the bed, careful not to wake John, and padded downstairs into the kitchen. Appliances hummed, and there was a single glass in the sink: John always had a glass of milk and a cookie before bed. I opened the refrigerator. My friends had loaded its shelves with meals yesterday, in anticipation of my arrival back home with a newborn. I was not going to touch a bite until I had a baby in my arms. I grabbed my Walkman and headphones and climbed back upstairs to the still-empty baby's room, next door to Nathan's.

This small third bedroom had been my practice room, and my cello and music stand were still in the corner, waiting to be moved over into the master bedroom when the baby came. My sister had friends at the Peabody and had found me a good teacher, and I'd enjoyed practicing while looking out the window into the leafy top of the oak tree at Home Base. Now, between its branches shifting and rustling in the dark, I could see Jessie's back door light shining for me. I sat down in the rocker John had decorated, put on my headphones, and rocked back and forth to the Telemann Viola Concerto. I looked around the room at the alphabet wallpaper border, the mobile over the crib, and the stacks of diapers on the changing table. A room all ready for a baby who wouldn't come. Who didn't want to come. Did this baby know something? Something about its future, or my past, that was making it hesitant? I spread Aunt Thea's baby quilt on my lap and rubbed my tummy with both hands.

I know I screwed it up with your brother, but I've picked a wonderful father for you! Don't be scared. He really wants to be your dad. We picked out all this furniture together. He put up the wallpaper. He's not like Larry. He's a real dad. He wants you. He wants you.

I want you.

I felt the faintest twinge. I stood up. *I'm not going to jump the gun this time*, I told myself firmly, *but maybe I'll just get back in bed with John.* A few minutes later I was sitting on the floor in the upstairs hallway and John was kneeling beside me. Had I called him? "It's time to go," he was saying. "Come on, let's get you downstairs."

Two contractions later I was on the first floor, leaning over the back of the couch, talking to Nancy on the phone. After another contraction, I put the phone back to my ear. "Okay, Nancy, it's over."

"That was sixty seconds, a good sixty seconds," she said. "That was a long, strong, contraction, Kim. You're doing beautifully. Let me talk to John." I handed the phone over and heard her say, "How are ya, Coach?"

"Great!" he said, with forced cheer. She said something else, and he responded, "I thought so," with much less bravado, and moved the phone so we could both hear.

"Kim, Baby's serious now, very serious. And that's just fine. You're doing great. But you are *not* driving to the hospital. At this point, if you want to transport, it's going to have to be in an ambulance."

"I don't *want* to transport." I waited through a contraction, then lifted my head. "I don't want to have my baby inside an ambulance going down Charles Street!"

"Dad, Kim is a perfect candidate for a home birth. She always was. She's progressing well. I can be there in fifteen minutes. Or you can call an ambulance, and I'll meet you at the hospital. Either or. I'm getting in my car right now. Just tell me where to go."

"John," I whispered, "this woman has delivered 963 babies at home."

"The house," John said firmly, then hung up the phone. "Let's get you back to bed."

I turned my head and saw Jessie tiptoeing in at the back door.

I doubled over at the bottom step. "I can't go up those stairs. I don't know why I thought I could do this again. I'm no good at it. I promised you there wasn't going to be any trouble. That we were starting fresh."

"We are."

"But—you don't understand! The last time I had a baby, my marriage fell apart!"

He took my face in his hands. "This baby is my heart's desire," he said, and then I was somewhere else: the same place, but also a different one, so I was in two places at once, and had to leave him behind in the old dimension in order to focus. I bowed down, gripping the newel post with two hands. To Jessie I gasped, "One on top."

Jessie said, "Tell her they're one on top of the other. Tell her she's in transition."

"She's in transition." John was on the phone again. "No, *she* doesn't say that. Jessie says that. Yes, her. The friend. She's a flight attendant. She knows how to do emergencies." He put the phone down on the floor. "She says get her comfortable where she is and unlock the front door. You do know how to do this, right?" John asked Jessie.

"Listen, John, I've had medical training. And I've had two babies myself."

They were talking all around me. I could hear everything. But they needed to stop fussing and they needed to get off the damn phone. I had things to get done. "John, I need to stand up now."

"Hold her," Jessie coached, "that's right," as he braced himself against the newel post, and we stood in that narrow space at the foot of the stairs as though locked in an arm's-length dance for which we'd run out of room. "Keep holding on to her. This is the position she wants. Take her weight." Her voice came from the floor, firm and confident. "Honey, we're all set. I'm all ready. You just go ahead and have that beautiful baby if he wants to come now."

And then it was utterly and completely still, as quiet as a moonless night in the remote wilderness, so far from city lights that the dome of sky was spangled and salted with stars, or at the bottom of the sea in depths where sunlight never reached, and the atmosphere was thick and sweet and sparkling. Sinuous flags of ocher, coral, and cornflower yellow circled delicately around me on the ocean floor, those perfect and living figures, glyphs of a language so deep and profound, it could only be read by the soul. The air thrummed with this silence. It was the music of time.

"Baby's crowning!" I breathed. "Don't let go of me."

"I've got you."

"Head's born!" Jessie sang. "You're doing great, Mommy."

"I knew there was I reason I did squats," John tried to joke, but then I exclaimed, "Baby's turning!" and he looked a little scared. "No, it's okay," I gasped. "Baby's getting ready. He's just going to push now. He's pushing himself!"

"Wish I had gloves," Jessie said from the floor.

John looked straight into my eyes. "You are the most amazing and strong and graceful woman I have ever seen," he said, his voice filled with excitement.

"This *baby* is graceful," I breathed. "If it's a girl, we're going to name her Grace."

And she was, and we did, after her godmother Jessica Grace, whose hands were the first to touch her, who gently caught her smooth beautiful jeté into this world with a Baltimore Orioles souvenir dish towel and cried: "It's a girl!" just as the midwife barreled through the door.

Chapter 7

Are You the Friend

IT WAS A SEPTEMBER MORNING LIKE ANY OTHER, EXCEPT for the fact that John was sleeping in. He and his colleagues Chip and Hank, Suzanne's and Jessie's husbands respectively, had worked late the evening before. This was unusual for corporate, and their boss Maureen had told them to come in late the next day.

At seven weeks, Grace was still nursing almost every two hours, but for some reason this didn't daunt me; everything seemed so much easier this time around with John by my side. As long as he took the feeding close to midnight, I was fine: 2:00 a.m., 4:30 a.m., 7:00 a.m.—this shift included getting Nathan up and dressed. It was a September morning like any other—until it wasn't.

Nathan wanted his rocket T-shirt and favorite blue shorts, so I laid them out and left him to it, going downstairs to make breakfast before Grace fell asleep again and I could buy a few minutes stretched out on the couch by putting on a cassette tape—Burl Ives and Woody Guthrie were our current favorites—while Nathan played quietly on the floor beside me.

In the kitchen I cradled the baby in a sling against my chest and swayed gently to and fro, singing softly, "*See saw, Margery Daw / Jack shall have a new master...*" I opened the refrigerator and pulled out the egg carton. *"He shall earn but a penny a day / Because he can't work any faster."* I peeled back the edge of the sling to check on Grace. Good: eyes at half-mast. I was ready to go down again, too.

Nathan clattered into the kitchen. "Sit down at the table, honey," I whispered. "I'm making special breakfast for you and Daddy!"

"Special brefkist with Daddy!" He climbed into his booster chair.

I gently lifted Grace out of the baby sling. As I laid her down in her bassinet, there was a yelp from upstairs. "Whoops!" I crooned, as I wheeled the bassinet into the living room away from the noise of the kitchen. "Sounds like Daddy just cut himself shaving."

John called to me over the banister, and I leapt to the foot of the stairs. "Hush! Baby's down," I said.

"You're not going to believe this. Some private twin-engine just flew right into the World Trade Center."

I craned up at him. "What? That's crazy! How could they possibly make a mistake like that in broad daylight?"

"I don't know."

I was beating the eggs with a fork when he ran down the stairs. "Another one. And they're commercial jets. Terrorists."

"Brefkist! Brefkist!" Nathan called impatiently.

"Commercial," I repeated, staring into the bowl. "Commercial. Which? From where? From where?"

"Boston. Out of Boston. They just took off."

"Out of Boston. Oh my God, Boston," I breathed. "Thank God. I mean, not thank God."

Jessie used to do Boston flights. Not anymore. What day did she leave? She left two nights ago, so she flew yesterday. It was yesterday. She's in LA right now.

John punched the button on the tiny clock radio we kept tucked into a corner of the counter, so I could manage Nathan's time-outs. Our only TV was in the basement. "Keep listening. I have to get dressed."

The phone rang. It was my best friend from Tulsa.

"Dana!" I blurted. "Oh my gosh. Did you hear what just happened in New York?"

"Yes, I'm in D.C., and they just grounded all the flights."

"D.C.?" I repeated stupidly. "Why are you in D.C.? You're not coming to visit until Thanksgiving." I lunged back to the eggs on the stove.

"We were in Paris. We're on our way home from Paris. We flew non-rev out of Chicago, and coming back they put us on a flight to Dulles. We were waiting for a standby to Dallas, but everything shut down."

Now I remembered. Dana's husband worked for American Airlines, and they went to France at the end of every summer using his non-revenue flight benefit, which entailed hanging around in the airport with standby tickets. I put Nathan's plate of eggs in front of him, browned-side down.

"Thank goodness you're on the ground!" I exclaimed. "You've got to come stay with us. But—Oh, Dana, Nathan is supposed to fly next week!"

She interrupted. "Don't think about that now, hon. Listen, I need you to give me directions to your house. I have a pen in my hand."

"The eggs are burnded!" Nathan chanted in complaint, as I narrated directions.

"Okay, Mommy will make fresh. See you soon, Dana." I hung up the phone. John was now in the kitchen, leaning over the radio while tying his tie. "You're never going to believe this," I told him, "but Dana and Dave are in the middle of coming back from their trip to Paris and they're stranded in D.C."

"They can cab it here in an hour."

"That's what I told her. They had their luggage and were hanging around waiting for a standby to Dallas, so they just ran out to the cab stand. I should go over and see Hank. I know Jessie flew yesterday, but God, that's horrible timing. I'm sure it's upsetting. Thank goodness she's not doing those East Coast puddle jumpers anymore."

"I'm going to turn the news on." John disappeared into the basement, where the television set lived in the company of two old sofas on ancient shag carpeting.

I dumped the burned eggs in the sink and turned the radio up.

"John!" I called down the stairs. "This guy's made a mistake! He's saying a plane went into the Pentagon. He means New York. This guy is saying that a plane just hit the Pentagon."

"No," he called up. "Another one. Kim, United, but also American."

I raced down and saw the scrolling banner: *AA Fl.77, Washington Dulles to L.A.* My legs felt weak, and I plopped down next to him.

His voice was raw. "They took the planes going the farthest distance. They have the most fuel."

"American?" I said stupidly. "I can't remember. I can't remember!"

"Remember what?"

"Jessie's route. I think it was two back-to-backs to the West Coast. She flew yesterday."

Yesterday. It was yesterday or even the day before. I was sure. Hank could tell me. I couldn't remember which, but either way it didn't matter. She was already in L.A. I hustled outside. The seven-foot sunflowers were coming off their prime, their heads beginning to droop, the whole wall shrinking, compressing. I could see past them, past the playground, to Jessie's back door on the opposite row. Hank was walking slowly across the green, phone to his ear, staring at my slate roof, and it stopped me cold. I didn't want to close the distance; something was pushing at me, like the opposite of a magnet. But I forced myself.

"Hey, Hank," I said softly, moving square into his field of vision, catching his arm, and the minute I touched him I knew. I led him to our picnic table under the oak, and he sagged onto the bench. Over his shoulder, I saw Mardie streaking across the grass toward us. I pointed at Jessie's house for her to get the kids, and she wheeled off.

Hank sat forward, staring at the ground between his knees, hands hanging loosely. "We talked about this, of course. Of course we talked about it. We're not dumb. We talked about this." He turned to me. "But not *this*."

Mardie hustled back, with Danny on her hip. Her face was ashen. "Baby's still sleeping."

I held out my arms. "Come over to my house for breakfast today, big boy. I'm making chocolate chip pancakes!" To Mardie I said, "His parents are in Ellicott City. They're the close ones. Hers are in Charlotte."

"Fucking terrorists!" Hank burst out as Mardie led him away. "This isn't the fucking Middle East. This isn't fucking Israel."

Suzanne came to the front door while I was mixing the pancakes. She was the only one who came to the front because she lived right next to me and it was shorter. I opened the door holding the bowl of pancake batter. She looked at me, and her face went pale.

"No," she said. "No. No. Please tell me no."

"Go over there. Mardie's there. I have Danny with me."

BY THE TIME THE AIRPORT cab pulled up, I'd already churned out a double batch of cookies to use up the rest of the chips. I shoved my wallet in my apron pocket, picked up the baby, and ran outside.

The cabbie jumped out of the driver's seat with an alacrity that belied his ample girth and ran around to open the trunk. When he saw me, he stopped dead. "She said you were about to *have* a baby. But you done already *had* it!" he exclaimed.

"No, no, this is the last one," Dana fibbed out the window. "She's got another one on the way. She's a fertile Myrtle, my sister is," then ducked back to resume her earnest interchange with the white-faced extra passenger in the front seat, who was twisted around awkwardly with his arms wrapped around his briefcase.

I offered Dave some cash, but he folded his hand over my wallet and calmly told me he had it covered, then added, "By the way, pretend you're the sister." He put his palm on Grace's head, and I gave him the baby to hold while Dana emerged from the back seat looking incredibly Parisian in a tightly belted black raincoat and leggings. She always looked Parisian when she came back from Paris.

"Sis!" I cried, throwing my arms around her, but at that moment felt myself crumble. "Dana—my friend was on one of the planes," I sobbed.

She hugged me tightly. "I'm here now," she said. "I'm here."

Then she detached herself to throw her arms around the cab-driver. "You get that man home and get yourself on home too," she admonished.

"Yes, yes, yes," he said. "This is family time, time for family. You don't never know what's gonna happen, you can't tell me that. I was in Korea. I'd do it again if they'd ask. By God, they're gonna get the bastards that did this. I'm glad you could come to your sister. You had to move so far away, and you with another baby coming! Yessiree. She's lucky she's got you nearby now. There's a lot of people goin' to be sleeping in the airport. I'm gonna drop this guy off and then go home. I got eleven grandkids and they're all in school. Can you believe that? Ever' one of them. I could make a lotta money going back to the airport, but that's not where I'm at."

The front-seat passenger tapped the horn.

"Yessiree," he said again, climbing back behind the wheel.

Dana put an arm tightly around my shoulders and walked me back inside. John and Dave followed with the bags and the baby.

"I bet you had to fight to get that cab," John said.

Dave cracked a smile. "It pays to marry a good-looking woman from Loosiana," he drawled.

"We just do what needs to be done," Dana said. "When another plane hit, I *knew* they were going to close down the airspace. I was like 'Hit the street, honey.' We were already out the door. I went up to the guy at the stand and I said, 'How much would it cost to go to Baltimore?' And he looked at me and he said, 'Lady, you don't want to go to BWI. *All* the airports are closed, all of 'em,' and I said 'I don't *want* to go to *B-W-I*. I want to go to Baltimore, to a personal residence in the vicinity of Towson, Maryland,' and he said, 'Well, ordinarily that would be about fifty bucks to go by cab, but ain't *none* of these drivers gonna go there today. They're gonna be busy going back and forth from the airport as fast as they can. Local only! Local only!' By this time there's a line starting, so I was like, I'm not wasting any more time with this guy, and we just got in the first cab in the line. I handed the driver the piece of paper with your address on it, and he looked at it and said 'Baltimore? Baltimore? I ain't going to no Baltimore. I can take you to the train station mebbe. Local only.' And I took the paper back and I wrapped three fifty-dollar bills around it and I said, 'This *is* local. On my map, family is always local. I'm from Tulsa, Oklahoma, and this is about as far as I would drive to go to the damn grocery store and this is my blood sister who's having a baby and I need to get there. You don't carry me to Baltimore to my sister at a time like this, you're going to fry in hell. I'll see to it personally. And I'll be down there myself after my sister gets finished with me for not making it up to Baltimore when we live two thousand miles apart now 'cause her husband got transferred and we're an hour away and look around you, there's no other way I'm gonna get there.'"

We laughed. It was the only time that day, but we did. We laughed.

"What did he do?"

"What *could* he do?" said Dave. "He took the money and said, 'Fasten your seat belts.'"

"And the guy in the front seat?"

Dana, who had caught Nathan, looked up from smothering him with kisses. "He came around the other side and got in the front seat. Said he lives in Ellicott City. Wherever that is. Didn't talk the whole way."

"You and the cabbie were taking care of that nicely," said Dave.

"Well, actually, you know it felt kind of good to be speaking English again. I mean just talking and not feeling embarrassed about it. Now give me that baby, *s'il vous plait.* I need to love her up. You know those French people they just don't like it when you try to speak French unless you're an expert." She grazed Grace's downy head with her lips. "I know I was French in a former life. But I've forgotten it all by now."

SUZANNE LENT US A PORTABLE TV to put in the living room, and we spent the whole day in front of it. Nathan and Danny took gleeful advantage of our inattention to build a train network under and around the dining table and then expand it into the kitchen. I'd suggested John get Nathan the Brio starter kit last Christmas, citing the wisdom of managing expectations for a toddler, but he'd insisted on the deluxe version plus some à la carte additions. I had to step over the ferry, the covered tunnel, the drawbridge, and the roundabout. This served as a distraction as I went in and out of the kitchen, ostensibly to refresh the drinks and snacks, but also to sit at the top of the basement stairs by myself for a few minutes each time, to cry very quietly. I couldn't get it out of my mind, that Jessica knew with an absolute certainty that she was about to die. I thought of her on the plane, calling Hank, leaving a voicemail, thank God for cell phones! He could keep it forever, couldn't he, her last words to him, or would it be too painful? What were they?

I would never know. I could never ask. Dana was monitoring me; if I was gone too long, she'd come out to the kitchen, wet a clean dish towel, press it to my eyes for a moment, and lead me back.

In the middle of the afternoon, I was standing at the stove, shuffling a fresh batch of chocolate chip cookies onto the wire cooling rack, when a woman wearing a golf jacket over a wrinkled shirt stepped in my back door. For a fraction of a second she stood there, holding the knob and looking at the floor. Then she turned her face toward me with effort.

"Are you the friend?"

Jessie's mother. I hadn't met her yet, and now it was too late. We embraced with reddened eyes.

"I've come to get Danny," she said, and clasping him to her tightly, she took him away, along with a plate of cookies, because what else could I give her besides that hug? What else could I do? And I went back into the living room with another plate, and we kept watching the television screen. We couldn't stop. We watched over and over, switching channels. We watched, even though we knew that when the smoke cleared, there would be nothing there, nothing at all, and that it wasn't even really smoke: that the heaving convulsion that rushed down the streets and bloomed over the buildings was the sinister kind of vapor made of thousands of tons of steel pancaked down, vapor made up not just of walls and glass and carpet and ceiling tiles, but of desks and chairs and file cabinets, of wastebaskets and framed photos and daytimers and birthday balloons...and people—and that it wasn't going to change, no matter how many times we watched.

I made the billows of smoke into real clouds, pure and puffy and white, but that wasn't enough. There was more; there were specks. Those specks were real, living people. Doomed souls in the moments before death instinctively jumping because the alternative was worse. I couldn't get past those specks. I closed my eyes. By force of will, I created a new world, and it was the kind of world a mother makes: a world where no one was alone, where all, not some, held hands, where laws of gravity could be reversed and downward falls arc upward into flight, where precious souls turned into butterflies—a beautiful, streaming cloud of butterflies, climbing up to heaven.

Chapter 8

I'll Be Home for Christmas

HOLIDAY SEASON HAD ROLLED AROUND AGAIN, AND I WAS pleased that at five months postpartum I could squeeze back into the green leather miniskirt Karen had helped me pick out for Harkin Guaranty's Christmas party the previous year. Leather was unforgiving, but I'd met my benchmark. This year, instead of a hotel ballroom, Harkin Guaranty had rented out the entire Hunt Valley Mall. The place was moribund; the anchor tenants had departed for greener pastures, while the get-rich-relatively-quick developer sat out the remaining leases, so in the meantime it was being marketed as an event venue.

Once inside, a cheerful woman presented us with a map and buffet tickets. We inched through the tight bottleneck at the entrance, which gave John the opportunity to pat me on the behind without being noticed. "You look great tonight," he said.

"Oh, thanks, honey!"

"You'll be beating them off with a stick," he teased. "I can tell. Just make sure you go home with me!"

"None other," I replied, thwacking him lightly with the ticket envelope while I craned around for Suzanne. Finally I saw her hailing us wildly, standing with Chip beside a forlorn trio of potted ficus trees, the only adornment in an otherwise empty atrium.

"Thank goodness John is so tall," Suzanne said, readjusting the bust of her red strapless dress. "I almost lost you."

And it's four of us this year instead of six, I thought, looking at the heart-shaped locket Suzanne wore. I had one beneath my sweater and felt for it with my fingertips. *Jessica Grace* on one side, *forever* on the other. John saw my expression and squeezed my hand.

"Thank you for doing this," he said softly in my ear. "I know you know it's important to me."

It had been only three months since 9/11. Hank was staying home, and this was our first time socializing as couples since 9/11, because we'd canceled the annual neighborhood progressive dinner the first weekend in October. Could we do this without them?

A clown moonwalking against the current pulled up and began to juggle; sensing a lack of enthusiasm, he shrugged, tipped his oversize bowler, and mimed directions to the bar.

I took a sip from the plastic cup John handed me and wrinkled my nose. "That's a thumbs-down on the merlot."

"You can't be a snob where free booze is concerned," Chip replied.

"She's just jealous," said John. "Her sister is swilling Veuve at the Four Seasons in Seattle right now."

"John, I couldn't care less. I'm perfectly happy here with you. You couldn't pay me to be in Seattle, anyway!" I exclaimed. "I can't even think of living in the same city as Larry. Your offer from Harkin was an act of God." I dispensed with the last half inch in my cup. "And now the court date is coming up, and we'll get the visitation settled for good."

"You bet," Suzanne chimed in. "And then *he'll* be the one getting on a plane."

In the immediate aftermath of 9/11, Larry had rescheduled Nathan's September visit twice, but I'd still refused to put him on the plane; my legs turned to jelly whenever I thought about it. In response, Larry filed a motion for contempt. When October rolled around, my attorney had made things clear. "As your lawyer, I have to tell you to put that kid on the plane. I understand your decision after September eleventh. I know there were two unaccompanied minors on that flight to Los Angeles. But Nathan is not traveling alone. If you refuse a second time, you could jeopardize custody. We have to comply with the existing order." So I did. But having cried in John's arms all the night before that first October flight, I was in no fit shape to drive to the airport, so he'd taken the morning off work and helped. Nathan had made two more trips since then, but I'd stopped crying.

We wandered down the concourse, where roving troubadours tried to combat the dispiriting effect of folding security gates in front of closed retail units. We parked at a café table tied with balloons. "I'm not quite sure that I get the overall, unifying theme of this party," John said, scooping a handful of mixed nuts out of a bowl.

"Ringling Brothers Barnum and Bailey?" said Suzanne. "We did see a juggler."

"Then there should be an elephant," John said. "If they can get an elephant onstage at the opera, they can get one into this building. No, really!" he protested, "There *is* an elephant onstage at the opera. In..."

"*Aida,*" I supplied.

"That's right. *Aida.* We saw it last spring. I am now an opera connoisseur, thanks to this young lady here," he said, putting an arm around my waist.

"Animals are a very long shot," said Chip. "But we've had a juggler, so if there's a flame-eater, that might seal the deal."

"Or a knife-thrower."

"No sooner said than done," Chip murmured, scratching his nose in a southerly direction, and we turned to see their boss

Maureen walking toward us in her "I'm the boss" work uniform—navy pantsuit with ivory blouse—which made her easy to distinguish at a distance. She was accompanied by her own boss, Gunther.

I found Maureen intimidating. I'd socialized with her a sum total of three times: at a baby shower the office threw for us, one cocktail party, and a progressive dinner in our neighborhood. Maureen had clawed her way through Harvard, John told me, signed on with a big-time New York litigation firm, but then, after her divorce, made a sharp left turn and gone corporate, so she could be home at dinnertime. She coached soccer instead of dating, and with the help of a live-in housekeeper, was giving her son the most comfortable, secure childhood she could manage, which was pretty damned comfortable and secure. I'd given up a law career to stay at home, and I was sure I'd be weighed in the balance and found wanting by someone like Maureen, who was doing it all, and so successfully too. About the only thing we had in common, I guessed, was that neither of us would ever dream of participating in an ugly Christmas sweater contest.

"Don't worry," Suzanne reassured me. "She doesn't see us."

"She's a *great* boss," said John.

"I'll have to take that on trust," I said, and, "Spoken like a true teacher's pet," warbled Chip, as Maureen, deep in conversation with Gunther, passed us by. "Okay, all clear," he announced loudly, tipping the remnants from the nut bowl into his hand.

John nudged his friend. "Hey. I've said it before and I'll say it again, but if you stopped being the class clown, she might not get on your case so much."

"Don't hold your breath on that," Suzanne said. "He can't help himself. You know what he said when I showed him the positive pregnancy test last year?"

"'That's a sell on Pfizer,'" Chip volunteered, then funneled the nut dust into his mouth.

"See what I have to put up with?" Suzanne crossed her arms. "Everyone knows oral contraceptives are not one hundred percent effective!"

"Well, I know that *now*, don't I?" Chip said. "But I promise I will never tell baby Joey. It will give him a complex. And I have to admit that while at first I was upset at having to give up the madcap life of young newlyweds sooner than anticipated, I have grown fond of the little tyke."

I remembered once asking John why Chip always went the extra mile to prove he took nothing seriously, and he'd told me that it was insecurity. That he was a third-generation Yalie, super smart, but he'd never be quite sure he got there all by himself, so he put up a front. Then John added that I didn't need to worry about him being insecure like that, because he had all the confidence of someone who came from nothing. To which I responded that he was a self-made man, and that was the best kind.

We ran into Maureen again at the Casino Room after dinner. She hailed us from the roulette table closest to the prize display, a veritable mountain of company swag. I noticed that the necklace she wore was a string of tiny white ceramic Christmas tree lights, her sole nod to the occasion. With a few smart gestures, she rearranged the seating around the table, then shook her envelope.

"Hey, kids! Drinks are on me. I filched a bunch of drink chits from the registration table. Figured Gunther owed me. How about it, John?" She handed him the chits. "I'll have another Manhattan."

John took drink orders and departed obediently.

Maureen fingered her necklace, deep in thought, then leaned over to us. "Do you know how to play?" she asked, eyes narrowed.

Chip waited a beat before replying, "You mean…roulette?"

She threw back her head and brayed. The dealer filled us in and spun the wheel. "There you go, there you go." Maureen nodded. "Let's get some beginner's luck for you guys." But only the stocky man sitting next to Suzanne had any success.

Maureen pulled the cherry out of her drink, ate it, and pointed the spear at us. "How old are your kids again?" she asked, and we blurted out their ages. "I remember now, right, right. Tiny tots."

John returned. Maureen traded cups with him and then threw in some more chips. "Do you *know* how hard it is to move kids while they're in school?" she went on, while the wheel spun. "I had to live like that when I was a kid, and I swore I'd never move him around like I had to. I told myself—the divorce move didn't count. We've stayed put. And now he's going into seventh grade! That's the worst!" She stabbed the green baize for emphasis. "The. Worst. Year. To move a kid."

Why was she talking about moving? We gave each other side-long glances, then paid studious attention to the wheel. Even Chip was silent. I tried to think: Was she this tipsy at last year's party? I didn't think so, but how would I know? We'd only stayed an hour.

The ball dropped.

"Five and five hits! Straight up!" The stocky man next to Suzanne punched his fist in the air.

"Damn," muttered Maureen. "I'm too cautious to bet like that. Maybe that's the problem."

"I'm out on that," said the winner. "Not gonna push. Let's quit while we're ahead," he said to his companion, a silent man expressing his inner self with a bright plaid bowtie, and they left.

"Yeah, a good strategy, if you've got a crystal ball," Maureen remarked sourly. She took another sip of bourbon, sloshing a drop on her slacks, then blotted her pants leg with a paper napkin. "You know, in my nine years here, I've never seen such a lavish holiday party," she said, then looked up and saw our expressions. "Don't mind me," she said abruptly. "I'm just upset because my horse has hoof-and-mouth disease."

She had horses; I remembered that. She commuted from Cockeysville because it was the closest she could get to Roland Park and still keep a horse. I remembered the conversation. *I like to be able to walk out the back door and go for a ride in the morning. Otherwise why bother?* Yes. I remembered her words, remembered how cool, calm, and crisp she'd looked while I was sweating at our baby shower, even in the air-conditioning, in a yellow flowered "it's all over below the shoulder" maternity dress. They'd all chipped in on a double stroller.

I racked my brain for something to say and chirped: "I think the circus theme for this year was a great choice."

"Circus theme. Is that what it was?" Maureen said dryly, rattling the cubes in her empty cup. "Well, time to saddle up. Maybe I'll hit that dessert buffet." She stood, but paused for a moment, cocking her head thoughtfully. "There's just something about it that reminds me of the children's ward at the Cancer Center. Clowns and balloons, to take your mind off. Have a nice rest of your evening, kids!" she finished, giving a little backward wave as she walked carefully in the direction of the prize table.

JANUARY 1 WAS CHRISTMAS DAY at our house because Nathan had been in Seattle for the holiday and readily accepted my matter-of-fact assertion on New Year's Eve that Santa was coming to Mommy's house tonight.

By two o'clock in the afternoon, the excitement had tapered. The smell of roasting turkey filled the house. Grace was napping; John and Nathan were playing quietly with the ever-expanding train set around the Christmas tree while I stepped around them, collecting wrapping paper.

The bell rang, and I opened the door to catch a sideways glimpse of a woman, a stranger, hands plunged deep into the pockets of an unzipped parka and staring over the front railing with a frown as though she'd just seen something unpleasant or unexpected in the bushes—a piece of trash? A discarded toy? But then she turned, and I recognized Maureen.

"Happy New Year!" she said.

"And Merry Christmas!" I said apologetically, tossing the wad of gift wrap behind me into the stairwell and smoothing my hair. John dashed up behind me, train engine in hand.

"Both," he said in jolly tones. "It's Nathan's Baltimore Christmas."

"Yikes! I didn't mean to interrupt," she said, stepping right in. "I was just in the neighborhood," she added, as though it were a frequent occurrence.

John ushered her to his prized leather armchair. She dropped into it without taking off her coat. She declined a drink but did unzip the parka. She was wearing an ivory cashmere turtleneck over her jeans: navy and white, again. Maybe it streamlined her routine, I thought, as we sat down opposite her on the couch. I pushed the baby's bouncer chair away with my foot.

For a long, awkward moment, she gazed at the Christmas tree with the same expression I'd caught on the doorstep. The tree did look strange, all the ornaments crammed onto the top branches, the lower part completely bare. I felt the need to explain.

"I had to put the ornaments out of Nathan's reach," I blurted, with a gesture.

"Oh—right." She took her arms out of her coat and went on. "Sorry to drop in like this, but I just wanted to chat for a minute. Something's come up."

John and I exchanged a wary glance: *Surely bosses do not make house calls for the purpose of laying you off?*

"Something's come up," she repeated, "and I wanted to talk to you—no, both of you," she said, putting out a hand as I started to rise. "I don't want you to read it in the paper tomorrow like everyone else. Like every other one of the twenty-five hundred employees of Harkin Guaranty," she said. "We're being bought."

John quickly sucked in a breath, and I exclaimed, "But Harkin just bought Ensign! Like, less than two years ago!"

"Moving up the food chain, I guess. But this one's going to cost jobs. That's what Gunther says," she added morosely, shrinking back into the depths of her parka. "Gunther told me. But you can't tell another soul."

"Of course." John sat forward and clasped his hands. "What's the deal?"

"It's Met Mutual. We're being bought by Met Mutual."

"New York." He nodded. "New CEO last year. Jack Terkel."

"Jack Terkel doesn't know shit about the insurance industry. They're going to keep our Chicago headquarters—it's the Midwest region they want. But us? Baltimore? We're 'redundant.'"

I thought back to our wedding day at Elmwood, when Mr. Freeman, Harkin's CEO, had likely put the Ensign CEO in the position of telling the majority of her Minneapolis employees that *they* were redundant. That's why her hands had been shaking when she'd tried to light a cigarette. They'd never make Chicago redundant, I thought bitterly. It's too big to be redundant.

I looked out the window at the thin layer of snow on the pear trees lining the parkway. If anyone should be made redundant, it should be Freeman, I thought. Maureen stared at me, and I realized I'd said it out loud.

"You're right there!" she exclaimed. "Sonofabitch. Don't tell me they all weren't in on it."

"Going potty," Nathan announced, mounting the stairs with an armful of his new stuffed animals. Maureen flashed him a quick smile and turned back.

"Listen, the only reason this deal went through is they agreed to maintain a presence in Maryland. Turns out they're going to keep the Round House as a corporate retreat and sell off the rest of the property! Presence, my ass. Prime real estate. Hundreds of acres. In a year, after the ink's dry and the state attorney general forgets all about it, they're going to sell it off and prance back to Manhattan with all the business."

"Just like that," John said pensively.

"Yep. Just like that. There were a few boardroom guys whining 'cause they're almost but not quite ready to retire to Florida, so they said okay, we'll keep a small office for a couple of years. But how can you have a satellite of a satellite?" She pinched the bridge of her nose. "I'm fifty-two. People like me do make lateral moves, but I have no leverage now. Gunther said he'd take me with him to Chicago. He's a great boss, but who knows? I want Colin to go to Calvert. I have to make some choices here. We all have to make choices."

"Two years," I said gamely. "We don't know what that will look like. Maybe we'll get lucky." But my stomach was churning. If Maureen was worried, Maureen of the top tier and the ivory cashmere, what did that mean for John and Chip and Hank and the rest of the corporate counsel office? For that matter, what did it mean for everyone who worked there, all the way down to second-floor data entry—the twentysomethings who'd worn sequined dresses and spike heels to the Christmas party? We knew what it meant. We didn't have a crystal ball, but we could guess. The dealer had spun the wheel, and the rest of us hadn't even known to make bets, but even if we had, it wouldn't matter. This had nothing to do with luck.

"I had my suspicions, and Gunther finally told me this morning. Harkin is one of the biggest employers in the Baltimore area. It's shutting down, and every Tom, Dick, and Harry who works there is going to find out about it tomorrow in the morning paper. It's just not right. I couldn't do that to you, John." She paused. "You know, actually...I think I would like that drink."

John brought out a bottle of wine. "This is what we had on tap for today," he said, holding it up.

"Oh God." Maureen groaned. "I'm ruining your holiday."

"No, you're not," John said, filling three glasses. "Here's to the future," he announced. "We just don't know what it looks like yet."

I could tell by the energy in his voice that he was trying to take the high road, like my road to Tahlequah. To go in the right direction. But secretly I wondered: Was this punishment for the choices we'd made? The choices *I'd* made? Subjecting my child to a damaging visitation schedule. Persuading myself that Larry would lose interest in Nathan so the distance wouldn't matter. Moving all the way to the East Coast for a seductively lucrative job that was evaporating less than two years later. If we moved again, Maryland would lose jurisdiction. And we'd be high and dry for yet another six months.

Maureen rotated the glass between her palms. "I know they gave Gunther your name as a potential new hire, but *I'm* the one that hired you. Now we're not even going to make it to your second annual review. And you just had another baby." She turned to me. "I was even hoping when you were ready you might be interested in joining the team, Kim."

She *had* been watching me. *Had* been evaluating, but in a good way. For a fleeting moment, I saw that future—the one in Baltimore. Trading our brick, slate-roofed town house for a brick, slate-roofed single-family home with a bigger yard. Dropping the kids off at the Calvert School, the most prestigious private school in Baltimore. Then driving to the office, together. I'd still have time to cook dinner, play with my quartet, maybe even coach Grace's…something…team. Lacrosse? Lacrosse was big on the East Coast. I'd still have Home Base. Our group would watch the children move together through the grades, then high school. I'd stay in one place. I wouldn't always be saying goodbye. In my mind's eye, this life suddenly rose, a waterfall of countless happy moments, sparkling in the sunlight, and then sank into the ground.

"Jack Terkel," she spat. "What does he know about this industry? He's thirty-five years old. He just shuffles money around. And now he's a glorified real estate broker."

She pulled out a business card and handed it to John. "Call this guy," she said. "He's a really good headhunter. This is coming out in the paper tomorrow. Believe me, it's hermetically sealed, but I don't give a shit. I'll be damned if I was going to have to look you in the face in the morning without warning you. Get in with him now. Call him tonight."

She drained her glass and left.

We sat back down on the couch again, side by side. It was intensely quiet. Nathan had disappeared upstairs, and the baby was still sleeping.

The oven timer went off. "Turkey's done," John said in a voice that sounded as though dredged from a gravel pit. Then he laughed. "*I'm* done. I'm done! Stick a fork in me."

"Ha ha," I said.

He tapped his fist on his mouth. "Do you have any idea the level of trust involved in giving me that information?"

"She really thinks highly of you," I agreed. I tried to joke, "Seems like you're always getting a business card at the right moment," but I couldn't pull it off. "We *have* to stay in Baltimore! We have court jurisdiction here now," I wailed.

"I know."

"I *want* to stay in Baltimore!"

"I know."

"What about Black & Decker? McCormick?"

A thought struck him, and he put a hand on my arm. "Geez. You can't say *anything* to Suzanne. We can't say anything today."

"I know. It's not going to matter to them anyway. They're not going anywhere. Chip's a native son. His family is here. He'll have connections. Hank too." I paused. "Unlike us..."

He put his arm around me. I looked around at John's prized leather armchair, the dining room set from the consignment shop on York Road, the geraniums struggling to winter over on the bay windowsill, a window without curtains. I hadn't even gotten to buying curtains. I'd been taking my time.

John slapped his knees. "Okay. You bring down the kids. I'll get the bird out of the oven, and then I have an email to send."

"The headhunter?"

He shook his head. "No. I'm contacting Dunwoody Scudder Ellis. In Seattle. I know I was only there a couple of months, but we parted on good terms."

I stopped at the foot of the stairs, hand on the newel post, and looked at John. I felt with my fingertips for the heart-shaped locket at my neck, beneath my sweater. *Jessica Grace* on one side, *forever* on the other. We all had them now. Our group.

Maybe it was all for the best. Maybe this place would always be covered in ash for me. Maybe a change was in the offing, a shift of key in a tune that would essentially remain the same. We looked at each other, John and me. He reached out, and I took his hand. We shook hands, formally.

Upstairs I found Nathan underneath his bed with all the stuffed animals.

I lay down on the floor. The Berber carpeting was unfriendly to my cheek. It had been sold to me as durable and long-lasting, but it was hard, unforgiving, institutional, not the kind of floor where little children could pad around barefoot and feel comfy. "Hey, there," I said softly. "What'cha doin'?"

He tucked the toys more closely around him.

Last month we'd gone to an open house for the Calvert School pre-K, and while looking at the application, I'd noticed there was a box to check to confirm the child was toilet-trained. I'd sidled over to one of the teachers and asked if that meant by the time the school year started next fall, and she looked at me like I had a hole in my head. "No, at the time of application! These children are all over three," she said frostily, so I skulked off, embarrassed and glad she hadn't asked me my child's name so she could immediately cross him off the list.

I didn't mind having to re-toilet-train my child. I didn't mind having to deal with his difficult, unsettled nights the first few days he returned home each time. I could manage all of that. It was this withdrawal that upset me, a more recent development. Nathan had always been an unusually sunny child, and now he was changing. He didn't belong under the bed.

I addressed the back of his head. "Kinda neat under here. Nice and quiet."

After a minute, he said: "I lost you."

That was a gut punch. I wanted to howl, to keen. I knew what he meant, because I felt the same. I thought of the Baltimore airport, of the kindness of strangers, of the prayer I now repeated to him each time before he left, clasping his little hands in mine, and then again every night while he was gone. Jessie had joked about keeping Miss Pink in a playpen until she was twelve, but the truth of the matter was that motherhood was an education in all the things in life against which you could not protect your child—which was most of them. We did what we could. I thought of Jessie racing to scoop up the tiny girl who'd fallen through the jungle gym, and I was convinced that on that flight to L.A., she'd done the same, at the end, taken charge of the unaccompanied minors, held them in her arms.

"I lost you," he said again.

"Well, I'm here now." I moved my hand just underneath the bed. "Here I am."

He gave me half of his face and one eye.

I walked my fingers closer, and he turned his head to watch.

"Here I am, and Smooshy, and Big Smooshy, and Smooshy Dan, and Smooshybird." It was not hard to remember all the names; either we were building a rainbow family here, or he just liked the "sh" sibilant. "We're all here," I went on, "every one of us. Mama is here."

His hand shot out, and he grabbed my fingers.

"C'mon out, Puddinhead. It's time to eat dinner, and there's special cake for dessert." Still holding his hand, I tapped a beat on the carpet with the fingers of my other.

Handy Spandy Jack-a-Dandy
Loved plum cake and sugar candy
Went into a butcher shop
And out he came hop hop hop hop!

He was watching.

"Hmm…let's sing. What should we sing?" I started his favorite, the one that in infancy had always made him burst into laughter at the end when the dish ran away with the spoon but we could never for the life of us figure out why. "*Hey diddle diddle, the cat and the fiddle / The cow jumped over the moon…*"

He let go of my hand and began pushing toys out one by one.

"*The little dog laughed to see such sport / and the dish ran away with the spoon.*"

He let me gently tug him out. I pulled him onto my stomach, wrapped my arms around him, and buried my nose in his hair. His ear against my chest, he listened to my voice through my bones as I lay on my back, singing.

Grace had fallen quiet in the other room. It was so quiet I could hear John's voice downstairs on the phone to Seattle. I'd eagerly discarded the idea of living there, even when it had actually materialized, because I didn't want to feel that Larry was still controlling me, controlling my new life, because—well, lots of reasons. Because I was anxious about how my new husband would react to living near him. Because I was too entrenched in thinking of him as the bad guy. I was too my-way-or-the-highway, too resentful of his abandonment and mistreatment during pregnancy. I couldn't believe I'd spat, "If he wants to see his child, he can get on a plane!" And now Larry had just won another motion to continue that would delay things for *another* four months. Eight cross-country trips so far! How much further damage would be done before we could put our Hopkins expert on the stand? My child was suffering, and it was all my fault.

John materialized in the doorway. He rubbed the doorframe with two fingers, then stood leaning against it, tapping the unused business card against his leg. I turned my head to look at him, and a tear slid into my ear. I wiped my nose with my shirtsleeve. We *had* talked about moving, usually in bed late at night, every once in a while, as things dragged on for Nathan with no relief. Karen and Frank had moved to Seattle a few months after our wedding. So that courtly handshake at the foot of the stairs, before I'd gone up to the children, had not been a sudden impulse. It was the outward sign of a healthy marriage, where genuine communication achieves unity of thought and mind. A real marriage. As I twisted my lips wryly, he was doing the same, and when I came out with it: "Goodbye, Baltimore—" he joined me at the finish: "Hello...Seattle!"

Chapter 9

Everybody's Dancing
with Everybody Else

FOUR YEARS LATER, EVERYTHING WAS GOING ACCORDING
to plan. John was on partner track at Dunwoody in Seattle; they'd
been happy to hear back from him, despite the fact he'd accepted
and then rejected their original offer before we were married. One
of the partners, Owen, who'd taken a shine to him during that
initial interview, was head of Intellectual Property. He told him
there was an opening in his group and persuaded him to move over
from insurance law; John couldn't have been happier. As for me, I
enjoyed being a stay-at-home mom, while also slowly continuing
to work my way back into music performance, a process that had
begun in Baltimore with private lessons and an amateur string
quartet and had now reached its probable apex with a seat in a
semi-professional chamber orchestra in Bellevue called Mostly
Baroque.

But by far the best part of living in Seattle was being near
my sister, Karen, again. She helped me find a house near hers in
Issaquah, so we lived only a few blocks away from each other. It
wasn't exactly in her subdivision, but tucked into a wooded ridge
behind it, the original 1915 farmhouse out of whose remaining

acreage the lots of Ogilvie Glen had been carved. Karen had been renting the remodeled barn as a music studio and was the first to hear about its availability. She called me right away. "It'll remind you of Elmwood," she'd said, and she was right. I'd flown out alone and fallen in love at first sight. But I feared it might be too big. "Your sister has a five-bedroom house, so why shouldn't you?" John had replied on the phone, a bit indignantly, but then his voice softened, and he reminded me that we wanted a big yard for the kids. "You have no idea how big," I said. "I see a riding mower in your future." He cracked back. "My secret goal in life has always been to own a riding mower."

The only thing that hadn't gone according to plan was Karen doubling her brood with the addition of twins, just this past year. They'd taken it in stride, but I'd fussed over her anxiously during her pregnancy until she sat me down in her second trimester and told me to stop; that yes, our mother had had a twin who died as a baby, but that was a long time ago, and medicine and prenatal care had advanced greatly in the intervening years, and that I needed to stop worrying. She was right, of course. After that I fretted less, but the fretting I did do was done in secret, because the miscarriage I'd had back when I was single, the one she didn't know about, was of twins. Karen gave birth without a hitch to perfectly healthy twins, and the first words out of her mouth to me were that she'd never been more glad that I lived practically next door. Two more children certainly made our two-women babysitting co-op a lot livelier, especially after she returned to the pit orchestra for the Seattle Opera when Michael and Molly were eight months old.

Tonight, the second Saturday in October, was opening night for *Ariadne auf Naxos,* so at five o'clock the whole crew was at my house. Four-year-old Grace sat in front of the refrigerator, arranging the alphabet magnets by color as she sang along with Burl Ives.

"There's a little white duck sitting in the water / A little white duck, doing what he oughter—"

Second grader Nathan, followed by his younger cousins, Sam and Tyler, raced through the kitchen with neoprene water bottles duct-taped to their backs. Nathan grabbed the cereal box off the counter as they veered around Grace and disappeared.

"He took a bite of a lily pad / Flapped his wings and he said 'I'm glad—"

The boys streamed through again, this time holding strings that were tied to their bottles, and I finally got it: parachutes! I grabbed back the cereal box. "Don't spoil your dinner!"

I shook out a handful of the cereal for each of Karen's twins, then turned back to the stove. Our kitchen remodel fit neatly into the back of the house like a puzzle piece, with large doorways opening to the dining room at one end and the den at the other. That it turned the first floor into a carousel, I did not mind one bit. It kept the kids where I could see them.

The doorbell rang. Grace ran out, just as quickly returned, and plopped back down on the floor. "It's not Daddy," she announced.

I checked the time. Yes, too early to be John; it had to be Frank. And it was. He leaned against the doorway and crossed his arms.

"Don't all cheer at once." He grinned, and his twins, catching sight, began to crow in their side-by-side high chairs. He side-stepped Grace and ruffled their curls. "I went home and it was so quiet I thought I'd walked into the wrong house. Then I remembered it was opera night." He pulled a beer out of the fridge and resumed his position holding up the doorway. "What are you making there, pumpkin?" he asked Grace, tipping his head sideways.

"Music!" she cried indignantly, with a dramatic flourish intended to emphasize the incredible stupidity on his part in questioning the obvious.

"Of *course!* It's beautiful." Frank had gained a few pounds since quitting smoking, but he was so tall he carried it well. In his heathered crewneck over a white dress shirt, he looked, as usual, considerably less drained after a long day's work than John. John knew *how* to relax, but Frank was *always* relaxed, which was why it was so easy for me to be relaxed with him. He was my brother-in-law, but he genuinely felt like a brother to me, and this laid-back quality might have been part of the reason he'd been so successful in the contemporary minefield known as Human Resources. He'd begun his career as a professional French horn player, which was how he'd met my cellist sister, but didn't seem regretful in the least about the career switch. That their third child had turned out to be twins only served to confirm the wisdom of his decision to choose a steady, substantial paycheck and plush benefits.

He did play in a brass ensemble on the state arts roster that toured Eastern Washington doing school concerts, for which his employer, Intelicomp, received charitable brownie points, but he liked to joke that he was living vicariously through Karen, to which I always responded: "You and me both!" But this was only partially true. In Baltimore, I'd had a couple of years of brush-up lessons and played in an amateur string quartet. By the time we moved to Seattle, I was ready for something more, and won a seat in a small, semi-professional chamber orchestra. Through all of this, I was making the beautiful discovery that there was much fulfillment to be had as a musician even without professional status, and I wondered why I had been so "all or nothing" at age eighteen. Teenagers tended to have more black-and-white thinking, I guessed.

The boys plowed through again and, with the additional obstacle of Frank in the doorway, stumbled over Grace, who promptly burst into tears.

"Sammy hit me in the bones!"

"Now, boys—"

"Daddy! We're in the future! You can't talk to us yet!" Tyler screeched, in the high-pitched tones of a kindergartner with low blood sugar being whipped into a frenzy by the effort of keeping up with the older boys.

I lifted Grace to her feet and reinstalled her on a stool at the counter out of the fray. She hunkered down and began scribbling earnestly on a notepad, pausing only to tent herself with her blanket as the boys ran around the mulberry bush again, which (the tenting) had the not unpleasant effect of slightly muting "There Was An Old Lady Who Swallowed A Fly." Then I went back to pushing plums and olives in around the chicken breasts in the dutch oven.

Frank stole an olive. "What are you making?"

"Chicken tagine. It's getting chilly at night now, so I got in a stew mood."

He leaned over for a whiff. "This is the silver lining for me." He sighed. "Dinner at your house on opera nights. It's impossible to persuade your wife not to go back to work yet when she can say it's part time. But that's cheating. Playing in opera orchestra is only part time if you average it over the entire school year. Really, it's full-time in spurts."

"I think Bill will like this dish," I said. "I'll save some for him." Bill Beery was our neighbor who lived in an old hunting cabin at the end of our unpaved road, conspicuously marked No Outlet at the back of the subdivision. It led up the valley past our house, turned sharply to cross a bridge over the creek, and dead-ended on the other side of the hill. We were the only two houses on the road.

"How come he never sits down with you?" Frank asked, popping another olive into his mouth.

"He's a rebel and a loner," I joked. "Actually, he does come over for dinner now and then, but only when it's just us. Bill doesn't like crowds."

The boys streamed through again, and Frank cracked, "I think I understand."

"Listen, thank goodness the rains have kicked in and all this has moved indoors. Poor Bill was almost ready to fall on his sword." Although his cabin wasn't visible unless we climbed the footpath to the top of the hill, noise carried.

"It's his own fault for building that playhouse in the woods. I think it's actually on his property, not yours."

"We're nonconformists over here in the back of beyond, Frank. We don't pay much attention to property lines."

My phone buzzed, and I leaned over to read the text. "Game's over, kids," I called. "Time to get ready, Nathan." Instantly Grace scrambled down from her stool, grabbed my leg, and put her thumb in her mouth.

Nathan began to whine. "But, *Mom*, I don't *want* to go right now! I'm *busy!*"

"I want to go with Daddy Larry too!" Tyler cried. "I want to go too."

His brother poked him. "Don't be dumb. He's not your dad. You can only go with him if he's your dad."

"But I want him to be! Why can't he be my dad too?"

Nathan put his hands on his knees and bent down to explain. "You can't have two dads, Tyler."

"Why not? You do!"

"Because I was *born* with them," he explained. "You have to be born with them. How 'bout, I'll bring you back a treat. I'll make Daddy Larry buy the Halloween candy this weekend, and then I'll bring a bunch home, okay?" He straightened up, detached his parachute, and handed it to Tyler. "Remember," he said. "*You're* in charge of the equipment."

"Okay," said Tyler solemnly.

Grace was still latched on to my leg. "Don't worry, pumpkin," I said, stroking her hair. "Nathan's going bye-bye, but you're staying with me." She relaxed her death grip and, when the doorbell rang, joined the stampede into the front hall.

This time I followed, wiping my hands on my apron. The boys wheeled off after opening the door, leaving Grace tottering on the threshold, staring at Leeza, who today was swathed in pale pink mohair, which made her look almost suburban. Except for the boots. The boots were the same as the first time I'd met her—those knee-high platform boots. Her hair was now a steeply angled shoulder-length bob in her natural color; the fuchsia-tipped peroxide had finally fully grown out, a tremendous improvement that had taken a few years. She did not look like a graduate student, and she wasn't anymore—this I had just learned from Larry's text about the pickup time. She'd failed her dissertation defense and dropped out of the PhD program. It had surprised me that he'd stepped out of his narcissistic bubble long enough to share this informational tidbit.

Grace backed up a few steps to the foot of the hall stairs and bellowed "Leeza's here!" quite unnecessarily, as Nathan was already halfway down, his overnighter thumping behind him. He towed it past us out the door, exclaiming: "Cool! The red car! Bye, Mom!"

By this time, I knew not to take either the reluctance or the enthusiasm of a seven-year-old personally. Nathan had had "play therapy" with a psychologist on the advice of our new pediatrician when we'd made the move to Seattle four years ago. After a few months, she'd reported no significant evidence of adjustment or attachment disorders but cautioned me to keep an eye out closer to his adolescence, because that's when issues often cropped up for children of divorce. So far things seemed to be going fine, despite the fact that he spent most of his time with Leeza and not Larry. Larry being continually unavailable. Or maybe things were going fine because of that.

Leeza was now picking at a thread on her coat. "Larry had a client emergency," she said, then stepped over the threshold, trying to get an eyeful of my living room without appearing to do so.

"He seems to have those a lot lately," I remarked, thinking that nothing had changed in the two weeks since she'd last picked up Nathan; I still hadn't gotten to curtains in the living room. Who was going to see into my first floor anyway? Bill was not going to look into our windows as he drove past a couple of hundred yards away. I'd been busy getting floors refinished, walls painted, and bathrooms remodeled. And why should I care about Leeza's judgment of my taste? I took a step closer to the door, and she edged back out.

"Well, I guess it's not such a chore to chauffeur when you can do it in a car like that," I said, and we exchanged fake smiles.

"Oh, it's *never* a chore," she chirped back, and turned to go but with a hunch in her shoulders that made me repent.

"Hey, listen. Larry mentioned what happened at your defense. I'm really sorry."

"Well, yeah. You know academic politics." Her expression was wan.

"You can still get a good job," I said energetically. "A master's is nothing to sneeze at."

"I guess one doctorate in the family is enough," she said with unconcealed misery, turning the diamond around on her finger.

How long had they been together? Seven years, all told, and at this point Leeza was probably the only person on the planet who didn't realize they were never getting married. He'd bought her off with a two-carat solitaire and was probably sitting there right now thinking, *Small price to pay*. When was she going to figure it out? Larry had used her shamelessly as a caretaker during Nathan's toddler visits. She had to be thirty-two at this point, and her own son about fourteen.

"Don't forget, basketball practice at ten tomorrow!" I called, as she bustled back to her car, and she wiggled her fingers in my direction. I blew Nathan a kiss as they pulled out, even though I knew he wasn't looking.

Grace followed me back into the kitchen. "She has a fuzzy coat," she said, then hugged my knees and cried, "Mommy, I want to stay with you! I just love you so much!"

"Oh, me too, Gracie! We're staying here together. But I don't want you standing right in front of the stove, please."

She climbed back up to the table and moved on to "Shoofly" with Burl Ives, while I dished out the second-shift plates of mac-and-cheese plus some cut-up roast chicken for Sammy, Tyler, and Grace. Plain chicken. Very plain. I knew better than to attempt anything spicy. If I did, I'd find tiny dried pieces underneath the refrigerator the next time I got down on my hands and knees to check, which was not often. They'd be in college before they realized what a sensational cook I was, and then they'd be sorry.

"Larry sure makes her do all the heavy lifting, doesn't he?" Frank remarked, mopping off the twins.

"And now look what's happened with her doctorate as well. I almost feel sympathy."

"This might well be the making of her," he joked. "You know what they say about academia: sheltered workshop for the psychosocially handicapped. I have to say," he went on, indicating Grace's baby boom box, "I'm glad that disc has migrated over to your house. I told Karen if I had to listen to the piccolo solo in 'Watch the Donut, Not the Hole' one more time, I was going to lobotomize myself with an ice pick."

Grace beamed up at him. "*Watch the donut, not the hole*," she caroled, over Burl Ives singing "Shoofly."

I stopped. "Catch that note!"

Frank looked up. "Which one?"

"The first. Do the first. *Watch...*" I sang.

"*Watch...*" He held the note with me; then I backed up to the matching track on the disc and pressed play.

"I thought so," I said with hushed excitement. "She was exactly on pitch."

He raised his eyebrows at me, and I held up an index finger silently. While the kids ate, I played "Shoofly" again, and then after a minute said craftily, "Honey, sing 'Watch the Donut' again." She obliged.

I picked up her note.

"*Watch...*" I sang, and Frank did the same, an octave lower: "Watch..." We held it while I switched back. Again, she was spot-on.

John walked into the kitchen. "What are you doing, starting a cult?"

The children scrambled down and swarmed over him to get into his jacket pockets.

"What's he got that I haven't got?" Frank grumbled.

"Candy?" I swiped it out of their hands and made a pile on the table. "Finish up, you guys. That's dessert. John, listen to this—"

But he already had his arm around me and was tipping me back for a kiss, then up again, all while Grace remained seated on his left shoe. "How's my beautiful wife?"

I prolonged the kiss in a standing position for another moment, then brushed my hair back in place. "Now listen, John, I'm serious. Listen up." I turned on "Shoofly." "Honey, sing 'Watch the Donut' again."

"I don't *want* to, Mommy."

"I think she's got perfect pitch," I said excitedly.

"What *is* that? I don't even know what that is. Is it gonna get her into Harvard? That's all I want to know."

Grace was not on his shoe anymore but still clung to his leg. "Oh, I can't stop loving you! All I want to do is love you and Mommy!"

"Gracie," said Frank, wiping beer from his nose, "You are just a living doll."

John got the three boys out of the kitchen by telling them there was a sabertooth moose cub in the front yard and they needed to investigate. Then he said he had a surprise. "A surprise!" Grace echoed, clapping her hands, as John pulled a bottle of Veuve Clicquot out of his briefcase and presented it to me with a dramatic flourish.

For a brief second I gaped. Then I launched myself at him. "*That* was the late meeting? You made partner! Congratulations!"

Grace bounced up and down. "What is it? What's the surprise?"

Frank said, "Your daddy just had a *really* good day at work today." He shook John's hand. "Right on schedule. Congrats, brother."

"It's a surprise! A really good day surprise!" Gracie burrowed in. John lifted her up on his hip so she could join our dance. Frank joined in, scooping up a twin in each arm, and we doh-si-dohed around each other.

"Look, Daddy! Everybody's dancing with everybody else! Why are we dancing with everybody else?"

He beamed. "Because I can't stop loving you and Mommy."

She put an arm around each of our necks. "All I want to do is love you! I can't stop loving you! Oh, Mommy! I'll do it! I'll do it now," she cried, and belted it out at the top of her lungs as we waltzed around the kitchen:

"*WATCH THE DONUT, NOT THE HOLE!*"

Chapter 10

At Least We Have Each Other

WE STOOD IN FRONT OF THE ELEVATOR AT BELLEVUE SQUARE, ready to launch our annual Christmas shopping trip. Ten-year-old Nathan and his younger cousins Sammy and Tyler pressed all the buttons they could find, while Karen and I stood behind them with the strollers and seven-year-old Grace. The chime rang, the doors opened, and a small gaggle of teenage girls looked out at our formation with visible dismay. "Don't worry. We'll take the next one," Karen reassured them.

She was pushing an old lightweight folding double stroller, which she still kept on hand for long outings, when the twins' three-year-old legs would get tired, but mine was a Cadillac single, cradling the Delightful Surprise, aka John Jr., known to his closest associates as Jackie. I peeked in, and baby Jackie beamed up at me, ruddy-cheeked and dimpled, from within the satiny recesses of the most obscenely plush stroller that the obscenely expensive baby store had carried. I had only pretended to object when John flourished his credit card and said, "We'll take *that* one." Of *course* I wanted that stroller. Jackie the Infant Wonder was our victory lap and completely unexpected.

John and I had visited Elmwood on our seventh anniversary last year. I'd arranged it with the caretaker, whose card, like that of the cowboy with the pearl-button shirt, I still carried around in my wallet. We'd left Nathan and Grace with my mother and driven up to Wisconsin by ourselves, wearing our swimsuits under our clothes. When we got there, we stripped down and took a running leap off the dock, holding hands—something we hadn't been able to do at the wedding.

As we toweled off afterward, the passage of time sank in. We'd been married seven years! The children were nine and six. We were sitting on the bench at the end of the dock with our towels across our knees. The afternoon sun was still high in the sky; it was a weekday, and few boats were out. "I guess that's it for us then, kid-wise," I'd said. "Well, Karen's certainly fulfilled the family quota. That's okay, right?"

He'd squeezed my hand. "I have two children, a boy and a girl. I'm more blessed than I have any right to be."

That Christmas, he'd given me the gold band set with their two birthstones.

And after New Year's, I'd discovered I was pregnant.

John had been so excited, he'd gone out and returned with a bottle of Veuve to celebrate, which I teased him was even more extravagant given that I was only going to have half a glass, but he told me not to worry; he'd just stopped by Karen's house, and she and Frank were on their way. Before they'd even arrived, we'd already talked it through. Our plan that I'd go back to work full time when Grace started first grade was now out. But I'd already signed up for the Washington bar prep course and the spring exam, and I'd go ahead with that. Although I enjoyed what Karen called "domestic engineering," I was chafing at the loss of professional certification: I'd had to drop my Oklahoma bar membership after three non-practicing years. I'd get the bar exam under my belt so that when the opportunity arose I'd be ready, even for part-time work as an outsider contractor. John couldn't have been more supportive; we were of one mind.

He never wavered, even when Dunwoody Scudder was acquired a couple of months later by international behemoth PSB (ironically known as Pillage, Slash, and Burn) and he and his mentor, Owen, left the firm to start their own boutique IP practice. John broke the news to me with a box of mini-chocolate cupcakes with banana frosting from the gourmet cupcake store. That was my current fixation for my third pregnancy, which was also probably why I was gaining much more weight the third time around. John reassured me that yes, we'd still be okay financially; this was a sure thing because they'd pulled out before the acquisition was formalized and were taking their book of business with them, so no, I didn't need to change course and get a full-time job with health benefits to back up the launch of a new enterprise. We were still Team Halvorsen. I had a second cupcake.

Another elevator chime rang out, and we regrouped. This time it was two women, seemingly bundled for a trip to the Arctic for the short walk into the parking garage.

"Oh my goodness," they exclaimed. "Those twins should be models!"

We were used to this. Not only were Karen's boy-and-girl twins picture-perfect with their strawberry curls, but they had been outfitted since birth in gorgeous hand-me-downs from Aunt Thea's twins. Luckily, the classics for little ones never went out of style. Today they were dressed in light blue snowflake-patterned cardigans with silver-colored buttons; the matching knit caps had yellow pompons. Who could resist?

"Just *look* at all these beautiful children," the women gushed, stepping out. "Are you Catholic?"

"No, we're just sisters." Karen grinned as we piled into the elevator.

I leaned over and whispered, "Oh my God, for a second there I thought you said 'No, we're just fertile.'"

"Mom!" Nathan scolded. "You can't *say* stuff like that in front of the kids!"

"It's a sexy word," Sammy added.

"Sexy, sexy," Tyler chanted.

"It is not, Sam." I knuckled the top of his head. "It's an agricultural term."

Grace turned to Tyler. "You can't say *saxy*. It's a *bad word*. It means you get all naked and kiss someone. Don't say that. It's in'propriate."

"We haven't even made it inside the mall yet," I said to Karen.

She grinned. "It's your fault if they run around saying that when Mom gets here tomorrow."

In the concourse we released the twins and stuffed all our coats into the empty stroller, except for the twins'. Karen left their sweaters on in case a modeling agent came along. We always hoped for this, but it never happened. Then I called for the buddy system, and Nathan and Sam each grabbed a twin's hand.

"No fair!" Tyler whined. "I want a twin! I *never* get a twin!"

"Sammy, give Tyler your twin this time. You buddy with Grace."

"*Mom!*" Tyler cried. "No fair. I want a *boy* one, not a girl one!"

Grace, meanwhile, was objecting to Sam on the basis that he was a pooty.

"What's a pooty?" Karen asked.

"I don't know and I don't care," I said, quickly making rearrangements until nobody was wearing a mulish expression. Karen gave a small notepad and pencil to everyone old enough to have developed a pencil grip. "Okay, everyone! Let's make our lists, so we can give them to Santa at the party."

Our holiday window-shopping junket was something Karen and I engineered once and once only each December, because, as Karen said, we were not nuts. The party afterward was a special addition this year: it would be the children's first visit to John's new office, and Santa was going to make an appearance. We were going to show up for thirty minutes at a designated afternoon hour, and if it went well, this, too, would become an annual tradition. The kids were excited about giving their lists to Santa in person this year instead of having to mail them to the North Pole. Karen was already finished with her Christmas shopping, so this was really a ruse, whereas I hadn't even started. I could not use my new part-time job as an excuse; Karen beat me hands down in that regard. With her opera schedule, quartet schedule, and a full private lesson teaching roster, she still had all her Christmas shopping done by Halloween. And she had more kids than me, if we were counting, which we actually really didn't.

While Karen got the procession going, I ran to get us lattes. I hadn't expected such a tempting part-time job opportunity to come along so quickly, but it seemed tailor-made. It was with an environmental nonprofit called Rivers Northwest and involved fieldwork averaging ten hours a week.

Rivers was active in the growing dam removal movement and currently focused on the John Day Dam on the Columbia River, which in 1957 had inundated the community of Celilo Falls and tribal fishing grounds that dated back thousands of years. The coalition wanted to sign on every Washington and Oregon tribe and band, fishing rights or no fishing rights, to lend weight as they tried to interest legislators in the initiative to decommission the dam for environmental and cultural reasons. It was a long-term strategy, and they needed someone to beat the bushes.

I'd gone downtown to interview, hugely pregnant. Terri DaSilva, chief counsel, had smiled sympathetically as I lowered myself into the chair in front of her desk. I found myself blurting out, "I haven't worked in eight years," perhaps because she was smiling so sympathetically.

For a moment she looked surprised; then she deadpanned, "I can see you've been a bit busy," and at that moment all my anxiety evaporated. She turned out to be a sterling example of

John's favorite axiom: *The boss is as important as the job.* I'd come for the job, but I'd stayed because of Terri, who kept our tilting-at-windmills endeavor together. In the five months since I'd started, Terri had become not only a great mentor but a good friend.

I caught back up with the group in front of Binnegan's Toys, where Tyler was asking his mother how to spell "light saber." Karen raised her eyebrows at me with a smug smile that telegraphed *Already bought!* as I handed her the snowflake-printed cup.

Our caravan continued down the mall. Karen came to a halt at Scent-sible Beauty, and I waved my hand in front of my nose.

"Please, do we have to stop here? It always nauseates me."

"I want to get a free sample of Tahitian Sunset."

"You're as bad as a teenager, Karen," I said, adding, "I think I had a Tahitian Sunset once at a Dartmouth frat party. It was deadly."

The wife of one of John's former colleagues walked out of the next boutique, hauling a shopping bag the size of a small doghouse. She recognized me and, swift as lightning, did a surreptitious head-to-toe assessment of my outfit, gave an overly effusive hello, and told us the twins should be models, in that order.

Since John left the firm, I'd seen this woman only once, in front of the organic kabocha squash at NewFoods, when she'd asked, "Why did he quit? I thought the whole point of making partner was to stay?" At the time I was in my first trimester and had zero reserves of bitchy energy to respond. And now, summoning up fake holiday goodwill, I introduced her to my sister.

"Goodness, you're brave to bring the whole gang out right before Christmas! My kids are ab-so-lute-ly climbing the walls." She rolled her eyes playfully. "I sent them to Holiday Camp at the WAC for the day."

"Well, this is the only time they get to come out all vacation," I said. "After this we take 'em home, lock 'em in their rooms, and give them bones for dinner. Right, kids? What's for dinner?"

"Bones!" they cried in unison.

She looked a little startled but recovered quickly, smoothing her hair with one hand. It was so shiny, it looked polyurethaned. I'd seen this woman twice a year, maybe. The Christmas party, an adults-only boozy open house with really good heavy hors d'oeuvres. And then the summer picnic, a lame attempt to project a warm and fuzzy family vibe, the strain of which was so great on the partners that it required an entire year, and another boozy Christmas party, for them to build up enough energetic goodwill for the next one.

Then she bent down to the stroller. "And how's that baby?" she cooed.

"This is *my* baby," Grace announced. "They're not babies anymore," she said, pointing at the twins. "*This* is the baby now, and he's mine. But now we can't get a dog."

Tyler placed a proprietary hand on the stroller to capture her attention and announced, "But Uncle Bill says when Shasta has puppies again, he'll keep one of them just for us. But at *his* house," and the kids started bickering about how to parse the future ownership of this future puppy.

My acquaintance stroked the baby's cheek once more, straightened up, and quipped, "You *do* know how this happens, don't you?"

Karen's smile became glacial. We'd heard it before, this dig, one too many times, always couched as a joke that seemed to preclude retort, at least for those of us with good manners. Quickly the woman wished us a happy holiday, hoisted her shopping bag, and sailed off.

"I didn't know there was supposed to be a quota system," Karen said dryly.

"We are rebels and loners. It is the way of our people."

She chuckled. "And that's another thing. Nobody understands our sense of humor. At least we have each other."

The children had wandered ahead.

"Anyway," I said to Karen, "geriatric motherhood has its benefits. Think of all the fun we had in our twenties!"

"True. Your friend there probably missed out on a lot of Tahitian Sunsets."

We cracked up again, to the extent we could while pushing strollers in public, while Grace bounced on her toes, demanding to know what a Tahitian Sunset was.

"It's this! It's a perfume," Karen said, plucking the sample she'd lodged in the bundle of coats. "Want to try it?" Grace rubbed it on her own wrists, then the twins' wrists, and almost got to the baby, but I stopped her.

We moved on to the food court for lunch. "I'm kind of glad we're out of that," I reflected as we carried our lunch to a table. "Dunwoody. John made the right decision to leave. It's not like they were the only ones who jumped ship. The whole real estate section peeled away too. That was four partners—Gracie, stop running around the table while you eat. You'll choke to death."

She plopped down between me and little Michael, who was plowing through his frankfurter like a woodchuck. Suddenly Grace slumped over in my lap. "Mommy, I'm gonna throw up."

I grabbed some napkins, and the boys started to chant "Upchuck! Upchuck!" All except Michael, who never stopped eating until his plate was empty—a defense mechanism often employed by youngest children in large families.

"Upchuck! Upchuck!" Anticipation was running high. A band of roving carolers in Victorian dress took in the situation at a glance and passed us by. After a moment, Grace emitted an anti-climactic little cough, and the show was over.

I collected the wish lists. "Let's make sure Santa can read these," I said, spreading them out on the marbled-plastic tabletop while Karen took the twins off to the restroom to give them a more thorough cleanup, in case any modeling agents walked by.

The first item on the oldest boys' lists jumped out at me:

1. Cell phone

Jackie was fussing in the stroller. I took him out and perched him on my knee. "Hmm. Now, Jackie!" I shook my finger at him playfully. "You know the rule. No cell phones until you're thirteen."

Tyler frantically stuffed the rest of his carrot into his mouth with the heel of his hand and plucked at his pockets. "I have a phone!"

"That's not *real*," Nathan scoffed.

"Yes, it is, yes, it is!" he screeched, shaking it in the air.

"Shut *up*, you baby!" said Sam. "It's *not*. It's Dad's old Berrypod, and it's *broken*."

Karen had already returned, quietly passed me the twins, and walked straight over to Sam. Taking his forearm firmly between thumb and forefinger, she pulled him down next to her.

I had a whole mental file folder, courtesy of Karen, labeled Techniques for Disciplining Your Kids While Dragging Them Around in Public Without Attracting Critical Glares, full of firsthand examples from our life together dragging children around in public. She was a master.

Tyler, though a third grader, was still easy to wind up, and tears were welling. I banked Jackie on my lap, put my arm around Tyler, and plucked the phone from his hand. "Okay, kids, look." I displayed the phone to the circle, on my palm, like a jeweler with a necklace on velvet. "This *is* a real phone. It's *not* a toy. You have a *real* phone. It's just defunct. It's a defunct...real...phone."

I presented it to him. Flushed but mollified, he stuffed it back in his pocket and folded his arms.

"Mom, *everyone* at school has a phone," Nathan complained. "Everyone. Everyone in the eighth grade. And some in the seventh."

Karen pushed her sleeve back from her wrist. "And you're in…Oh wait, let me check my pretend watch…Fifth grade! And *you're* in fourth, Mister," she said, turning to Sam, who quickly swallowed his laugh. "You guys know the rule. No cell phones until you're fourteen. So cross that off your list."

JOHN'S NEW OFFICE DOWNTOWN WAS in a prime location. He and Owen had cut a great deal at the prestigious Bateman Building, where a blue-chip firm, needing to trim some fat when the recession hit, had backed out of its lease on an entire floor. The boys hauled open the doors to the suite, and we advanced toward a black marble reception desk that was so big and shiny, I could see our whole entourage reflected in it. Eric, the receptionist, jumped up from behind his desk, radiating a compact, pink-cheeked energy that Karen and I knew to be authentic stage presence, as he actually *was* an actor, on the local repertory scene, and had the requisite almost-shaven head and stubbled beard to prove it.

"Now, who have we here?" he asked in an impressively musical baritone. "Do you have an appointment?" He came around the desk and knelt in front of twins Michael and Molly, whose eyes were glued to his face. "I knew you were coming. Look! I wore my Christmas outfit. Just…for…you!" He gently tapped them on their rib-knit sweater cuffs.

"*That's* your Christmas outfit?" Tyler said, wiping his face with his hand.

Eric snapped his green suspenders and readjusted his red bow tie. "Hey, what's wrong with it? You're hurting my feelings."

"We like it." Sam sniggered.

Down the hallway I saw the firm's female partner, Larissa, stick her head of tight, impressively sculpted curls out her office door. Larissa took pride in considering herself above fashion, but her hair was so thick and wavy, she was forced to pay attention to it. That and a heavy application of mascara appeared to be the sum total of her concession to feminine style. Our eyes met, and she flashed me a slightly bucktoothed smile for a nanosecond, which I tried to return. I had never really warmed to Larissa but couldn't quite figure out why. It might simply have been her marked inability to smile, which appeared to be physically painful. Owen had worked with her before and persuaded John to take her on board as their third partner. *Litigation is not a beauty contest,* he'd said. *We're not looking for Miss Congeniality. We're looking for a ten-plus years' experienced crack litigator, which she is. And we need a third named.*

Eric took Grace by the hand. "So, let's see who's going to help me with Reception today." He led her behind the desk and helped her with the headset. "Just push this button," he whispered, then coached her to say: "Mr. Halvorsen, you have important visitors at reception."

John appeared immediately and Grace barreled into him. "Daddy! I had a demi-puke! I almost threw up, but I didn't!"

"That's good news," he said seriously, and led her by the hand into a conference room with floor-to-ceiling windows and a table big enough to be an ice rink for midgets, on which sat a small boom box and enough snacks to produce the requisite holiday sugar coma. I took a disc out of my purse and put it on the boom box: Tchaikovsky's "Nutcracker Suite," the only holiday music Karen and I could listen to in an endless loop without wanting to slit our wrists with a nail file. Meanwhile, the other children were being helped out of their jackets by a young woman with a tight black ponytail. She turned around, and I realized from the dark purple lipstick and triple ear studs that this was the new hire. She shifted her burden to extend a hand.

"I'm so pleased to meet you, Mrs. Halvorsen. I'm Paisley. I've heard so much about you. A lawyer and a musician!"

"It makes me tired just to hear that," I said, but I was flattered. It really wasn't as busy as it sounded; Mostly Baroque, which

John liked to refer to as Mostly Broke, only had a four-concert season. "Let me help you with those." I took half of her load, and she bustled down the hall in front of me. Her plump derriere was encased in a black skirt short enough to merit opaque tights, and the long sleeves on her chartreuse blouse were on account of the six-inch Lady Justice, which was inked on one bicep—John had told me this.

She opened a door. "We can put them in here, in the cloakroom," she said, then flushed slightly. "I guess you know where that is. Oh my gosh, I just *have* to tell you I think your commitment to nonprofit is so totally awesome. Indigenous rights are just *hot* right now. I think what I do is, like, meaningful and everything," she said, busily inserting hangers into coats, "but I just really admire your passionate commitment to the environment. I mean I love what I do," she rushed on. "I love working here. I just have a lot of tuition debt to pay off first."

If she had the impression I was some sort of lifestyle attorney who didn't need to worry about income, I wasn't going to disabuse her. It made John look even more successful. And the bald fact of the matter right now was that I was the support spouse to an upper-bracket professional. Right now. But the implication stung. "Oh, I'm only part time with Rivers Northwest," I said, "just enough to keep me in the game." I was going for humorous self-deprecation, but my smile was tight.

She pushed up her horn-rimmed glasses and changed the subject. "Let me take you back to Santa." She led me down the hall to the very last door, and I realized that the firm's existing space was all staffed up. It hadn't even taken a year to exercise the option they'd negotiated to expand for the same rate per square foot within eighteen months of the original lease start date. Owen and John had begun with significant brand-name recognition and were now doing a land-office business. It had been almost too easy, and this despite the gap in social skills represented by

Larissa, who was at this moment electing to sit out the half hour of frivolity by volunteering to be Reception.

"I'm so glad John hired me first," Paisley enthused, opening the door. "They're interviewing for two more right now. I'll make senior first. He's such a great boss. Oh my gosh."

"Oh my gosh," mimicked paralegal Jason, swiveling around behind the desk, where he'd been staring out the window with his chin in his hand. He readjusted the Santa beard and cheerily continued: "Best boss ever—I'll agree with that as soon as I can get out of this suit."

Eric the actor/receptionist had wanted the Santa role, but Jason fell into the Big and Tall category and did not need any padding, so he had been pressed into service.

Jason stood up to shake hands with me. "I have no idea what kind of petrochemical was used to produce this fabric," he said, "but it just does not breathe."

"I didn't pay attention to the fabric content when I ordered it," I apologized. "We'll get a better one next year." I looked out the window. Our twelfth-story office was directly across from the top floor of a much older building.

Jason turned and tapped a gloved finger on the glass. "Isn't that a beautiful building?" he said. "I'd rather be here looking at that than over there looking at this. Excelsior Bank Building. Beaux Arts. 1914. National Historic Register. I know for a fact those are fifty-inch wide sash windows with the original glass. I've been over there. All operable—just pop the sash locks and up they go. A banker actually jumped out of those windows in '29. That's a documented fact. There weren't as many suicides after the crash as people think, and most of them weren't from jumping. But some were. This one was."

How desperate could a man be to climb out there? I thought. How desperate, not to think twice, to think of what he was doing to his family?

Jason touched my arm. "Are we on soon?" he asked.

As if on cue, the intercom buzzed, and Larissa, otherwise worth her weight in gold, announced in tones leached of enthusiasm: "John says battle stations. He also says to tell you 'no cell phones.' He said you'd know what that means, Kim."

I clapped my hand to my mouth. "He's seen the lists. Santa, the boys are going to have cell phones at the top of their list. Do not, I repeat, do *not* make that promise. "Nobody's getting a cell phone before age fourteen. That's in stone."

"Got it," said Jason. "No cell phones till age fourteen. I'll have to remember that myself for the future." He gave Paisley a toothy grin.

"That's optimistic," Paisley replied. She circled around, smoothing the shoulders of his coat and adjusting the belt. "Hope springs eternal!"

Jason picked up the small sack of locally handmade gourmet candy canes, large enough to be walking sticks for hobbits, which Karen and I had decided were the appropriate pre–Big Day party favor. "All righty, then!" He slung the bag over his shoulder and fidgeted one last time with the mustache. "Let's get this show on the road!"

Chapter 11

Christmas Bonus

THERE WAS STRENGTH IN NUMBERS, ESPECIALLY WHEN "numbers" meant a passel of small children whose parents were quite reasonably disinclined to drag them around on long airplane flights during the Christmas season. So it was that over the years, the center of holiday gravity inevitably shifted to what my brother, Doug, called the "hacienda" in Seattle, as in "Cassie and I have to road-trip to Seattle to spend Christmas at the hacienda." To which I routinely retorted that it was not our fault that he didn't like to fly and that they loved road-tripping.

As for my mother, Bobbie, it was just as easy for her to fly from Mexico to Seattle as it was to fly from Mexico back to Chicago for the extended MacLean family holiday jamboree at which her own grandchildren would not be present anyway. She'd sold her mother's home in Fort Lauderdale because she felt it wasn't warm enough there in the winter and bought a house in Puerto Vallarta instead. It had been built by the widow of Montgomery Ward Jr., so we called it the Monkey Ward. The nickname had a double meaning, we did descend on her there with our increasingly large brood at regular intervals.

My mom and Doug always coordinated their travel to arrive on the same day, but this year, for some reason, on my way home from the airport with Bobbie, I got a cryptic message from Doug that he had been unavoidably detained on the road and would be arriving not today but tomorrow. We were used to cryptic messages from Doug; "All will be revealed," my mother intoned. I actually didn't mind because it alleviated my guilt at not being finished with my Christmas shopping. I'd made dinner this evening, and Karen was in charge of it at her house the next day, so I determined to get it done before then.

Which I did, just barely. It was half past four when I arrived back at Karen's with a car packed with baby Jackie and multiple shopping bags, dark enough to set off the motion-sensor light tucked into the eaves over the driveway. "We're here!" I caroled, and Jackie kicked his feet excitedly.

Our current third grader, Tyler, opened the front door to Chez Massey clad in a bathrobe with three strings of Mardi Gras beads around his neck. "I'm in charge. That's what the beads mean," he announced, as Grace and little Michael skittered up behind. They were similarly attired, but wearing swim goggles instead of sunglasses and sporting gladiator armbands.

"That's nice, honey, but just let me in—we're getting wet."

"Back to the tower!" he cried with a flourish, and they thundered up the circular stairway in the parquet-floored foyer, which was naked except for a doormat and a chandelier. I kicked my shoes off. On either side of me, arched doorways opened onto small, graceless boxes, one bereft of everything but a grand piano and the Christmas tree, the other containing a dining table. Karen and Frank had been on the verge of furnishing the living room when they'd found out the third baby was twins and had decided "Why bother?" I lugged Jackie through the dining room, past a closed door that muffled the unmistakable sound of middle-school boys video-gaming, and entered the great room in back, where all the action was, and most of the furniture, too. My mother was sitting at the oak trestle table in the bay window breakfast area.

Molly was beside her, hunkered over crayons and paper, with Grace's doll in her lap.

The spindle chairs and Waverly prints gave the room a Colonial look. Karen's house was more old-fashioned than mine, even though mine was almost a hundred years older and actually had a name: Cedarly. John had unearthed a wooden plaque in the basement with Art Nouveau lettering, which he'd sanded, stained, and hung proudly over the front door. The name was appropriate, because the back of the house, banked against a wooded ridge, appeared mantled in evergreens, which were held in abeyance by a small retaining wall for a sliver of backyard. In compensation, there was a long porch in front with an expansive view over a saucer of lush meadow to the next ridge west.

I delivered my heavy baby into my mother's outstretched arms. "All done! I felt like you, Karen. Made my list, put my visor down, and went in. Totally mission-specific."

My mother widened her eyes at the baby. "Good job!" she cooed, then set him on her knee and began singing. "*See saw, Margery Daw / Jack shall have a new master...*"

Here we go again, I thought, downing a glass of water. *Good job I got it done, or good job I was like Karen?* I was not going to let her rain on my parade. I bent to inspect six custard cups cooling on a wire rack on the counter. "Karen," I said, "is this what I think it is?"

"Yes. It is, in fact, what you think it is."

"I brought the packets with me," Bobbie interjected.

"Have tapioca, will travel!"

"Are you girls laughing at me?"

"We're not laughing *at* you, Mom! We're laughing *with* you," Karen said, and Bobbie flapped her hands in a humorous concession of defeat.

I sat back and popped a cheese straw into my mouth. "Molly, did you tell Grandma about the Santa visit?"

"We saw Santa! We gave him our Christmas list-es."

"You wouldn't believe how the baby started to scream when he saw Old Saint Nick," Karen said.

I gave Molly another cheese straw and took one myself. "Poor Jason felt so guilty. He saw his Christmas bonus passing right before his very eyes."

"Who's Jason? What's a Christmas bonus? I want one!" Molly cried. "I want a Christmas bonus. What's a Christmas bonus?"

"*You're* a Christmas bonus, dolly. Oh, Mom!" I turned to her. "I met our latest new hire at that party. She was so cute. She told me how she admired my work with Rivers Northwest, and I gotta tell you, it made me feel good."

"Stop filling that child up with cheese straws," Bobbie said sharply. She took the package away, then resituated Jackie on her lap and said in milder tones, "So, how is your little project going?"

Your little project. This was why I hadn't even told my mother about the job—not right away. It had taken me a full month to work up the nerve. Karen was a natural in the confidence department, but I'd had to work hard to develop even a fraction of what she had. And at every turn, there stood my mother, in the way. She'd always been like this, even before I became the Daughter Who Got a Divorce—long before. It was subtle, but it still hurt, the way she'd trivialize an accomplishment, or damn with faint praise, or deliver a direct criticism as a throwaway afterthought. It probably hurt more because it wasn't constant. I never knew when her darts might arrive. That's why she hadn't exactly been the first person I'd told when I had my first success on the job and felt confident the job was going to work out.

I WAS STILL HIGH ON adrenaline when I got home after that first meeting with a tribal council out in Yakima County. I was saving the good news for John until suppertime; I knew Karen was in rehearsal. So I dropped my purse in the kitchen, traded my shoes for boots, and took the winding path up the hill behind the house to see Bill. We had a hangout spot on the saddle of the ridge, where two Adirondack chairs, positioned to catch the western view, sat in a small clearing bounded by some embedded boulders and an old felled Douglas fir. We called this spot Procrastination Station because it was where we rendezvoused when one of us was trying to avoid something: for me, perhaps starting dinner during a heat wave, for Bill, maybe tackling an engine reblock. John hung out there with Bill too, but usually *after* he'd finished some house project or other, so technically, as he often and helpfully pointed out, he was not procrastinating. These chairs were sacred and reserved for adults only. The kids had other places to frolic, including the playhouse Bill had built for them in the woods, and they frequently trod the path over the hill and back to his house on the off chance that he had some shoestring licorice on hand. But Procrastination Station was grown-up territory.

I pulled out my phone and called Bill. "Come on up. I've got great news!"

"Sure thing. You got coffee?"

"No. I was too excited. I forgot."

"Well, hold your horses, I'll heat some up. Be there in a jiffy." Bill always had a saucepan of coffee on the stove ready to heat up; he claimed he couldn't drink it fresh.

I was still pacing when Bill appeared over the brow of the hill with his red plaid thermos and two mugs. He was shirtless and wearing suspenders to hold up his jeans because he was so skinny and was enthusiastically accompanied by his dog, Shasta, a husky/shepherd mix.

"Hey, missy! What's so all-fired exciting?"

"Bill, it works! It worked. I mean my job is going to work out."

"Well, of course it will, darling. Why wouldn't it? You're the smartest lady lawyer I know."

I sat down and took the mug of coffee he poured with hands that had perpetually grease-blackened nails, despite the rag he tied to a belt loop to wipe off the engine oil as he worked. Bill was a commercial trapper, but in the summer he made ends meet with mechanic work.

"Bill. You can't say 'lady lawyer' anymore," I chided him, and he grinned. Shasta was curled up between us, and I reached down and scratched her behind the ears. "The thing is, I wasn't sure," I went on. "We're a small nonprofit. We don't have any lawyers with tribal affiliation at Rivers. Native American law school grads get snapped up by top law firms in Seattle, Anchorage, and D.C. You can't blame them, I guess."

"Follow the money." He nodded. "It's the way of the world."

"I got this gig because I'd taken a few courses in federal Indian law in Tulsa. I wasn't sure what kind of a reception I'd get."

"Sounds like it went well, though?"

I took a gulp of coffee. "Not at first. They were not smiling. I could tell what they were thinking: Here's another *Dances with Wolves* white chick wasting our time. I told them I know they'd heard of us because we were part of the Klamath River Restoration Agreement. That dealt with *four* dams, Bill! But they shot that down. They said the John Day is different because it's in good shape, that PacifiCorp is only agreeing to take down the dams on the Klamath because it would cost them more to do the remediation and comply with the regs. That it was a purely economic decision. Well, *I* knew that. They knew that. So I told them that after the Oregon legislature's Day of Mourning last year and the admission on the record that the dam was a mistake, there'd been a groundswell and we're trying to capitalize on that."

Bill picked up a twig, snapped it, and threw it aside. "I remember when they opened that dam," he reflected. "I was just a kid, so I never thought about it. It was all about progress and hydroelectric power and how that was so great. Nobody ever said anything about anything else. I'm not surprised that the council was skeptical. But things are changing all the time. Look at all the wind farms in Eastern Washington. All those turbines going up along the Gorge."

I nodded. "I just spoke from the heart, Bill. I didn't give up, and I kept the conversation going until it more or less turned around. I really wasn't sure when I walked out, of course. But then they called me while I was driving home and said they were in!" I heaved a big sigh of satisfaction. "If I hadn't pulled over to take the call, I'd probably have driven off the road."

"Congratulations, dear. People get entrenched—heck, governments get entrenched. Good for you for helping to push a rethink. I'm not surprised you got them to participate. You're one smart lawyer. See—I didn't say *lady lawyer* this time, did I?"

I levered myself up from my Adirondack chair. "There's hope for you yet, Bill," I said with a smile, and handed him my empty mug.

WHY WAS IT SO MUCH easier for me to talk about my new job with everyone but my mother? When I finally picked up the phone, I'd anticipated that she'd criticize me for getting a new job halfway through a third pregnancy. Instead, she accused me of being a dilettante. Well, not accused, perhaps; she voiced a concern that I would *become* a dilettante.

I was so shocked I spat back, "Is Karen a dilettante?"

"No, of course not. She's a *professional* musician. And a *teacher*."

I was familiar with this tone of my mother's. It was gentle yet deliberate, asserting objectivity in so reasonable-sounding a manner that it foreclosed remonstrance. Which of course infuriated me even further.

Ever since we were little, Karen had been the golden girl. And truth be told, Karen was the golden girl for me as well. But it hurt to have my semi-professional status thrown at me. I was perfectly happy with my reputable string orchestra and being on the sub list for a few local groups if they needed a ringer for a small honorarium! I'd never *intended* to be a full-time concert musician. That ship had sailed. Nor was it what I wanted. She was aware of that. I'd carved out a niche in the law, and it was my own. I was not dabbling.

And now. *Your little project.* I pressed my lips together in disgust, letting the words hang in the air. My sister quickly joined us at the table. "Tell the story again you told me," she said encouragingly. "Tell Mom. About when you started."

I took another cheese straw. "Oh, that first conference? Yeah. It was tough, Mom. They just sat there. I felt like I was a prisoner up for parole review. I talked to them about the Oregon legislature putting it on record that the dam was a mistake. Mom, they actually said, 'If it were today, we wouldn't have done it.' So then this older guy in a plaid shirt—Monroe, he's my friend now—said 'humph.' Well, at least someone said something!" I looked at my sister, and she nodded. "I figured I had nothing to lose, so I put my papers away and said, 'I want to talk to you about water.'"

Bobbie sighed deeply, transferred Jackie to her other arm, and rubbed the back of her neck. "Talk about water?" she said dubiously. "What do you mean?"

Karen leaned forward, chin in hand, and gave me another encouraging smile.

"I told them this," I said, closing my eyes. "That I know what it's like to be flooded. Waters come, and waters go, and sometimes it's a good thing; those waves get you where you need to go, they move you, like wind moves a boat. But sometimes it's a bad thing. A mistake. And when you see that and realize that and know about that, then you have to do something about it. You're bounden to do it. It's never too late. You can't worry about lost time. Why I took this job—I went to the bank of the river. I drove out and stood on the bank of the river, and I could hear the silence. The music of running water was not there. But it wasn't an absence; it was a presence, like a corked bottle. The voices are still there. Sometimes towns get wiped out because a river changes its course or there's a flood or something. But that's not what happened here. We didn't ask permission, not of the earth, the water, or the people who lived there and the people who had the fishing rights and got their living from it. So we need to correct that. Those voices need to be honored. They are still there, and if you let the water loose, the voices will reappear. This will be done. That time is starting now, and that's why I took this job."

I opened my eyes.

"Then I thanked them and got up and left, and I thought, like, so much for this job, but then I got a call, and I answered the phone, and Monroe said: 'Pretty poetic for a lawyer.'"

"'Yep. That's me, I guess,' I said. 'Take it or leave it.'"

"And he said, 'We're taking it.'"

"I blurted out, 'Why?'"

"And he said, 'You talked about the ancestors.'"

"'I did?'"

"'Yes. We just needed to see where your group was coming from. You talked to us about the earth. You talked to us about the ancestors. We can work with you.'"

Tyler and his two junior gladiators sprinted into the kitchen. "Mom! What's for supper?"

Karen, chin in hand, still looking at me, rapped out, "Bones. Go back upstairs!" They sprinted off.

Bobbie said to me, "You talk too much."

I flinched. I turned to Karen with teeth gritted. She sat up, tapped the side of a glass custard cup to check for coolness, then picked it up and handed it to me.

"Have some tapioca," she deadpanned, as Frank walked into the kitchen.

"Hey, Mother Mac!" The children flocked in behind him, led by Tyler, who was now barking into his real yet defunct cell phone. "What's that boy doing?" Frank asked, picking up Molly and turning her upside down.

"Making dinner reservations?" I suggested, but Frank, seeing the box of mac and cheese, turned a giggling Molly upright, grabbed the box, and shook it. "No, he's calling his stockbroker! Tell him it's a buy on Kraft!"

Karen plucked the box from his hand. "Do *not* draw my mother's attention to this packaged food."

John arrived and lifted his arms so the children could raid his coat pockets. His eyes lit on the mac-and-cheese box as well. "Not again!" he exclaimed in mock horror. "That stuff is toxic."

"Turns their tongues orange," Frank said.

"I ate a cupcake once with blue frosting on it, and it made my poopoo blue," Michael volunteered.

"Thank you for that, Michael," John replied seriously, loosening his tie. He had been slow to adapt to West Coast casual, but his wardrobe had expanded by now to include dress shirts in an array of soft pastels. "Heck of a day. Partner meeting. Think I win the worst-day contest. As usual."

"That's right," said Frank, "All I do is put my feet up on my desk and watch those paychecks roll in!" He did a drumroll on the countertop. "Thaaat's Intelicomp!"

"You mean, 'In-Hell-icomp!'" Karen dished out mac and cheese.

"I think Karen should win," I suggested. "Did you ever think of that? She had to make tapioca today."

"What's so bad about making tapioca?" Frank asked.

"There you girls go again," Bobbie said, handing me the baby. "The word 'tapioca' is now officially banned."

THAT EVENING, AFTER DINNER, AFTER the kids had been sent off to put on their jammies, Doug announced the reason for his and Cassie's late arrival by handing our mother a snapshot of the two of them standing in front of the Little Church of the West in Las Vegas. Apparently, after eighteen years, they'd suddenly realized that they'd forgotten to get married, so they turned around and selected the appropriate venue among the many available, because one thing they did remember was that they'd promised Bobbie a church wedding. Frank jumped up and brought out two bottles of champagne that Karen, being Karen, had already lain in for Christmas dinner, and Bobbie, after taking off her glasses and pinching the bridge of her nose, because this was not *exactly* what she had meant by a church wedding, accepted a glass because it was not every day that your one of your children tied the knot after an eighteen-year engagement.

The children, bathrobes flapping, stampeded back out of the kitchen past us, knocking over their grandmother's cane again and making the chandelier in the empty foyer tremble audibly. They hunkered down underneath the piano in the living room, next to the Christmas tree, and all was quiet until we heard Nathan, whose remark rang out like a bell.

"These Popsicles are good. They don't have the aftertaste of packaging."

"Popsicles!" Karen shrieked. "My carpet!"

Frank jumped up and windmilled his arms. "The piano is a DMZ! Repeat, the piano is a DMZ! Finish those in the kitchen." At six foot five, he would have been a formidable figure to any other children except these, who inured through long familiarity, floated past him in unhurried compliance. Molly brought up the rear.

"Grandma," she said, hanging on the arm of Bobbie's chair.

"Yes, honey?" Bobbie dabbed a streak of blue juice running off her chin, then cupped her hand underneath the Popsicle. "Lick the bottom."

Slowly and carefully, Molly shored up the bottom of her Popsicle, then smacked her lips. "Grandma," she said again, casting a sidelong glance at Cassie, "I *know* something." We all leaned forward as she looked around shyly, took a deep breath, and then leaned over and whispered loudly in Bobbie's ear, "Aunt Cassie is your Christmas bonus!" Then she scampered off as a chuckle rolled around the table.

Bobbie examined her glass. "I think I need just a teensy bit more." She sighed and looked up at her son-in-law as he carefully poured another inch. "John! Do you never get tired of this large and goofy family?"

"Never, Mother Mac!" he declared. "I was an only child! What's not to love?"

Chapter 12

Sisters Eating Leftovers

"John, what are you saying? Do you mean I should quit and take a full-time job with benefits?"

"No," John answered. His reluctance was audible, even over the phone. "Then we'd have to get a nanny."

"Exactly. Those couples you keep bringing up, honey, they all have full-time live-ins. I mean—they do payroll." A yellow light at the intersection caught me by surprise, and I braked quickly, throwing a glance in the rearview mirror at three-year-old Jackie. He'd just finished his preschool gymnastics class and was listening contentedly to the Classical for Kids disc Karen had given me. The light changed, and I turned onto Snake Hill Road.

"I want *you* to raise our kids."

That had been our plan from the beginning, but if we were going to change it after more than ten years and with a preschooler still under the roof, we were going to have to have real discussions, not these vague little conversations that seemed to manifest some degree of financial anxiety but then petered out. We'd always had discussions. We'd always worked things out together. We were a team, or had been, until he closed down, except for these occasional moments when he briefly ran up the flag of concern, then just as quickly ran it down again. Was he really anxious, or was he just grousing? The first time, it didn't really register, but when it happened again, I put it on the back burner. I was way too busy to sit around and think about it, because it was obviously transitory, the result of the events of September, and who could blame him; it had really been a one-two punch.

First, Owen had suddenly and privately announced to John and Larissa that he and his wife were both going to retire at the end of the year because she'd just been diagnosed as being in the early stage of Parkinson's. They had embarked on a clandestine search for a new partner, with Owen's help, but hadn't landed one yet, and on top of that, John had felt duty bound to fly out to Connecticut when he'd been informed of Claudette's death. He'd returned looking gray, less from the seventy-two-hour round trip, I guessed, than from the ordeal of attending the funeral of a mother he'd hardly known, alongside a bunch of relatives he'd never met.

But now it was after Thanksgiving.

"What if we can't find a replacement for Owen?"

I tried for levity. "Hey, I'm supposed to be the worrier, re-member? Remember what you always tell me: 'Let's not play the what-if game.'"

He did not laugh.

"Honey," I continued, "we've had this conversation, like, three times in the last whatever, and it always ends up like this. Of course you'll find one. And bottom line, I know you want three partners, but there's nothing wrong with a two-partner firm. If revenue drops, Terri DaSilva is the most understanding boss in the world, and if I have to leave Rivers and go full-time at a big firm, she'll understand."

"I don't want you to. I want to make this work. I'm not going to let my wife bail me out."

A pickup came toward me, the driver instinctively cleaving to the middle of the road to avoid the dubious-looking embankment guardrails. "Whoops. Wait just a sec." I put the phone down to get a two-handed grip on the wheel. "Okay, I'm back. Sorry, I'm on Snake Hill."

"Snake Hill? On your phone? Why aren't you using the hands-free? That's exactly why we got that option in the new car."

"I know." I glanced in the rearview mirror again. The timpani heralded the opening of "Fanfare for the Common Man," and Jackie was beating on an imaginary drum. "I know, but I don't want Jackie to hear us arguing."

"We're not arguing."

Technically speaking, he was right. We weren't arguing. Because we weren't speaking. We were mostly just breathing at opposite ends of the phone line. Jackie was the only one who was enjoying himself.

Finally I said, "Hon, you've got so much on your plate right now. But I feel like I'm not any help. We just go in circles. Are you talking about this with Dr. Markarian?" I'd asked Karen and Frank for a recommendation in October, and in November John had finally agreed to see him. "That's actually why I called." I adopted a humorous nasal tone. "'Mr. Halvorsen, this is your courtesy reminder for your one p.m. with Dr. Markarian!'"

"I'm not seeing Dr. Markarian. I canceled."

"You mean for today?"

"No. I'm not seeing him today or any day."

I shot a glance at Jackie again and spoke carefully. "Is two visits enough to tell if he's a good fit?"

"One."

"You mean—wait, what? You didn't go last week? Why didn't you tell me?"

"I didn't want to get into an argument. I just don't like him. I don't like what he said to me. I don't need to pay some fancy-schmancy therapist with a degree from NYU who's never been in the real world trying to carve out a living to tell me how to run my life."

I refrained from pointing out that Dr. Markarian himself was also carving out a living in the real world and also from mentioning that he *had* agreed to pay some fancy-schmancy therapist, and if he was going to change his mind about it, when was he going to share that nugget of information with his wife? Next Thronsday? But I'd been learning over the last couple of months that sometimes silence was the better part of valor. So instead I responded: "I'm so proud of you for starting your own business. Not everyone would have the guts."

"You can give me the 'Many are called, few are chosen' pep talk, but I'm thinking more along the lines of 'Fools rush in.' I should have gone back to corporate. A W-2 sounds like a really nice thing right now. Frank made the right choice."

"He's happy being a company man. It works for him. You're entrepreneurial. That's what I've always loved about you. You're a self-starter. Remember?"

"Yeah, well, being a self-made man means when things go wrong, you've got no one to blame but yourself."

"Horsies! Horsies!" Jackie cried, bouncing in his seat.

"Yes!" I enthused. "The horsies are there today." We'd passed the string of subdivisions on our road and were now driving along the peeling fence that marked the Warner farm. Ogilvie Glen was next, and the last stop on the road. As I turned in, I noticed the water feature at the entrance was dry, and a maintenance truck was parked on the shoulder. "Something's up with the waterfall," I reported.

"Again? That thing breaks down once a year. It's false advertising anyway. That creek doesn't even go through Ogilvie Glen. It goes through Bill's property, and ours."

I pulled into Karen's driveway. "Why don't we ask for some new names from Frank? Just in case you change your mind."

"That's another thing. It's embarrassing to ask my brother-in-law for headshrinker recommendations."

I pulled into Karen's driveway, threw it into park, and banged my hand lightly on the steering wheel. "John. It's part of what he does in HR. He knows people. He has lists."

"I'll think about it," John said. "We can talk about it tonight. See you at dinner."

I hung up and sat for a moment, persuading myself that we'd ended well, simply because he hadn't said he wouldn't be home for dinner.

KAREN AND I HAD LUNCH together every Monday. We'd been doing this for a couple of years now, since the twins started school, and it had quickly become sacrosanct. Evie joined us when she could. Evie was Karen's stand partner in the opera orchestra and our mutual best friend. Her real name was Yvette, but she'd reinvented herself after leaving Winthrop, Minnesota, to study with János Starker at Indiana University. Evie had presence: long black hair, high cheekbones, penetrating violet-blue eyes, and a deep voice. She owned an honest-to-goodness 1910 velvet opera cloak that she wore to work on performance nights, just for fun; it was so voluminous, we called it the "Cloak That Ate Manhattan."

I set Jackie up at the table with two slices of bologna on a plate—he was currently on a bologna kick—and some carrot pennies. "Now, don't keep me on tenterhooks," I said to Karen. "Did you accomplish the mission?"

"Yes, indeed!" She pulled out two smartphone boxes. The formidable cultural pressures of middle school had forced us to accelerate our initial electronics timeline. Nathan was going to receive his first cell phone this Christmas instead of at his eighth-grade graduation in June, and Sam, a year younger, would get his now as well. "These kids don't know how lucky they are," she added.

"I doubt they'll look at it that way. Remember: We didn't *cave*. We just made a minor adjustment to our principles."

Evie swept into the kitchen, having let herself in, laden with take-out containers. "Make sure to get the talk and text package," she said, nodding at the cell phone boxes on the counter as she disburdened herself. The delicious aroma of Thai food filled the air.

"Yes, ma'am." I filed that away under The World According to Evie. Although Evie was our age, she'd embarked on motherhood much earlier and was a veritable font of helpful parenting information. Her only child was a morose mid-twenty-something named Eugene Jr.—morose, perhaps, because he was named Eugene Jr. This made him even older than Karen's stepson Frank Jr., who was now a college sophomore and, to clarify, not morose in the least despite being a Junior. Evie's son had become our primary official Test Child. It always helped to widen the pool.

"As you can see," Evie said. "We are not eating leftovers today. You're welcome. Is he finished?" she asked, nodding at Jackie as she unloaded the containers on the table. "He's not going to want any of this, trust me. It's too spicy."

"There's your answer," I said. Jackie was already climbing into my lap with a book.

"Beach book, Mama," he announced, then put his thumb in his mouth.

"'A Happy Day at the Beach,'" I began in a singsong, but he was asleep before we got to the end. I carried him upstairs and put him down gently onto the spare bed in Michael's room, where he slept on overnights. Molly had a trundle bed in her room for Grace. There were plenty of extra beds at Karen's now, which made things easy on those occasional Saturday nights when John and I went out for dinner and dancing.

Jackie roused long enough to say, "Three kisses, Mommy!" I planted them on forehead, nose, and lips, and he dropped back onto the pillow. I stood at the window, looking out at Karen's small backyard, waiting to make sure he was settled.

Occasional Saturday nights—who was I kidding? I tried to remember the last time we'd gone dancing. At least a few months. No. It was probably six or eight. Even *before* the start of the new partner search. It was a shame, because dancing was such good exercise and so much fun—one of the few times he really relaxed. We'd won a series of ballroom lessons at the Saint Thomas school auction when Nathan was in first grade. We'd bid on a whim and discovered we loved it. Maybe if we'd kept up with that, he wouldn't need a therapist.

I flipped the blinds shut and went downstairs, where Karen and Evie were setting up our lunch. Karen had her cranberry relish container out as well. "What's this?" I asked.

"I felt duty bound to put something that was a leftover on the table," Karen said.

"I'm tired of leftovers," I said. "Even Bill Beery won't take a turkey sandwich from me."

"That's your cue," Evie said, digging into the rice. "At this point you should just throw them all out. I mean, it's been ten days."

"Our Scandinavian genes forbid it," I said. "We're forced to make soup."

"I don't know what I'm going to do with you girls," Evie said. "Anyway, listen. Cell phones. Back in the Stone Age, when texting was invented, they charged it at a dollar per text even if it was only one word, like 'Dude,' or 'Whassup?' Gene almost had a heart attack when that first bill came in. It was for four hundred dollars."

"Oh my God," Karen and I said simultaneously.

"Yeah. So take note. Do not make it even remotely possible for them to screw up. You have to go fail-safe. Remember what we say: 'You can lead a preteen to water...'"

"'But you can't make him *think!*'" we chorused in response.

After lunch Karen got out the wrapping paper. "I got two different-size boxes for the phones. That ought to throw them off the scent." She turned on the electric teakettle, and leaned against the counter, arms crossed, studying me. The room was silent, except for the rising whoosh of the electric teakettle. Karen exchanged a quick glance with Evie, then asked, "How's John?"

I turned sideways to avoid eye contact and swung my feet up on the window seat. "Fine. He's…preoccupied."

The kettle clicked off.

Karen was forcing me to drink herbal tea because she thought I drank too much coffee, which was, of course, true. She brought over three mugs and sat down. "He is, isn't he," she agreed. "Preoccupied. Quieter. I'm sure it's a challenge to find a new partner under cloak of darkness, so to speak." This was a secret, but not from Evie. We had no secrets from Evie; she was part of the inner circle, even if John and Frank did not know this. She was *our* inner circle. We were a sisterhood. Evie had named our club Three Cellists on the Verge of a Nervous Breakdown. This was something we had in common with Evie: We named things.

"But it's not really that." I fingered the fringe on the woven mat that held a wintering-over geranium on the windowsill. "He's said to me more than once that he's not ready to be senior partner. I've never known him not to rise to a challenge. I mean, he's the epitome of resilience! Now all of a sudden he's losing his confidence."

Evie bobbed her tea bag. "He's older," she offered. "More kids. Bigger mortgage. More at stake."

"I think it has to do with Owen. It has something to do with Owen leaving."

"I know he's been a mentor to John," Karen said. "Like a father, when you think about it. But is it…?"

I turned my mug around. "I don't want to talk about his mother."

She persisted. "It doesn't matter if they didn't have a relationship. It's still going to have an impact. It *is* having an impact. We can see that."

"He doesn't want to talk about her, either. Not to anyone. Not to me. Not to Dr. Markarian." And I certainly didn't want to talk about Claudette. Claudette, who'd never even met her grandchildren. The story of her departure from the earth was that she'd returned home early from the U.S. Open complaining of headache and nausea and holed up in her Chestnut Hill mansion. She didn't go to the doctor for a week, at which time she was diagnosed with a high-grade malignant glioma. She was dead eight days later.

I reached for the wrapping paper, but Karen stopped me, covering my hand, and I slumped. I could never avoid her drill down. "What more can I do? I can't force him."

"You could go by yourself."

The larger box we were going to use to fool the boys was an empty chocolate sampler. I plopped Nathan's phone inside and wedged crumpled tissue around it, packing it in tight. "Okay. Here was the conversation around Claudette. I said, 'I'm sorry about your mom.' He said, 'My mom died a long time ago.' I'm like, 'What do you mean?' He goes, 'My real mom. My grandma. Twenty-six years ago. When I was in college. And my dad, my grandpa, died when I was in high school. And my birth dad died when I was a baby. Claudette means nothing to me.' That was the conversation." I grabbed the roll of gift wrap and sheared it.

"Stop." She took the scissors from my hand.

"I'm *glad* she's gone," I protested. "She never even acknowledged her grandchildren. I mean, how crazy is that? She couldn't even put a baby card in the mail. I mean, you met her at the wedding."

Karen nodded. "She seemed like such a nice lady. A little high strung, maybe. But..." She emitted a tiny puff of air from between her lips.

"I only ever saw her the once, and that was enough," I said.

Evie raised her eyebrows and quipped, "Now tell us how you *really* feel."

Karen started wrapping her box. "At least she went fast. That's a blessing."

"Yeah." I reached for my own box. "Maybe fast is good. And now he can exorcise her from his mind. With a clear conscience. She even left him out of her will. I mean, not that we were surprised. Left everything to the Philharmonic."

"Sounds like there wasn't much to leave?" Evie remarked, busying herself handing out strips of tape.

"Yep," I said. "That second husband really buttoned things up tight. He left her the house, but she only had the income from his trust. It sounded like that man's kids were damn glad she died before she figured out a way to get around the trust restrictions."

I scissor-curled my ribbon with two brisk flips and fluffed it with my fingers. Karen stowed the wrapped gifts in her Christmas decoy box, an old Georgia praline carton labeled "Brokerage Statements 1990s."

"John did get her IRA," I said hesitantly. "He told me that was sixty thousand."

"At least there's that," Evie said. "Imagine if there hadn't even been...It's a saving grace."

"He said it must have been a mistake, or she'd forgotten she'd done it. But at some point, it was a deliberate decision made by someone. And shouldn't that have made him feel better?"

"Of course. And sixty thousand is nothing to sneeze at."

"But it didn't seem to make him feel better." I shook my head. "He was embarrassed even to tell me. And he's so worried about money now, and you know what? I'd rather not have gotten the tennis court." John had announced that gift when he came home from the funeral. I told him no, but he insisted, so I'd agreed because I figured he needed a fun project to oversee and to assuage my guilt I'd suggested we add a basketball hoop to the setup for the kids. And there was plenty left over for the business transition fund. We knew full well that after Owen's retirement, his clients could stay or leave.

Owen's clients. I turned anxiously to Karen.

"You'll help me with my dress for Winter Ball, won't you? John says it has to be a knockout this year."

"Of course. So you're doing it? I wasn't sure…"

"They bought a table, just like always. They have to be business as usual."

And now "they" meant John and Larissa, because Owen was retiring. Owen's wife, Melody, was a Microsoft millionaire, a lucky early investor, which was how they'd already purchased their future retirement home in Tucson, into which they would now be moving earlier than expected, due to Melody's Parkinson's diagnosis.

"She's only fifty-five!" I blurted. "She barely has a tremor at this point!" Then I put my head in my hands. "I just hit a new low. I'm jealous of someone with Parkinson's."

Karen reached out and put her hand over mine. "We'll go shopping this weekend. You're going to look great at that do."

"Larissa is bringing the Bridegroom this year to fill a chair," I said gloomily. "I'm surprised she ever got married, but I'm not surprised he's an anesthesiologist. I'd need to be anesthetized, too, if I lived with her."

"You are *so* bad." Evie grinned. "If we didn't love you so much, your reputation would be in tatters."

Chapter 13

Invisible Boundaries

John spun me out, and my skirt twirled around my knees. "You look great!" he said, and gave a slight tug to my right hand, the signal for another turn.

"All the credit goes to my sister, as usual," I replied. She'd persuaded me to get this tightly fitted dress with some flare to the hem. "The one-shoulder thing is going out on a limb for me. And plaid? I guess plaid got trendy again."

"I can tell you from here, plaid is definitely sexy." We did some breaks in the shadow position, then went back face to face, fingertip to fingertip. *One, two, cha-cha-cha.* Couples nearby glanced at us admiringly.

"Karen said I needed to be more unconventional. Actually, she's gone a little bohemian since moving out to the West Coast."

"She doesn't run around in a tennis skirt all summer like you do."

"Because she doesn't play tennis."

"I'm glad you do." His hand was warm on the small of my back. "Anyway, I can't wait to unconventional you right back home."

I blushed and wondered if we might even have sex that night. It had been a while. "Isn't it great to be dancing again!" I exclaimed. "We've *got* to get back to dancing. I mean..." I looked up and smoothed his lapel apologetically.

"I know. We're almost there. I told you, I think we've finally done it. We're zeroing in on that third partner. Then I can sit back and relax."

He seemed pretty relaxed now, and I was glad to see it, because I'd caught him being testy with Owen during their pre-game huddle in the lobby—Owen who walked on water, Owen of the partnership match made in heaven and why they'd absolutely sailed through the first three critical start-up years. They *never* argued, much less in public. I hadn't caught the whole exchange. When I caught back up with the men, I heard John snap, "Well, *you* tell her then," and Owen reply calmly, "It's not my story to tell."

"Oh, no, what's she done now?" I joked, to lighten the mood. Larissa was a crack litigator, but she'd never been to charm school, and I was sure she'd created the occasional moment of frustration for them during the search process. But Owen said nothing, just gave my arm an affectionate squeeze and walked away.

The dance ended. John laced his fingers through mine, and we threaded our way back to our table, strategically positioned in the middle of the ballroom to maximize casual en-route schmoozing opportunities. On the way we passed our guest Bernie Mayer, table-hopping in his trademark '70s tux while his wife was otherwise occupied dancing with Larissa's husband.

Bernie was one of the firm's most high-profile clients. Bright-eyed and bushy-tailed at eighty-two, he maintained an iron grip on Caffe Delice, the chain he'd founded "for fun" after his early retirement from the wholesale food business. Tonight, Owen and Melody were in charge of the Mayers and had lovingly tended them during cocktails. But they'd departed after dinner as early as possible without raising eyebrows, their appearance being in the nature of an emeritus cameo, although this was not public knowledge.

The firm's other showpiece guest was Diane Wozzeck, whose company, Puget Sound Player, had been midwifed three years ago in John's office. Larissa had just crushed an infringement suit from a small mom-and-mom company in Portland over the popular Lululegging, which our client had been marketing for a full year before that company had even existed. Once Larissa had sneezed that out of the way, John and Owen had been busy brokering a deal to open stores in Boise, Missoula, Jackson, and Salt Lake and, to top it off, were in secret talks with Galloping Gwen (the flinty-eyed grandma of athletic wear merchandising) down in Portland about brand licensing, which would make the already rich Wozzecks (her husband was a lumber heir) even richer.

Diane had broken her ankle at Whistler on New Year's Day so was more or less table-bound this year. Without her husband, whose policy at such affairs anyway was to spend as little time as possible with his wife and as much as possible trying to mooch Cuban cigars off his friends. So Diane was pinioned there alone with Larissa, who was valiantly trying to talk athleisure. It was obvious from both their faces this was an uphill battle. In a town where people conferenced immediately before, after, and even during workouts, Larissa perversely prided herself on her non-athleticism. Diane was visibly relieved as we sat down.

"We've just got to get going," she drawled, ruffling a hand through her short hair, coiffed in the take-no-prisoners weekend warrior style du jour and then draining her glass decisively.

"Of course! I can't believe you lasted this long in the first place," I said while shooting visual darts at Larissa.

"I wouldn't have missed it. And I'm not on painkillers anymore. As you can see," she said, reaching for her husband's glass and emptying it as she swiveled her head to scan around the room. Abruptly, she grabbed one of her crutches to barricade a passing woman.

"Oh my God! Maya! You stop! How are you doing? Look at this!" She turned in her chair and for the umpteenth time that night pulled aside the slit in her floor-length dress, gleefully displaying her surgical boot. "First day on the slopes—can you believe it?" Her strapless gown had clearly been chosen for its thigh-high, sequin-edged slit in order to showcase this badge of honor.

Her husband, standing close by and puffing on a Cohiba, pivoted back. "Don't break anyone else's ankle, Diane," he said, reaching for his wineglass but arresting with surprise when he saw it was empty.

Quickly John lifted the bottle of red and leaned over to execute a flawless left-handed pour, which the husband acknowledged with a grateful toast.

Diane claimed John's other arm with a ring-studded hand. "John!" she said coyly, "You know that's not my reputation."

In truth, her local nickname at the negotiating table was the Grim Reaper.

John quipped, "I wouldn't say an *ankle*-breaker," and as she guffawed, he put down the bottle, straightened up, and deftly unfastened himself by picking up her hand and sandwiching it warmly between his own.

She didn't notice, merely tightened her grip. "Everything I know about negotiation I learned from you, you rascal!" she said, while he gave her hand a last playful squeeze and let go.

"Nice move," I breathed in his ear as we sat down.

"The left-handed pour?"

"No, the other one." I'd seen it once before, and it had impressed me enough that I'd mentally filed it under John D. Halvorsen's Etiquette Tips (sometimes also titled How to Succeed in Business Without Anyone Realizing You're Really Trying), and now had enough information to file it under the subcategory Deflecting Flirtatious Behavior of Slightly Inebriated Women Old Enough to Be Your Mother.

"Top o' my game tonight, baby!" he joked. "It's all thanks to you and that plaid dress."

Diane's husband tucked her purse under his arm and organized her crutches. "You should have gone with the knee scooter, babe," he said. "That you couldn't use as a weapon."

As he towed her away, she turned and scolded John gaily, "Don't forget our lunch tomorrow!" in a voice much louder than the distance merited.

"I think maybe she still *is* on painkillers," I whispered to John, and he murmured, "They're leaving a little early, but that's okay. We got the pictures." John had squired the Wozzecks around during cocktails in the lobby, making sure to bump all the right elbows and get enough shots to ensure they'd see one in print.

A man I didn't know took Diane's empty seat. John's eyes brightened, but before he could say anything, the man put an arm on the back of my chair and leaned across. "Aren't you going to introduce me to your wife?" he joked, and then invited me to dance.

Buoyed as I was with optimism—about the partner search drawing to a close, about my marriage, even about my outfit—I waded right back onto the dance floor with him. We started swing-dancing to "In the Mood." He was a passable dancer but a lazy one and had the kind of full-lipped mouth that usually inclined me to distrust. But my job at this event was to be the Sociable Wife.

"So, Tom," I asked brightly, "How do you know my husband again?"

"You mean you don't know?"

"Know what? Oh my gosh, I'm sorry!" I rushed on. "Were you at our party last year? I usually never forget a face!"

Faces were easy for me; names were a different matter—I memorized the annotated guest list backward and forward every year for the firm cocktail party at the Harlequin Vineyard. This I would not have been able to do without the color-coded notecard system I'd developed for taking the bar.

"No, I wasn't in town then. I moved from Boston a few months ago," he supplied, without naming the firm, then surprised me with a left-side pass and an inside roll. "You really *don't* know who I am, do you?" He put his mouth close to my ear. "I had dinner with your husband on Thursday."

"Aha! So you're the one. I knew there was a prospect. But I didn't even know if it was a man or a woman."

"Impressive. Quite a firewall."

"Of course! I know that drill. I'm a lawyer too. Only part time," I added. "I consult with an environmental nonprofit. Also, I'm a musician." I usually didn't gabble like this but the breath in my ear was disconcerting.

"A musician! That must be why you're such a good dancer."

"We've had a lot of practice," I said lightly. "It's our thing. We won some lessons at our kids' school auction years ago and got hooked." A reference to children, I knew, sometimes did the trick to arrest any flirtation, but he just laughed and shook the waves back from his forehead.

"Sounds great. Probably a lot more fun than Miss Wilson's Dancing School in sixth grade. Listen, I'm flattered they tapped me. Your firm is hot. Terrific client list. But with Owen leaving, it'll be a whole new firm, won't it? There's always a risk with that."

Keep your voice down, I thought, while replying mildly, "A lateral move from a firm like Reeves Dwight is a big decision."

"Oh, I'm just of counsel. Seemed a good enough berth. I was partner at a megafirm back East, and I've had it with that kind of pressure. I mean, it was the wrong kind of pressure. It was never really about the actual work. Just about the competition. So." He pulled me a little closer. "What's the inside line? Why is Owen *really* leaving?"

"You're not going to pry it out of me," I said. "But it has nothing to do with interpersonal dynamics."

"Actually—they did tell me," he admitted. "You really *can* keep a secret."

A bit alarmed, I tapped his shoulder. "Listen, that's closely held. It wouldn't be kind to Melody. She has *not* given notice yet at the art museum. She's very private and has no interest in a pity party."

But he wasn't listening. "You're really good at keeping secrets," he repeated. "We should go out sometime."

The look was unmistakable. I smiled cheerily. "What a great idea! I'd love to double-date with you and your wife."

"I meant just the two of us." He did the Wagnerian hair toss again, a move probably invented at Miss Wilson's, which had apparently served him well since then. Most of the time.

"I'm flattered, Tom, but I'm a married woman, and the only man I go out with is my husband."

"Okay," he replied. His nonchalance was infuriating. Suddenly it occurred to me: If everything had been so swell back in Boston, what was this frat boy with his tassel loafers doing out here on the other side of the country?

I went on smoothly. "And, anyway, what would your wife think about that?"

"We have an agreement."

I gave him a smile without teeth. "Well. I'm not built that way."

He shrugged again. "Okay. Let me know if you change your mind."

The dance was winding down. I dropped his hand and plowed back to my seat, inwardly seething, hard-pressed not to turn around and slap him in the face right in front of a Nordstrom scion chatting with our newly elected congressional representative.

John stood up to pull out my chair, but I put my hand on the back of it instead and reached for my water glass. I took a gulp, dragged my eyes up, and slid them in the direction of my husband, who was not-smiling at Tom, which prompted Tom to take a step closer. He put his arm around me, sandpapered my bare tricep with his palm, and then squeezed it. "You've got a great little dance partner here, John."

I compressed my lips and got very, very still, to give him time to back out of his mistake. He was not picking up on it. The whole host of possible reasons this obviously intelligent, experienced business professional had been booted to the hinterlands rose again on the horizon, but now was not the moment to indulge in idle speculation, deliciously spiteful though it might be. Right now I was trapped against my chair. There was no way I could wriggle out of this by a graceful slide into my seat.

John looked pointedly at Tom's hand on my arm, inches from his own, and then at Tom, who merely grinned and tightened his grip.

"Get your hand off my wife," John barked. "She's not part of the deal."

The air currents in the nearest concentric ring of tables shifted, and into this conversational lull, Tom dropped two words.

"What deal?" he said, then sauntered off, smirking.

We sank down into our seats. "Sonuvabitch," John breathed. Mortified, I stared across at Larissa. She rose and moved over with the coffeepot.

"I don't want any," he said.

"Oh, yes, you do," she nodded, busily pouring. She smiled and looked around the room. "He wasn't going to come on board anyway."

John bent for a took a quick slurp. "I did not get that read."

"Owen didn't either. But I did. I suspected. At the very end of that meeting." She stirred in her sugar, then pretend waved to an imaginary someone across the room, while I sat numbly in my chair with my hands in my lap. I was impressed. Larissa was revealing hidden depths. I felt guilty for ever thinking she was borderline Asperger's.

"He just wanted another free steak at El Gaucho," John said glumly.

"He wasn't stringing us out, necessarily. I think he decided that night but didn't say. I think he'd liked the idea of the freedom but hadn't realized how much he'd have to put in," she said. "Not money, I mean. Effort. He wants a lifestyle practice."

I sipped my coffee. "Not a good fit, then. For us or for him."

She leaned forward and folded her arms on the table. "Maybe it's a good thing. Maybe we need an up-and-comer. I mean, he is older than we are, and we could have gotten into another early retirement situation again."

"I think he's already early retired. Here they come," I warned, catching sight of Larissa's husband, Joel, squiring his dance partner back to the table. Mrs. Mayer plopped down, visibly glowing.

"I'm just having the time of my life with you young people," she panted. "Who knew this firm was so full of good dancers?"

"I never thought about that before, Rosemary," John quipped. "Maybe we should make that a hiring requirement!"

"It's easy to dance when your partner is light on her feet," Joel added gallantly.

Mr. Mayer returned to the table and sat down, chuckling. "I just watched Diane's husband wheedle another Cohiba out of the president of the Bar Association on their way out."

We seemed to have come to rights, but I was still mortified with embarrassment at John's outburst and couldn't meet Larissa's eye. I excused myself and escaped through the nearest door into the lobby. Milling around me were dozens of people who had *not* just witnessed my husband lose his temper in public. I stood there a moment, drawing a lungful of air.

There was a light touch on my arm, and I turned to see an old acquaintance.

"Natasha!" I exclaimed. This was a more sophisticated Natasha than I remembered—sleek updo with wisps, short empire-waisted column of mocha chiffon—but then again, I hadn't seen her in several years. "Don't you look terrific! How are things at Dunwoody? I mean, PSB?" I racked my brain for her husband's name. He'd been a new associate during John's last couple of years…They had one child, younger than Grace…lived in Wallingford…

"Great! Things are great! I'm so glad I ran into you. I've been thinking about you! You and me—we're in the same boat!"

You were propositioned on the dance floor? But then she made a quick, unmistakable gesture—hand cupping smooth silk against a slightly rounded belly—and went on. "I have a surprise on the way, after an eight-year gap!"

"Congratulations! And you've got a sitter-in-training. I'd love to send something for the baby. Let's trade contact information. Is it a boy or a girl?"

"A boy. Cameron is thrilled."

Bingo. With the first name came the last, and I typed her in under H for Hodges.

"This was completely out of the blue," she said. "I mean we were *floored*. I'm telling you."

"Family planning. Contradiction in terms!" I joked. The problem was thinking you *could* plan when really that was an illusion. But you could take surprises in happy stride if you had a good relationship. *So much of marriage is just dumb luck*, my mother had said years ago. I understood that now. You never knew what was coming down the pike.

Natasha tucked her phone away. "Listen, they were talking about the Puget Sound Player deal at the table. Piper said he wished John and Owen were back, with that book of business, but Andy said he got the feeling they really liked running their own shop, *and* they're looking to add partners, so fat chance." Inwardly I gave thanks to heaven that the situation was still successfully under wraps, while Natasha sighed and went on. "It would be so great if you guys came back. I miss you at the firm events. You were always so nice to talk to. A little safe haven." She chuckled.

"It is kind of a fishbowl, isn't it? He's on partner track now, right?"

That had been a confident guess. One of Seattle's Big Three, Dunwoody had always taken two tables at the gala, and in the post-merger years, three, but in a large firm plenty of partners would opt out, and favored rank-and-file were invited to fill in.

The roving photographer bore down on us. "Now, what are you two attractive young ladies conspiring about?" he jollied, as he sized up the shot.

Natasha brightened. "This is the first time for me!"

"Well, here we go, then." I put my arm around her waist. "You never know if it will make the cut," I cautioned.

"I can't *wait* to tell Cam," she said, beaming, as the photographer clicked away.

Chapter 14

A Question of Upbringing

JOHN HOOKED HIS THUMB ON THE STEERING WHEEL, piloting the car like a little boat in a dark sea as we crossed the I-90 floating bridge toward the lights of Mercer Island. The dashboard cast a milky glow on his face. His brows were knit.

I hugged my fake shearling coat more snugly around me. Why was formalwear for women always gossamer-thin, no matter the season? I wondered. I reached for the water bottle tucked into the passenger door pocket, but it wasn't there.

"Sorry," said John. "My fault."

"No, no, I'm getting like the kids, always expecting a water hose on hand." Farther east now, outside the city, the traffic was thin, the sky inky enough for a few stars to be visible. I began to sing softly.

After the ball is over
After the break of dawn
After the dancers' leaving
After the stars are gone...

"You are the world's foremost repository of obscure show tunes," chuckled John.

"Hey! Obscure? That was one of the greatest popular hits of 1891."

"I rest my case."

"Anyway, the world's foremost repository, that's not me, that's Hudson Flame. Undisputed king."

"Who?"

I registered his look of perplexity. Of course he didn't know Hudson. Why would he? All the fixtures of my childhood were utterly unknown to him, as were his to me. No matter how long you'd been married, there was a whole swath of your life forever cloaked from your spouse, a little private universe, richly stocked and peopled, that you could never share. I leaned back against the headrest. "A friend from Glencoe. From when I was little." I'd take Hudson over Tom What's-His-Name any day. At least Hudson was mannerly. He'd also given up drinking on his thirtieth birthday.

Wells of light on the pavement ahead seemed stationary in the distance but sped up as they advanced, flashing into the past too swiftly for the eye to catch. In my vanity, I'd thought myself equal to any occasion, but now it was apparent how truly thin my resources were. What did I know of John's childhood? Little. I knew he'd gotten a bicycle for Christmas when he was eight, a secondhand Sting-Ray, and the big boys had grabbed it away, rode it down the block, then dumped it and ran off laughing. That, I knew.

In my imagination, I made the bike that bright metallic green so popular when we were kids. I gave it a crack mended with tape on the banana seat and a couple of dings on the fender; I saw him leaning it up against a scrubby piñon pine in the dusty yard of the Los Alamos ranchette, close to the kitchen door but not under the carport, so his grandfather wouldn't hit it. But even thus embroidered, it was nothing. I couldn't will myself into his childhood, even the simplest pieces of it, so how could I possibly fathom what it had done to him to know that one whole side of his family had completely ignored him his entire life? Because it wasn't just his mother. He'd had another set of grandparents he'd never met. And an uncle and aunt, plus two cousins in their thirties, that he had—just last year, at Claudette's funeral.

A late-model sedan passed us on the left, and a cigarette dropped out of the passenger window, hitting the pavement like a tiny bomb before we sped over it. Our similarities were suddenly superficial; our upbringings, on different planets. But like all married couples, we—the two of us together—were the foundation for the formative years of our own children.

And we did have a past together: the past of us. We'd built it for twelve years. We'd gripped each other's arms and made that bridge. We had to strengthen that. We would strengthen it. It was important for the children.

Children. "Guess who I ran into in the lobby? Natasha."

"Who?"

"Cameron Hodges's wife. You remember."

"Oh, yeah." He signaled, then took the Front Street exit. "Nice guy, Hodges. I always liked him. Smart. Didn't run into him tonight. He's still there, right? At Dunwoody? Or should I say Pillage, Slash, and Burn?"

"Yes, senior associate now. His wife buttonholed me in the lobby," I went on. "They're having another baby. After an even longer gap than us, and—she wanted my advice! I was flattered."

"Advice, advice, I'll give 'em advice, cereal in the bottle at four months," he cracked, then rubbed his chin thoughtfully. "You know, I always liked Cam. We were aiming for someone more seasoned on board. But I should run it by Larissa. Like she said. Maybe we need to change our approach."

Natasha was quitting her job, so this might not be the right moment. They might feel more secure right now with the devil they knew. On the other hand...

He pulled up at the red light off the exit and shook his head. "We were *this* close," he said, pinching thumb and forefinger together. "This close. We were at the point of 'we'll draw up the papers.' I'm so tired of these Ivy League shits. They play with you and take what they want. It's because they grew up wealthy."

"I don't think—" I interjected. "It's not all about money...It's a question of upbringing—"

But he ignored me and burst out: "Now he knows Owen's retiring!"

Owen's short list of three hadn't panned out. They'd never gotten far enough with them to reveal the real reason they were seeking another partner. Only Tom...

He read my mind. "He pissed all over us. He's lucky I didn't punch him in the fucking nose. And now *I'm* supposed to be embarrassed?"

"Of course not," I said quickly. "But really, that was nothing. You can't fill a room with lawyers and not expect some lively banter. Nobody really noticed, I'm sure."

He punched the accelerator a little too hard when the light changed, and I turned in my seat and folded my arms. "Listen. He certainly showed his true colors. You couldn't possibly trust him after that."

He looked at me finally, a thoughtful and appreciative look. "True. He'd be a total liability. In this climate, you can torch a deal with even an innocent remark. If the gal takes it the wrong way, that's it. Down the toilet."

He caught the yellow at the next intersection and made the left turn smoothly, but leaning into his door, seeming to deflate. We were well and truly in the darkness now, driving along an invisible Lake Sammamish. After a moment he straightened up and glanced over again. "Besides the fact I just want to punch him in the fucking nose. I'm sorry you had to go through that."

"That's okay. Glad to help. Due diligence, no extra charge," I joked, but he didn't laugh.

"I should have done law school at Stanford. People wouldn't treat me like that."

"But you couldn't have! You couldn't have afforded it!"

He palmed the wheel, looked at me, and shifted in his seat. "Maybe the money was there."

"What do you mean? Claudette would never have forked over. That much is clear. She is—she was—the absolute epitome of selfishness."

"I hope you don't think I take after her in that way."

I grabbed his arm. "What? Of course not. I'm shocked you'd even say that."

"Well, you know the old saying about the apple not falling far from the tree."

"But she didn't *raise* you. She had zero influence on you. Zero. What a horrible woman. I don't even know why she came to the wedding."

He snorted. "Maybe just to see if I was someone she could fleece."

"Well, Tulsa gave you a free ride. Law school at Stanford wouldn't have made a bit of difference."

"Not in the education, I know, but it's like getting your ticket punched. I mean, I did go there for undergrad. Maybe people are wondering why I didn't do law school there. Maybe they think I didn't get in...I should have pushed it with her."

"You were young. You hardly knew her. Wasn't that like only the second time you'd ever met her? You're not the adult you are now. Don't beat yourself up for not being brassy. It would've been a lost cause anyway."

"Yeah," he said, but in such a bleak tone I felt guilty for voicing the ugly truth.

"And anyway," I teased, "if you'd gone to Stanford, you wouldn't have met *moi*!"

"True. What would I do without you? I gotta say, you were very calm with that asshole."

"I was probably just in shock."

"Take the compliment," he said. "And now I know you'd never be unfaithful," he added.

"As if *that* was in doubt," I joked, and drummed on my knees.

But he went on. "You'd never abandon me, would you? Like Owen?"

For a moment I floundered in perplexity. "Owen did *not* abandon you. People retire. He's that age."

That goddamn trust baby. He ruined everything. Things were going so well tonight!

In darkness we drove past the Warner farm. Its faded white fence, caught in John's high beams, led toward the brightly lit entrance to Ogilvie Glen. Its center waterfall burbled merrily, twinkles of spray caught in the illumination from spotlights hidden on artfully placed boulders, and on the flanking pillars, carriage lanterns flickered in imitation of candles. We turned into the golden light.

Grace and Jackie were bedded down at Karen's; Nathan was on a sleepover, even though it was his dad's weekend. In eighth grade now, he was starting to win the occasional battle on this score. Karen had predicted this. Silently, we passed her house. Frank had just gotten wind of his larger-than-usual bonus this year. "Where do you want to go?" he'd asked Karen.

I remembered those days, the days of Christmas bonuses, of being an employee at a big firm. But we'd made the decision to trade that for greater freedom and potentially greater reward.

When Karen picked Miami, I asked her why. "It's so different from here," she'd said. "Kind of like leaving the country, without leaving the country."

I didn't want something different. I wanted the same. I wanted everything to be the way it used to be. It wasn't the money I was jealous of. It was that Frank was happy. He came home at dinnertime every night and he didn't see a therapist. Need to see a therapist, I corrected myself.

John pulled into the driveway and stopped outside the kitchen door, facing the backyard and the wooded slope beyond. Last year, after Winter Ball, we'd scampered into the empty house like teenagers and littered the floor with each other's clothes. Now we sat in the car, quietly watching the rising moon begin to silver through the spindles of fifty-foot trunks like light from another, happier room, and we both leaned forward, hungrily, waiting for it to arrive.

"How many other kids do they have?" John said suddenly. "Cameron and Natasha?"

"Just the one. A daughter. Year behind Gracie."

"Two, then." He nodded. "That's manageable."

I looked at the familiar silhouette of the treetops on the ridge, gentle, watchful, full of nodding kindness during the day. Now, in the dark, they were a harsh row of black spikes, an impenetrable line of sentinels jealously guarding what lay beyond. Abruptly, I turned my head to the passenger window, where beads of moisture clung in perfect stasis: heavy enough to well but not to succumb to gravity.

"Remember when we jumped off the dock at Elmwood that time? On our seventh anniversary. And we said it looks like we're not going to have any more kids, and we said that was okay. And then—you're not sorry, are you?" I blurted. "That we had Jackie. I mean—of course not *that*—but maybe…if…we were further along with things…it wouldn't be so complicated. You could make these changes with less pressure…"

He put his arm around me. I leaned into him, burying my face in his shoulder, breathing him in.

"I've said it before and I'll say it again." His voice was husky. "You are my heart's desire. You, and Nathan, and Grace, and now Jackie."

No man ever wanted children in his life more than John. No man wanted family in his life more than John, an only child of an only child, raised by his grandparents. Regret another baby? It sounded absurd even to say it out loud.

"Each of those kids, each of them, is the best thing that ever happened to me," he said, and kissed me, the real John again, long-awaited, long-desired. "I'm not feeling burdened, if that's what you mean," he said, then, "Look!"

I lifted my head.

The full moon, which had been resting on the spiky tops of the evergreens, had just risen clear. Close by, like a large, unwinking star, was Mars.

Reverently, he said: "Once every fifty-five thousand years."

Once, years ago, he'd called me out to look at the moon. It was shortly after we'd moved in; Grace was about nine months old and had started to sleep through the night, and we didn't need to tag team it anymore. We sat together on the front porch. Everything—our little valley, our front meadow, the front of the house, everything—was bathed in soft, clear light, bright enough that you could even, faintly, discern color. "This is why I wanted to live on a road without streetlights," he said. I went inside, opened the window, and put on "Song to the Moon" from *Rusalka*, and we sat on the porch watching its transit. "I like the connections you make," he said, and when we went inside, he made love to me, not vigorous and enthusiastic, but tenderly, and looking straight into my eyes. And I knew—I knew into the marrow of my bones—that he loved me.

He still had an arm around me. I didn't want him to let go. I wanted to get as close as possible to that place, that time, before I ever knew there was or could be even the smallest of gaps, the tiniest of chinks letting in the opposite of light. This was the real marriage. Like my grandmother's, my mother's, my sister's. It was healthy and strong. It had flourished for years. It would flourish forever.

Nestled against him, I spoke tentatively. "You know, Natasha said people were talking about Diane's deal. They said you had a great book of business, and they wished you'd come back. Maybe we should consider that."

"Yeah, I know. It feels like going backward, though. I'm sure we'll find someone." He flipped the wiper once, to clear the sheen of drizzle.

"What was the name of your best friend again, when you were little? Your best friend before. I was just trying to think of his name. Bob?"

He roused. "Rob. Robbie. Ives." A tiny smile flitted. "What made you ask that right now? That's so weird! I was just thinking about him. I was thinking about summers growing up. Maybe because we were talking about jumping off the dock. It made me feel like a kid, you know?"

"How were *you* anywhere near bodies of water when you were little?"

"Hey, there was a big pond right in the middle of town. Ashley Pond. We swam in it…Not sure if you can do that anymore, but we did. There was also the pool, but you had to pay to go there." He scratched at the oil change sticker in the corner of the windshield. "I spent the whole summer outside. When school got out, my grandpa got the clippers and gave me a mohawk, and every morning my grandma gave me a sack lunch, a towel, and fifty cents, and off I'd go on my bike. I wouldn't be home until dinner. Outside, all day long. There were kids that went to summer school, day camp…but we always felt sorry for those kids. We never ran out of things to do. We were all over the place. It was awesome. They didn't even make me go to church in the summer."

He sat forward, laced his hands together on top of the steering wheel, and gazed intently into the sodden woods. "I don't know what kind of a man I turned out to be, but I was pretty good at being a boy." His smile was so wistful, it broke my heart.

Backward, John had said. Returning to Dunwoody would feel like that. You couldn't go backward, you could only go forward. Perhaps "backward" was only a way of saying you were moving forward, just in a direction you didn't like.

The moon rose higher, bathing more of the yard in light, but beyond still lay a wedge of blackness, a companion darkness on the ground slowly shrinking back toward the gleam of the retaining wall. We sat there in the car, suspended, watching this shadowy bluish patch of light increase, unsure if it was advancing or retreating, if we were facing the past or the future.

I turned to John. His face in profile was closed, no longer familiar territory. As I watched, he receded inwardly; he was going where I could not follow, leaving me behind, alone in the wilderness of this world, a pilgrim stripped of faith. *Don't!* I begged in silent anguish, then cried: "But you made Bright Lights three years in a row!"

He turned. I felt the pull of him willing himself to meet me, willing himself back into optimism, and he was able to say, "You *bet.*"

It rang a bit hollow, but I kept it afloat in my mind, reaching for my purse on the floor, saying brightly, with relief, "Oh, I forgot to mention! I got my picture taken. In the lobby. With Natasha. Cam's wife. Isn't that nice?"

He pulled the key out of the ignition. "Why did you do that?" he snarled. "He's only a senior associate." Then he stomped into the house.

I sat, frozen, in the ugly silence created by a slammed door in a small space. I hated the rain, the trees, the dark sopping days, the false promise, the false charm. I longed for the flat planes of my Midwestern childhood, where the sun shone all day even in winter, a wide and generous landscape imparting an optimism I hadn't realized people raised elsewhere might not possess.

A kitchen light went on, and his face appeared at the door. I turned away. When I looked again, he was gone.

I squeezed my eyes shut and stood on the train tracks with Karen, heard the two-note clang of the crossing gate, a chime of C-sharp and B-natural, a childhood constant, so embedded we heard it not only during waking hours but while asleep, percolating gently through our dreams at night. I stood on the tracks, holding hands with my sister, looking north to Wisconsin, south to downtown Chicago, thirty miles, clean and clear, each way. We could see things coming.

When things are flat, you know where you stand. I'd always thought of the landscape of my marriage as a plain, with visible gentle hills and valleys. The terrain in Seattle, so picturesque when I'd first arrived, was now irritating, seemed, even, faintly menacing. The topography was muddled. Too many hills, too many blind corners; too much was hidden.

I heard a sound. My eyes flew open. John was there, bending down, one hand on the door, the other braced on his thigh, tilting his head with the same little smile he'd sent across the room at the first law journal meeting in Tulsa when I'd thought, *Who is that? How come I don't know him?* It was all there, all the years of him, and it was real, and there, and mine, collapsed like a tiny invisible telescope safe in the palm of my hand.

"I'm sorry," he said.

My heart leapt, but I pouted.

"C'mon inside. I'm sorry, I'm sorry, I'm sorry. That was very not cool. I don't know why I'm acting like this. This is just a process. We'll get through it. Listen, I laid a fire and I found a bottle of Kahlua. Let's make White Russians and party like it's 1999."

I pursed my lips to keep from laughing.

"I promise you I will not let this impact you anymore. Heart and soul. I promise not to take it out on you. It's not fair."

I sucked in air and let it out through my teeth. "And I promise... not to stick my foot in my mouth. Every time I open it."

"That's hardly true, O my silver-tongued nonprofit corporate counsel." He opened the door wider, beckoned, and I stepped out, a little sheepish, but he was smiling at me. He gave me his arm and drew me safe to shore.

Part Two

Universe of Lost Answers

Chapter 15

Breakfast of Champions

He bore no resemblance to Claudette. That was my first thought as his somber face hovering above the appropriate dark suit swam close enough for his voice to be heard, for recognition to gel, which was very close indeed, close enough to see the pores in his nose and to catch the expensive smell of Italian wool as he leaned in to introduce himself as John's uncle, giving my arm a gentle apologetic squeeze as he did so to temper this fact—that he had to introduce himself.

Embarrassed, I looked down. His dress shoes were tassel loafers, probably as sartorially rebellious as a Main Line banking executive would allow himself. John disliked those; he never wore them.

"...tiring...matters..."

Why was this man almost whispering? I shifted on my feet. My black pumps were not new; I'd spent years dancing in them. But it was different when you had to stand still.

"...an overwhelming time for you, but I'd like to meet briefly next week."

"I'm sorry?" I looked up, eye level with him, a little taller, actually, which was how I could examine, once again, the pores on his nose. It wasn't that he was short, just that I was used to living around very tall men.

"Just some documents to pass along. A family business matter. I wanted to take the opportunity to do it personally. Nothing to worry about."

He'd stopped talking, and the last phrase registered. *Nothing to worry about.* If there was nothing to worry about, then what was the big deal?

"Of course," I replied stiffly, and he moved on. I hadn't meant for there to be a receiving line, but when I'd walked into the guild room and stood still, one had simply materialized, and I was at a loss. There was no guidebook for this, no app or social media platform. John left no instructions. One night after my father died, Bobbie got out her knitting bag and, along with the yarn, pulled out a piece of paper. She looked at it, then handed it to me: 1. MAKE NO SNAP DECISIONS.

"We were at the hospital," she said. "He wanted to make me a list." She gave a faint smile. "He wanted to make me a list...but then he got too tired."

My father had been dying of cancer and knew his time was coming. John had not anticipated suffering a fatal heart attack while working late at the office one weeknight. But not to worry. I didn't feel capable of making any decisions right now. Except that I needed to get off my feet.

A fellow basketball mom was next. A tight hug, and then she drew back, clasping my hands. "How are you managing?"

"Drugs?" I cracked.

She gave a sympathetic little shake of the head and shot a glance at Karen, who was standing by my side. Karen put her arm around my shoulders.

"Sorry," I said. "That just came out."

"We're going to take *good* care of Grace," she said. "Don't you *worry*," and the three of us turned to look.

The entire eighth-grade girls' basketball team was clustered on the other side of the room, in front of a row of leaded glass casement windows framed by heavy drapes. The girls, subdued by the occasion, hovered quietly around Grace, as a few rays of pale winter sun straggled in on them. Off to the sides of this Caravaggesque tableau, the mothers of these girls stood in small, stricken clumps, trying not to cry about seeing lightning strike so close to home. I realized this particular mother had been deputized.

"Don't you worry," she said again.

"Good," I replied, tears springing to my eyes. "Because she'll hardly say a word to me."

I didn't want to talk to people. I wanted this to be over. I wanted to be back in my own kitchen with my sister and Evie and Dana, who'd flown in from Tulsa, and Mardie, who'd flown in from Baltimore. I wanted to be sitting around the kitchen table with them. With our shoes off. Maybe taking drugs—there was a first time for everything.

John's doctor *knew* about his father's heart attack. It was in his medical history. They'd determined there was nothing to worry about! He'd missed his physical last year. He'd said he was too busy. Should I have hounded him to reschedule, and if I had, would this have happened? And that doctor! He'd actually said to me on the phone: "Your husband's father died at thirty-five, so your husband got almost ten more years than his dad. That's something to be grateful for," and I had said, "Gratitude is not a word you should be using with me right now," and hung up on him.

I looked around for Jackie and located him at the coffee urn end of the room. He was in my brother-in-law Frank's charge, and luckily Frank was big enough to hold a very small six-year-old on his hip if circumstances required, which they did at the moment, while he chatted with my brother, Doug, and his wife, Cassie.

Did I need to have my children checked for heart defects?

"I can't stand up anymore," I said abruptly. Karen and her daughter Molly led me to the only couch in the room, in front of a fireplace that had likely never been used, flanked by two intimidating wing chairs. The only other seating was a row of straight chairs, lined against one wall as though for a dance, but they were empty.

Everyone was on their feet, milling about, as though this were an unusually quiet cocktail party with a small youth contingent sprinkled in. I watched Frank move on to Melody and Larissa. He prompted Jackie to return their greeting, and Jackie lifted his head off Frank's shoulder and gave them each his hand in turn.

"Oh, Karen. I'm so grateful for Frank. He's doing yeoman's service. He's got to be hurting."

She nodded silently, then squeezed my hand.

"At least we have each other," I said, attempting a smile, but it didn't work. It was a tiny twitch in the left corner of my mouth, which she for her part returned, exactly. I looked back at Frank, rocking gently from side to side as he held Jackie, as a parent will do with a child on the hip.

Jackie wouldn't really remember Larissa, and he wouldn't know Owen's wife Melody at all. We'd never been big on kids in the office. That's why the firm's Christmas party had always been such an event for them. Melody, smiling, charmed him into a bit of conversation. She reached out to pat him and then put her hand back in her pocket, probably, I realized, to conceal the slight tremor I'd noticed before the service.

Oh, Melody, I'd blurted, *I'm so glad Owen isn't here to see this!* which she'd thankfully not only taken in exactly the right way but with such kindness and genuine sympathy, it almost bowled me over. I regretted losing touch with them when they'd moved to Arizona, and I especially regretted not accompanying John to the memorial service when Owen had passed away unexpectedly the previous year. That had hit John hard, and I should have gone with him.

Close to Melody I saw my mother talking to Dana. It had been more than twenty years since she'd been widowed, twenty years since she'd cried out to me one night in anguish: "All I want is what I had!" Now, though deep in conversation, she sensed my glance and looked over at me, her face riven with new grief. *All I want is what I had.* I understood that now. It hurt too much; I looked away.

The boys were clustered at the buffet table, trying to figure out how to juggle a smartphone in one hand and a plate of little triangular sandwiches in the other.

"Those boys shouldn't clump up in front of the refreshments," I fretted. "They're in the way of other people."

"Are you hungry, Aunt Kim?" Molly's expression was that of a forlorn puppy. I reached out both hands.

"Oh, honey," I lied, "I'd love a little plate of sandwiches. Do you think you could get me one?"

"Yes," she breathed, and bustled off. She was wearing the purple velvet dress we'd only just recently bought for the annual family group portrait: jewel neckline, embroidered empire waistband, just the right thing for a fifth grader in that awkward stage. We always scheduled the photo shoot for right before Christmas, when Bobbie, Doug, and Cassie came into town. I watched my boss Terri help her put a plate together.

Dana materialized. She handed me a tissue, then took it back and said, "Just let me real quick," fixed my mascara, and gave it to me again. She looked very continental. I didn't know how she did it. It had something to do with scarves.

I grabbed her sleeve. "Oh, Dana! Thank you so much for being so nice to my mother."

"My *God*," she said. "You know I *love* your mother! We go back. We're sticking together. For some reason, we're always, like, the only two people in the room who aren't lawyers." She handed me a fresh tissue, this one to wipe my nose, then bent down and picked up the card that had fallen to the floor. "What's this?"

"Oh—that's John's uncle. Paul. The uncle he barely knew, come all the way from Connecticut. If you can believe it. He wants to talk to me. Don't lose that."

∽

AND THAT'S HOW I FOUND myself at the Sheffield in downtown Seattle on a weekday morning, three days after the funeral, having breakfast with this uncle of John's. The hotel's tablecloth restaurant occupied one entire corner of the lobby level. Unimaginatively named the Dining Room, it hovered above the street like the prow of a ship breasting the intersection and heading downstream toward Smith Tower. This was someplace I'd never been, but it was beautiful. A curved, underlit bar and a handful of round booths were tucked into the interior recesses. We sat at a small table for two among the many tables sprinkled generously out in the open to catch the light from two soaring walls of windows. The sun was shining brightly; Paul remarked on it, and I made haste to assure him that yes, this was unusual for the second week in February.

"Perhaps you brought it with you," I added.

"Well, if that's true, it's the least I could do," he remarked, straightening his fork on the napkin. He seemed more relaxed today. Maybe it was the clothing—slacks and a crewneck sweater instead of a suit—or maybe it was just me. Maybe I was more relaxed. Nothing like having to shake hands with dozens of people on the occasion of your physically fit forty-four-year-old husband's dropping dead of a heart attack at the office to key you up.

"Thanks for making the trip into the city," he added. "I'm sorry to take you away from your kids."

"They went back to school today."

"Probably the best thing," he nodded. "And your mother?"

"She's staying as long as I need her. My brother and his wife left yesterday, but my sister and her family live here, so I have a lot of support."

"Your sister…That would be Karen." He nodded again. "A close family. That's a good thing." He realigned the document envelope that sat beside his place setting.

I checked again for any signs of resemblance to John but found none. He had close-set, bright blue eyes, and a receding hairline that accentuated his bullet-shaped head. His hair was the kind of blond that turns gray unremarked. He looked a bit like a Prussian rabbit.

The food arrived, mine a yogurt and berry parfait. I'd ordered it because it was soft. Yesterday, I'd eaten nothing but two bowls of vanilla ice cream. My mother was concerned, I could tell, but it had not yet risen to the level of visible irritation. It was all part of that gracious leeway I kept noticing from her. Which was nice, because it wasn't like I was doing it on purpose, which of course she knew. It put me in mind of the unstinting and unremitting emotional support—and help with the baby—she'd given me during the two long years of my divorce from Larry, which I knew had to have been an emotionally devastating time for her as well. When the chips were down, that was when my mother showed me best how much she truly loved me.

Paul lifted his hands admiringly as his Denver omelet was placed before him. It really was beautiful; not the huge flat crescent you'd get at a diner, but an elegantly crafted pouch with edges folded in as lovingly as a mother would swaddle a newborn. A tiny, delicate bird's nest of hash browns nestled beside, and a sprig of cilantro and squiggle of salsa verde completed a presentation that I viewed with the complete detachment of someone who'd lost her appetite long enough to drop eight pounds in a week.

He adjusted the plate with a finger on each side, then applied salt with a liberal hand. "This is an indulgence. My wife polices my egg intake. But I worked out this morning, so I earned it."

That explained the glow, I thought. I smiled thinly and carved a minute spoonful of yogurt out of the parfait swirl. Would policing John's diet have helped? He hadn't been a pound overweight.

The server refilled our water goblets, the ice making a musical sound as he poured. I lifted the glass; it had weight and heft and was cold to my fingers, and I felt the ice cubes against my lip as the cool water went down my throat. Ordinary things now seemed amazing. But the server wasn't done; he returned with the coffeepot. The rich stream splashing into the china cup, the rising steam that came along as different air temperatures collided, proved we lived on a planet with an atmosphere and breathed oxygen. I thanked him, grateful.

"You're welcome," the server replied, meeting my eye, and I saw a young man who resembled Nathan but ten years older: same coloring, same energy, same hair, but with a little bit of a beard. I took a sip to conceal the welling tears and was suddenly angry at Paul. He'd acknowledged the waitstaff with just the barest of nods. How could Paul not see this was all a miracle—the sound of the ice, the steam from the coffee, the omelet, the server, the air we breathed in and out every minute of every day? Paul was seventeen years older than John, carrying an extra twenty pounds, and had to watch his cholesterol; why was he still alive and not John, who'd looked fit as a fiddle?

"John was fit as a fiddle," I said.

"I'm sure he was," he replied.

John had taught me—had taught us—that the atmosphere around the Earth was thin and fragile and that the very edge of it was called its "limb," which the children thought was funny because to them it meant an arm or a leg. But John said no, it was more like a rainbow.

A group of men in their thirties, engaged in energetic conversation, sat down close by. They were all dressed in expensive sweats. I saw Paul notice and adjust the collar of the blue dress shirt peeking out from the neck of his sweater.

"I'm sorry—you were saying?" I took another spoonful.

He told me he'd just worked out at the Washington Athletic Club down the street. He belonged to the Union League in Philadelphia and had reciprocity, and he could have stayed at the WAC, but when he traveled, which wasn't all too often, he liked to hunt out small hotels with character. Otherwise why bother?

I don't want to be here. Why on earth are we here? What kind of business can you have? What in the heck is in that folder—Great-Uncle Roscoe's genealogy chart for Chrissake? Not interested, I thought, but he kept up his line of conversation, and oddly enough, I began to feel buoyed, and I repented. There was this way, I'd noticed lately, that people had of keeping you afloat with their chatter so you could just sit there and breathe and feel the ground under your feet and keep realizing, because you kept forgetting, that although your life was over, you were still alive.

The athletes were eating hearty breakfasts, just like Paul. If one of those young men, full of vim and vigor, keeled over right now, with all these people around, there would be a flood of 911 calls, and the EMTs would arrive in a jiffy. He'd be bundled to the hospital, where he would be joined by his family, who would thank the doctors for saving his life. But not John. *John was alone.*

"You have to stop that."

I turned my head back. I'd said it aloud.

Paul laid down his knife and fork. "You have to stop doing that," he repeated quietly, firmly. "Yes, John was alone. But I'm telling you. You just can't...dwell."

"I know," I said miserably, and he sighed and palmed his head, reminding me that we all had past moments of pain, regret, and disappointment, and I had the sudden insight that for him, just as for John and me, some of these may have had to do with Claudette. A window opened in my mind, and I saw his youth sketched out before me in crystal clarity: Claudette, running away as soon as finals were done her junior year at Vassar; Claudette, having a baby that had to be swept under the rug; Claudette, returning home, conveniently without the baby; Claudette, rejecting two consecutive suitors ginned up for her with great effort but finally accepting the third when her father threatened to cut off her allowance, a B-grade candy company executive. Claudette: sucking all the air out of the room. And all this while, Paul had been there, eager to please and dutifully treading his father's path, all the way down to the monogrammed cuff links.

Paul talked about his children, unfolding parallels to his own youthful family history, of which he appeared completely unaware: older daughter, younger son; the daughter throwing away her MBA from Wharton to abscond to Florida and build yachts for a living, the roman-numeraled son going into banking and producing his own requisite two children. Perhaps ignorance was bliss?

The server returned. "How are we doing here?"

"Just fine," Paul responded, bestowing a smile that precluded further pleasantry, and the plates were whisked away. Paul then brushed a few nonexistent crumbs from the tablecloth and placed the folder front and center. It was one inch thick, brown, its flap tied with a fabric ribbon the color of dried blood. He folded his hands on top.

"I'm glad I got the chance to meet John."

That would have been the once, four years ago, at his mother's funeral, when John was forty. Involuntarily, my fingers clenched the gaudily striped drawstring case for the drugstore readers I'd just retrieved from my purse.

He leaned forward. "Families are different," he said, spreading his hands as though in general appeal to this universal truth.

"Yes, they certainly are," I replied coldly. "My sister's kids practically live at my house, and vice versa."

"You're very lucky. I don't think that's quite as common as we'd like to believe nowadays, with people being so mobile."

The silken tones with which he compressed a lifetime of estrangement into something as thin as a dime was breathtaking. I had no energy to object and simply remarked sadly: "When Claudette died, all I could think of was that she'd never seen her own grandchildren."

He pressed his lips together. "I know. It's not what I would have done." He untied the string, then smoothed the folder gently as though to iron out wrinkles. "I'm glad *I* saw them."

Any trace of indignation deflated. We all had lost opportunities to regret. As for me, I just wanted to take a break from it all. I wanted to crawl under a rock. With my children. I wanted to lie on my bed with my kids all tumbled together and watch old cartoons. Like we used to.

Yet another group was being seated nearby, all in athletic warm-ups. Paul looked puzzled. "Are they training for a marathon?"

"This time of year? No. These guys are just the diehards. Here for some conference, and no matter where they are, they're going to get in their five-miler."

"Aha." He shot his cuffs. "I was thinking this might be business dress in Seattle."

"No, it's just always Breakfast of Champions around here," I said sourly.

The first table was done eating. They sat with their chairs pushed back and their legs crossed, finishing their green tea and poking at their phones. These people must schedule all their meetings in the afternoon. Or maybe Paul was right; these *were* their meetings.

He took a breath. "Let me just say this, Kim. I was very impressed when I met John. He seemed solid. Amazingly so, given the early circumstances. And he was obviously devoted to you and the kids. And I see now what a wonderful family he has. It's a real testament," he said thoughtfully. "Not just to you, not just to the grandparents who raised him, but to *him*." He cleared his throat. "To who he was inside. Inherently. Not everyone would have turned out that way."

In the pause that ensued, we stared out the window as a stoplight cycled from green to yellow to red. Paul had his lower lip tucked in. Whatever possible Halvorsen loose end that needed tying up could easily have been accomplished by mail, I thought, but Paul had flown all the way across the country.

The chink of my coffee cup on the saucer roused him from his reverie.

"Now it's time for me to hand over the reins. After all, they're your children. You should be the one managing the trust."

"What trust?"

He patted the folder. "John's trust."

"Oh, we don't have one yet. I mean, we started college savings accounts for the kids. We were going to set up a *trust* trust, but we hadn't gotten around to that yet."

I caught the slight frown and pursed lips as he glanced quickly away and then back, making it obvious he'd just won some unfortunate internal bet.

"You don't mean Claudette's IRA, do you?"

"No," he said slowly, deliberately, drawing out a thick stack of typewritten pages. They were affixed to a blue paper backing by two brads at the top. "John's trust. The one my parents set up for him. They set up three, one for each grandchild. Claudette and I were each the trustees for our own kids and successor trustees for each other. That's why I'm the current trustee. I took over when Claudette died."

He swiveled it around and pushed it across.

William Mayhew Halvorsen and Eleanor H. Halvorsen Trust FBO John Diaz Halvorsen. I put my finger on the names. I hadn't even known their names.

"He never mentioned this."

"John didn't know about it either. Until his mother died."

"He didn't say anything about this when he came home. I guess because it was something you were in charge of? Everything is at the office. I mean, not just the firm stuff. All our financial stuff. When I had Jackie and was overwhelmed with three children, John took over all the bookkeeping. He managed everything from the office..."

I stopped babbling. I put my glasses on and placed my index finger beside the first paragraph, the way I used to read cases in law school. "Well, of course you should resign as trustee.

Obviously," I said, running my finger down the page. A thought stopped me, and I looked up. "But John was forty years old when his mother died!"

"The trust was pretty restrictive. It didn't terminate until age forty-five."

"Restrictive? *I'll* say." I'd taken that class. "I guess forty-five is the new thirty-five is the new twenty-five."

A little smile bloomed. "It is a bit excessive, but when your parents are handing your kids two million dollars, you just smile and say thanks."

I swallowed. That class I *hadn't* taken. The one on how to understand why a husband consumed with financial anxiety would also conceal an inheritance of such large proportions from his wedded wife.

I pretended to be Karen, arranging on my face the expression I imagined she'd adopt: blasé yet businesslike, as though bandying about seven-figure sums in conversation were a daily occurrence. Karen never let them see her sweat. I slid my fingers under the assemblage, lifted it an inch, and held it there in front of me while I looked him in the eye. "So what, in fact, is the actual value of the corpus here? Today?"

"Like I said...at the beginning, two million."

I sensed he was hedging. "In total?" I asked.

"No." He hemmed a bit. "For each child. Each. There were three trusts. At inception, each trust was two million."

"Each?" I squeaked.

"Yes, each. My parents had a major capital event in the mid-eighties and were in a position to spread things around a little."

"That's a lot of money in the eighties."

"That's a lot of money anytime. You can see the need to remove it from their estate. The federal exemption was only about half a million then. This would have been, let's see, when John was seventeen, and my kids were three and five."

This had happened when John was applying to college. I folded my arms tightly. "John worked his way through Stanford."

He shifted in his seat. "That's exactly what *he* said. When he found out." After a moment he went on. "Now, when Claudette died, the value of that trust was somewhat under one million."

He knew: I was no dummy. I knew investments grew over time and large investments had large growth over time, especially if untouched. How could two million become less than one million after twenty-five years of growth?

Answer: There were not twenty-five years of growth.

As I remained silent, embarrassment rouged his cheeks, then resubmerged. I had thought my out-of-body experience was complete, but it wasn't. I now found myself looking down almost with pity on a sixtyish business executive after he had conveyed to a suddenly and freshly widowed mother of three to whom he was only tenuously related that his blood sister had fleeced her own son of millions of dollars. While he, the sixtyish business executive uncle, had remained willfully blind.

Slowly I said: "How do you even *spend* that much money in twenty-five years?"

He snorted. "My God, that's easy, if you set your mind to it. Very easy, I'm sure, for her." He paused, then said sadly, "And the lost earnings. To put it another way, my kids' accounts, even after I paid for all their schooling and down payments on their houses, are still over five million." He pulled at his bottom lip. "I'm not trying to make you feel bad. But the facts are the facts. She just thought it was her money to use. So she did."

"But she was already wealthy!"

He nodded. "And that second husband was even more so. But when she died, this portfolio was worth nine hundred thousand."

I stared at him aghast, speechless, as the vastness of Claudette's deception sank in on me. Claudette bought jewels, Claudette bought furs, Claudette donated big bucks to the opera, all while John worked his way through Stanford. While he lived on ramen noodles until he got his first job after graduating from law school. We had scraped together the down payment for our twelve-hundred-square-foot rowhouse in Baltimore.

Then it dawned on me: This was the *second* time Paul was being forced to go through this enormously awkward and unpleasant conversation, and through the goodness of his heart, or guilt, or perhaps both, he had decided it couldn't be done except in person. And this was why he had flown out.

He plucked at his bottom lip again. "And now it's about five hundred thousand," he said.

Now I was really confused. "Where did you put it?"

"No, I mean, John took distributions. Over time. He asked for it. Of course I let him call the shots. I'm not going to tell a grown man and an experienced attorney how to manage his money. After all, there was plenty of it."

What in the world had John done with this money? I hadn't the least idea what to think. I only knew I wanted to leave the table as soon as possible. I said quickly, "I know you wanted a copy of the death certificate, but I don't have it yet. It probably won't come until next week. They had to do an autopsy. They have this new rule in King County for unattended deaths because of the opioid crisis. It was sudden cardiac arrest, but they had to do it."

He nodded.

I looked at my hands folded in my lap. "So. He took regular distributions?"

"Not at first. But in the last eighteen months or so, we fixed on quarterly deposits. Of twenty-five thousand."

"His backup attorney is taking care of things in the office," I said. "I'm sure all the financial details will be included in John's letters of instruction. I haven't really gotten into the office yet. There's been so much to do."

"Of course," he said smoothly. "This is a lot to take in. Unfortunately, when people pass away, it brings all this business upon us. I've been through it a couple of times…So many details. It's confusing. Not because things are in disarray; simply because you're tired."

He really was a good businessman; I could see him, in the boardroom, normalizing a disturbing visual when everyone around the table saw the arrow on a graph cratering and then plummeting down, all the way off the page. He would casually rearrange the crease on his trousers and persuade everyone that what they were seeing on paper was not, in fact, what it looked like.

For example, that John had *not* been sucking huge amounts of money out of a trust fund he kept secret from his wife, the most likely reason for which would be that he was in some sort of financial difficulty and keeping that secret, too.

I was grateful for the simple artifice. Paul didn't need to be nice to me. In a couple of hours, he could dismiss me from his thoughts entirely. But he was behaving kindly. Despite the toxicity of his family dynamic, he had turned out this way. And John—John too had turned out well, in spite of it. Paul had pointed that out. I clung to that. To the John I knew. There would be an explanation for the way he had organized this money, and I would find it.

He leaned forward and paged busily through the document. "You can see here, a third successor trustee was not originally named, but I was given the discretion to name one. If I do not do so, the bank becomes trustee upon my resignation, and you do *not* want a corporate trustee, believe me." He pulled out some loose papers tucked in the back and swiveled them to face me. "So, I've amended to name you successor trustee, and then"—he turned a page—"*I* withdrew. And now"—another page, his finger hovered; then he speared another line—"all *you* need to do is accept the substitution and have that signature notarized, and you're the trustee. Then change the title on the brokerage account, and we're good."

Beside us, the table of five stood up to go, and it suddenly hit me.

"Rain or Shine! The Rain or Shine Run. That's what those guys are doing. I remember. John heard about it in the locker room. A half marathon along the waterfront."

Paul nodded politely, then leaned forward. "I know I didn't need to tell you all the gory details," he said, speaking with hushed intensity. "And maybe I shouldn't have. Maybe when I realized John hadn't filled you in, I should've just said, 'Merry Christmas, here's a windfall for your kids! Here's a five-hundred-thousand-dollar trust your husband saved for your kids!' But you would have found out anyway. Claudette acted in bad faith. I'm not saying John did," he hastened on. "Clearly he kept these circumstances to himself for whatever reason. I assumed he was setting up another vehicle, he had a plan, and he just hadn't shared that with you yet. I'm just guessing. I don't know.

"What John was *not*," he continued, "was like Claudette. Claudette was an unqualified bitch. I have no idea how she turned out the way she did. She was the most spoiled, selfish person I ever knew. She was born spoiled. I've never seen such a sense of entitlement. I don't know where it came from, and I don't know why my parents gave in to it. She claimed she was a sickly child, but that's a lot of bullshit. She was a little bit asthmatic, and she milked that to the hilt. My mother had an eye for luxuries, but Claudette was my mother on steroids. She'd go to Wanamaker's and charge anything she wanted, and my parents never said boo. Once my dad kicked up a mild fuss when she brought home a mink jacket, but even then they let her keep it. Whatever she wanted, she got. She wanted Christmas in Bermuda, we did Christmas in Bermuda. She wanted to go golfing in Scotland, we all went golfing in Scotland. She was a horrible manipulative materialistic bitch and made my parents' life hell on more than one occasion and not just when she ran off to that stupid commune in Taos and not just when she had a baby out of wedlock. I *watched* all this. I just *watched*. I'm not surprised she spent all that money, Kim—she considered it hers! She gave up her baby in order to be taken back by my parents. She gave him up! Thank God she never had any more kids. Now that I think of it, not wanting any more kids might have been a requirement for my parents when they were shopping for a husband. She was already a handful enough. They already knew."

He sat back. "It *had* to have hurt your husband," he continued. "It had to have hurt him that his mother more or less abandoned him. For all these years, I just told myself he was well out of it.

"And then when I met him, I realized I was right. I mean, Claudette hadn't warped him. I know that's cold comfort. But—he was solid. He'd made a good life for himself. The first year or so, we had some nice conversations. Talked about our wives and kids, a little bit of getting-to-know-you. After we set up the auto-deposits, of course, I didn't hear from him as much."

I turned my water goblet around by the stem. The ice had long melted; no music left. "She helicoptered in a few times," I told him. "Came to his college graduation, I know that. Showed up at our wedding—that was my doing. I thought we should invite her. I'm not sure if that didn't just make things worse."

"Who's to know?" he said. "I'm sorry I had to be the one to deliver that blow four years ago. I'm sorry he had that experience and I'm sorry I was the one to give it to him. She left that to me." His voice had a bitter edge, and he broke off to take a sip of water, then went on in a more controlled fashion. "I believe that whatever happened with John, his ambivalence about discussing this money was because it really brought up those ghosts. He was struggling with the ghosts."

I nodded, fumbling with the papers, and he took them from me while making it appear I was giving them back, a deferential, almost obsequious, sleight-of-hand. Slowly he neatened and compressed the stack, slid it back in the envelope, and tied the string, with an abstracted, meditative expression, followed by a barely visible hardening of his visage, no more than a ripple, into professional opacity.

"You don't know how my wife suffered through this for years, silently. She accused Cynthia of stealing my mother's jewelry! More than once. After a while, we just tried never to see her. But my *God* those people who were friends with her thought she was great." He paused. "I guess…that kind of person…it comes out most with their own family."

"Wait—" I said. "That kind of person? What kind?"

He stared at me as though it were obvious. "Narcissists. That's what my wife says." He shrugged. "Narcissism. It cuts a very wide swath," he said, and lifted his hand to signal for the check.

Chapter 16

Haunted by the Question

I STOOD AT THE INTERSECTION IN A LIGHT DRIZZLE, WAITING for the light to change, with Paul's folder tucked inside my coat. Beneath my feet, brass letters spelled out UNION ST. My world might be tilting on its axis, but in downtown Seattle, at least, I knew exactly where I stood. At the next corner, Pike, conference attendees swirled around the broad pyramid of steps to the entrance of the Convention Center. My car was parked in that garage, but I knew I needed to keep moving, so I turned toward Puget Sound. Fourth Street, Third, Second—I walked steeply downhill, straight toward the Public Market sign towering over the low building at the brink, its bright red neon letters deadened even further by the backdrop of graying water, graying sky. The fickle sun had disappeared.

My first husband, Larry, had abused me financially as well as physically; I'd had to hold out my hand for cash on grocery days, because he wouldn't allow a joint account, and he'd also blithely forged my signature on checks for real estate proceeds and tax refunds and then hidden the money. This, however, paled into insignificance compared to the monumental, callous fraud that had been worked on John by his own mother. A million dollars! Perhaps that was part of the reason he'd concealed it. Did he think

"What's done is done," so there was no point in talking about it? Or was this too humiliating to confess, even to a life partner with whom he shared a mutual low opinion of his mother? Or maybe he thought that like Claudette, I'd steal his money if I'd known about it. *I don't want your stinking money!* I wanted to scream. *I didn't need this coat! I didn't want the sport court! The kids can shoot hoops at a park.*

He'd never had a basketball hoop. He'd grown up in a home where he'd never had friends over, because of the oxygen tank his grandfather wheeled about the house, because of the absence of toys, of mothers who wore pretty clothes and plied his friends with home-baked after-school snacks. But that was the past. He'd built his own life as an adult, a successful one, with friends and colleagues and family. I wasn't ignorant of the fact that his childhood hadn't been altogether happy, as I considered mine to be. He didn't talk about it much; he lived in the present. I thought he'd left those painful echoes behind. We'd adopted him into our tribe, and in my arrogance, I'd thought the matter resolved.

When I was seventeen years old, I sat with my mother in a diner in southern Minnesota, listening to her reminisce after a visit to her grandparents' home, which was now a museum, where other people, other families, walked through the rooms, touched the furniture, listened to the gramophone. Suddenly she stopped, midsentence, gazing out the window; then swiveled, looked directly into my eyes, and said to me, in the gentlest of voices: "The past is just the present of another day."

Now I was as old as she had been then and realized for the first time that even if he couldn't remember it, John *had* known his mother as a baby. He'd known her warmth, her feel, her smell, her songs. And then one day she was gone. Her voice was gone.

In my mind, I held my cello in the crook of my thumb and from among the infinity of tones on wire-wrapped catgut found just the right one, then reached with the little finger, a gentle breath, not a pressure, for the harmonic: the single delicate place on each string, where the tone was a ghostly whisper containing within it echoes of the lower octaves. Harmonics were shadows, shadows thrown back by the future or forward from the past to the place where time meets timelessness, eternity. This was where I wanted to be: the place where I could be whole. Whole in myself and united with the generations. There are those for whom remembrance of things past is a matter of free and easy movement through always-open doors. I knew my mother was one of those people, and I strived to be one too. I tried, and I was, sometimes. I craved those moments, whenever and wherever they appeared—often through music—because I knew they were gifts from the universe of lost answers, even if those answers did, sometimes, contain a note of bittersweet pain. But John? He couldn't stand in that place. He couldn't weather that pain. The hurts were old but deep, and it was too much for him. He could not weather the unity of time.

The Bremerton Ferry was nosing out across the bay past West Seattle, which from this angle looked like an opposite shore but wasn't. Bainbridge Island, behind it in the distance to the north, could be considered the opposite shore, but even then you were still stuck in the Sound; you were still on the same side of the ocean. You'd have to go beyond and beyond and beyond, inlets and straits and peninsulas, the whole big messy estuary, before you really got to the open sea and found the true horizon.

I grew up on Lake Michigan. Simple by comparison. The points of compass were obvious, the choices clear, so it was easier to make decisions. Years ago, one bitter winter day, I walked to the beach. I walked straight to the end of the pier, into the wind, the spray, the cruel whitecap ruffles, straight into the elements, and buried my wedding ring at sea.

Things seem easier when you're young. I drew out Paul's folder, fat with financial promise, tied with its sickly pink ribbon, and wished I could fling it into the Sound. Of course I knew I couldn't.

I was in my forties, with three children to take care of. This thick document represented something bigger, more complicated, with a life of its own, going back years, going back decades. In a way it had nothing to do with me, but I was responsible for it now, because this reckoning my beloved husband had avoided would be my children's emotional inheritance unless I somehow vanquished it. Why had his mother run away when he was a toddler and then secretly fleeced him of most of this large inheritance? In these last three years, since he'd discovered this betrayal, he'd been haunted by the question, one arguably of greater depth and importance than any of my issues had ever been—like, *Why was my mother so critical?* or, *Why did I give up the cello as a career?* or, even, *Why did I marry an abuser?* His question dealt with primal abandonment.

John and I had lawyerly minds, always organizing, categorizing, searching for the "why." In this we were alike. But this question had ultimately proven too much for him, and I, for my part, had been of this genuinely or willfully blind, or perhaps a bit of both.

To my eternal sorrow.

John had been haunted by the question, but he'd run out of time, so now his question was mine. I tucked the folder back into my coat and turned away from the water. I had to get back to my mother. I had to get back to my kids.

Chapter 17

Two Women Exchanging Glances

I STOOD IN THE EMPTY FOYER STARING AT THE BIG, BLACK reception desk. Faint sounds emanated from the file room: the soft click of a file drawer, the muffled scrape of chair legs across carpet. They startled me out of my reverie, and I walked down the hall to investigate. Larissa's head popped into view.

"Thought I heard someone," she said, stepping out tentatively. Larissa had been John's designated successor attorney and had driven out to Issaquah the day after the funeral to pick up a set of office keys. I'd given her mine by mistake; only John's unlocked the desk.

I put up a hand to ward her off, then, embarrassed, turned it into a little wave. "I'll be in the office. I'll visit in a minute."

"I'm here if you need me," she replied with visible relief, and withdrew.

I was left staring at the watercolor at the end of the hall. It was a streetscape, a narrow jumble of whitewashed plaster punctuated with dark dabs of windows, against a background of blue sea. It fit the space exactly. I'd purchased it off a high-end corporate art platform by plugging in my required dimensions. John had suggested this; I hadn't known you could buy art that way.

This wall had come down and then gone back up after John negotiated his way out of the additional space he'd negotiated his way into seven years ago. I wished I didn't remember crowing about getting that extra space, because now that was all I thought of when I looked at the painting.

Karen had wanted to come with me to the office today, but I'd said no. I was just going in for a few minutes to touch base with Larissa, I'd said. Get a few papers for Paul, I'd lied. I didn't want to make a big deal about it. She and my mother exchanged glances. I knew that look. When my father died, Karen and I helped our mom through it. We were the ones who took her hand, walked over thresholds with her, through doors. Now it was my turn. But I'd told them no. And that was when they'd looked at each other, weighing whether or not to insist. Two women exchanging glances.

All right, they'd said. *All right*, they'd said gently, and smiled.

I opened John's office door. There was his large, old-fashioned desk, and the rest of the furniture, all Danish midcentury modern: a couch and two armchairs upholstered in dark peacock blue—distinctive yet tasteful—picked out by his decorator, who was me. Over the couch, an arrangement of small contemporary Tlingit and Salish silkscreen prints of animal totems. Nothing seemed strange, which in itself was strange. Motes of silence floated about, and when I breathed them in, they grew and charred my lungs with frost, chilled my legs, and I knew I had to move before I was encased altogether, so I took one step, and then another, and achieved the couch, where I sat down.

After a moment I turned sideways and swung up my legs, just like I did on date nights, when I'd come downtown to meet John at the office. I'd kick off my heels, put my feet up, and read the paper while I waited for him to return from a meeting or finish a call. From this position I could see my favorite painting, *Two Leggings in the Headlights.* The old man filled the canvas like a plinth, his huge moccasined feet rooted to the ground in rough provisional strokes, almost lost in the scrub grass and brilliant dabs of wildflowers dramatically silvered by the unseen headlights. His monumental body stretched upward to meet the night sky. The bright white fringe on his elongated jacket sleeves led the eye up and across green fields darkening as they receded toward the horizon line where Two Leggings's now-tiny head, topped with a red feather, was silhouetted against a deep purple-blue sprinkled with stars. That was what John liked, the night sky and stars.

I registered the date on the newspapers on the coffee table—the day time stopped for him, his last—and turned them over.

The Wozzecks of sportswear fame had bailed even before Owen's retirement. That was what that lunch date with Diane had been about, after the Winter Ball—to let him down. We were philosophical. We already knew this was in the nature of things. A boutique firm was sometimes a victim of its own success, when a client's fledgling business was bought out by a larger one with its own corporate counsel. But if it was hard to keep the pipeline full in a small firm, it was even harder for the solo practitioner John had become after he and Larissa had been unable to find a third partner, and they parted ways. She'd moved to a big firm across town but had agreed to be the designated backup John required as a solo practitioner to comply with bar regulations.

Two Leggings stood gravely with his hands clasped in front of him, a calm and detached witness to untold numbers of confidential conversations. I imagined that despite an understandably jaundiced view of our legal system, he would never break attorney-client privilege.

Date nights. Twice a month on Fridays. We'd made a point of it…until we didn't. In our busyness, we fell silent, which settled it more definitively than would have words of an actual conversation, like, *Looks like we'll have to put this on hold for a while,* or some such other casual acknowledgment. The silence made it worse.

Two Leggings was observing me quietly, in the manner of all wise elders; waiting for me to arrive at the truth on my own, the truth that I'd been willfully blind. I was getting there, slowly. I remembered John's cryptic allusions to financial anxiety during the partner search after Owen retired. I'd chalked that up to general uncertainty at the time and felt confirmed in that when the comments disappeared after the transition. John had elected not to go back to Dunwoody, and professed himself happy as a solo practitioner. But now it was becoming clear. For some reason he hadn't made a resounding success of it, and had concealed that from me. The inheritance had allowed him to do so. But so had I, because I hadn't probed. He'd consistently told me he was pleased with solo practice, that he was focusing on fewer clients, but bigger ones. In retrospect, that sounded like a euphemism for losing business. I didn't know who it was more impossible for me to forgive: him, or me?

I swung my feet off the couch. Larissa was standing at the door, trying to pretend this was just a normal day, but then she couldn't. She hugged her elbows and said, "I'm sorry. It's hard to believe we're doing this. It just doesn't seem real."

Until the funeral, I hadn't laid eyes on her in almost three years. She had new glasses.

"You have new glasses," I said.

"I'm sorry," she repeated feebly. She took her glasses off and drew her fingers across her forehead. I saw a surprising depth of sorrow in her eyes and also regret. I traveled into that and realized she meant sorry for everything. Everything.

John the talented, John the brilliant, John the contract whiz. John the winner: Bar Association YLA, 40 under 40, Fifty to Follow—*What's next?* we used to joke, *Sixty Still Sexy?* John the best boss in the world—that's what Paisley and the whole crew had said. John who'd crashed and burned, John who was now spared the embarrassment of the virtual office, the client meetings at coffee shops or at the Athletic Club, the working in slippers from home, the "Whatever happened to John?" Now it was all tidied away, now they could say, *Poor guy. Heart attack at the office.* I was the last to know what had really happened. But even now I wasn't certain—I was resistant. Surely it couldn't have been *that* bad? There was always money in the checking account. John had put everything on autopay, and checks for school tuition or summer camp never seemed to be a problem. We didn't take fancy vacations, but he never made a peep about spring break in Puerto Vallarta every year…

Two women exchanging glances.

"I never thought," Larissa said. "In a million years. I agreed to be his assisting…but I never thought I'd actually have to do it."

"Thank you, Larissa," I said. "Thank you for everything." I averted my eyes. "Everything."

She put her glasses back on. "Well. I'm going down to get something at Saint Sandwich. I always loved that place. Heh-heh. Want anything?"

I stood up and smoothed my skirt, which hung on me. To think I'd fretted about a few extra pounds when I'd had a living, breathing husband sleeping next to me in the bed every night. What I wouldn't give…"A coffee would be great," I lied. "How about a mocha? When the going gets tough, the tough need chocolate."

She heh-heh-ed herself out again, and I sat down at the desk and fished the bag out of my purse, the plastic ziplock they'd given me at the hospital.

AT THE HOSPITAL, I KNEW it the minute I saw him. Real dead people look nothing like what's shown on TV or in the movies. Those people are just pretending. A real dead person you can tell in an instant.

"He's not there," I said. The room was hard and bare and the fluorescent light ashed his face and grayed his temples. He'd joked when he'd started to show some salt-and-pepper, "Now I can raise my rates." I panicked. It was all wrong. It was ugly. "Frank. He's not there." Frank put his arm around my shoulders.

A police officer who told me to call her Rowena gave me the plastic bag with his wallet, keys, comb, and loose change. She put it in my hand. I took it. But then I realized—that was it. It was all I had. So I looked at it. "Where is his cell phone? Frank! Where is it?"

Rowena said, "Maybe he didn't have it on him," and I said, "He always had it on him," and then I said, "Where is his ring? They took it off, but it's not in the bag! I know they do that at hospitals! They steal things. My father said! My father told me!"

She looked at Frank, put a hand on my arm, disappeared, came back. "Sometimes this happens, Mrs. Halvorsen. I'm thinking, maybe we should go take a look in your husband's office to see if we can find the phone? Would you be up to that?"

She gave me another quick friendly touch, to show she wasn't patronizing, but addressed the question as much to Frank as to me, and he quickly said, "Yes, if you think that's necessary."

"I think so. We need to check that nothing else is missing. Even with natural causes…I'd like to make sure. It would be important to know."

So we went. They both seemed to think it was wise, and I was just doing what I was told. After all, his office was just an empty room. His cell phone was, in fact, not in evidence, and then I noticed the Golden Gavel Award was gone too. Quite matter-of-factly Rowena said it could have been the cleaner, maybe even the one who'd placed the call about finding him. They'd have a chat with him, because unfortunately temptation sometimes got the better of someone, especially if it was something small that could be slipped into a pocket and easily disposed of on the street, and that included anything precious metal or anything that looked like it. They could monetize that pretty easily. Frank bundled me out, and that was the only time I'd been in the office.

But I decided not to count that visit. *This* was the first time.

I laid John's key ring on the desk. I moved aside three door keys, then the one I recognized as belonging to the small lockbox we kept in our bedroom closet for important papers. That left the small keys for the two bottom desk drawers. I knew the right one was the whiskey and cigars drawer, so I tried the left one first.

As expected: accordion file for bills, petty cash envelope, and two three-on-a-page business check ledgers, one for each account—regular and escrow. I leafed through them with trembling fingers, but everything seemed in perfect order. It was all in his bookkeeper's hand. We'd stopped using a service after Larissa left; he'd said there was no need. He'd found someone semi-retired who came in twice a month to do billing right out of the conference room.

I pushed these materials to the front of the desk. These were the account books I needed to give Larissa.

Here were the household accounts, too, segregated in a typing paper box; as I'd told Paul, John had taken over that chore after Jackie was born without a word of complaint. It was a relief to me, even though almost everything was on autopay by that time. I put those back to be dealt with another day and locked the drawer.

So. Nothing mysterious here. And I knew what was in the other one. That cut-glass decanter on the breakfront was part of a presentation set Cassie had found at an antique expo in Chicago. It held a cheap single malt just for show. The good stuff was stowed in the desk. I opened the drawer, and there it was, the bottle of Lagavulin 16, almost full. It had been a gift from the Wozzecks when Jackie was born, the same year it won its fourth consecutive double gold medal in San Francisco, which was why John called Jackie his gold-medal baby. There was also a box of Cuban cigars he'd bought under the counter in Miami on a business trip.

I didn't need to fuss with the whiskey and cigars now; account books were the order of the day. But something made me take both these things out.

Behind them, there was more: two one-inch white binders and a standard personal-sized checkbook. I lifted open the pebbly green plastic cover and read the name: *John Diaz Halvorsen.* It was the "Diaz" that got me. He never used "Diaz," only the initial. Ever since his third year of law school. That's how I knew this was it. That's what he would have done, as a visual to help keep things separate.

Nervously I paged through the check register. It began with a $20,000 deposit two months after Claudette died. Complete inactivity for nine months, then a check written in July, for $13,000 and change to Loyola Academy. I recognized this as the full tuition for Nathan's first year of high school; Larry made us pay up front, then reimbursed for his half.

Maybe John hadn't really done anything with this money. The whole thing had been a surprise, after all. Perhaps, as Paul had suggested, he was trying to decide what to do. In a few short years, when he became his own trustee, he could elect to take full distribution by transferring the portfolio into a new trust account for his own children. He had time to think about options.

But it still didn't explain why he'd said nothing to me about it.

I returned to the checkbook. After the tuition payment, there was another absence of activity for ten months. Then deposits of increasing size began to appear at irregular intervals. I tapped my finger on the page. This would have been when Larissa left, taking Paisley with her. After that the regular quarterly deposits that Paul had referred to began and, correspondingly, checks made out to our joint account. Obviously he was making up for a reduced draw. With a sickening thud in my stomach, it registered: I'd enabled this subterfuge when I'd completely relinquished all the household bookkeeping to him.

I forced myself to leaf through the binder of credit card statements. There was a similar pattern: barely any use for the first two years, then activity began and increased over time: a lot of restaurants and a lot of air travel. Dublin, Singapore. He *did* have clients; he *was* working! I knew that. He wasn't sitting around twiddling his thumbs. Some of his clients had cross-border contracts. I knew he had to travel more—I was the one who drove him to the airport! But...no lawyer would mix personal and business expenses like this. John would never have done that. Why would he do that?

Books on my lap, I swiveled to the window. Beneath a dark sky, the city was impoverished, its buildings grayed, shrunken, bereft of swagger. The windows across the street that had been spanking with late-afternoon sunlight at that long-ago Christmas party were dull and opaque. I realized: It was this bank, the one I was looking at across the street, where this account was held. I remembered Jason in his Santa suit talking about this bank, the National Historic Register building, built in 1914, ancient by West Coast standards, which had allegedly seen jumpers in the aftermath of the '29 crash. I was looking straight across at the top-floor ledge.

In my mind, I filled the gray stone canyon with invisible flood-waters, so those diving men bobbed to the surface and were carried safely away to where the concrete ended and the water gently spilled out into ever-widening, ever-shallower channels, until, finally, they felt solid ground beneath their feet and stumbled up, shaken yet whole, gifted with another chance.

The building stared back at me, bleak despite its post–Clean Air Act rehabilitation, and this made me angry. So I had to open another mental file folder. It was much smaller than the one I'd had for Larry. It only had two entries. But it was much more im-portant, because John had been the real husband.

LIES MY HUSBAND TOLD ME 2.0

1. Told me he got no inheritance

2. Kept a secret bank account

Larissa tapped on the door.

I swiveled back to the desk, ledgers hidden on my lap, and smiled brightly as she set down my drink. Then she held up her little white bag and said, "I'm going to eat this now, but I'm ready whenever you are."

She left. My pulse was beating wildly. She hadn't seemed to notice anything, perhaps because the two of us were in a kind of behavioral no-man's-land. I dumped the ledgers in an empty box, added the whiskey and cigars, and put a lid on the box. On top of that, I piled the regular ledgers and some rolls of colored stickers and awkwardly made my way down the hall.

In the file room, Larissa sat hunched over her phone on the tabletop, delicately tapping and scrolling between bites of her Saint Sandwich deluxe veggie wrap. "Oh good—the books," she said, as I dipped my knees to slide them off onto the table. "Thank goodness. I'll take those with me today."

I put my box of dirty secrets on the floor and shoved it under the table with my foot. Then I peeled off a sticker and applied it to a chair, rubbing the edges with my fingernail to affix it completely. "Okeydokey. As for the furniture, anything marked in green is for Rivers Northwest. I already talked to my friend down in Yakima about what they could use."

She crumpled her sandwich wrapper into a ball. "Great. Donation or sale?"

"Rivers is a nonprofit. We're going to donate."

"That's fine. Make sure you establish a value and keep a list. You need a paper trail. It's not going to be all that critical…" She trailed off. Scrounging every possible deduction wasn't going to be much of an issue because there wasn't that much to offset. Everyone but me had known it: John hadn't been doing much business.

"But we should be thorough," I said briskly. "I understand."

"Every little bit helps. I want to do my best to minimize taxes."

I nodded. "So yellow is for the Deer Lake Band," I said, applying those stickers to four horizontal filing cabinets. "They're going to rent a truck. There are certain things they don't need, and they're just going to take everything I give them, and what they can't use, they'll parcel out to other places." I paused. "Larissa?"

She looked up.

"We're going to be okay," I said. I wanted to reassure her and quell that look of pity on her face. "John had a good life insurance policy."

She took a small breath in relief. "Oh, good. I'm glad to know." She busied herself cleaning her hands with a pocket wipe, then cleared her throat. "So. Now. Just to let you know. The first thing I did was go through and pull the ones that absolutely needed immediate action." She placed her hand on a stack of files. "That was four. I've filed substitution of counsel motions and motions for continuance on three and handed one off to a new firm as per the client's request."

I resented her matter-of-fact competence. To her, the closing of my husband's practice was simply a project to be tackled like any other. She was being fully paid for her time—three weeks of Thursdays and Fridays—to clean up someone else's mess. Smith Jacobs, where she was now ensconced, would log her hours as pro bono. Paralegals were jumping in to cover for her; admins were marshaling her schedule to accommodate. Her paychecks would still be autodeposited like clockwork; and every night she'd go home to her anesthesiologist husband, who was a nifty dancer and still alive. She had her life ahead of her, just as she'd had thirty months ago when she'd left, a completely amicable parting. After all, she'd had her own career to consider. As had Paisley, and Jason, and Eric, and…

"…These are the accounts receivable I'm taking back to Smith Jacobs. They're going to take care of them—" She stopped.

Belatedly, I registered the silence and looked up.

"I'm sorry. Is this too much? It's probably too much. I don't need to go into the details of every aspect. I just want you to know everything's in hand and you don't need to worry." Her look was sympathetic. I realized why John had asked her to be his assisting attorney—designated signatory on his accounts, authorized to take over and wind down a solo practice in case of incapacity or death—and I realized as well why she had said yes. Their relationship, though prickly at first, had developed over the years. What a bitch I'd been about her. I pulled out a chair and sat down.

"No, no, no. This is good. This actually helps me. The details, I mean."

Reassured, she went on. "So, this last pile—I already did triage on the four most needy last week, like I said. These are the remaining, and I've separated them out. They'll all get letters. I'll follow up. I'll see that they find a new berth, and then I'll document that."

I put my finger on top of a pile. "Is one of these the international? Wasn't he working on something in Singapore? That sounds complicated to sort out."

"Singapore? Oh, no. That was a closed-end deal. We finished up a few years ago. We closed that file right before I left."

"Aha. Just wondering. Good. That might have been more of a hassle for you." *Dublin? Singapore?* All of a sudden I needed to get out of the room. I was never good at dissembling. I blushed too easily. I picked my box up off the floor. "I better get home now."

Larissa tucked a thick curl behind her ear. "Are you sure you don't want me to negotiate with the landlord? I'd be happy to. It's all part of what I'm supposed to do. I'm almost buttoned up here. I've ordered the service to get the files moved tomorrow."

"No, I have a meeting with the guy next week. I want to do it in person. I'm going to see if I can wring a sympathy concession out of him. In this I was trained by a master."

"You certainly were." She smiled in recollection. "He was an awesome negotiator. The best."

As I descended in the elevator, it occurred to me for the first time that the contents of the box in my arms had potentially made my need to economize at home slightly less critical. It was not a happy realization. On the contrary, it was as bitter a one as it could be.

BACK HOME, THE LIGHTS WERE on in the kitchen. Nearby was the trellis John had built a couple of years ago to create an entrance to the patio. In that short time, the wisteria planted on one side had climbed all the way up and across; its naked tendrils now leapt forward, an immobilized spray of fingers grasping at thin air. In the spring they'd realize their job was to gravitate down the other side and so complete the frame. Things grew fast in this climate, almost faster than one could manage.

I regarded the box on the passenger seat as warily as a crate of nitroglycerin. I was not taking it into the house. Gingerly, I lifted out the whiskey and cigars and sat holding them in my lap, staring at the wooded hill in the backyard. It seemed preposterous that this towering, dripping regiment of firs and cedars was contained, and had been for decades, by a four-foot wall of concrete block, plastered and painted white. Above the ridge I saw the trail of woodsmoke that meant Bill was home in his cabin on the other side. I propelled myself out of the car and, because of the box, locked the door behind me. In the kitchen, Jackie was doing his homework under my mother's supervision. First-grade homework was clearly an arduous task: He was kneeling on his chair, practically draped across the table, resting his head on his arm and clutching a candy bar.

"How did it go?" Bobbie asked, then looked up at me and folded her lips in. She could read me like a book.

I tried to seem a little more animated. "Oh, fine," I said, sitting down beside her. "I'm fine. I gave Larissa what she needed, and she showed me everything she's doing. She's got stuff well in hand. I brought home some things that I wanted to show you.

But first I want to take this over to Bill," I said, indicating the whiskey and cigars.

"What a lovely idea. He's been such a good friend to the family all these years."

She reached out and stroked my hair. She used to do that to neaten me up, even well into my twenties, which, of course, by that time I hated: It felt like she was tamping me down, that I didn't fit some picture of me she wanted. But now I didn't duck away. We weren't there; we were somewhere else, somewhere even farther in the past, when a mother could so easily console a weeping toddler—early childhood, when things are simple between mothers and daughters, before the complicated, unconscious frame of expectation has been set. At the same time her hand, warm and gentle on my head, carried me past the intervening years to the moment I'd fully understood her anguished cry after she lost my father: *All I want is what I had.* Now I met her eyes along this path, a path that was the longest in the world but also the shortest, and I saw how it grieved her, this unlooked-for communion.

When I was a teenager, I sometimes sat on the kitchen counter after school and retailed some petty indignation while my mother stood at the stove cooking dinner, and she would turn to me and say: "Into every life a little rain must fall." At the time it absolutely infuriated me, but now I understood: It wasn't dismissive, but preparatory, in anticipation of just such a moment as this, when misfortune might arrive, when tragedy might shove me beyond the evergreens even farther, even more rudely than in the past, and she would be able to do nothing more than stroke my hair, as she did now.

This is what mothers can do for you, as long as you are both alive, no matter how old you are. It's all they can do.

Upstairs, I showered to wash off the office, pulled on jeans and a hooded sweatshirt, then grabbed a tote bag from my closet pile: bright red, with WALK FOR THE CAUSE stamped across it.

Back downstairs, my mom was rooting around in the refrigerator. She pulled out an avocado-green casserole dish I recognized from musical potlucks as belonging to Evie.

I put the whiskey and cigars into the bag. "Evie makes good lasagna."

"Maybe you'll eat some, then."

"Sure," I replied, and she looked at me pointedly. "I promise you," I said. "A little slice." I slipped on rainboots and escaped.

Two tree trunk steps got me on top of the retaining wall. Brushing past dense wet blackberry bushes, I hurried up the path to the top, then stood for a minute, getting my breath back, looking at a view that was long familiar but now seemed newly vast: west over layers of ridges, beyond which, in the inscrutable distance, lay the ocean, a hundred miles away. Between each ridge was a little creek just like our own, joining to flow into the Tolt River, then the Snoqualmie, and then the Snohomish, until they emptied into Puget Sound, ending the journey to the sea. It was all dizzyingly expansive. I wiped off the chairs with a towel, sat down, and dialed Bill's number.

A couple of minutes later, Shasta and her daughter Socks tumbled into the clearing, followed by Bill himself with mugs and thermos. He poured the coffee. "Almost time for the Show. Looks like we're gonna get a good one," he pronounced, handing me my mug.

I anchored it to my chest and we settled back to wait in companionable silence, the dogs curled at our feet. The Show was not a guaranteed event, as it often failed to appear altogether, but today augured well. We sipped our coffee and watched as the pale, late-winter sun shyly made its first appearance of the day, escaping beneath the clouds to give us its last sweet slanting rays. When the entire sphere was visible, Bill gave the flat arm of his chair a small triumphant slap, as he always did, and said, "Well, *there* you go."

My eyes welled.

I reached for the thermos to top off my mug. "Bill," I teased, "you're going to need to upgrade this thing soon or we're going to get lead poisoning, and then where will we be?"

"Yes, dear," he countered affectionately.

I opened the tote bag. "These are for you. I know John would want you to have them."

"Ah, the good stuff." He held the bottle in front of him like a baby. "Now, isn't that thoughtful? And yes, I know these cigars." He took one out and weighed it in his palm. "Yep. We used to smoke one up here end of every summer. It was our own little ritual." He reached out and rested his hand on mine. Now it was his eyes that looked moist.

Individual raindrops glistened in rows on nearby branches; on the opposite ridge they appeared as faint brush marks of glitter. The entire world was being gently glazed by the setting sun, everything but the mystery cabin, whose east-facing windows were dark.

He put his gifts down on the stump and sat forward. "So, how's it going?"

"Okay, I guess," I mumbled.

"Bad day at the office?"

That was always his line, but I burst into tears.

"Oh shit, honey. That was just—I'm sorry."

"I know," I blubbered. "I mean—it *was* a bad day at the office."

"Oh, sweetheart. You actually did go to the office."

"Yes. For the first time. It was okay, but— Oh, Bill! John had a bank account with a half million dollars in it he'd never told me about!"

"Listen now, don't cry." He patted me helplessly, then rose from his chair, knelt on one knee next to mine, and got an arm around my shoulders. Once, when toddler Gracie was wailing inconsolably and at high volume in the backyard, before I could even get to her, Bill had bounded over the hill, shirtless, in jeans and suspenders, hands creased black with grease, to shoo off the offending big boy and kneel beside her, put an arm around her tenderly, in just such a way, and take her hand as he took mine now.

After a minute he let go to lean on the chair arm and shift his weight to his other knee.

"I'm sorry," I cried, gasping for breath. "It's—you don't understand!"

"Well...what the hell did he *do* with it?"

I flung my arms out. "He *supported* us!" I wailed.

"Well—" He squinted at the ground and rubbed his forehead hard with his wrist. Then he sat back on his heels and exclaimed, "Thank goodness!"

This made me laugh, and then I started to cry again, but not as much. More along the lines of having trouble breathing evenly.

"Thank *goodness*," he said again. He stood up and knuckled the small of his back, turning from side to side. "Geez. I can't bend over like that anymore. Listen, I thought you were gonna say he gambled it all away or he spent it on a woman or was paying off a blackmailer. Here." He poured a generous tot from his gift bottle into both our mugs. "This is *not* what we should be doing with whiskey of this quality, but we're going to anyway. Take a sip. No, wait a minute." He rummaged in the pocket of his unbuttoned field jacket and pulled out a wrinkled bandanna. He inspected it, then handed it over. "Keep it."

I wiped my nose and stuffed it in my hoodie pocket.

"*Now* take a sip."

I did, and then another.

"Now, missy, we're gonna sit here and think about this for a minute. We're gonna figure it out. 'Cause that's what we do, isn't it?"

I nodded.

Bill was always there to help, all day long in the summer when he ran a Scout repair shop out of his yard, and even in the winter, because when he ran his traplines he left before dawn and was home by two. Bill was always home. Ambling over the hill on his own—to borrow a couple of eggs, or a postage stamp, or once, inexplicably, to have me knot a necktie for him and then loosen it, after which he carefully carried it back—or following on the heels of a child I'd sent over to fetch him for emergencies small or large—*Tell Bill if he wants some coffee, the cookies just came out of the oven,* or *Can you go tell Bill I can't start the car,* or *Run and get Bill NOW!*

Now he combed his hands over his head. "I mean, it could be worse. You could have discovered he was half a million in debt."

I laughed hollowly. He was right.

The sun was almost gone. The gentle wash limning damp naked branches was now compressed in that thinnest sliver of sky below the clouds. A hundred miles away there was a long slow sunset over the ocean, but here, this was what you got. This was the last sparkling moment, the one you couldn't catch, the moment you thought you had back the day and then it was dulled and gone, and the changeling twilight began to advance, transforming everything in the landscape, even the things you thought wouldn't change.

"So. His life insurance was enough, even though the IRA wasn't huge." He ticked them off on his fingers. Bill had family-level security clearance. And I'd told him immediately about the life insurance anyway, because he'd come over in a barely suppressed panic and said, "Don't move! You won't have to move, will you?" And I'd assured him we wouldn't have to.

"So, this is a good thing," he went on. "The whys and wherefores we don't know, but we know John. He was a man who took his responsibilities seriously. He used this money for the family, and now he's left it to you to use on the family. He was probably planning to tell you but hadn't done it yet."

"For three years?"

He buried his chin in his hand. "Well, if business was down…"

I could tell he hadn't confided in Bill, either. Which he might have. "It really was, Bill. I'd say it was down by half."

"I can tell you for a fact that sometimes it's easier to back away from hard family issues." Bill went on. "I mean, look at me," he said, and I nodded. Bill's dad had been chief surgeon at Swedish Hospital but also a raging alcoholic who'd driven his wife to drink and to an early death. Bill had been expected to become a doctor, but when his mom died, he dropped out of college, jobbed as a miner in Montana for a while, then came home and got a trapping license. He took over his dad's hunting cabin and never spoke to him again. "The longer you wait, the easier it gets not to. And then sometimes things get to be too late, but you don't know. You can't know that."

Our sunset show was over. I knew it was beautiful because it was fleet, but I wished that wasn't so. I wished that I could bend the arms of time, enlarge that space to make it last, and sit on the ridge with Bill forever. In the dusking light, we finished our mugs and shook the last drops out onto the ground. I put the gifts back in the tote. "Keep the bag," I said.

He took it, tucked the thermos under his arm, and whistled to the dogs. "G'bye, dear. Holler if you need anything," he said, as he always did, and started down the path, then stopped, and turned around to add, "There's no comparison, of course. My dad was a son of a bitch."

Chapter 18

I Belong to this Club

THE CHECKBOOK DISCOVERY HAD BEEN TWO WEEKS AGO, and the worst was over. My brief foray into drinking had lasted only three days, because I'd felt horrible in the morning. After that, there was the cocoon phase, wherein I stayed in bed watching old movies and eating my mother's homemade macaroni and cheese: seashell pasta, baked, with cheese crusty on the top, underneath soft, tender, and melty, with an ever-so-slight hint of separated oil at the bottom. That phase lasted four and a half days, until Bobbie told me to take a shower and get dressed because it was time to act like a grown-up for my kids' sake, and I was not the only person in the world to whom sad things had happened. So I did. In retrospect, I think I was hiding out in bed waiting for John to come back, but that didn't happen. Met as I was by such conclusive, resounding silence, I was forced to accept that it wasn't going to happen.

EVERY FIRST GRADER WORTH HIS salt knew the gift wrap was as important as the gift, and Jackie had picked out a doozy: bright blue with a red rocket exploding through stars, stuffed with plenty of colored tissue, and two star-shaped mini-balloons on sticks. Given the size of the present—the diminutive build-your-own action figure du jour—it was obscenely large. It wobbled enormously on the seat beside him as we pulled up at the entry gate, and Jackie started bouncing in excitement. He didn't know it, but we were a full half hour late. My mother had gone back to Puerto Vallarta. It had to happen at some point—she couldn't babysit me forever. But the admission required to step into the walk-in closet every day and get dressed—that half of these clothes belonged to someone who was simply not here anymore—was monumental. I'd hear a door closing or a step in the hall and discover I'd been sitting on the edge of the bed with a sock in my hand for twenty minutes. It was as though a big hole had opened up right next to me. I didn't fall in; falling in would have been easier, but I didn't. So I stayed where I was—lost in a state of confusion.

I stretched an arm out to steady the gift bag. "Don't let that present on the floor," I warned Jackie, then turned to smile and wave at the security camera.

Years ago when I'd started on this circuit, birthday parties were kid-only events. Gone were the days. And this one? I knew for a fact that there would be no carpooling for this one. Every single mother in the first-grade class was going to show, because Wesley's mother was a Post, and her childless great-uncle was allowing her to use his pool while he was out of town, and even though we knew we weren't going to see the house, we were all salivating just to set foot on this Mercer Island property.

I gave my makeup a quick check in the rearview mirror. I'd had to apply under-eye concealer with a hand trowel, but my lipstick was okay, and my hair was brushed. I usually sidestepped my fashion inferiority complex by running around in tennis clothes, but unfortunately, that was not an option in early March, so I'd done the best I could: pale gray jeans and a soft pink cashmere sweater set. I'd even changed my purse to coordinate.

The gate opened slowly. Clusters of balloons tied to laurel bushes at strategic intervals led the way down the gently curving drive. The pool complex came into view, a three-sided pavilion with a rugged fieldstone fireplace in the back and a dramatic cantilevered roof in front that covered half the terrace. Buffet tables were set up around the fire pit. I turned in to park, and there was the pool itself, linked at a right angle. It had sliding glass walls and its own dedicated patio area, where a group of first-grade mothers sat at a clutch of umbrella tables while their children shrieked and splashed in the water, completely ignoring the beautiful view across Lake Washington.

The birthday mom, Angela, detached herself and hurried over, ruffling Jackie's hair as he raced past her with his swim bag. I apologized for being late.

"That's o*kay*," she said. "We were just worried about you." She turned to wave at the other moms, who lifted their plastic cups in greeting, and I realized she'd headed me off at the pass to do a preliminary status check. Based on our recent interactions in the parking lot of Saint Thomas, my fellow first-grade moms were at a total loss with someone in my situation, especially someone who looked like she'd just been run over by a truck, which was probably what they were now whispering among themselves as they sipped their berry refreshers. *Did you see her at pickup yesterday? I felt so bad. She looked like she'd been run over by a truck.*

It wasn't their fault. They weren't really my cohort. They were so much younger than I was—most of them ten years younger. My cohort was in Baltimore—except for Sita, whose husband had taken a job at UCSF Medical Center and was in the same time zone. We kept up with phone calls and the internet and saw each other when we could. This new group here would have its own patterns, go through its own set of triumphs and tragedies through the school years, which might or might not create a Home Base of the kind to knit them together for the long term.

Or maybe Angela wasn't sparing them, but sparing me. If I hadn't felt up to it. This sudden realization brought me to the verge of tears, and I felt ashamed for telling Suzanne on the phone yesterday that these moms were all too young to understand.

"How *are* you?" Angela had a wonderful voice: deep seated, well oiled, possessed of the kind of textural range usually heard only in mature singers or actresses. *How are you?* It was in anticipation of just such a question, just such scrutiny—which I now had my head above water enough to notice—that I'd selected my earrings, brushed my hair, put a dab of color on my lips. I toed the crushed oystershell in the drive and said ruefully, "I just got a little behind," which was what I was supposed to do: dissemble, let us all off the hook. What were they looking for? I couldn't give them what they wanted. Whatever that was. The whole thing was exhausting.

Suddenly I thought: *What the hell.* I put down the obscenely large gift bag and confessed, "Actually, I fell asleep with Jackie in front of the cartoons this morning after breakfast, and I only woke up again at eleven! Can you imagine? I was all dressed and everything and ready to go. It's just…I'm not always sleeping at night."

Angela cocked her head and ran her finger along the gold chain at her neck.

Should I have said that? But yes. I could see. It was almost a relief. *Here* was something she could hang her hat on, an opportunity for concrete action.

"Can I get you anything?" Her voice had dropped to a lush alto.

"I'm good." I grinned, holding up my paper cup of coffee.

She took charge of the gift and led the way along the flagstone path. "You know," she continued in unnecessarily hushed tones, "I have three Vicodin left over from when I had my dental surgery after Christmas, and I'd be happy to give them to you, truly. My sister told me to save them in case I hit my thumb with a hammer. Not that I'd ever do that. But they're so hard to get now. If you took one tonight before you went to bed tonight, you'd *definitely* get a good night's sleep."

"That's so sweet." I could always go to the doctor and get a prescription if I wanted to. If it came to that. Or even go back to that counselor, the one I'd seen a few years ago, by myself, on Karen's suggestion, when John wouldn't go with me. But I didn't want to. "I'll be okay. You save them. You're so thoughtful."

We walked around a bank of camellias almost past their bloom and under a trellis of clematis not quite there yet and arrived at a gift pile big enough to require its own designated patio area. It came home to me what it truly meant to invite every child in a class of thirty to a birthday party—yet another trend that had not fully developed when Nathan and Grace were little.

Takes all kinds, I quipped silently, but the sarcasm soured as it ricocheted around inside my head like a free-radical pinball. Who would get my jokes now? Who would laugh? John would have laughed out loud. Then he would have said, shaking his head, "Yep. There goes the neighborhood!" And that would have made *me* laugh.

Stop it, I told myself sternly. Plenty of people would get it. Karen, and Evie, and my friends from Home Base who'd come all the way from Baltimore for the funeral, except for Suzanne who was coming for a week in the summer instead, with Joey and the baby, who were now fourteen and eleven and annoyingly insisted on being called Joe and Emma. Lots of people. *These are your longtime friends, and you still have them. They're still there. Stop feeling sorry for yourself.*

I took another caffeinated slug and turned to the pool, where the children were bobbing up and down in the water. All the sliding glass walls were open, but their voices seemed unusually muffled. As did Angela's. I dragged my eyes back to her.

"You have every right to feel sorry for yourself," she repeated, lips pursed in sympathetic indignation.

"Did I say that aloud?" I tapped my cup against my lip, feigning confusion.

"Every right in the world," she said with slow emphasis.

And she didn't know the half of it, I thought, watching the words come out of her mouth as though behind glass. "I think this haul needs its own security guard," I joked, taking the gift bag from her and wedging it into the pile.

"Oh my gosh, you're so funny. It *is* way too much, I know. It's just…" She sighed. "What can I do?"

Goodwill drop-off? was on the tip of my tongue, but instead I laughed. "Hey, don't worry about it. He's going to have a ball. In a few years all he's gonna want is a sleepover with his four best friends and all you'll have to show for it is empty pizza boxes and orange soda stains on the carpet."

"Good to know!" She fingered an earlobe, tightening her stud. "Kim, what would we do without you? You are just a gold mine…"

She thought she knew what I was going through, but she didn't. She didn't know that the invisible hole I faced wasn't getting smaller with time but bigger, that it was now enormous and deep and had razor teeth around the edge.

"…truly a *gold* mine of information," Angela was saying. "So much experience, in every area…" She trailed off and and put her fingers to her lips in a gesture so obviously spontaneous, it was bereft of contrivance. "I didn't mean…"

My eyes wandered toward the pool again. I was looking for Bitsy, our vacation nanny, and then I found her, standing at attention in her red tank suit, arms akimbo, a tubular float laced behind her back. She must have felt my glance, because she looked over and waved, then reanchored the float, rocking on her toes a few times before settling back into position. Bitsy, with her tight yellow curls and muscled energy, standing at the edge of a swimming pool, rocking on her toes: a familiar sight. Relieved, I turned back to Angela.

"What a great setting for a party!" I said brightly. "And if you're talking about a goldmine—then that's Bitsy."

She pivoted deftly. "Oh, your nanny is *awesome.* Thanks for the lifeguard recommendation! I really didn't know where to turn."

This conversation, the one in which I'd recommended Bitsy, had taken place only two months ago, but I could hardly remember it. It seemed years. I certainly didn't remember calling her a nanny. I made a mental note to tell Bitsy she'd been promoted.

"Just don't steal her away from me!" I teased. "She's like a live-in camp counselor at spring break. I couldn't manage without her. My sister and I together, my God, that's seven kids."

"That's right. You go to Puerto Vallarta at spring break, don't you?" she purred, in tones intending to convey *I belong to this club.* Admiration of that sort from a fourth-generation Post who could throw such an opulent party for a young child's birthday confused me, but there was no mistaking it.

"Oh, yes. Yes, we've gone at Christmas a couple of times too, and I'm telling you I would not set *foot* without Bitsy. She takes such a load off. Do you know she taught all those kids how to play water polo? My nephew Sammy's on the team now at Loyola." I chattered away as we stood watching kids cannonball down the slide, one after another, on Bitsy's signal. "Listen, next time we're there at the same time, you'll have to bring everyone over for lunch and a swim."

She couldn't conceal her delight. "That would be so much fun!"

Suddenly I was tired of playacting that everything was all right. I was bone tired and lonely and jealous of the young moms at the umbrella tables. I wanted to go back to my Home Base. All the way back—back in time. But I couldn't. We were older. Our kids were older. We lived in different places. Some of us were dead. We paid visits until the kids had gotten older and life had become more complicated; we still sent our daughters to summer camp together in Michigan, which did earn us a girls' weekend together at the end of the season. But the real days of the group were gone.

I'd had that, though, really had that. And this was that for them. I couldn't begrudge them.

Abruptly I said: "I really can't stay. I have to get Grace to her French horn lesson. My nephew is going to pick Jackie up."

I got back in the car. My cup was empty, but I hadn't wanted to ask where to throw it out, so I put it back in the holder. I turned the Saturday Met broadcast back on—*La Forza del Destino*—and drove out, this time passing a golf cart and two landscape technicians weeding impeccably mulched beds. It occurred to me that if they weren't so impeccably mulched, they wouldn't need to be weeded every day because the weeds wouldn't be so noticeable. Perfection was such a taskmaster. Even thinking about it exhausted me.

MUFFLED SOUNDS OF DISTANT CANNON fire emanated from the basement when Grace and I walked in the back door after her lesson. Standing on the threshold, I rested my hand on the basement knob. It vibrated with a rolling wave of thunder. At the next pause I opened the door. "Hi, kids!" I called. "Who's down there?"

"Us!" a voice identical to Frank's boomed out—Sammy—followed by hyena-like laughter attributable to the two younger boys, whose vocal cords were as yet considerably shorter.

"Thanks for clarifying." I turned to roll my eyes conspiratorially at Grace, who was wedged behind me with her horn case, but she only barked: "Move!"

I stepped forward, and she eased her way around just as Molly walked in from the den. "And...that makes four," I remarked with compensatory cheer, plopping my bag down on the counter. "All Massey offspring accounted for. Why don't you girls hang out for a while?"

"I got some stuff to do," Grace muttered, swiftly exiting the kitchen while Molly pretended not to mind.

"What do you say we do some baking, Molly? I'm getting rusty. Whatever you want. We're going to do a Betty Crocker Bake-Off." I opened the basement door again to shout: "Turn it down, please! The glasses are rattling up here." There was more hyena-like laughter, but the volume went down.

Post-banana bread, Molly mixed up peanut butter cookie dough while I got my loaf bread started. After baking one sheet of cookies, she washed her hands.

"I think I'll practice now."

"That's a good idea. When Jackie comes home from that party, he might need a nap." I set my dough to rise, then went out and stood by the piano. "Do the repeat again," I said. "There—" I put my finger on a measure. She stopped. "Take a breath here, and the broken triad is a throwaway, honey—focus on the top note at the downbeat." She started again.

Out of the corner of my eye, I saw Grace slinking down the stairs. She stopped at the bottom and hung her arm around the newel post. "Wanna do manicures?" she asked casually in the direction of Molly, who jumped up with alacrity. They went upstairs.

I'd given up trying to figure it out; whatever had prompted this offer from Grace, even if it was only the desire to put an end to the Clementi, I was glad to see it. I sat down in the den and put my feet up.

Photo albums were stacked on the coffee table, along with a shoebox of loose prints I hadn't gotten around to. About three years' worth—from before we'd gone digital not too long after Jackie was born, after which there were never any rolls to develop. I pulled a fat album onto my lap and turned a few pages. It felt good to look at them but also difficult. I regretted not having kept up to date, but at this point it was hard to imagine that I might be up to it someday.

JOHN AND I WERE AT Elmwood, standing by the row of cedars where Cassie had taken our wedding photos. We were running down the hill, and I thought, What are we doing? Then I realized: Oh, we're going to jump off the dock again just like we did that time before, when we came back to visit, before I got pregnant with Jackie! We turned younger and younger as we ran down the hill toward the lake until we were two little children in swimsuits. It was deeply satisfying: I got my wish! We'd known each other as children! We scrambled down the limestone steps and ran to the end of the dock, which was much longer than I remembered it, and still holding hands, we jumped off the end—but when I came up, John wasn't there. He wasn't anywhere around. I climbed out alone, dripping, anxious, and then I saw him, going back up the hill, hurrying away in the distance, his real age now, hunched over, in a suit, and I called to him and tried to catch up, but he would not look back.

THE PHOTO ALBUM HIT THE floor and woke me. A small body had landed beside me on the couch. I smelled chlorine, felt Jackie's damp hair, and heard the soft voice of Frank Jr.'s girlfriend, India, apologizing for waking me. She and Frank Jr. were dropping Jackie off and would be back later to take Michael to his basketball game.

"Thanks so much for being on driving duty today," I said. "I'm down a few." My mother had gone back to Puerto Vallarta three days ago, my brother-in-law was out of town, and Nathan had driven himself to his own basketball game.

"No problem. I enjoy it. It's fun being around kids for a change." India was an in-home physical therapist, so she spent much of her workday with the elderly set.

"A birthday party, a horn lesson, and two basketball games on an opera day when Frank Sr. is out of town...It's a perfect storm."

"I don't know, Kim, it sounds like business as usual around here!" India laughed. She hugged me and left.

I laid a dish towel over the loaf pans for a brief second rising and expedited another sheet of peanut butter cookies. It was going to be Carbohydrate City around here for a while, but it felt good to be baking again. This was a positive sign. Slowly, I was picking up my feet and slouching toward normal. I was already back to the cello. I'd only needed a sub once. Cassie had managed to get me back out on the tennis court, and now I was forcing myself to go out and hit balls for fifteen minutes each day.

Jackie ran in from the den and laid a small photograph down on the clean part of the counter. "Hey, Mom! Mom. Who *are* these kids?"

I craned over. "That's Nathan and Grace."

"No way!"

"Yes way." I remembered the clothes—matching Hanna Andersson outfits, orange-and-white checked seersucker—sundress for her, shortalls for him. They sat together on a wooden bench holding snow cones at a veterans' memorial park, next door to a corner gas station in a small town in Idaho we liked to stop at on the way to the Rockies. They made real snow cones. I remembered everything in great detail, except the name of the town.

"But..." he spluttered, "they're so *little*."

They were. Impossibly little. Nathan, who had his driver's license now and shaved pretty regularly, was younger here than Jackie was today. The stretch of family life that had occurred before Jackie's birth suddenly became vast and poignant. We'd thought it was merely a chapter, but it was almost the whole book.

Jackie scrutinized the picture with a frown. "Where are you?"

"I'm not in that picture."

"Where's Daddy?"

"Behind the camera."

He edged the photo back and forth on the countertop with a finger, tucking in his bottom lip. I recognized that expression. Quickly, I washed my hands, pulled out a stool, and took him on my lap.

He buried his head in my chest. "I wish he was here. I wish it wasn't forever."

"Me too."

"It *is* forever." A statement, but with a slight interrogatory lilt.

"Yes. Yes, it is."

"I knew that." Voice muffled in my apron bib, he said, "I wish it wasn't. I wish he could just visit."

I rocked him, closing my eyes reflexively. "Me too. I wish he could visit. But he can't. We can't see him again because his body got too sick. But he loves you very much, and he's watching you from heaven."

"I know." He loosened his grasp, straightened up a bit, and turned his head to peep at the photo. "The snow cones are orange."

I put my finger on the print. "I see that now! Do you think Mommy picked orange so the drips would match their outfits?"

He tried not to laugh, then said importantly, "I know where that *is*. That's on the way to Col-yurado."

"That's right! Remember the time Nathan got snow cone all over his favorite T-shirt?"

"Yes!" Jackie had only been three, but children always remembered dramatic spills and vomiting incidents.

"That time when you were in the middle and Daddy was giving you your snow cone through the window and it went all over Nathan?"

"Yes! It was a red one!"

"And *you* said, 'It's a good thing he's wearing the tie-dye shirt,' and everyone laughed?"

"I was funny!" He straightened up, planted palms on my knees. "And Daddy laughed loudest of all!"

"That's right! And Daddy said—he said, 'Hidden depfs. The boy has hidden depfs.' And then *I* said, 'I wanted a blue one anyway,' and Daddy went back and got me a whole 'nother blue one." He bounced on his toes.

"That's right. A whole 'nother blue one."

"Hidden depfs! That was the first time I ever had a snow cone ever. I don't know why I wanted a blue one!"

"I don't, either. I love that story."

"Me too. That's a good story." He reached forward, rocked in my arms another moment, then sprang away.

I walked back into the den and dropped the photo in the box. I put everything back in the cupboard, the albums, the shoebox… They could wait. What I needed to do now was to get prints made of all those post-Kodak-era digital images and build an album for Jackie. He had so much less to remember than the others of his time with his father, so it was all the more to be treasured. He belonged to this club, and deserved an album of his own.

Chapter 19

Last Words

THE PIZZA ARRIVED RIGHT AFTER MICHAEL RETURNED FROM the basketball game and right before Sam left for a concert and sleepover. I ran out to grab the pizza, stepped back, and windmilled my free arm to direct traffic. The kids wanted to have a picnic in the den, so I spread an old tablecloth on the floor and issued a dish towel to each child with words of stern admonition about preserving the carpet. I left them to it and went to bring the laundry up from the basement. I liked to fold it upstairs where there was more light, but when I walked into the living room, I caught some conversation from the den that stopped me cold.

"You don't *have* last words if you die alone." Michael was speaking with authority. "There's no one to say anything to."

"Maybe he talked to God." This was Molly.

"Like, why? Why would you talk to God? You're about to *be* with God. What would you say? 'Hey, God, heads up! I'm coming!'"

I lowered my basket to the floor and stood, arms tightly folded, staring at the jumble of clothes still exuding that warm, fresh, just-out-of-the-dryer smell.

"Your last words would be to other people," Michael continued. "Because those are the people you won't be able to talk to anymore after that."

"Unless you're a psychic," said Tyler.

"What's a psychic?" That was Jackie.

"Someone who knows how to talk to dead people."

There was no sound from Grace. She should have been top of the pecking order here, despite the fact that Tyler was a year older. Nathan and Sam would have put paid to this line of conversation, but Nathan and Sam were not there.

"I think if you're dying, your last words might be 'Call nine one one!'"

"That's only if someone else is there. To do it. If you were alone, you'd just call nine one one by yourself."

"Yeah, people do it all the time. Even if you can't hardly talk, they instantly know where you are and can track you and send the paramedics so maybe you could get saved."

"But that didn't happen with Uncle John."

Silence followed. Should I intervene? Or was this healthy? I couldn't remember my own father's last words to me, which must have been on the telephone, in the last couple of weeks before he died of cancer. With Jessie, though, I knew exactly. She'd called me, as usual, and, as usual, we went out onto our back decks with our phones to wave across the green; I could still hear her voice in my ear. I could still summon it up: *See you next week, sweetie!*

Jackie piped up. "I know what Daddy's last words were. 'Bye, honey, have a good day at school!'"

"That's not last words," said Michael. "That was in the *morning*."

"It is, too, last words. It's the last words he said to *me*."

"But he said *other* things all through the *day*. So it wasn't important. It wasn't the real last words."

Tyler took charge. "What's most important, kids," he said, "is your very last words. 'Cause that's the last thing you ever say in your life. Sometimes people are gathered around, like if you're really old and sick and die in bed. And if the person can't talk, sometimes they write it down. They ask for a pen and paper and they write a note. It's important. They're saying goodbye."

"It *was* his last words," Jackie insisted.

"Jackie, those are his important last words to you," Molly said. "They're very special. You get to remember them forever."

Good girl, Molly.

"Yeah! See? I *told* you guys. It was *my* his last words."

I couldn't remember with mine. I'd forgotten if we talked that day; I thought I remembered, but then I forgot. It was all murky.

There was a pause, and then Michael said, "I can't remember the last time I talked to Uncle John. I can't remember what he said to me. Maybe it was at pizza night? He came in and said, 'Oh no, all that's left is pepperoni?' I remember that because we laughed. Because we only ever got pepperoni. He always said that. I think maybe that was my very last words. My very last time of words."

"Do you think he left a note? A note for Aunt Kim?"

"I don't know. She didn't say anything."

"Well, maybe it was private, idiot!" That was Tyler.

Grace started yelling. "Shut up! Everybody just shut *up*!" She exploded out of the room past me and ran up the stairs. Then there was a colossal slam, the kind you can only achieve in a house built in the early 1900s with solid-core doors. I walked into the den. The children stared at me.

"Maybe let's talk about something else now," I said gently, into the pin-drop silence.

Another burst of screams was heard, this time in stereophonic sound: muffled through the floor but also floating down the stairs from the cavernous upstairs hall.

Molly put her arm around Jackie, who stuck his thumb in his mouth and with his other hand gathered a handful of her shirttail. I knelt on the ground and rubbed a couple of the backs close to me.

"It's okay, kids. Sometimes when people feel sad, they get angry. I'll go up and make her feel better."

But before I could get to the foot of the stairs, she was already thundering back down. I put my hand on the newel post to block her. She pushed past me halfheartedly, then stopped. She was shaking with adrenaline and seemed a little frightened at her own rage.

"I'm getting rid of this!" She brandished a framed photo at me. It was from the Saint Thomas daddy-daughter dance. "I *hate* it. It's *dumb*. I don't want it anymore."

"Oh, this one," I said calmly, putting my hand out to take it from her.

She was having none of it. "It's *my* picture, and I can do what I want with it!" she shrilled.

"Of course you can, honey. It's yours. But what's dumb about it? You look so nice. Daddy was so proud of being your date."

"It's stupid! This is eighth grade! It's from *eighth grade!*" She shook it like an errant toddler. "Middle school! That's not even the *real* daddy-daughter dance. It's the *fake* one for little kids. High school is the *real* one. At Loyola they have a real dance floor and real music and a chocolate fountain! They have a dance contest! We were going to win that next year. He *told* me! We would have *won!*"

She was right. They probably would have.

Suddenly she became very still. Not quiet, but intense: marshaling her energy, gathering it into a taut coil. "I hate him," she said, low and harsh, then repeated the blow with slow, deliberate emphasis. "*Hate* him."

I took a step back.

"He never even left a note. He never said goodbye, and that's forever. He just *left*. Nobody else's dad is dead. It's not fair. He just died and left, and he wasn't supposed to. I *hate* him."

She tore away from me and jerked open the French doors in the dining room. She went out onto the terrace, then across the lawn.

"Oh, honey, don't—" I cried, following her. She dropped the picture on the soggy grass and stepped on it, then picked it up and ran to the retaining wall and flung it with a mighty overhand into the woods. "I hate you! I hate you!" she bellowed. She turned around and threw her hands out. "All of you!" she cried, then raced back into the house. The children were pasted against the matching set of French doors on the other side of the terrace. They saw me looking and scrambled away.

I went inside, kicked off my sodden shoes, and walked back into the den, leaving damp sock prints across the kitchen floor. I checked my watch. Right now was probably second intermission, and Karen was probably eating her chicken Caesar salad with a plastic fork while the other strings traded diva jokes, because they didn't like this soprano. *How does a diva screw in a light bulb? She just holds the bulb and the world revolves around her!* I was pretty sure she wasn't having much fun and that she wished she were here with me. I know I did.

I took a deep breath, let it out, and put my hands on my hips. The children sat there on the floor, silent, uneasy, cowed. Open pizza boxes held thin, gnawed crusts like the rib bones of tiny animals scattered in a fine sifting of Parmesan sand.

"What did she *do*?" Michael breathed. He wiped tomato sauce off his cheek. He was still in his basketball uniform, and his sweat-dried bangs clung to his temples like spit curls.

"She broke her picture and threw it in the woods, stupid," said Tyler.

Jackie was sitting on the edge of the couch, looking from one to the other and sucking noisily on his thumb.

I started closing and stacking the boxes. "Gracie's having a bad day. She's pretty sad. She'll feel better soon. Jackie, why don't you pick out a book, and we'll snuggle on the couch and read a little. I'll come in a minute."

Tyler swung Jackie's legs up, covered him with his blanket, and took Michael off to play video games. Molly gave me a hug.

"I'm sorry," she said. The top of her head just fit under my chin.

"Oh, honey, you have nothing to apologize for. Uncle John wasn't able to say goodbye. I know he probably really wanted to, but he just couldn't. Sometimes it happens that way. We need to remember the happy moments. Those are the ones that count. I know in my heart that before he passed away, he thought about each and every person in this family and sent us all love." I took her by the shoulders and looked right into her brimming eyes, magnified slightly by her glasses. She had the beginnings of a small acne breakout on her chin.

She wiped her nose with her sleeve. "Mommy Kim," she said, a toddler conflation I hadn't heard in years. "I bet we can find it. She's gonna want it back. I know she'll want it back."

I nodded, and together we slipped on our rainboots and went outside to see Bill stomping down the path, Shasta and Socks leaping beside him in excitement. His shirtsleeves were rolled up to the elbow, and his hands were black with automotive grease.

"What in the Sam Hill is going on over here?"

"Gracie got a little upset," I said.

"A little? You could hear that clear up to the Canadian border!"

"She got angry and threw a picture into the woods," Molly said.

"Framed," I said. "A nice one. We're looking for it."

"Well, shoot," he said, wiping his hands on his grease rag. "Lemme help you. I'll be right back."

"But it's practically dark," I fretted.

"This is the best time to look. You'll see." He came back alone, wearing gloves and armed with a flashlight and a machete. I showed him the general area as best I could. He started whacking around in the underbrush, but gently, using the machete as more of a crook than anything else, and just as I called, "I think it's a lost cause," he came wrestling out of the blackberry brambles, cradling the picture in his gloved hands.

"Got it. The light reflects on the glass," he said, and slid it into my open palms.

The frame and glass were broken, and the print was smeared and marred where the shards had fallen out, scratching it and exposing it to the damp.

"Oh, it's ruined—" But as soon as the words were out of my mouth, I remembered. "I have another one!"

I'd bought double prints. So they could each have one. John's was in the office. On the shelf. Wasn't it? They were on the middle shelf of the wall unit. Four framed photos.

Bill's face brightened. "That's good. This one might be okay, though."

Suddenly I realized: They hadn't been there—the photos on his wall unit. And that's why I hadn't noticed they weren't there, because they weren't there. I was only paying attention to the desk. I'd only noticed the Golden Gavel missing from the desk. But—why would anyone steal family photographs? It didn't make sense. I had to be wrong. I just wasn't remembering it right. Which was understandable.

"Everything okay?"

"Yes. Fine. Bill, we made cookies. Want some coffee?"

"Nah. Trying to cut back," he joked. "I'll take a few cookies home, though." He put his arm around Molly's shoulder, and the three of us went inside.

Chapter 20

In the Night Kitchen

It was 1:00 a.m. on Saturday morning, and the sink was polished to within an inch of its life. The counters were clear, the dishwasher emptied, and I'd even cleaned the toaster with an old toothbrush. There was nothing more I could do. The house had never been cleaner since my insomnia had returned, courtesy of the daddy-daughter picture fiasco the previous Saturday. All week I'd been torturing myself: Was that other print in the office, or not? Was that row of photographs still there? Why did I think it wasn't? But I was not going to make a special trip to find out. Tomorrow was the day we were planning to move the office furniture, and I would check then.

I leaned against the counter to survey my handiwork in the soft glow of a pair of sconces close to the ceiling. These were the lights I'd leave on for John when he came home from work late. They sprinkled the faintest cloud of illumination over the kitchen so he could see his way to the leftovers. I'd had more than one discussion with the architect about the lighting and had even done drawings on graph paper: plentiful ceiling cans, under-counter strips to brighten dark corners...It all seemed so trivial now.

He'd only had the daddy-daughter picture in the office for a week. The prints had just come in; I'd framed them and given him one. I'd seen him put it in his briefcase. I'd searched around the house, too, to make sure, but no: I'd seen him put it in his briefcase. It was going to be there.

I tightened my bathrobe belt and opened the fridge. A single casserole dish occupied the now-denuded second shelf. I pulled it out and levered the last slab of Bobbie's macaroni and cheese onto a plate with a spatula. I'd saved it. It had kept well in the freezer.

John didn't leave me with debt; he left me with money. This was what my mother and Karen and Frank had said. Bill, too. I knew that was true, but I wanted to know why, and the why was forever relegated to the universe of lost answers. Don't borrow trouble, people said. Speculation was pointless. You knew he was a responsible family man—just look at the life insurance...Clearly he thought he was going to turn things around, but it got worse instead of better...and then maybe he was too embarrassed to say anything...He wasn't spending it on a yacht or a motorcycle, now, was he? He named you as the payable-on-death! He wouldn't have done that if he'd intended to keep it a secret!

It all sounded reasonable, and I tended to agree, but I wished I could hear it straight from him.

I tugged at a deliciously charred thread of cheese I'd scraped intact off the outside of the casserole dish. Why would anyone steal family photos? The wedding ring wasn't bad enough? I *knew* it. I knew this would happen. A wristwatch, a phone, these I could understand. Even the Golden Gavel, if you're a crack fiend and the metal was good for twenty bucks. But family photos? Did they think the frames were silver? Well, guess what? Only one of them was.

I couldn't bear to think of those prints tossed in a dumpster. My daughter's last fun memory with her dad, thrown out like trash.

I heard the key in the front door, then the soft sound of sneakers being kicked off. Nathan, the Long-Lost. I heard him pad upstairs, then back down. My heart rose. I quickly resumed eating.

He pulled out his earbuds and put his phone down on the counter. "Hey."

"Hey," I replied, casually flipping a page of my magazine. Then I glanced at his phone to see what he was listening to. Porcupine Tree. Another group I'd never heard of.

He got out the cereal, a bowl, and a spoon, and bumped the drawer shut with his hip. "You're up," he remarked. He circled past the aquarium and bent down. "Hi, fishy."

I peeled off another pasta seashell and popped it in my mouth. "I thought you were spending the night at Iain's." *For the third night in a row.*

"Yeah. I decided to come home. I wanted to sleep in my own bed."

Iain was his best friend since kindergarten and the only one whose mother always made sure to check with me every year before scheduling birthday parties. Larry never allowed Nathan to do anything social on "his" weekends, driving a tiny little wedge that brought us back to the psychologist when Nathan hit adolescence, just as the psychologist had predicted years earlier. The only exception to the rule that we'd ever achieved was games during basketball season, starting in fourth grade. I'd enlisted the support of Leeza, who was also aghast, and together we'd achieved Larry's grudging acquiescence.

Nathan walked back to the island, cradling the bowl against his chest and spooning cereal rapidly into his mouth without a drip. "I can't believe you're eating that cold," he said, between slurps. "You're like a teenager eating cold pizza."

"Hey! It's great this way. There's the crusty exterior and then the soft interior. I can't explain it."

"Isn't that from when Grandma was here?"

"I saved the last piece in the freezer. I didn't want it to be over."

"How come you never made it for us, then? If it was your favorite when you were little, like you said?"

"I don't know. Good question. Maybe I should start." I opened a new mental file folder: BETTER LATE THAN NEVER.

"Whatcha reading?" he asked.

I wiped my fingers on a paper towel and showed him the cover, then flipped back to the article. "It's a story about the Hubble Telescope picture of a comet going by Mars."

"Cool." He bent over the picture. "Dad always gave us his *Science News* when we needed a current events article for school," he remarked. "It was great. No one else had it."

We both turned our heads to look at the telescope in the corner of the den. It was John's pride and joy. He and he alone was allowed to move it, onto the terrace in back or the porch in front. His fingerprints were probably the only ones on the chrome tripod. I thought of us listening to Dvorak's *Rusalka* while we tracked the planets late at night after the kids were asleep.

Mesicku, postj chvili / Reckni mi, kde je muj' mily...
Moon, linger for a moment / Tell me where my beloved is...

In the silence, the aquarium's hum was loud, until it was overcome by the *creak-tick-tick* and faint *whoosh* of the furnace cycling on and then the purring rush of air through all the registers in the house. All these sounds, in daytime barely audible and as familiar as one's own pulse or heartbeat, were now magnified by the night kitchen.

Fingerprints. I touched the stainless-steel counter, so shiny its machined whorls were almost invisible. A lemony antiseptic scent still lingered in the air. I'd given this kitchen a thorough cleaning, and in so doing, had scoured away John's presence, even to the tiniest, most vestigial trace. Soon all the rooms would be empty of these traces. I'd scoured this kitchen furiously, thinking that if only I could clean the slate, the real John would rise to the surface, the one who shared his heart with me, instead of leaving me with secrets locked in my own. If I could scrub down to the pure bone, I'd find him: the real husband. And his last words would rise, shimmering, and appear before me in the air.

But it hadn't worked.

Talk about the universe of lost answers.

I flipped the magazine shut. "Don't forget you're helping move furniture at the office tomorrow. Today, I guess. Remember?"

He put his bowl in the dishwasher and pulled out the stool next to me.

"I remember." He sat perched there for a moment, hands on knees, then blurted, "I know I've been gone a lot."

"Listen. No explanations needed. I'm just glad to see you—"

"For a while, I wanted to be away, away from the house, with other people, not family." He put his chin in his hand. "Just be where things weren't different, you know? Everyone kept asking me if I wanted something to eat. I mean everyone was paying so much *attention* to me." He hesitated, pulled in his lips. "But on the other hand—did you remember I took the SAT last Saturday?"

"Oh God! That's right. How did it go?"

He gave a big shrug and clapped his hands on his thighs. "Okay, I think. Scores aren't out yet. But I slept over at Iain's on Friday and we went over to Eastridge together Saturday morning, and I knew you forgot because you didn't say anything when I came home. Nothing."

I lowered my head to the table. "Oh...my...God." I groaned into the stainless steel. "Oh God. That day. It was *that* day. It was a horrible day with the kids."

"Mom, it's okay. I get it."

"No, it's not okay. I'm sorry." I scooted closer and put my arm around him.

He turned and wrapped me in a tight hug, burying his face in my shoulder. "I know you think I'm grown up, but I'm just a kid!" he sobbed. I felt his breathing, irregular and jagged, against my neck. "I'm still a kid!" It turned into a moan, traveling through his cheek, his jaw, into my own bones, penetrating to my very core.

"He won't see me graduate!" The stubble on his cheek scratched my neck, and his nose was running onto my shoulder. "He's never going to see if I get into Stanford. He's never going to know *anything*! We used to go camping when I was little. We haven't in a long time, but I never thought we *wouldn't*, again, ever! And now it *is* ever. It's all over!"

"Daddy saw the man you were," I crooned, rocking him. "He saw the man you had become. He got to see you become an adult. He knew you as an adult. I'm so happy about that. We're blessed in that."

His face was hidden, but I could tell he was listening.

Our little pirate, then dinosaur explorer, then astronaut, then a lawyer like Daddy, even though he didn't really know what that meant except going to an office with a briefcase. Lately he'd told me he might be interested in journalism instead. Had they talked about it? The discussion was over.

Softly, I said, "He saw you, he saw you, he saw you."

He lifted his head and wiped his nose on my paper towel napkin. Despite the experimental sideburns, he looked so young, like a little boy, his eyes puffy and bruised-looking. "Remember when Dad made us blood brothers?"

He'd been in second grade when Grace started kindergarten, and a bossy classmate had told him that he and Grace had different last names and why. "She's my *whole* sister," he'd spluttered when he came through the door after school that day with a pink slip for fighting. "And Daddy's my *whole* dad!" That evening, John took Nathan outside, built a campfire, and solemnly conducted a ceremony for just the two of them, the apex of which consisted of Dad taking his pocketknife and making a tiny cut in his own palm, then Nathan's, and clasping hands. "We're blood brothers now," he'd said. "We share the same blood."

John had told me about it, afterward.

"I remember," I said now.

"Okay." Nathan straightened up. "So. I want to change my name. I want to. I know I've said it before, but I really mean it now."

He had. He was twelve when he'd sidled into the kitchen after a weekend at Larry's and asked. I'd explained to him that he—or we—couldn't do anything without his father's permission until he was older, and maybe it would hurt his feelings to bring it up. "I don't care if it hurts his feelings," he'd said bluntly. "But I'll wait."

Now he was seventeen and hadn't seen his dad for two years, since Larry had broken up with Leeza and moved to Savannah. Nathan kept up with Leeza—she'd done the real parenting, after all—but refused to get on a plane to visit Larry. For his part, Larry seemed not to care.

"I see," I said now, carefully. "Well, it won't be long until you're eighteen and you can do what you want."

"I'm *his* son," Nathan went on. "I want to be his. I've been thinking about it for a while. I just never said it to him. I meant to. I'm sorry I didn't."

Nathan was starting to make adult decisions now. Adding some things, erasing others, he was building his own reality, which, at his age, had more to do with the future than with the past. With the moral clarity of youth, it was easy for him to scour Larry away, to affirm John as the real dad.

"Wait!" I lifted both hands and placed them on the countertop. "Remember that time when you brought it up before?" I asked. "I *did* mention that to Daddy. He knew."

"Are you making that up?"

"No, I just remembered! It was a long time ago. You were in sixth grade, right? It was sixth grade." He nodded. "After spring break. But I told him. He knew," I said, and a change rippled across his face, a lightening.

The furnace cycled off.

After a moment he nudged the *Science News* with a finger. "What's the date on that thing?" he asked casually, and I flipped it over.

"January 12."

"So maybe he saw that one." He gave a little sideways grin. "That would be cool. I know he was into Mars. He probably read that one."

"Yes," I said softly. "Yes. He probably did." I placed my hand on the cover. Not everything had been scrubbed away.

Chapter 21

It All Adds Up

JOHN'S BRIEFCASE WAS COSMIC RETRIBUTION FOR MY whimsical obsession with mental file folders. Now it was full of mine, not his, and they were real, labeled by yours truly: EXECUTOR, TAXES, BUSINESS ACCT., OTHER ACCT., LEASE, DONATION RECEIPTS, INVENTORY FURNITURE, INVENTORY BOOKS, INVENTORY OTHER. My husband died, and all I got was this lousy briefcase, I thought. I pressed the elevator button. A tastefully muted chime sounded, the doors whooshed shut, and up we went to the twelfth floor.

I walked through the suite, flipping on lights. It was moving day and the first time I'd been back since meeting Larissa to give her the books. Thanks in part to the Secret Bank Account Discovery, I was sleeping only about four hours a night, so I'd wisely scheduled nothing before noon. Rivers Northwest was getting everything in the conference room. Frank Jr. and Nathan were coming at one o'clock to help my boss, Terri, because I'd promised her some muscle. The conference room table was fifteen elegant feet long. Luckily, it came apart in three pieces. I'd thought it was a giveaway from the previous tenant, but apparently Owen and John had had to purchase it from the landlord, a little fact I added to THINGS THE WIFE DIDN'T KNOW.

The bulk of the furniture was going to the Deer Lake Band. Monroe, my friend from the tribal council, was coming at two. I'd taken to driving out whenever there was business to do, as an excuse to visit with him, instead of talking on the phone. So I'd seen them prepping for the new double-wides. They'd been offered three portables by the county after a bond issue for a new high school had passed. They'd need to furnish them, and this would help. Monroe was bringing his own helpers, who would load not only their own truck but mine, with the things I was taking home to the barn. And Paisley was sandwiched in between. I'd asked her to stop by; John had been fond of her, and I wanted to give her a memento.

In John's office, a short stack of banker's boxes was leaning against the coat tree. I sat down at the desk, took a sip of coffee, and fished out my file folders. I squared them up. Another sip of coffee, and then I moved the folders two inches to the right. Finally I raked my eyes across the wall unit, trying to take it by surprise. I'd remembered right: The photo shelf was empty.

How could this be? I took out my sandwich and fussily unfolded a napkin for a place mat. Then I raised my eyes again and went around the room methodically. Door. Coatrack. Lectern— actually, one of our music stands, so he could work standing up if his back was bothering him. Tripartite wall unit, which he called the sideboard because it held his birch drink tray. There were cabinets and drawers below, shelves above, holding books, a tiny jade plant, and in the middle—yes. Still empty.

I walked over, touched it.

Did he take them all to be reframed? How would I know where? He usually left those tasks to me. Dying was complicated. I was learning a lot. Don't make assumptions. Leave lists. Leave letters. Leave instructions, explanations. Clean out your papers. Throw away the trash, the unimportant, the things you don't want anyone else to read. Say goodbye. My father's list to my mother had been short, because he'd gotten too tired to continue. *Make no snap decisions.* At least he tried.

I constructed a banker's box, opened the desk drawers, and loaded everything in. The flotsam and jetsam from the shallow top drawer I swept into a big plastic freezer bag, sealed, and labeled. One done. I built another box for the sideboard and worked from the bottom up, jerking open the stiff cabinet doors, but they were empty. Then I opened the drawer in the middle, and there were the pictures. My heart ballooned.

I took out the first two: me with baby Jackie, the daddy-daughter pic. I opened the drawer a little further, and there was our favorite camping picture, the two boys hunkered in the door of their tent with the snow-capped Wallowas in the background, and then a really nice shot of John and Owen with the governor. Four photos, all present and accounted for, four pieces of lost time. Then I discovered his cell phone. His phone? Another mystery solved. To be thorough, I brushed my hand along the front edge of the drawer and came out with his wedding band and a crumpled facial tissue. I stared at the ring in my palm, then closed my fingers over it and pressed my hand to my chest. It wasn't lost! Not lost!

Then I picked up the tissue I'd flung aside. A smear—nosebleed? John always kept a box of tissues at the ready, even though he didn't have that kind of client, those kinds of weepy cases. He never used them. He used real handkerchiefs; he'd adopted my father's habit. And I ironed them for him, just as my mother had done.

I looked at the tissue again. It wasn't blood; it was lipstick.

My brain ground to a complete halt.

People think you're not married anymore after one of you dies, but that's not really true. You're more tightly bound than ever before, because you're bound to however things were left, and that's permanent.

I'd come early to give myself time, so I could nose around for the pictures in privacy, but I hadn't really thought I'd need it. The privacy. But now I did. Because I was trying to understand the lipstick. I picked up each glass on the presentation tray until I found the one. Right there—he was right there, in front of the sideboard—Rowena had said. I don't know why I'd asked. It seemed important at the time. But the most important thing was to see if there were any valuables missing, and there were. From the security camera, Rowena had had stills printed of each person that had entered the building from 8:00 p.m., which was when the concierge left, to 2:00 a.m., when the cleaner had found John. I'd looked through them cursorily. She'd given them to me.

Rowena. Rowena's folder. I fanned the stack on the desk and scrabbled it out. Police Photos.

And there she was. *I never forget a face.*

When had that evening been? I tried to remember when, exactly. Had it been a year ago? At that point, date nights were vanishingly rare, but I had a downtown hair appointment on a late afternoon, so the timing was right, and I pushed for it. I was going to bring up couples therapy. John had settled into solo practice, but he was hellishly busy and the sense of disconnect had not abated. He didn't seem to regret his decision not to return to Dunwoody— or any other large firm, for that matter—but this produced in me a lingering sense of unease: If it wasn't work that was troubling him, then it had to be us. I vacillated between thinking something was wrong, but I didn't know what, and nothing was wrong, and I was making it all up. I wore one of his favorite outfits, a pink satin miniskirt and a slouchy sweater with long belled sleeves. I'd had my hair curled. I felt very fashionable. "Come on," I said, "let's go—don't you want to take me out and show me off?"

We walked two blocks to the Cheshire, a brand-new hotel that had taken over a now-defunct department store. The whole of the soaring center atrium was given over to see-and-be-seen, including the dining venue, defined by a row of large majolica jardinieres whose palm and fern plantings exuded Victorian whimsy. The rest of the lobby was dotted with intimate little conversation areas. We chose a ball-and-clawfoot settee, the better to people-watch. I sat, showing quite a lot of leg and dangling a glass of wine, while John finished up a piece of work on his laptop, which I hadn't known he was going to do. *I could have brought work too*, I'd thought in irritation.

A petite woman with a mass of long brown curls and an over-size shoulder bag walked across the lobby. There was something about the way she was ambling—both casual and purposeful—that caught my eye, and feeling my look, she glared at me with hostility, then did a double take and dismissed us, all in a fraction of a second.

For some reason—maybe the knee-high boots she was wearing—I figured it out. "John," I said in a startled whisper. "I just saw a prostitute!"

He looked quickly up, then down. "Here? Nah. Not in a place like this."

But a few minutes later, there she came again. Upper stage left, exact same circuit, only this time there was an embarrassed-looking twentysomething in jeans slouching along, a pace behind her.

I elbowed John. "See! I told you. There she is again. *With* someone."

He looked up. "No. Don't be silly."

"I'm telling you, that woman gave me a look that could kill. She thought I was the competition."

He stared after her then. "My God, this place has only been open three months!" Then he turned to me, closed his laptop, and joked, "I'm going to have to stop taking you out! I have my reputation to consider," and we had a good laugh. And a nice evening, too, actually, both before and after we went home, and I never ended up mentioning couples therapy.

It was my own fault. I'd practically introduced them.

I guessed he'd stood at the sideboard that night...after. Opened the drawer to take the pictures back out, put his ring on, retrieve his phone. Then he'd seen the lipstick on the whiskey glass he'd given her. Instead of using his own handkerchief, he'd walked over, plucked a tissue from the desk, walked back, and with two decisive swipes, cleaned it off, put it back down on the tray. And then he'd had a heart attack.

I closed my eyes. I saw Nathan, young, tumbling about on the porch as he tried to keep the new puppy, Shasta, out of his Lego box. I saw the man who was my husband leading Grace by the hand with some wildflowers from near the creek, walk her up to the porch, where he released her and accepted a beer and put his feet up on the railing. That world was gone. It was irretrievable. I couldn't say, "Yes, I had this." It didn't matter that it had been for such a long time and that it had been so good. I saw now: It had been running through my fingers like sand every minute of every day since we'd met, running through my fingers every second but I hadn't known it, and now it was all gone, like something written on a flag that whips away in the wind and disappears, leaving only the echo of voices saying *What's for dinner?* or, *I love you, Mommy* or, *Where are my shoes?* little wisps of sound that trail away long after the flag has blown out of sight.

I hadn't just lost John; I'd lost this. This loss was just as profound, just as deep. The anguish was tinged with guilt. How could I have known? What should I have done?

My phone rang.

"We're here," Nathan said. "But the guy says you have to come down to sign out the hand truck."

"Give him your phone," I said. Holding the crumpled tissue in my open palm, I went on, in tones carefully calibrated to be both stern and suppliant: "Harold. Can't you please let my son sign for the equipment on my say-so?"

"Mrs. Halvorsen, I'm sorry. But he's not eighteen. I asked him."

I pulled two more tissues from the box and gently wrapped them around the mystery tissue. "He's almost eighteen," I said. "He'll be seventeen next month. Which makes him almost eighteen."

He thought for a moment. "You got a point there, Mrs. Halvorsen, but he told me. If he'd a' *lied* to me, I could've written that down and we'd be good."

"But, Harold! Isn't this better? He told you the truth, so since he did that, he's probably more trustworthy than if he'd lied, so it should be okay to let him sign it out."

There was another brief silence while he digested this. Harold was a notorious stickler for formalities, even under the best of circumstances, which would have been *not* having been grilled mercilessly by Call Me Rowena about a theft in the building that had occurred hours after he'd clocked off, which really wasn't fair, just because it was his own nephew on the janitor duty, who was on work release, which was also not fair, it was profiling. I was very fond of him, but at the moment I had no bandwidth left to devote.

"Then let Frank Jr. sign it out." I held the newly reinforced tissue ball gingerly on my open palm. "He's my nephew. He's twenty-five."

"I already told them. He's not related to you."

"How is that not related?"

"He's not immediate. The rules say immediate family. He's *extension* family."

"Harold! I'm very busy up here." *Busy going into shock because I just discovered my husband saw a prostitute the night he died.* "Please don't make me come all the way down again." I used a begging tone and sensed a gain of advantage, so I pressed on. "Look at them! Do they look like they're going to waltz out the front door with a dolly and two hand trucks and hawk them on the street corner?"

There was a pause. "Okay, Mrs. Halvorsen, but he's got to sign *his* name, and then *for*, and then your name. I think I can get that to work. Gotta get it done right."

I'd worn him down. I thanked him and hung up. Then I opened my purse and zipped the tissue ball into an inner pocket. My mind went blank again. I could actually feel large banks of switches in my head being thrown into the off position. I had just enough juice left to open one new mental file folder:

Symptoms of a Nervous Breakdown
1. Brain shuts down.

Nathan was standing in the open door.
"WHAT?" I shrieked.
"Don't yell at me!"
"*You're* yelling at *me*."
"I'm *not* yelling at you. I just said—all I *said* was, we're here. Mrs. DaSilva is here too."
Terri placed a reassuring hand on his arm and stepped around him with a small tote bag, which she put down in order to wrap me more fully and completely in a long hug. Then, without speaking, she opened the bag and withdrew a small bouquet of T-shirts in bright candy colors. She unrolled one to display the three lines of block-lettered printing:

IT'S THE
ECOSYSTEM,
STUPID

"Isn't that a little sarcastic?" I asked.
"That's what we're going for, remember? This is the one for Gen Z. It went through committee." Committee was her daughter, the perennial terror with whom I was intimately yet indirectly acquainted. She lifted her reading glasses to read the size tag and remarked, "This one can be for Grace." I wasn't sure how old Terri was. Old enough not to care about wearing her glasses on a chain around her neck, also old enough to know what to do with a widowed colleague. She'd taken me out of the house at least three

times in the last few weeks: twice for coffee and once on a long scenic drive to Leavenworth in Eastern Washington, where we'd split a schnitzel platter for lunch at the Bavarian Haus.

"Anyway," she said. "We'll make others for *our* demographic." She slid the tees back into the bag. "Should we get going?" Nathan and Frank Jr. had already dismantled the conference room table, and we began the process of maneuvering the pieces into the hall.

And suddenly there was Paisley, standing in front of me, dressed in wide-legged stretch pants the color of mud and clunky T-strap shoes. Though still curvy, she'd lost ten pounds of baby fat; the post-law-school trudge through her twenties had thinned her out. How old was she now? Obviously still young enough to dress sloppily and still look chic. The boys repositioned the dolly and got it onto the elevator. Terri squeezed in with them. I told them to be careful, otherwise Harold would have my head, and the elevator doors closed.

Paisley had been clutching a tote bag to her chest and now drew out a framed picture. "I wanted to give you something," she said. "We wanted to—Josh and I. We looked through all the old photos and found this one. We thought you might not have it."

There was a close-up of John in shirtsleeves and loosened tie, leaning over the podium as only the very tall can do, dangling a mic in his hand. His expression was animated. "That's from a Q and A session when he chaired the IP symposium that year."

I thanked her. Pictures were missing; pictures had arrived. And now pictures were leaving again. I lifted a small box onto the seat of a folding chair and pulled out two small David A. Boxley silk-screen prints of a raven and a wolf. "These are for you and Josh."

"Are you sure you don't want to keep them?"

"There's *so* much art in here," I said. "I really stuffed this office full of it. And listen, Paisley—you were special to him."

Older she might have been, but she was still subject to blushing. "I've had two bosses since then. Well, maybe two and a half, so I can *say* now. At the time I had no idea. Not all lawyers…" She trailed off. "Being good at your profession is one thing, but being a good boss is another. He was the absolute best one I ever had. But how could I have known that?"

She wiped her nose. "I'm so sorry for what happened—" She gulped. "I didn't know—"

Me neither.

"I didn't want it to happen."

That makes two of us.

I saw her out. Ten minutes later, while Terri's furniture was crossing town in a U-Haul with the boys, my last appointment arrived, my friend Monroe from the Deer Lake Band with his crew of three: two, tall and burly with long ponytails and one short, wiry kid with two teeth missing on the top deck and an abstract shave pattern at the nape of his neck.

"That guy downstairs didn't like us so much," Monroe remarked.

"Yeah, no shit." That was the short kid.

"Language," Monroe warned.

"That's just Harold. Don't mind him. He practically wanted my own son's fingerprints before he'd let him bring the hand truck up here."

"And I even wore my sport coat," Monroe said, lifting a cuff with the fingers of one hand. "Hides my tattoos."

"Harold's had a hard time," I said. "He's trying to be extra se-curity conscious. There was some stuff stolen out of here before the paramedics arrived, so they put him through the wringer."

"Shit," said one of the tall ones.

"That's like fucking *grave* robbing," said the other.

"Didn't know Anglos fucked over Anglos like that," added Little Guy.

"What did I say?" Monroe snapped, and they apologized again, calling him Uncle, which I knew didn't necessarily mean he was really their blood uncle. We left the three of them to figure out their system for moving the furniture, and I sat him down in John's office opposite *Two Leggings in the Headlights.*

"I recognize this guy," he said. "I've seen his stuff. He does crow pictures too. Intense." I supplied the name. "Yeah, Ric Gendron. He's big-time. How'd you get one of those?"

"I saw it on exhibit at the Tamastslikt Cultural Institute in Pendleton a while back. I made a note of the owner's name and looked him up. Wrote him a letter, in case he ever wanted to sell it. A few years later, he contacted me."

He settled back in his chair, looked around the room, landed back at *Two Leggings.* "Standing in the headlights. Kind of a joke. Except it isn't."

"I like how he is so big and rooted to the ground. His feet have become part of the earth." I leaned forward and clasped my hands between my knees. "Actually, it reminds me of my great-grandfather. His heart was in farming, but his family had to sell, so he ran a hardware store instead. During the Depression, nobody could pay cash and he couldn't say no, because he knew folks needed the supplies to keep their farms going, so he sold everything on credit. He lost everything. He used to drive out to the old family farm in the Model T and just sit there. One night he didn't come home, and they found him out there the next day, sitting in the driver's seat. He'd had a heart attack. I think he went back to the homeplace and died of a broken heart. This painting reminds me of him, but in a good way. Two Leggings, there he is in all his glory. He knows who he is, and he's not giving way. He doesn't care if the world has changed around him. He is the world."

I bent over and put my head in my hands.

Monroe was silent. That was one of the things I liked about him. He was comfortable with silence. After a moment he said: "This grandfather, he's part of your roots now. You carry his legacy."

Head still in my hands, I nodded.

After another minute he said, "Something's changed."

"Yeah, well." I sat up and tried for humor. "When the shock wears off, the reality sets in."

He wasn't fooled. "No. Something else. Something more."

Yes, something else and something more. Reality was more and more, pocked with concealed bank accounts, secret business trips, the entertainment of prostitutes.

Gently, he said: "We're all trapped by circumstance," and tears of embarrassment sprang to my eyes. What right did I have to fall apart? I knew that besides the obvious abiding effects of historical injustice, Monroe had already in his lifetime buried one wife, one adult daughter, and two nephews. I brushed a tear from my eye.

"It's just—going through my husband's things—there are things I don't understand now. About him. I have questions. But I'll never know the answers."

"Sometimes you don't get answers," he said thoughtfully. "But if your ancestors want you to have one, you will. They'll send a sign, a message. You just have to pay attention."

I remembered the cloud of butterflies. I thought of my grandmother in dreams, of how the air was singing when I met John, and saw again those perfect and living figures who danced around me at the moment of Grace's birth. "Yes!" I exclaimed. "I try to. I understand what you mean. I've had that before."

"If it's important, you will again." He lifted his chin at the portrait of Two Leggings. "But remember—this grandfather, who wanted to stay on the farm, you carry his story in your bones. With your husband, it's a little different. His trail on earth has ended. And you have no ancestral ties with him. You're the mother of his children, so I understand your desire to find answers. But don't forget that you have your own story. That's the only one under your control, and that's the story you have to focus on, because that is the one you will leave to your children."

He reached into his inside breast pocket and pulled out a tiny fabric bundle, no bigger than one of my grandmother's dresser sachets. "I brought you something. I made this for you."

Suddenly it registered that he was wearing a sport coat—the same one he'd worn to the funeral. With the same blue dress shirt and bola. Did he always put on a sport coat when he came into the city? I realized: This was a formal visit.

"We're grateful for the furniture. But I have gratitude for you personally. You have good balance. You don't talk just to be talking. Not enough people understand this, that they have to take care of the earth. Through physical action, not just posting junk on the internet. Personal action to restore right relations with the earth. You are sharing this message. And you're sharing it in a persistent way. You have valuable work to do for this, as well as for your family. I am sorry for your time of turmoil. Know that through this process, you are being forged into a stronger metal."

He leaned forward and held out the sachet. I rubbed my fingers over the little cloth bundle, then lifted it to my nose. It smelled sweet and fresh.

"I trust that you will be able to move forward with the guidance of your ancestors. When you do your prayers, pray for clarity. Don't hold anything back when you talk to the ancestors. You have to be very clear with them when you pray. Keep emotion out of it. Speak clearly, and listen. I'm praying for peace, tranquility, and healing for you and your children. For courage. That's the intention I'm holding for you."

"Thank you," I said softly, and tucked the bundle in my purse.

When we went back out into the hall, the boys were fitting the last of the vertical filing cabinets into the elevator. They were lightweight but bulky. Monroe waited patiently, then stepped in himself. "I'm here if you need me," he said, pressing the button.

Done. I checked the rooms that were now thinned of furniture, made a list of what was left. Back in John's office, I opened my handbag and put in Monroe's tiny medicine bundle. My hand hovered over the inner zip pocket. I pulled out the wad of tissues I'd hastily stuffed in there, unwrapped it, brought myself to look at it. Some brands were more perfumed than others. I was in luck: It had a definite scent. Dior? Shiseido?

Monroe believed in me. He was praying for me. *Clarity and courage.*

"I'm matching it as a surprise for my sister," I could say at the makeup counter. *What do they care? They just want to make sales. They're on commission. Who cares if they don't believe me. I'll just brazen it out.* I locked up and left the office quickly to walk the two blocks to Nordstrom before I could change my mind.

Chapter 22

Day of the Iguana

A LITTLE STONE GIRL PRESIDED OVER THE ORNAMENTAL pool in the courtyard of my mother's house in Puerto Vallarta. The wide flat planes of her featureless face were set off by a stylized corona of hair. Her arms cradled a large bird, and at her feet ran musical rivulets of water from three tiny spigots. The wall behind her was so thickly papered with orange trumpet vine that its pink brick was all but invisible, and on its other side, a young palm tree belonging to the uphill neighbors formed a small umbrella. Its branches hung low, dappling light and shadow across her form, the pool, the ceramic pots of croton and caladium tucked all around it.

Bobbie sat in the full shade below the mission-tiled roof over-hang, wearing her conical palm-leaf hat, otherwise known as the Hat We Loved to Make Fun Of. Karen and I had thrown caution to the winds and sat in the full sun, our feet propped on the wide fountain ledge, our heads greedily buried in lowbrow reading material. The noonday silence was thick and drugged. It muted all sound: The delicate splashing of water and faint ostinato of birdsong barely penetrated, and a car backfiring in the street below sounded like distant cannon fire.

Bobbie remarked, "I hope you girls put sunblock on the backs of your necks."

"Yes, Mom," we lied, and adjusted the brims of our ball caps.

"You're as bad as the Canadians. You'd better get some on. It'll be worse up at the pool." Every other sentence out of our mother's mouth in Mexico had the word "sunblock" in it, but we were only on day four of our break from the Land of Clouds and Rain and were still greedy for the sun. I turned around in my pigskin barrel chair. Mom was reading an impressively thick book that was clad in an expensive-looking pearlized cover with a neoclassical painting wrapped around the spine.

"Glad to see you're keeping up appearances," I said, to change the subject. "What's that?"

"*A Dance to the Music of Time.*"

There was a rustling from the courtyard wall, and a ripple traversed diagonally down the curtain of trumpet vine until it divulged the resident iguana: Millard. The name had been bestowed by a child in a distant year who had had to memorize the presidents right before spring break. This Millard, likely Millard IV, was the largest one yet, which attested to the excellent survival instincts that had obviously seen him through to ripe and wise old age.

Having arrived on the ground, he paused to assess the terrain, while Bobbie regarded him calmly from beneath her wide brim. Nothing could make Bobbie look undignified, not even The Hat, which she defended on the grounds that her housekeeper, Maria, had given it to her and she couldn't hurt Maria's feelings, but we knew for a fact that she loved it anyway. With a slow movement, so as not to startle Millard, she lifted her book to show me the cover. "Anthony Powell," she said.

"Never heard of it."

"The British *Remembrance of Things Past?*"

"It's called *Return to Lost Time* now, Mom," I said.

"I prefer the poetic to the merely literal," she replied.

Karen raised her eyebrows behind her magazine. "Can we please just say 'recherché' and leave it at that?" she said dryly.

I reached for her magazine. "And how is 'Beauty Secrets from the Produce Aisle the Cosmetic Industry Doesn't Want You to Know?'"

She yanked it away, rolled it up, and smacked me on the arm. "Look at you, with that ancient Agatha Christie you've read like four times already. The pages are yellow."

Millard, meanwhile, was taking stock from within the hibiscus. When Maria returned from the corner store, the metal door into the courtyard clanging shut behind her, he skittered off into the hedge of croton lining the path to the swimming pool.

She crossed to the kitchen with a milky yellow plastic bag, holding it up as she passed. "*Limones.*" We gave her a *gracias* and a thumbs-up and returned to our reading.

A breeze rasped dead leaves out of an unswept corner, and the vine-covered wall trembled. A car backfired three times, then chugged laboriously up the hill. The little stone girl in her long plain dress was unperturbed. That her features were only hinted at had never bothered me. Just because she had no eyes didn't mean she was blind; on the contrary, it gave her an air of wisdom and serenity. From her nothing was hidden. She saw everything, and with complete composure.

Something was afoot. There was the shuffling of many little feet, then a skitter and a pause. *Shuffle, shuffle, skitter...Shuffle, shuffle, skitter.*

We looked over, and Maria stuck her head out the kitchen window just as Millard shot back down the path, completely skirting the hibiscus, and leapt through a small potted butterfly palm into the lush wall of trumpet vine. Jackie was careening behind him. "Whoa!" he cried, braking dramatically on the fountain ledge.

"Incoming!" Karen drawled, and turned another page.

"You shouldn't devil that poor thing," said Bobbie as the other children spilled into the courtyard. Maria gave Nathan the benefit of a cuff on the head as they surged past her window.

"*¡Por el amor de Dios, déjalo en paz, niños traviesos!*"

"What's she saying?" I asked.

"She's saying they shouldn't devil that poor thing," replied Karen without lifting her eyes from the page.

Nathan bumped against Jackie and passed along Maria's knock, then sat down on the ledge and twirled his goggles. "Watch out. You could get arrested for that. He's an endangered species."

Jackie rubbed the back of his head indignantly. "You were doing it too!"

"That one is clearly endangered," Bobbie murmured.

"Honey, he's teasing," I said. "Nathan. Don't scare him."

Bitsy brought up the rear, carrying a large rubberized tote in both arms and throwing her feet out slightly in the way of compact, broad-shouldered women with a low center of gravity. In earlier days, the tote had held water toys and inflatables; now it contained water polo balls and goggles. She set it down. "They were egging Jacko on," she reported, tucking her towel more firmly around her waist. The children flopped in a row on the fountain ledge, all but Jackie, who rotated around the tree trunk pillar with one arm, singing to himself.

Bobbie closed her book. "Who won?"

"Stanford." Bitsy gave Nathan a fist bump.

I gave her my credit card for lunch down on the beach, where they liked to get ringside seats under the thatched roof of the café and watch the parasailing. Bitsy detached Jackie from the pillar and steered him away. "Let's go, kids!" she called. "Rinse off and get dressed! I'm hungry!"

"That girl is just a saving grace." Bobbie tucked her book in her knitting bag. "I'm going up now, Maria," she said, starting toward the hibiscus path, while we went into the kitchen.

"Mom! You're forgetting your cane," Karen said.

Bobbie scowled and retrieved it, then thrust her knitting bag at me. "You'll have to carry that up, then. And you girls get something proper to eat!" she added as we rummaged in the refrigerator.

Maria, whipping up Bobbie's gringo lunch, winked at us but didn't smile, due to her divided loyalties. Maria was quiet and stayed out of all plots and conspiracies. She laid two carefully washed lettuce leaves on a plate, then placed a scoop of chicken salad on top. "I have left," she announced.

"Oh, goody, Maria! *Gracias.*" Maria's American chicken salad was not to be turned down. She made everything fresh from scratch, and rarely were there leftovers. Karen and I, on the other hand, in our own kitchens, were the queens of the double batch. Still holding the knitting bag, I watched out the window as Bobbie tackled the upslope to the pool. The path was just steep enough to need the occasional step as it ascended to the upper terrace, and I saw her switch her cane to the other hand so she could hold the railing, almost concealed by the abundant flora.

Mom! You're forgetting your cane. Karen could get away with scolding like this not because she was the oldest but because she hadn't lost any respect in Bobbie's eyes by making the kinds of stupid mistakes I had. She was an adult. I was a child in constant need of reprimand and guidance.

I turned away. One of my favorite photos, hanging next to the window, caught my eye: Nathan and Grace sitting on the curb outside Bing's, holding their ice cream cones. Ice cream, that time-honored strategy for getting kids to sit still for the camera. How old were they in this one? Six and three? The sidewalk was high; Grace's tiny dangling legs didn't even touch the cobbles. This was a long time ago. Before Bitsy, before Jackie, even before the twins. I was presented with the past at every turn, and each time, there was an initial bloom of pleasure, followed by a tiny pang as the years pancaked down and hit ground level. I was getting used to it.

So much of marriage is dumb luck, Bobbie told me long ago as I sat at her kitchen table with baby Nathan, waiting for Larry to be served with divorce papers. Luck. She'd had it. Karen too.

And I thought I'd joined their happy club, the club of those for whom remembrance of things past means free and easy movement through always-open doors.

How long he had been cheating? How many times? Why? I wanted answers to my questions so I wouldn't be forced to humiliate myself. If he could return from the universe of lost answers, it could stay a secret. Just between us. The last thing John would want would be for me to tell his secrets. I wanted him to explain. And then I'd ask: "What should I do?" That was what I really wanted to get to. *What should I do?* We used to work things out together. Now he was going to be stuck with whatever I did.

After I discovered the secret bank account and talked it over with my sister, Karen had told me my fifteen-year marriage was not a mistake. I'd asked her. "No," she'd said, gripping me by the arm. "The mistake was with Larry; this was not a mistake."

Now I wasn't so sure. Overworked husband has heart attack in his forties? Act of God. Husband inherits a bunch of money and fails to tell his wife? Peculiar, maybe not unheard of. But this lipstick-stained handkerchief? This security-camera footage of that woman going into John's building that night, the night he died? This was deception on a whole new level. What do you do when the things that only happen to other people happen to you?

You run to your mother.

When I'd told Karen, she'd gotten very quiet and still and said in strangled tones, "No, no, no," and then, "I had no idea things were that bad," and then burst out with: "But he *loved* you!" Karen couldn't help me; she was at a loss. "You have to tell Mom," she said. "We have to ask Mom."

Bobbie reached the top of the path and switched her cane again, to open the pool gate. It sang on its hinge, and suddenly I realized: She hadn't used to do that. Hold the railing. When had that started? When had my mother grown old—when had handrails become important? I'd missed this. Probably because I was busy with my own problems, or, more accurately, busy denying them. I'd been busy ironing handkerchiefs. In this, I was like her. I'd tried to be different, but it hadn't worked.

Behind me, Karen exclaimed, "Don't tell me we're out of tostadas!"

Maria reached under the counter and brought out a fresh bag. "No nine one one," she said, handing it to her with a straight face. That was the children's favorite phrase this year. *Nine one one, chip emergency! Nine one one, salsa emergency! Nine one one, towel emergency!* We'd complained about this until our mother pointed out we'd started it, which succeeded in shutting us up, because it was true. Maria continued in my direction: "You have ironing?"

She knew that word. I must have spoken aloud. I hastily reassured her not and took the proffered bowl of chicken salad. I put a spoonful on my plate, added a tiny dollop of guacamole, and slid one large, crispy tostada out of the bag.

"That all you're having?" Karen asked as she peeled mandarins.

I twirled the plastic cylinder shut. The truth was, after the second bomb had hit on moving day, I'd lost what appetite I'd recovered, but I just said, "Nothing like wearing a bathing suit all day every day to remind you to eat lightly."

"But you're as thin as a rail!" she exclaimed, and Maria frowned at her. I pretended not to notice. Karen hurried on. "We're going to have lots of *bistec* shish kebab tonight, aren't we, Maria?"

"*Si, chiquita!*" She picked up the tray. "*Vamanos!*"

We climbed the stairs to the upper terrace. The swimming pool was on the order of a chain-link-wrapped bird's nest perched above a sea of descending rooftops. In this aerial basin, Bobbie was gliding slowly back and forth in an elegant breaststroke with her palm-frond hat still atop her head. Not a swimmer in her youth, she had taken it up in her fifties on the advice of her doctor in order to preserve mobility and was now a religious adherent. Quietly she swam, her arms skimming the water's surface, while beneath it, she propelled herself forward, polio handicap invisible.

Maria set down her tray, covered it with a dish towel, and left, latching the gate gently behind her.

Karen and I pushed our lounge chairs against the bougainvillea-covered backstop to enjoy the full sweeping view of Banderas Bay, from Mismaloya tucked beneath us at the south end all the way to the northernmost misty blue tip with its mountainous profile of the Sleeping Woman. The mini cooler sat between us. I stripped paper from two straws and handed one to Karen.

Bobbie emerged carefully, using the wide shallow corner steps that also conveniently served as the designated penalty box for water polo. She sat down on the end of her lounger, took off the hat, and fluffed out her cap of gray waves with her fingers. "Oh, you girls. Look at you. You and your Mexican Coke."

At home, soft drinks were banned; but at the Monkey Ward, the moms drank Mexican Coke. The cooler was just big enough to hold four small glass bottles, two highball glasses, a baggie of citrus wedges cut from the whole limes Maria sanitized every morning, and a baggie of ice.

"Count your blessings, Mom," Karen said. We popped the straws in our glasses and clinked. "Other gals our age, it would be a cooler full of margaritas."

"At this hour? Over my dead body," she responded, and started in on her lunch.

Surreptitiously, we rolled our drinking straw wrappers into little balls in furtherance of our traditional childish prank on the downhill neighbor, which we traditionally kept secret from our mother, because her second favorite line after "Are you girls wearing sunblock?" was "Why do you girls regress when you're down here?" and we didn't want to give her any more ammunition, even though she'd given us the idea in the first place.

Due to some complicated property shenanigans effected by the Montgomery Ward heir, we actually shared the pool with his friend to whom he'd sold the lot next door in the seventies. Friend was now absolutely ancient of days and never used it anyway, so it worked out well for us, but Bobbie knew the family—had gone to Wellesley with someone's niece. At some point, probably on a rare evening we'd successfully persuaded Bobbie to enjoy a margarita, she had confided the sordid details of this friend's divorce, which left his wife of forty years saddled with the house in Lake Forest, dependent on their two adult children, while he'd moved full time into the house in Puerto Vallarta and changed his will to leave everything to the housekeeper.

Bobbie's tones of hushed vehemence revealed an impressively deep vein of suppressed disgust, and thereafter, in indignant solidarity, Karen and I had taken to pressing our noses to the chain-link fence at quiet moments and pushing little projectiles through the metal diamonds. We made sure never to do this when the children were around, so as not to give them ideas, and likely these little projectiles—dead blossoms, rolled-up leaf balls, candy wrappers—were never even noticed by the owner, sitting below in his wheelchair in the courtyard surrounded by the housekeeper's ever-expanding extended family. Most of it simply became lodged in the vine-covered wall. Nevertheless, this subversive operation gave us a juvenile sense of satisfaction.

Bobbie took a sip of iced tea. "Bitsy is just a saving grace," she said, picking up her previous beat again.

"Truly," we agreed.

"I'm so glad she's going to college. In all modesty, I'd like to hope that some of that was our good influence."

After a gap year working full time as a YMCA lifeguard, Bitsy had done two years of community college and was now transferring to Washington State University for a degree in exercise physiology. She would be the first in her family to earn a four-year degree. We'd encouraged her.

"Remember how shy she was at the beginning?" I asked.

That had been eight years ago, when the twins were three and Karen was ready to start traveling again. Bitsy's mother was one of Frank's admins, and when she heard that we were looking for a babysitter who could swim, a star was born.

"Shy? Maybe," Bobbie remarked acidly. "I think she was just scared of you." She finished her lunch and pulled out her knitting. "But that was my suggestion. A mother's helper," she added, with some satisfaction.

"You mean an *au pair*," Karen said. "That's what they're called today," she said, "except *we're* the pair!" and we fell all over each other laughing.

I leaned over to hand my bottle caps to Karen. She gave me a meaningful glance, which I ignored. My sister had been picking up on the meaningful glances lately, which telegraphed *When are you going to talk to her? We've been here four days already... five days...six...*

"I'll have to knit Bitsy a scarf in the school colors," Bobbie said, while she clicked away on a layette set for our school auction. It was pale blue; this was her third year running contributing her beautiful handiwork, and the chair had asked me if she could do two this time, one in pink and one in blue.

"That's a good idea," said Karen, adding the bottle caps to our prank pile. "It gets cold in Eastern Washington."

Above us a cacique burst out in a scold. I catapulted out of my lounger, did a surface dive to the bottom of the pool, and in that underground silence, swam fast all the way around. Then I grabbed the ladder and climbed, and my head burst out of the water, the world exploding around me in bright shards. I gulped mouthfuls of air as the water stilled to glass and the noises reassuringly organized themselves into sound: the trill and bark of the cacique in the tree, the tinny murmur of the neighbor's radio, a child singing. I stood on the top rung, holding the ladder with both hands, and looked down to the bottommost blue depths, where a painful ball of shame, grief, and humiliation was crouched, waiting to uncurl and shoot its quills again, ripping up my insides.

You could tell yourself until you were blue in the face that you didn't need advice from your mother anymore, that you were too old for it, but that wasn't true. I was back in that place, balancing on the top step, the octave, the same note I'd begun on: a painful conversation that would break my mother's heart.

I hoisted myself out, lay down, and put my hat over my face. A tiny wisp of mariachi music floated up from the street far below, and the water dried on my skin. *The water is the air of the ocean, and the air is the water of the sky*, one of the boys had told me excitedly once, here at the pool, long ago. Which one was that? Tyler? Michael? I drifted off.

I WAS SITTING IN THE upstairs studio in the barn. The "Qui Tollis" from Bach's Mass in B minor was on the stand, but I wasn't looking at the music. I sat, bow in hand, hand on knee, watching dust motes dance in the air, tiny specks rendered momentarily visible by the slant of the late-afternoon sun. Why? My cell phone had rung. John saying he wouldn't be home for dinner.

It's beef stroganoff, your favorite...

Save me some. I just have to get these contracts done. It's the new client, I want to be on the ball for them, I promised them tomorrow...

Oh, by all means! The new client. Of course...

Bye, hon, love you...

Love you too...

I lifted my bow arm but couldn't make the arc, touch the string, start to play. A groan bubbled up from my throat, but it was okay—there was no one in the room. The children were elsewhere. There was no one to hear.

MY EYES FLEW OPEN.

Bye, hon, love you.

I had them, his last words, the last I heard in my ear, but now I didn't want them because they were a lie. Or had turned into a lie? I wanted to know, to pin down a single answer. There was still a piece of lost time, and now it was worse. Now it would dog me. I almost wished I hadn't remembered.

Above us palm fronds whispered and clicked, casting splinters of gray onto the bleached concrete. Hidden in the tree, the cacique began calling again, urgently.

There was always the next thing to get ready for in our lives. Life just kept barreling along. I'd never had time to sit down and figure it all out. Figure out what was wrong. I swung my feet to the ground and turned.

"Mom! Mom, I need your advice. I have to talk to you about something. I need to tell you…something."

She looked up. Her knitting descended to her lap. Just as I knew her every permutation of tone, so did she mine, and a shadow passed over her face, dank and heavy with the multitude of possible variations on a theme. She bore it lightly, tipping her head, not down but up to meet it, then exhaled sadly. "You mean there's more? Something more?"

More? More than the concealed inheritance and sadly concealed career downslide that I'd already had to tell her about? Yes, more.

I'd thought the worst moment in my life had been confessing to her seventeen years ago that Larry had sexually abused me while I held baby Nathan, but it wasn't. This was. Even though my sister, who already knew, was beside me for support. This time was the worst. Because we were older, because of the weight of that accumulated time, because she'd loved my husband. This one, she'd loved. As I spoke, telling her about the prostitute, about the mysterious business trips when there was no business, I watched her recede into herself, deeper than I'd ever seen, so deep, I despaired.

Until, unbelievably, she came back.

She homed in on me with the open face of an equal, a face full of unconcealed grief and unbounded compassion. She took my hand and anchored it on the blue layette. "I am so sorry," she breathed.

For a moment, none of us moved.

Then suddenly Bobbie exclaimed, "Does anyone else know? Have you told anyone else?" And we, alarmed at her alarm, swallowed the lumps in our throats and cried, *No, no, no one else, just us.*

"You can't tell anyone," she said sternly, pointing an index finger at each of us in turn. "It would be very damaging if the children ever, ever heard anything about this. They must never know. And the only way to ensure that is to tell no one. No matter who. Not even Frank. You didn't tell Frank?"

Karen shook her head quickly.

"I can't tell you how important this is, girls. No one."

"Okay," we said, cowed. "Okay."

Behind us the fence rattled. Millard's head appeared above the tapestry of flowers, then the rest of his body. He froze on the top of the fence, solemnly regarding a distant point to the north, then turned a gimlet eye on me in harsh speculation. Was he stalking me to see if I told his secrets? I couldn't tell. He looked in the other direction, paused again deliberatively, and then withdrew. Karen was still holding our drinking straw paper balls. She was shifting them nervously back and forth from one cupped palm to the other. I could tell it was unawares, because her eyes were glued to me.

"Mom." I sat forward. "This is the thing. I don't know what to do. Should I hire a detective? A private investigator? To find out? What was going on? I don't know what to think now. About anything. It's eating me up. The spending, the traveling. I don't know what to think anymore."

From high above, we gazed out at the relentlessly silent ocean, dotted near the beach with tiny specks of colorful parasails. At the far north end of the bay, La Mujer Dormida slept calmly, implacably, her long hair trailing into the sea.

Finally our mother said, "I'm not going to answer your question. Because nobody else can tell you what to do. You are the only one who can make the decision. Never in my life have I been more grateful that you went through what you did, before, with Larry—not that it happened, I mean...but...I *saw* you go through that. So I know you have the strength. I have complete confidence that you will deal with this with your children in the forefront of your mind. The decision is yours, and I know that whatever decision you make, it will be the right one."

She was leaving me behind. It was for this that she'd returned to me from inner recesses: to tell me that I didn't need her. With the accumulated grace and strength of a lifetime, she'd shared the simple truth that had been forged within it, one transformative for her as well as me: that I would do this on my own.

Karen looked between us. The lower half of her face was crumpled in a way I'd never seen before, like tissue paper dissolving in water. We sat there, suspended in the peculiarly silent no-man's-land between *before* and *after*, which suddenly thrust the greatest of distances between us and the nearby, the quotidian: a rooster's halfhearted crow, the knife grinder's flute, sandaled feet slapping bare ground and a snatch of children's laughter; all were pushed aside into the dimensional vastness necessary to allow both daughters to make this tremendous shift into a new key. To stand for one last eternal moment at the brink, to stand at the train tracks holding hands, snow boots firmly on the ground, and look south, look north, mark the points of compass, see who we had been, had become, and still were.

Karen tried to speak, but only gulped. She tried again.

"I love you," she said bravely, aloud.

"I love you too," I replied, and Bobbie returned to her knitting.

Chapter 23

Three Cellists on the Verge
of a Nervous Breakdown

ONCE WE WERE THROUGH THE DOOR OF THE HOTEL, EVIE took charge. This was why we needed Evie. We'd known this. And it wasn't really disobeying our mother, because she was the closest thing to another sister we had, and we trusted her completely with the secret we'd promised to reveal to no one, not even Frank. Which we hadn't.

She scanned the lobby and led us to a seating area in the corner, distant from the action but with an unfettered view. It was a bit early for the after-work crowd, and servers were milling about aimlessly. We sat down, unbuttoning our coats but leaving them on, as though this tufted velvet sofa was but a temporary mooring.

Karen fingered the handles of her recycled Nordstrom shopping bag, which held two of her own sweaters, neatly folded and wrapped in pristine tissue paper. "Maybe nothing will happen," she said lamely.

Evie waved off an approaching server. "We're waiting for a friend," she said.

I had a hot flash and shucked off my coat.

The sofa was steel gray; a few magenta throw pillows brightened it up, and, when the copper tray table was taken into account, achieved a look that might be called "harem moderne." Eclectic would be a nice way to put it; I'd just call it out of place.

"Remember. This is just an experiment," Evie reminded us. She slipped off her coat and sat there, legs crossed, perfectly calm, looking like a model with her high cheekbones and long straight hair. She claimed she had Indian blood through her French-Canadian mother, and this was likely true, as it was of probably everyone in northern Minnesota. "We're just going to sit here for a while. We don't need to do anything."

"We're not going to see her," I said. "No chance. I mean, what's the chance?"

"Let's change the subject," Evie said brightly. "Hey, did I tell you guys the Coho asked me to do the Brahms Sextet with them? The first one. For the autumn series." The Coho was the faculty quartet at Seattle University.

Karen took up the thread. "I don't think so. That's great! Who's the other violist?"

"Kevin." He was one of their colleagues in the opera orchestra.

The dull pain in my temples began to trudge across my forehead. My eyes were already getting tired of scanning. "I don't like Kevin," I said. "He's too full of himself. He'll schmaltz it up. You can't do that to Brahms."

"He is," Karen agreed. "Kevin. You're going to have to militate against that a little bit."

Evie clasped her knee thoughtfully. "I don't know. He's not *that* bad. You know, hmm. Basically, they all have a chip on their shoulder. Violists. They don't even have their own solo repertory. Everything's transcribed from the cello."

"Yeah," I said, as I looked around. "We should cut them a little slack. That's got to wear on your musical self-'exteem' after a while," deliberately mispronouncing the word. That was John's joke. Whenever we got too esoteric for him, he'd kid, *You guys are giving me low musical self-exteem!* Then I felt a low-voltage zip as though I'd just hit an invisible electric fence and remembered why we were here.

Evie had promised she'd take it to the grave. Just as Karen was never going to tell Frank, she would never tell her husband, Howard. *I'll take it to the grave*, she'd said, then joked, *That might be sooner than we think.* At which point we'd softly pummeled her on the arm, one of us on each side: *It was only stage one. You're fine. Stop!*

The server returned, this time staking his claim with little white napkins, embossed with a retro navy monogram encased in a diamond: *H* and *C* for Hotel Cheshire.

"It's going to be a few more minutes," said Karen.

"Okay, perfect," he hummed, and floated away.

"'Perfect,'" I said. "Why does everyone say 'perfect' all the time? What in the world does that even *mean*?"

Karen wasn't listening. She had placed her fingertips on one of the napkins and was moving it about absently as though it were a Ouija planchette, then noticed what she was doing and lifted them quickly, as though from a flame.

It was the waiting. There's the idea and then there's the waiting. The waiting is the hard part. It's like being pregnant, at the very end, when it seems like it's been ten months. On the other hand, some people have to wait and wait and watch their husbands be sick and waste away and die. That's what my mother did. Which was worse?

After fifteen years, I was left with John's closed face beneath fluorescent lights. It pushed aside all other images and formed a blank, impenetrable shroud through which I was unable to stretch my hand to reach the living flesh of my earlier life. I wanted the man who kept the pocket Yeats in his bedside table, because he'd majored in poli sci and hadn't taken any lit courses and wanted to be well rounded—not the man who lied to his wife and telephoned a hooker.

Lately, our newlywed years rippled through my dreams like flashing glints of silver in the distance, half-buried in oceanic silt: the Baltimore parties, the birth of Grace, the cross-country move to the big new house in Issaquah. If I knew the end—not just the beginning but the end—then perhaps I could get back the whole. See it all the way through, like a finger on the page scanning a poem. I knew he was gone. But I would have the beauty of it. And I was greedy for that, because without it, I had nothing. I'd be empty inside, scraped hollow, unable to nourish my children.

After a minute, Evie said: "Oh, for the days when your friends only asked you to do the easy things, like to be your bridesmaid," and we laughed again, less resoundingly but appreciatively.

"Perfect," Karen and I said together, then "Jinx!" we cried, and the server again advancing upon us almost altered course but didn't. It was hard to tell if he was the same one as before; it wasn't just the uniform of jeans, crisp white shirt, and navy bow tie, but the fact that—male or female—they were all incredibly slender, with quiffs and stud earrings. It might have been a requirement.

"We need to commit. Three glasses of the house white?" Evie said, glancing over for our nod of assent.

"You got it." He hurried off.

"Well, we made *him* happy."

"Whatever happens, he's gonna get a gigantic tip." Karen looked at her watch. "God, it's only been twenty minutes. We said two hours."

"Next time one of you can wear my wig," Evie offered. "Change it up a little."

"There's not going to be a next time," Karen exclaimed.

"I am *not* going to wear the wig, Evie," I said.

"Me neither," Karen chimed in. "Wear the wig? Why can't you ask your friends to do the *easy* things? Like not wearing the wig?"

Evie had never even used it. She'd gone out and bought it right away, even before the lumpectomy. We'd tried to tell her some people do not even lose their hair. Mrs. Weickert, Nathan's English teacher at Loyola, did not lose a single hair off her head. But Evie had retorted that she didn't want to go shopping when she was bald and nauseated. *I want to be proactive. I want it to look exactly like my own hair. I want to* nor-ma-lize *the situation,* she'd said, drawing out the word as though we'd never heard it before, so it had turned into our word of the week.

And then she'd never needed it.

The seating areas filled up as the after-work trickle increased to a stream, and the room filled with a murmur of voices. The servers no longer wandered but moved purposefully back and forth. I lifted my newly arrived glass, thought better of it, and put it back down. "What if I don't recognize her? Or what if I get the wrong person?"

"But you're good with faces," Karen said.

Evie chimed in, "You got a real good look that time, it sounded like."

But I *could* get it wrong, I thought. I could pick the wrong person, I thought, and, suddenly, there she was. The right person.

Karen felt it. "You found her!" she whispered. I took another quick look, and she followed my glance. "There? By the pillar? With the long brown hair. Is that her?"

"Where? Where?" Evie joined in.

"Don't look don't look don't look!" I said urgently, softly banging the flat of my hand on the sofa. "Be quiet. Pretend we're talking." We put our heads together while I scrabbled in my purse for the lipstick, saying, "This is insane. Insane. I'm not doing this."

"Wait." Evie ducked out and back in. "We're being stupid. Nobody's paying any attention. We're just three gals who went shopping, and now we're having a drink."

"Just three cellists on the verge of a nervous breakdown," I croaked. Then coughed, then emitted a giggle.

Karen put a hand on my knee. "Kim. It's okay. Do you want me to do it? I'll do it if you want."

I held the tube of lipstick and looked at her. I looked right into her eyes. A lot else was different, but we had the same eyes. "No. I just need you to be here."

"Okay. So, um. Pretend you're going to the bathroom." She leaned forward and took a casual sip from her glass.

I froze, just as I had that first time, afterward, on the threshold of John's office.

"Come on, Kimmie. Just go," Karen urged. "If you don't, you'll always wonder. What's the worst that can happen? She blows you off."

"*Go, go, go,*" said Evie softly, lifting her wineglass.

"Okay." I stood up and began working my way around the perimeter of the lobby toward the woman who might actually be the very last person to see my husband alive on this earth.

She was hovering by the restaurant entrance, marked by a gap in the row of jardinieres: near to, yet apart from, as though not wanting to step up until her fictitious companion arrived. The head of brown corkscrew curls, swept partially up and back, was what I remembered most clearly. Standing up, as I was now, I saw she was very short. Small-waisted, broad-hipped, wearing a turtleneck sweaterdress; I started to wonder how I'd so easily identified her, before, as a prostitute, but then she took a few steps, shifted her bag to her other shoulder, and crossed her arms, and I realized: It was the way she moved. She knew she was sexy.

And her purse was cheap.

Clutching the lipstick tightly, I sauntered closer. She had a kittenish prettiness, and her makeup was well done. She looked a good fifteen years younger than us, but when her eyes darted in my direction, I saw a tightness in her face that betrayed long-term deprivation. I could tell she'd had to go to more than the usual lengths of inner exertion during the formative years to give people what they wanted, while simultaneously covering a large hole located somewhere, invisible, behind her sternum, and this had aged her.

I stopped very close to her, in the grip of terror, trapped in that thin wedge of space, the proscenium, with nowhere to go.

Suddenly I was fifty feet above, perched in the skylight dome. Up close it was a marvel, a many-paned shell of varying alabaster hues, probably originally intended to be a Tiffany mosaic. The varying opalescent sheens—some warm, some cool—wrapped me in a kind of quiet vanilla calmness that allowed me to look down and observe the urban professionals in the lobby, wandering around, sipping their craft cocktails and shopping on their smartphones as they waited for their friends to appear. Among them I saw the two of us, separated by just a few feet: me, rooted to the ground; she, standing there with her arms crossed. The sight flooded me with compassion, not just for her but for myself as well. For both of us, and then suddenly I was back in my skin, stepping up just as she began to move off.

"Excuse me, hey, is this yours? I think you just dropped this."

She gave me a quick up-and-down, then took the tube and squinted at the label, "Uh, yeah, I guess, thanks," she said, opening the flap on her bag as she kept moving.

"I'm sorry to bother you," I babbled. "Can I ask you something? I just need to talk to you for a quick sec."

"No, you don't." She dropped the lipstick into her bag, then was arrested by something she saw inside. She pulled out the tube again and uncapped it. "What the fuck? This isn't mine. It's my lipstick, but it's new." She looked around furtively. "Who the fuck are you. Detective? Lawyer? You're a lawyer."

I glanced over at Karen and Evie, who were sitting at attention in the tufted steel-gray distance, radiating encouragement. "No, ma'am," I said smoothly. "I'm a musician."

"What...the...fuck?" She said it quietly. It registered on me that she was hampered by a visible reluctance to make a scene.

"I'm not here to make trouble," I went on quickly. "I just have a quick question for you, and then I'll be out of your hair." I touched her arm confidently for a second, indicating the direction we should go.

"Who are *they*?" She'd followed my glance.

"My friends. We're cellists. They're kind of my support group."

I steered her over to our table. She perched on the edge of the sofa, hunched over, as though protecting her handbag from the cold, then set the lipstick on the table and ostentatiously pushed it away. "Okay, so what's the deal? Talk fast 'cause you got like one minute 'cause you're all creeping me out."

We sat speechless, not having thought this far ahead, not even Evie. Three cellists having a nervous breakdown.

She popped her lips over her teeth. "So, like, what are you staring at? What's the fucking deal?"

It was Evie who spoke.

"This is the deal. My friend here is trying to gather a little information. Her husband is gone, and she's trying to fill in a few blanks. It would be helpful to her, is all."

"Okay, *I* get it. Listen. I don't have nothing to do with anything, and what makes you think...? Lady, I'm sorry your husband took off, but that's got *nothing* to do with me. So I think you just gotta leave me alone now."

"We mean—" said Evie.

But I put my palm down on the table calmly. "No," I said quietly. "We mean gone. As in passed away."

"Well, *shit*," she breathed, then said quickly in stilted fashion, "I am sorry for your loss," then cradled her purse again.

We were silent.

For the life of me, I couldn't understand why she wasn't jumping up to leave. I could only conclude that the situation must have been so foreign that it completely defeated her relatively limited social skill set.

She frowned into her lap, then looked up. "How? Car accident? Kill himself?"

We shook our heads.

"Well, w*hat* for Pete's sake? Just died? That sucks."

Karen said, "All we're trying to do…We're just trying to piece together some stuff so we understand what was going on. There are a few gaps."

"But I don't get—what makes you think—"

Karen cut her off. "Security footage. At his office building. Elliott Tower?" She showed her a photo on her phone.

"Shit. That guy? Yeah, I remember him. That guy. I saw him a few times."

I winced, and Evie said quickly, "We don't want to know about that—"

"Oh, for Chrissake," she spat in disgust. "Listen, I can tell you jack *shit* about this guy. The manager here is my friend," she added, averting her eyes, not even fooling herself.

"We owe you a drink." Karen caught the server's attention. "Let's get you a drink. What would you like? You're really helping."

This mollified her. "Double vodka tonic," she said.

Without a word, Karen smiled up at the server, a smile that telegraphed *Quickly*.

"You guys are, like, really creeping me out. I wish to God I could smoke in here." She looked around. "God, I really need a smoke. Don't have any left though."

Karen drew a five out of her wallet and laid it on the table. "This is for a pack afterward."

She eyed the bill on the table. "It's more than that."

Karen added another five and said, "We're just glad we can talk to you. We're glad you gave us a minute. It's been a relief somehow, you know?"

"Hey, that's way more than enough." She drew the bills toward her with an index finger, then stuffed them away. "Thanks. It's just, it was more than five." She sat back a little, recrossing her legs but still clutching the handbag. I started wondering what she had in it. "Well," she said, flattered. "Kinda like closure, huh? I get it." She eyed the drink, which had just arrived.

"Exactly. Closure. Big help. Do you think you can remember when you might have seen him last?"

"God. Who knows? Been a while."

"Maybe…mid-January?" Karen suggested.

"Second week of school," I said. "January seventeenth. A Tuesday. In the evening." I looked up to see her staring at me.

"Shit," she said slowly. "You mean…?" She looked from one to the other of us. "Oh…my…fucking…God," she croaked. "You're shitting me." Then she bolted half of her drink. "I gotta go. I got nothing to do with this. Ab-so-fucking-lutely nothing. He was fine when I left."

"We *know*," Evie said firmly, reassuringly. "It's *okay*. We know you've got nothing to do with—it. We're just trying to get an idea… Do you remember anything specific? Did he look okay? Anything."

"Please don't," I whispered. "Don't go."

She eyed me and took another slug.

"Anything," said Karen. "Listen, this has nothing to do…This is totally private. My friend never said anything about…She recognized you from the security camera just 'cause she's seen you around. This is just totally for her peace of mind."

Evie leaned forward. "I mean, think about it. It's not something she wants anyone to know about."

"Yeah, I get it. I get it," she said. Then she screwed up her eyes. "Okay, fuck. I'm thinking."

"That's great." Evie nodded. "Take your time. Anything you remember—"

"Yeah, yeah." She flapped her hand. "I'm thinking. Really. I'm thinking." She picked up her glass, frowned at it, took a small sip.

"I do remember, and I'm not making it up. I remember, because—I'll tell you why—he was nice. He walked me to the door. Like a gentleman." She shot me a glance, hurtling on. "Okay, yeah, this time it was really late. He stood at the door, and I said, 'You look tired. You should go home now, get some sleep. It's late.' I mean, it was late. And he kind of stood there in the doorway and he, like, rubbed the side of it with two fingers and made a little face and he said, 'I've got to go'—no." She shook head, remembering. "He said, 'I'd love to go home to my family, but...I've got a lot left to do.' That's it. 'I'd love to go home to my family, but I've still got a lot left to do.' I shit you not. So then I told him, 'You're definitely a type A workaholic,' and left." She sat back and nodded. "Yeah. That's what he said. He never called me again."

My heart soared to the top of the dome, then plummeted like a flatiron and smashed in a bloody mess on the lobby floor. Here it was. What I'd asked for, right in front of me. Now it was mine forever.

"Listen, I am not shitting you," she said, after a moment, in formal tones. "I didn't make it up."

"I know," I replied.

"You do?" she blurted incredulously.

I nodded, sadly, at the woman sitting before me, who clearly had never, ever gotten anything in life but the short end of the stick. "Yes." I lifted my two fingers to touch an imaginary doorframe. "He always did that. We asked him, 'Why do you always do that?'" I turned to Karen, who was nodding. "And he made a joke, like, 'I don't know. In a past life I must have grown up in a shtetl.'"

Our gal said: "What's a shtetl?" and then: "Can I have another drink?"

Karen flagged the server again and made a crisp circle with her hand. He made no chitchat but hastened away, *Make mine a double* trailing pathetically behind him.

A lot left to do? Yes, of course there was a lot left for him to do. And the number one thing was to *talk to me*. Tell me what was going on, share his troubles, maybe before they got so bad and painful that the mistakes seemed like they were past fixing.

"Got kids?" she asked.

"Yes," I responded.

She nodded into her lap.

For no reason I could fathom, this woman had invested in us, if only for fifteen minutes. I felt like it had to do with something more than two vodka tonics and a pack of cigarettes, but I had no idea what. This was the thing I'd wanted, the thing I'd so desired, the thing I'd told myself would make such a difference. A gift, but an ugly one, wrapped in slime and dirt and ash, born with a caul—permanent, toxic, indecipherable.

The last word.

The first word came while I stood outside the Top of the Town Café in Springfield, Illinois, talking to John on my cell phone from inside that decommissioned phone booth, and he asked me to marry him. I saw it, flitting toward me in the sky, dancing over green treetops and past the gold-tipped courthouse dome sparkling in the sun, until it landed: *Yes.* That was the first word, the word that began it all, that started our life together. And now I had the last.

What good was it? How was it going to make anything better? What had I been thinking?

The server came back and switched out our drinks.

She reached out, faltered, looked at us. "That help?"

"You *betcha*," said Evie energetically, so the woman took ahold of her glass and drank.

Karen scrabbled a pen out of her purse. "Please," she said. "Say it again. I just need to remember."

She wrote it down exactly.

I would not have had the presence of mind. I would simply have said to myself, *Oh, of course I'll remember that, how could I forget?* But I would have. I would have forgotten. It would have flown right out of my mind like the tail end of a dream, and later, I would have agonized, *What was it—what was it exactly?*

"Thank you," I said.

She popped her lips again. "Well, shit," she said, then, "I think he looked kind of sad. I mean, about it," she rushed on, "about not going home." She looked down at the floor, around the room, then up into the skylight dome. "If it makes you feel any better, the guys who *really* hate their wives—they're the ones who have affairs." Then she looked straight at me, at everything about me—the expensive coat, minimal makeup, unmanicured nails, suburban purse—and her face hardened back up. "Well, here I am with the ladies who lunch. What the fuck do I care about you?" She drained her glass with a jerk and put it down a little too forcefully. "I don't ever want to see your fucking faces in my life ever again," she said, and marched off, clutching her purse.

Chapter 24

The Music Lesson

Miss Lindgren looked up at my tap on her open door.

"Ah, there you are!" she exclaimed, rising from her chair and advancing toward us with a brisk grace that was the hallmark of those long used to the stage.

"Thank you so much for making the time," I murmured as she took my hand and, despite the sense of bustle, enveloped me in an atmosphere so warm and tranquil, I fell in love instantly. *Pleasepleaseplease take my child*, I begged silently.

But she had already turned on this child the full force of her dimpled beam. "So, *this* is Grace!" she said, and put out her hand in the general vicinity in a manner so skillful, it made it inevitable Grace would choose to take it, upon which Miss Lindgren covered it snugly, as though netting a butterfly that had been gently coaxed to alight on her palm. "I'm *so* glad to meet you. I've heard such good things about you from Mr. Newell."

At this, Grace, who'd made no movement to extract her hand, pinked up and almost smiled, and I breathed an invisible sigh of relief. Getting her in the car for this meeting had been touch-and-go; these days my daughter said no to practically everything, even things she would enjoy and/or had previously been excited about.

Miss Lindgren led us farther into the room, a long, narrow space squeezed between two full-size orchestra rooms. One entire wall held the music library—forty feet of slotted shelves—and a small thicket of music stands was pushed into a corner for quartet rehearsals. But the collection of opera posters over the desk clearly marked the room as Miss Lindgren's demesne.

Grace put her hands back in her hoodie pockets, then took them out again and toyed with her visitor badge. "Are you from Sweden?"

"No, but I *am* Swedish. Here, let's take that off. You don't need to wear that in here. It's just in the way." Miss Lindgren took the lanyard, coiled it neatly, and laid it on her desk. "My parents are from Sweden," she continued, "and I spent every summer there with my grandparents. I have lots of stories to tell if you decide to take lessons from me. You should probably take off your sweatshirt, too."

"Do I have to? I want to keep it on."

I busied myself folding the map of the school into ever smaller rectangles while pretending to look out the windows at the far end of the room, which were wall to wall and ceiling height and showcased a row of very old maple trees along the sidewalk.

"Well—" Miss Lindgren put a finger to her cheek. "It *might* get in our way. Let's just take it off for a little bit at first, and then you can put it back on."

Compliance was immediate; clearly, this was a woman used to dealing with nervous adolescents. She took one end of the upright piano. "Mom, help me turn this around," she directed, and we maneuvered it on its squeaky wheels. "Thank you! And now—we'll be done in about twenty minutes."

I'd been trying to decide where to sit but recovered quickly. "Of course! Time for Mom to go! Have fun," I chirped to Grace. Her eyes slid away.

Out in the hall, I saw a folding chair, picked it up, and tiptoed back to the open door. I placed it out of sight and sat at attention.

Voices murmured; obviously, they were having a preliminary chat. My own teacher, my cello teacher, Mr. Baumgart, had been cut from sterner pedagogical cloth. Collegial warmth had taken years to earn. But this was the twenty-first century, and times had changed.

I stood up and examined a bulletin board. The orchestra had just done *Pictures At An Exhibition* at their spring concert, and the musical this year would be *Into the Woods*.

Chords were struck. I folded my arms and stared through the glass-windowed fire doors to the stairwell, listening to warm-ups on "ah," ascending from root to fifth and back down, then repeating the full octave in triads. A couple of students came down the stairs and pulled a fire door open, and a snatch of piano scales from a practice room in the upper reaches momentarily escaped. The girls walked down the hall past me as though I were a lamppost and left the building. That door fell closed with a heavy *ka-chunk*, sucking in a swirl of pollen that added to the already-thick accumulation on the mat. At Saint Thomas, the children's elementary school, and Loyola High as well, youngsters always politely acknowledged parents they might see in the hall. I knew that for a fact. I liked Loyola, but Eastridge was our local public high school and happened to have one of the biggest and best performing arts programs in the Seattle area. At the beginning of the school year, Mr. Newell, the new and enthusiastic middle school choir director at Saint Thomas, had suggested we consider whether Grace might benefit from Eastridge's higher-caliber opportunities and to contact Miss Lindgren about private voice lessons. When I did, Miss Lindgren pleasantly enough declined to audition her, suggesting we bring her back in the spring before freshman year. At the time, Grace had found this prospect flattering, but lately, she'd become very hard to read.

Miss Lindgren had moved on to a five-note descending scale on "e-o-e-o-e," striking the chords with verve and singing along. She dropped out and Grace went on by herself. To me, she sounded like a bell, but Miss Lindgren stopped her. It was quiet for a moment. I heard Grace laugh, and then they began again, and the sound was even better. I couldn't resist and peeked in the door.

Miss Lindgren, her face animated with encouragement, was vigorously striking chords with both hands and then lifting one to describe a sweeping arc, like a chubby ballerina doing an arabesque. Grace stood with her back to me beside the piano, resting the fingers of one hand on the upright case. I couldn't see my daughter's face, and I suddenly realized why Miss Lindgren had turned the piano around. Chastened, I retreated to my chair. It became maddeningly silent again, a silence in which the lingering scent of floor wax, comfortable and familiar at Saint Thomas, took on an ominous aspect. I stood abruptly to get a drink of water.

The water fountain was in its own tiled niche near the retro-fitted stairwell fire doors with their honeycombed safety glass. I regarded the stream of running water for a moment. *Please don't say no. My daughter doesn't need that right now. She needs a yes. A yes, a yes, a big fat yes. She needs someone to say yes to her,* I prayed, then bent down to drink. The water was shiveringly cold.

Someone turned the corner at the other end of the hall and walked briskly toward me with a clipboard under his arm. He wore trendily oversize horn-rimmed glasses and had a comb-over verging on the drastic, signaling someone with a long-past background in musical theater aiming for an un-tweedy academic look. As he drew abreast of me with a pleasant smile, "Oh, What a Beautiful Mornin'" came belting out of Miss Lindgren's open door in an unaccompanied mezzo-soprano, displaying the acoustics of the wide, empty hallway to terrific advantage. He stopped in his tracks.

"My God! Who *is* that?" he exclaimed in a stage whisper, beckoning conspiratorially as he took a few steps back, leaned to look in the doorway, then straightened up and repeated, with widened eyes: "Who *is* that? How come I don't know her?"

I put a finger to my lips to tame a smile. "That's my daughter. Grace Halvorsen."

"What year is she?"

"She's not in high school. She's graduating eighth grade."

"Ah, that explains it!" He clapped his clipboard to his chest and pumped my hand. "I'm Dr. Franchini, and I'm chair of the music and drama department here at Eastridge, and let me just say I'm looking forward to working with your daughter."

Maybe, maybe not, I thought. *All the other kids go to Loyola. We haven't decided yet.* Feeling it would be churlish of me to disabuse him, I merely nodded and murmured something nice about Miss Lindgren.

"Alma Lindgren is a *gem*. She doesn't usually give freshmen private lessons, but I can understand why she's auditioning this young lady. We've got...She's got...three girls graduating this year." He tapped a finger on his upper lip. "Two sopranos and an alto. So it's good timing."

Miss Lindgren stuck her head out the door and said sharply, "We're almost done. We're just going to do a little sight-reading."

Dr. Franchini lowered his voice. "Sorry to disturb, Alma," he said deferentially, and she gave us, but mostly him, a look and shut the door all the way. "Grace Halvorsen, I'll remember that," he said, nodding pleasantly, and left.

I paced the hall while Grace attempted "Voi, che sapete" from *Figaro*. I knew for a fact that Mr. Newell did very little sight-reading with the kids at Saint Thomas, and there was a lot of stopping and starting—that I could tell. Finally Grace poked her head out and said flatly, "We're done. You can come in."

Miss Lindgren was busy with paperwork. She neatly extracted one sheet from each of four folders and tapped them back in place in her file drawer.

"Now, Grace. I've explained to you what it would be like to study with me so you can decide, and now I'm going to tell your mother the same and give her the paperwork. Why don't you go return the visitor badges to the office and then come back?"

Grace gathered the lanyards. I could see that Miss Lindgren was waiting for her to leave the room. Nervously, I ran my hand along the top of the piano, looking out the window behind it, where the lowest maple branches, dotted with soft yellowy buds, bobbed gently in acknowledgment of the gusts outside. My mother had studied voice. She hadn't made a career of it, but she'd continued private lessons through our early childhood. I remembered hearing her practice while I played in my room. I'd hear the pitch pipe and knew she would begin to sing, and I'd continue with my dolls or blocks or crayons to the accompaniment of Italian arias, floating a cappella up the stairs.

The hall door closed. Miss Lindgren put the sheets down on her desk and leaned on them with one hand. "Well. Yes. How long have you known?"

I was startled, then saw the dimples. "Oh! Known. A while, I guess. I found out she had perfect pitch when she was about four. But her voice—it was my husband, actually."

She smiled encouragingly.

"Last winter, I guess. He came and got me in the kitchen and I thought something was wrong, but he took me halfway up the stairs. She was singing in the shower. 'Out of My Dreams' from *Oklahoma!* He said, 'I thought it was the radio, but then I realized it wasn't! That's good, isn't it? Tell me, that's good, right?' And I said, 'Oh boy, yes.'"

Grace knew all the tunes. She'd watched all the old musicals with her dad. He claimed it was because he was tired of watching Disney sing-along videos over and over, but I knew he had a secret weakness for classic musicals.

"He told me at New Year's, 'Don't forget, this spring Gracie's going to do that meet-and-greet with the voice teacher.'"

I blinked back tears. He'd called me from the office apropos of nothing, one January afternoon, just to remind me. "It's awhile yet," I'd said, and he'd reiterated, "It's not too early to get on her calendar."

I hadn't mentioned this to Grace, I realized. I should have.

I was full of things that I had forgotten to say.

Miss Lindgren cradled her laced hands against her stomach and regarded them pensively. "I am so sorry for your loss." Then she squared up the papers and slid them into a fresh Conn-Selmer music folder illustrated with shiny brass instruments. "This is a tough time for teenagers in general," she added, "even without losing a parent." Then she patted her hair and said, "I treat my students like the young adults they are. My relationship is with the student, and I would never say anything to a parent that I would not say in front of the student, but I'm making an exception in this case, right now." She handed me the folder. "She has a lovely instrument. Quite the potential. She is ready for lessons. I would like to teach her."

I nodded, thinking, *What's the "but"?*

"But. Lots of kids have talent. It's like anything. They have to make choices. You can't do everything. Whether it's sports or music or drama or debate. And they have to really want it. The decision has to be theirs. Otherwise it won't work." She reached out and put a finger to my cheek to stop me from nodding. "You're making me dizzy," she said, and we both laughed.

"There's something she has to work through. It might be the obvious, or it might be something completely different that neither of us has any clue of. I've worked with teenagers long enough to know that! So please be patient. She'll let you know if and when. They can't be rushed. Because I'm telling you, she has promise."

Grace reappeared, and Miss Lindgren pivoted gracefully. "So, your mom has the parent contract, student contract, tuition sheet, and the studio expectations. Miss Halvorsen, it was a pleasure to meet you. You just let me know. If you're going to go to Loyola, I'd have to give you lessons at my home studio in Ballard on Saturdays. So bear that in mind."

We left and were buffeted along the row of maples toward the parking lot. Grace bounced a fist lightly on top of a waste can at the corner, then got in the car and shut the door quickly.

I put the keys in the ignition. "Well," I began, but she cut me off.

"I just want to go home." She pulled up her hood and buried her hands in her pockets.

Suddenly I wanted to cry. To hide it, I pulled the water bottle from the door pocket and took a sip.

"I don't know why she's a Miss and not a Ms. That's kind of dumb," she said as I pulled out of the parking lot.

After a few more chilly blocks: "She was just being nice to me."

I looked out my side window and tried for a neutral tone. "I doubt that. She told me you had a lovely voice."

In response, she swiped the folder off the dashboard and tossed it into the back. Then she shrank down even further in her seat, squeezing against the door as though trying to meld with it. A front air bag probably wouldn't have even made contact.

"She made me sing in *Italian*. Why did she do that? I don't know Italian. It was too hard. She only went through the words once. I didn't even get to start just doing it on 'la' at first. I totally screwed it up."

Tryouts were really scary in high school, I reminded myself. And she wasn't even in high school.

"*And* she's not from Sweden."

We approached the drive-through Starbucks at Highlands, and in a sullen voice, she asked, "Can I have a berry refresher," more as a statement than a question. I tightened my lips and made the turn.

The sugar seemed to revive her, because after a few minutes she elected to speak again. "You know what? Her mom, like, got sent from Sweden to Seattle to stay with her aunt and uncle for a year of high school, and then, like, when she got there, they said, 'Don't come back.' Because of—the war—" She hesitated.

"World War II?"

"I knew that."

"Of course you did."

She slotted her obscenely large plastic cup into the holder on the console between us. "Mom. You do the *Civil* War in eighth grade. I know *that* war. You don't do World War II until high school."

"I wasn't saying anything, honey. It's just there were a lot of wars, and it's hard to keep them straight—" But she ignored me and plowed on.

"So, anyway, so, like, she never even lived with her parents again, because then she went to *college* in Seattle, and then she got *married* and stuff."

"That's too bad. But she did see them again, didn't she?"

"Yeah. She did." Forced to reveal this pedestrian ending, she deflated for a moment and played with her hoodie strings, then sat back up. "The point is...the point *is*, why Miss Lindgren spent all her summer vacations in Sweden with her grandma was 'cause her mother *sent* her there. 'Cause she had to *work*. I mean, at a real job. She was a single mom. Her dad died when she was five. He was some Swedish dude her aunt and uncle picked out for her 'cause they had clubs and, like, neighborhood Swedish stuff, but they really loved each other, and when he died she *never* got married again the whole rest of her life and never had any more kids, just Miss Lindgren."

That was a long speech, and I was not going to presume I understood what was behind it. The possibilities were legion. Miss Lindgren was absolutely right: You never really knew what was going on in their heads once they hit puberty and decided you weren't up to date enough to merit serious conversation.

Grace took a long pull on her drink. Chin in hand, she gazed out the window: Binnegan's Toys, Saint Sandwich, Bad Habit

Burgers, the 28 Shop. We'd been in every one. The refresher was so pink, it was practically fluorescent, as radioactively pink as children's amoxicillin, which John had once gotten all over his jacket lapels trying to help me administer to Grace when she was two. It was the first dose for strep, and she was screaming in pain. It was definitely a four-handed affair.

When I was sure nothing more was forthcoming, I said, "That's very sad, I'm sorry to hear that," but got no joy of it.

It seemed so long ago that I'd fought my way out of an abusive marriage by rediscovering my voice. I'd assumed that, forever after, as long as I stayed true to that, then all would be well. But I was wrong and was being actively and repeatedly reminded of just how wrong every day since my husband died. I kept saying the wrong thing, hitting the wrong notes, sometimes even playing from entirely the wrong piece of music.

We went through two stoplights in complete silence, then left the stores behind us and turned onto a smaller road through a large tract of old growth that had yet to be developed. It was long and arrow-straight, with a deep, well-mown drainage ditch on each side that held back the encroaching woods and kept the horsetails at bay.

"Your dad knew you were going to see Miss Lindgren," I ventured. "He reminded me to make the appointment, actually. He was excited about it. He was all over it, honey. He told me, 'Don't forget!'"

"What-*ever*," she muttered.

"Daddy knew you were going to do this," I persisted.

"Can't you ever just shut up?"

"Well, honey—"

She turned, rewarding me with a close-up and unmediated view of her fury. "Shut up, shut UP, SHUT UP!" she cried, pounding a hand on the dashboard each time to accompany her violent crescendo.

So I did.

I just kept driving.

I had so many stories to share, so many songs to teach. About her grandmother and the pitch pipe. Her father, dumbstruck by her voice in the shower. But what do you do when your daughter is thirteen and doesn't want to hear it? She'd throw them back in my face. How old had I been when I started having adult conversation with Bobbie? Seventeen? Grace was too young. But now was when she needed hear this. I was a married woman when I lost my father; Grace was only a child. It wasn't her fault.

I opened the window an inch, letting her encapsulated fury flow out and fresh air flow in. Then, in my mind, I took hold of my cello, neck in left hand, bow in right, and started in on Ravel's *Pavane for a Dead Princess,* filling the space with music instead. Hands on the wheel, I concentrated intensely.

The initial phrase was softer the second time around, so more difficult—forte was always easier than piano. But it wasn't just a repetition. No. It was more. It was something else altogether. It was its own thing. You had to listen, closely. There was so much mutability in the circumstances if you really, really listened. Then you could hear all the differences. It wasn't identical. So few people realized this! Because the notes on paper looked the same. It was difficult to get across. Impossible? I looked at Grace, frantic with urgency. It was important to get this right. Every note was part of the bridge of sound. Maybe I'd failed with John, but I couldn't fail with Grace. I wished I were better. I wished I were a better musician. Because it wasn't the same river twice. The phrases were, at one and the same time, identical and completely different. I was not the same as Karen, and Grace was not the same as me. And if I—if *she*—could understand this, then she would be free in the world and could exercise her gift. Who was she trying to measure up to? She was good enough, even if she didn't feel like that after her tryout. She was her own person, her own artist, and that was good enough.

I pulled into our driveway, up to the kitchen door, where the wisteria was now in flower on the arbor, and I turned to her, to try again, but she was already unbuckling her seat belt, and as soon as the car stopped moving, she was out the door and running into the house.

Chapter 25

Easter Parade

GRACE SEATED HERSELF AT THE TABLE WITH EXAGGERATED primness. "Paper place mats? I thought you said this was a nice place. A *real* restaurant." She waited a beat, then turned to me. "How is this different from fast food?"

I smiled an apology at the patient hostess, who handed us our menus and left.

"We're on the Olympic Peninsula, Grace," Nathan snapped. "Put a cork in it." Grace harrumphed in response, then dropped that tack; instead, she folded her arms on the table and propped her chin on her hand the better to display sophisticated ennui as she drawled, "Oh my God. What's with the ginormous empty bird feeder collection?"

"Stop," I hissed. We'd had a great day, capped by Frisbee on the lawn after check-in, so I could only guess this performance was due to the fact I'd just said no to Chicken Licken for dinner, because the nearest Chicken Licken was fifty-three miles away and I was not going to make a ninety-minute round trip for a fast-food dinner.

I looked around the long, sunporch-style dining room with timbered shed roof and beadboard walls. Admittedly, Meriwether Lodge fell into the category of "rustic." I thought it was charming.

And the boys certainly weren't complaining. But Grace clung to her sulk for the entire meal. Afterward, she sequestered herself in ostentatious solitude at the puzzle table in the rustic lobby, away from the tempting sofas in front of the fireplace to which the rest of the family had instantly gravitated.

I made one attempt to join her, but when she saw me coming, she pointedly got up and left. Hoping no one had noticed, I returned to the sofa and my knitting and gratefully watched Nathan play pick-up sticks with Jackie on the coffee table, which was a four-inch-thick slab of western red cedar trunk.

It may not have been Chicken Licken. Chicken Licken may simply have been a stand-in for other, secret, outrageous complaints impossible for an obtuse parent to intuit and therefore hopelessly unresolvable, therefore unresolved, therefore triggering the inevitable downward spiral into the dark mists of adolescent futility and gloom.

The next morning, as the hostess ushered us to yet another table by the window, I sensed her winding up again and headed her off at the pass. I'd had a sleepless night punctuated by bad dreams and was in no mood.

"Whatever you're about to say, don't."

She gave me a withering glance and plopped into her seat.

She was only a teenager. How could I blame her for the dashing of my own expectations for this trip? Initially they hadn't seemed unrealistic. Things had augured well from the start. The sun appeared as soon as we left the metro area and, unusually, shone brilliantly all day long. The two-hour car ride hummed along pleasantly. Next to me in the front seat, Nathan slapped percussion on his knees while playing for us, at acceptable volume, a custom mix tape that included such time-tested crowd pleasers as the Gorillaz's "Superfast Jellyfish" and the theme song from *The Good, the Bad and the Ugly*. In the back, Grace looked out her window, thoughtfully but not unhappily, and Jackie busied himself with his shoebox full of Lego, using the lid as a tray.

I'd wanted something to get us out of the house on the holiday weekend, and the Elwha had occurred to me. The Glines Canyon Spillway Overlook had opened over the winter. I thought it might help, somehow, to return and see how things were moving forward since the day almost three years ago that we'd gone to watch the removal process. John had hoisted Jackie on his hip, explaining how dams worked and what was about to happen, and how I had been a part of it: "This is what Mommy does." After the blast, he'd cried excitedly, *My mommy blows up dams! My mommy blows up dams!* to much amusement in the general vicinity. This he would remember.

At the very least, it would keep us, for two nights, from being marooned, each in our own part of the house, isolated, plugged into our own digital devices.

So we'd stood at the overlook and watched the restored Elwha release out of the wide valley that had been Lake Mills into the deep narrow canyon that was now, once again, a flowing river. We'd walked the trail down onto the former lake bed. I'd explained the process of ecosystem restoration to the best of my ability, courtesy of the education I'd picked up at Rivers Northwest: In this valley, the river would find its own way. It might be different from its former path, the channels would change, but that was all right. It would take its own time.

"We're going to see a lot of robins," I explained. "They favor what's called 'early-stage' habitat. They're bringing in lots of seeds and stuff that's going to grow. Then the mud flats will fill in. In a month this place will be full of lupines. They were planted on purpose a couple of years ago because they nourish the ground and help other plants grow."

As we stood at the water's edge, I spotted a small, flat black stone and instinctively reached down, remembering as I did so my childhood summers on Lake Michigan, walking along the beach with my friend Laura during day camp, combing the water's edge for skipping stones. She'd dipped a black one in the water and tipped it back and forth in the sun, to show me all the colors. "Look! See? It's the black ones that have the rainbow in the stone," she'd said.

I did the same now with my children, and they exclaimed over it. Grace had even pocketed the stone. *Thank you, Laura.*

Our waitress arrived. Older, grandmotherly, clearly a regular and not a seasonal employee. Catching Grace's look, she nodded at the window. "I know, I know. We just opened back up this weekend after winter closure, hon. We haven't gotten around to filling those feeders yet. But, boy oh boy, you should see those hummingbirds when we do. They're all over them like white on rice." She rested the water pitcher in one hand. "Will you want coffee?"

"White on rice," chirped Jackie. "What's white on rice?"

"Yes, please," I said, "and two milks over here."

"I don't want milk," Grace said flatly.

"What's with the no-milk thing?" Nathan scoffed. I could tell he was getting a little irritated with her irritation.

"It's not *good* for you. It thickens the mucus in your throat. It's bad for singers."

I gave her a look that was too quick and too interested, so I got the back of her uncombed head. I turned to Jackie. "Oh, my! Look, Jackie. I think there's something underneath your chair!"

He scrambled down and pulled out a Seattle's Best Chocolate deluxe Easter basket which, sleep-deprived though I was, I had actually carried all the way into the dining room in a brown paper grocery bag and passed to the hostess completely unnoticed by the children, who, being children, paid absolutely no attention to anything that was not in front of their noses and didn't directly affect their immediate comfort or convenience.

"The Easter Bunny! The Easter Bunny!" he cried. The basket was so big that when placed on the table, its green woven handle reached the top of his head. This was *not* overkill, I reminded myself staunchly. We all oohed and aahed, even Grace, who ruffled his hair and said, "Lucky duck!"

Jackie bounced on his toes, peeling the colored foil off a tiny chocolate egg. "Mommy! How did the Easter Bunny know to come here?"

"Well!" I shook out my napkin with pleasure. "I *told* him! I told him that we weren't going to be home but we'd be here, at Meriwether Lodge, so he came here instead!"

A crease appeared in his brow. "Instead?"

"Yes! Instead. Remember I told you we were going on this trip Easter weekend."

"But—he came to our *house,* right?" The unwrapped egg was warming in his hand.

"Well, honey, he came *here*!" I said cheerily. I looked over at Nathan for assistance, but his face was peculiarly expressionless.

"The Easter Bunny didn't come to our house? But the Easter Bunny has to come to our house! He *has* to come," Jackie gasped, the words tumbling out as he sped from horror to panic to utter desolation: a six-year-old confronting the abyss. He slid over the edge and began to cry, and diners turned to look at the table where the mommy had made the little boy cry at Easter Sunday buffet brunch.

"Shut *up*, you baby!" Grace hissed.

Nathan sprang up, lifted Jackie, and put him on his lap. "Hey, hey, Jack-a-dandy, Mom didn't mean that!" He pressed his cheek against his brother's and shot me daggers at an angle. "Mom meant *yes*, the Easter Bunny *is* coming to our house. But later, 'cause he knows you're not *home* right now. And this, this"—he said, placing a hand reverently on the gaudy, oversize basket—"this is your *pre*-Easter basket! That he dropped off here because he knew you were here, right now, at breakfast time. He wanted you to have something right away."

Jackie, still clutching the chocolate egg, looked at me for confirmation.

"Yes, I meant he was coming here *in the morning* instead," I said, chastened. I leaned over and took out the package of jelly beans. "Hey! Can I have one of these?"

He nodded, and I ate a jelly bean, which I really didn't want, then gave one to Grace. Jackie immediately put the melting egg in his mouth to free his hand. "Me too."

"When we get home," Nathan went on, "the Easter Bunny will have come. He put us on the end of the route, see, because he knew we wouldn't be home till this afternoon."

"That's right," I said. "I got a little confused."

Jackie knuckled his eyes, getting melted chocolate all over his face, then inserted his thumb in his mouth.

I wet the tip of my napkin in my water goblet. Jackie took his thumb out and tipped up his face as I ministered to mouth, cheek, and hand, while Nathan affirmed, "That's right, buddy. This here is a pre-basket. You're the only one who gets one! You're special. Now. Why don't you and Grace go get your waffles?"

Grace had been watching, transfixed, bowled over by the recognition that someone else's needs, if only momentarily, outstripped her own. She now snapped to attention and took Jackie's hand, giving me an *are-you-noticing* look designed to emphasize how happy she was to cooperate with anyone who was not her mother, and off they went.

Nathan scooted in and leaned forward. "Mom, what the fuck?" It was all one word: *Momwhatthefuck.* His breath smelled like jelly beans.

"I told him!" I bleated. "I told him. He *knew.* He was okay with it," I insisted, but he only shook his head.

"I should have paid more attention. I should have been paying attention. You really fucked it up," he said, then leveled me with a Karen look. Manifestly; he'd inherited it. "What," he enunciated. "What. *Exactly.* Did you tell him?"

"That—that we were going to do something different. That we were going to take a trip and we weren't going to go to church."

"You *idiot!* Did you actually, specifically, *tell* him that the Easter Bunny was *not going to come?*"

I shook my head miserably.

"No! You didn't! You told him what you knew he'd like. That we weren't going to church. Because you knew he'd like to hear that."

I looked over at the buffet. The children were loading up on waffles. They seemed fine. The waitress delivered the one milk. She bore the coffeepot as well, but when she saw my face, she had second thoughts and retreated. I pleated my napkin in my lap.

"Mom. Mom. Look at me. You didn't tell him the Easter Bunny was not coming to our house. Because you *knew*—you *knew* that was wrong."

"But I thought we'd be better off with a change. Right now. Wasn't it good for us to do something different?"

"We? You. *You* couldn't do it. But he needs that. So does she, by the way, even if she won't admit it. You're the grown-up. He's the kid. You have to do what he needs. Which is that everything stays the same. And we've got to give it to him. So we're gonna to have to figure out how to do that."

"Okay," I said. "I can borrow Karen's eggs and reuse them. But what about everything else? Should we stop at a grocery store? They'll probably have stuff left."

"It's gotta be the good stuff. Just like every year." He sat back and pulled out his phone. "I'm gonna have to mop up after you here."

Sensing the moment had passed, the waitress homed in again.

"Bit of excitement," she remarked, nodding at the basket while she poured my coffee.

"Yes. Well. We got a little overwrought."

"Kids and holidays. I remember. My husband used to say, 'As long as nobody throws up or bleeds from an open wound, we're ahead of the game.'"

Nathan turned over his cup and gave her a charming smile. "I guess I'll have some of that, too. She's driving me to drink."

"Those waffles are going to fix everything up, I guarantee." She smiled back.

Nathan stirred in copious amounts of cream and sugar, while moving his phone around in the air with the other hand. "Wi-Fi sucks here. I can't get any bars."

"You have to go out in the lobby—" she began.

"—I know, and stand under the portrait of Calvin Coolidge by the brochure stand."

"Trust a teenager to have that figured out, right?" The waitress chuckled. She gave my shoulder a gentle pat as she left. I felt absurdly grateful.

"What is it you're trying to do, anyway?" I asked Nathan.

"Find a Seattle's Best Chocolate that's open. Today. On a Sunday. On a major holiday." He stood, lifted his cup overhand, took a hasty slurp, then left.

The kids returned. Grace's plate was double-piled with waffles topped with so much fruit she had to carry a separate little bowl of mucus-producing whipped cream to avoid a landslide. Rail-thin, long hair unbrushed—a recent campaign to annoy me—and solemnly delighted, she looked for all the world like the Little Match Girl after she'd struck the second match.

"Oh my goodness!" I blurted. "People are going to think I don't feed you," then wished I could swallow it back as I saw her face fall.

I stood up abruptly and escaped to the buffet, where Nathan, mission accomplished, joined me and assembled his own heaping plate: scrambled eggs crowned with a log cabin of bacon strips. Two waffles were wedged in at the sides as an afterthought. I looked at it, opened my mouth, shut it again, and he gave me a toothy grin.

We ate our meal in a not-unpleasant silence as rain drilled down outside the windows and beat on the roof, which made things feel cozy. Nothing makes children happier than sitting in front of a full plate of hot food, and as for me, scrambled eggs, a couple of links, and coffee, especially after little sleep, made everything right with the world. Memories of the night began to fade, a night spent wallowing in self-pity while staring at Grace in the other bed—her back resolutely turned to me even in slumber—and wondering why in the hell I was spending money on therapy for her because clearly it wasn't working.

Departing diners stopped by our table to admire Jackie's basket, which pleased him no end, but after the first sympathetic smile in my direction, I avoided eye contact. They all probably thought I was divorced.

Unlike her possibly less discriminating brothers, Grace had made less headway on her meal. She was prodding her waffles with a look of dissatisfaction. A small, soggy peach slice flipped off her plate and landed on the table.

"We're not wasting food, are we?" I said archly. What was her problem? And Karen wanted *me* to go into therapy? And Mardie and Suzanne had agreed! They were all ganging up on me.

"They're not *like* Aunt Karen's. We always have waffles at Aunt *Karen*'s on Easter after church. I didn't *know* what they would taste like. Hers are better."

I shot a quick glance at Jackie, but he was in the initial, quiescent stage of sugar coma, eyes glazed, mopping up a last bit of syrup by hand with a leftover piece of waffle.

I took a tiny square, dipped it in the puddle on his plate, and popped it in my mouth. "You're absolutely right. Hers *are* better," I said brightly, then produced the room keys. "Why don't you kids go brush your teeth and put your stuff together?"

They left, Jackie hugging the basket like a newborn puppy. Once they were out of sight, I made a beeline for the lobby. In the library corner, I pulled out my phone, and dialed Karen's number.

Pick up, pick up, pick up! I willed, staring out the window at the sodden lawn rolling down to the concrete brink of Hood Canal, where a clutch of Adirondack chairs were perched, catching the rain.

Suddenly there she was. "Happy Easter!" she said, in a voice so cheerful it robbed me of speech.

I turned away from the view. The shelves built into the wall were stuffed with books, clothbound in a previous century. I ran my finger along the mildewing spines as though searching for a particular title, or perhaps a hidden spring. Maybe there was a secret door. It would pop open and I could disappear.

"Take your time, Kimmie. I'm listening."

I emitted a sound like the mewling of a kitten, then coughed, then said, "I think I need to see a therapist."

"Okay," she said in the placating voice we'd employed with our toddlers, back in the day.

"No, no, I really mean it now! I *mean* it this time—"

"Yes, okay," she said quickly. "We can do that! Good idea."

I plunged a hand into my hair. "Am I interfering with you famous waffles?"

She went on reassuringly, "No, no, we're done. I'm all yours." After a moment of silence, she ventured further. "Sounds like things aren't going as well as you'd hoped."

I let go my grip on my scalp and swiveled to make sure no one was within earshot. Then I pressed myself into the bookcase, cupped my hand around the phone, and whispered fiercely, "You can say that again. I am absolutely *the* worst mother on the face of the earth. And I fuck *everything* up."

She chuckled gently. "You know, we all get to say that once in a while, but I think you've used up your quota for the rest of the decade."

She was not going to take me seriously. Even if I swore. I sat down at the infamous puzzle table and ran my hand over the surface.

"Tell me *one* nice thing that's happened on this trip," Karen coaxed. "Just one."

I put my palm on a cluster of jigsaw pieces and shifted them idly, then realized someone had organized them, perhaps even Grace, and shifted them back. "Okay," I said. "It was sunny yesterday."

"Awesome! Pretty lucky for the Olympic Peninsula. Okay. How about another?"

"We went on a hike and nobody whined," I dredged up. "During the hike, I mean."

"The whole hike? Congratulations! Okay. Just one more."

"Well. Okay. Jackie liked his pre-Easter basket," I admitted.

"What's a 'pre-Easter basket'?"

"Long story. But here's the deal. The real reason I'm calling is because the Easter Bunny *has* to come to my house when we get back, so I need to borrow your eggs."

I didn't need to draw her a picture. She was already there. "Sure! I've got three dozen. Boxed and in the fridge." Karen always packed her eggs away immediately, so we could have leftovers of egg salad, which she and I ate like dip with pretzels, whereas at my house, baskets with spoiling hard-boiled eggs adorned bedroom dressers for weeks, like Miss Havisham's moldering wedding cake. I just couldn't bring myself to rob the baskets, and the kids didn't like egg salad anyway; Karen and I were the only ones who ate the leftovers.

"I can go in and do it for you before you get home, if you want."

"No, that's okay. You don't know all the special places. Just stick them in the fridge, and I'll run in and do it quick before Jackie gets in the house."

"What about the rest of the booty?" Karen asked. "Can you stop at a grocery store somewhere out there? There'll probably be leftover stuff."

"We have to go to SeaTac. Apparently the airport is the only place where a Seattle's Best Chocolate is open on this day. It's got to be exactly the same candy as we always get. This is what my seventeen-year-old parenting expert has impressed on me."

She sighed. "Yeah. God. Listen, Kimmie. It's a tough gig, but you're doing a good job. The day is going to end well, and that's what they'll remember."

A young family walked past me: mother with baby on her hip, father carrying a duffel, and a very small boy proudly towing his own wheeled suitcase behind him. With a stab I remembered those teensy wheeled suitcases. Hardly big enough to hold a pincushion, but the kids had loved them so much. I felt like a bicycle missing a wheel, and all the reassurance I'd gotten from my sister drained away. But she'd already hung up the phone.

THE RIDE HOME WAS DEADLY quiet for the first half hour. In the front seat, Nathan registered his in-it-but-not-of-it prerogative by wearing headphones for an exclusively personal listening experience. In the back, Jackie had fallen asleep, likely out of sheer nervous exhaustion. Grace was hunched over her phone.

I glanced in the rearview mirror and caught her delicately removing the basket handle from Jackie's limp grasp. She wedged the prize securely against his booster seat, then pulled the edge of the train quilt over his arms. My heart leapt, and I tried to formulate a benign, casual "thank you," but when I looked again, she was snapping photos of him with her smartphone. His little head was lolled back and turned toward her. His closed lids stretched like delicate membranes over big, long-lashed eyes, and a tiny drop of moisture trailed from the corner of his mouth onto his soft pink cheek.

Click-click-click, she went, then, with a maddeningly gleeful smirk, began furiously typing with her thumbs.

"Hey!" I whispered. "Stop it! Remember the rule."

The rule was hard and fast: DO NOT EVER TAKE PICTURES OF SIBLINGS WHILE THEY ARE ASLEEP. AND POST THEM ON THE INTERNET. EVER.

Karen and I may not have allowed our crew to jump on the digital bandwagon until later than most, but once we did, we'd caught on pretty quickly.

She ignored me. I flapped my hand to get her attention, and she looked up with a scowl.

"It's just going to my friends," she whispered loudly. "It won't last. It'll disappear. I just want them to know where I am and what I'm doing. Don't you *support* that?"

She certainly had all the lingo now. It really was time for me to go into counseling, I guessed, if only so I could keep up.

"You mean, support breaking the house rules? Uh, no," I drawled, then quickly folded my lips in. *I take it back.* Too late. Now it was Mom who was breaking the rules, and this was a cardinal one: NEVER USE SARCASM WITH SARCASM-PRONE TEENAGERS. EVER.

Whatever came next was my fault, and come it did.

"What house? It's not the house anymore. There's no house. The Easter Bunny doesn't even come there."

Jackie shifted in his sleep. Beside me, Nathan pushed back one headphone with a quizzical expression.

"I didn't even want to go *on* this trip," she continued. "Olivia and Charlie went to see *Cinderella* this afternoon, and I couldn't go. It's almost out of the theaters. I'm always having to do stupid family stuff."

John would know how to talk to her. He was the one who could do it: retain objectivity, humorously deescalate. He'd treated Grace as an adult from the time she was nine or ten, whereas I'd never stopped treating her like a child. I realized now that I was trying to protect her from the world, but he was teaching her how to be *in* the world. He had the kind of relationship with her that I had with Nathan; maybe that was the way of it between fathers and daughters, mothers and sons.

Fathers and daughters. When John died, I lost something I'd already lost, but she lost something she'd had. For her, there had been no invisible shifting of tectonic plates, no insult to injury, no Original John and Recent John; for her, he was unchanged, steadfast. Loss upon loss. She was utterly bereft.

And not only did I have to sustain that John, for her, but I had to figure out how to give her all those things she'd gotten from him but could no longer, from the toddler clutch of wild-flowers, to the movie musical popcorn and snuggles, to the funny bunknotes sent to Camp Nemahbin. Obviously I couldn't fill that void, but I had to try. *That* was my job; pursuing detective work to satisfy my own childish purposes was not. The realization hurt like hell.

Meanwhile, Grace was not going to stop flaying me. "This was the stupidest trip ever. You thought it was going to be some kind of *bonding* experience, and it was all a load of"—she hesitated as Nathan removed the headphones entirely and turned around—"a load of bullshit."

My hands tightened on the wheel. Nathan put a restraining fingertip on my arm and glared at her.

"Bullshit," she repeated. "And *you* know it," she spat at Nathan. "*You* just won't say it. Mom, you suck. All your ideas suck. This whole trip sucked." She grabbed her backpack and rummaged in it blindly. "I missed *Cinderella*. We missed everything, even Aunt Karen's waffles. Which you can't even make. Cuz you're so lame. You're like so 'wah-wah-wah, look at poor me!' All your ideas are lame. And I'm *not* going to take stupid voice lessons." She jabbed her hand into the front seat to make sure we saw the small black stone on her palm, then flung it out her window. "You and your stupid rainbow!"

I started to weep.

"Pull over," Nathan said, low and fierce.

"I'm sorry," I pled, scrabbling for a tissue in my jacket pocket. "I can't take it anymore!"

"Mom! Pull over."

I did so at the nearest approximation to a shoulder I could find, a track that had been worn into the ground for the mailbox at the foot of a paved driveway. Nathan removed Grace from the car and gave her a lecture by the back bumper. When I craned around, he caught me looking; holding Grace in abeyance with one arm, he stuck his head in the open door. "I'm not done," he said fiercely, then to her: "Stay here."

Amazingly, providentially, Jackie was still sleeping.

He got back in the front seat and turned toward me, gathering his limbs and folding his hands. "*You* can't take it anymore? *You* can't? *I* can't take it anymore. This shit stops *here*. I have to get good grades because Stanford is going to look at *all* my grades. Not just the SATs. I'm not gonna let anyone, or anything, fuck that up for me. Pull it the fuck together and stop babbling like a baby every time your thirteen-year-old daughter hurts your feelings. She's a teenager! She's acting like a teenager! Get over it! When *I* did teenage shit, you never batted an eye. When she does it, you go bat-shit crazy or you get all weepy. Can't you just pull it together?"

I folded the tissue in half and wiped my nose again. "Yes," I whispered.

He reinstalled Grace.

Shame washed over me. I'd read the books Karen gave me. I wasn't supposed to let this happen—let the child become the parent. I snuck a glance at Nathan, who was putting his head-phones back on. He met my eyes and clapped his hands softly on his knees. "Let's boogie. Next stop SeaTac, to buy the fucking Easter candy. And yes," he said, breaking into a wide grin, "you owe me big-time."

I DREAMED A DAM BROKE and John was washed out to sea. Jackie and I scanned the horizon anxiously and finally saw him float back in, miraculously unhurt. But he wouldn't look me in the eye, so I knew the marriage was over. "But we *didn't* get a divorce!" I cried aloud, still tangled in the nets of the dream, and woke myself up. I was on the couch in the den, with Jackie, wrapped in his blanket, wedged against me at the other end, napping peacefully.

I looked at my phone. It was still Easter Sunday. 5:03 p.m. Three texts from Karen. I texted her back a smiley face, then made my way into the kitchen, stepping over Jackie's eggs and candy, which were arranged in rows along the geometrical border of the Oriental rug. Then I brewed some coffee and called Bill. I couldn't raise him, but I slipped my phone into my pocket, filled two mugs, and headed up the hill. Socks greeted me halfway, tail wagging furiously, and escorted me to the top, where I found Bill already ensconced with Grace.

I gave him a mug, then turned to Grace and said cheerfully, "I'd have brought something for you, but I didn't know you were here."

"Was I supposed to get your permission? Do you want me to go?" She put her hands on the wide chair arms, but I didn't take the bait, just perched myself casually on the stump table and sipped my coffee with a benign expression, looking out at the next ridge west. The sun had not yet descended below the clouds, but the strip of clear sky above the horizon was there, auguring an actual sunset and another show.

"Anyway, I didn't *go* anywhere," Grace went on. "I'm just *here*." She leaned forward with a stick and drew hieroglyphics in the dirt. I sensed a private interchange lingering in the air.

After a minute, Bill rubbed his hands together. "Well!" he announced, and we both turned toward him. "It's good your mom showed up, Gracie. Because we definitely need to get her permission for this."

Grace's mouth opened slightly, but her expression was cautious.

"Yep." He nodded. "Mother, I think it's about time I took this young lady along on a trap run. I've been thinking about it lately. I think she's definitely old enough to do it and big enough to keep up."

Grace beamed, then looked back and forth between us, her excitement tempered with anxiety. Today, everyone but me knew best how to deal with my children, and I was going to have to accept that. I nodded, pretending to mull it over. Then I said seriously, "Nathan didn't get to go until he was fifteen, but if you think Grace can manage, I see absolutely no problem."

She gasped in delight, unconsciously clasping her hands together under her chin like a small child. "Can I go tomorrow, Uncle Bill? Mommy—can I go tomorrow? There's no school."

Bill glanced at me for confirmation. "Well, sure," he said.

"You'll need a good night's sleep tonight," I added.

I knew a ride-along with Bill was grueling, because John had told me so, right before he fell asleep in the bathtub. That Bill had invited him, a few years after we'd moved in, was a true indication they'd cemented a friendship. Bill didn't walk, he ran; he had a lot of territory to cover, a lot of gates to open and shut, a lot of traps to check: beaver, fox, bear. John had seen a bear that day, and the story was legend with the children.

"Why don't you go get all your stuff ready, honey," Bill said. "Lay it all out, and have your mom check it over. You're gonna need layers. Regular boots. I have waders if we need 'em," he called, but she was already running down the path.

I reclaimed my chair. In answer to the unspoken question in his twinkling yet sympathetic eyes, I raised an index finger and declared, "This was a day which shall live in infamy."

"So I gathered."

"Don't tell me. I don't wanna hear."

"I wasn't going to, so don't worry. I keep the secrets of the confessional," he said with a smile, indicating all of the great outdoors with the sweep of a hand. Socks jumped up, thinking he was going to throw a stick.

"Don't I know it," I said wryly. Socks turned in a circle and lay back down.

"So…do I need to go get that bottle of Lagavulin?" Bill chuckled.

"Not necessary and perhaps not advisable."

We settled back into companionable silence, sipping our coffee as the sun began to finger out beneath the long, padded lid of cloud. "I'm wishing John hadn't made such a big deal about the bear," I remarked. "I don't want her to be disappointed."

"I know. Don't worry. Nothing like a day out in the fresh air. I'll tire her out. It'll be a good time." He combed his beard. "To be honest, that was spur of the moment, but I have been thinking about it. She brought it up a couple of weeks ago. Don't know why."

More of the sun's rays escaped, slanting across the landscape. They'd been there all along, just withheld from us above the clouds. In late April they were pretty, but delicate. You could call them pitifully weak, or you could call them hopeful. I decided: hopeful. We watched the last rays ebb away, then stood up.

"Looks like we're having Chicken Licken for dinner tonight. You interested?"

He bent over, pretending to scrutinize Grace's scratchings in the dirt. "Might be. Just you guys?"

"Just us."

"Okay then."

In fourteen years, Bill had never once directly accepted an invitation. He always came in, as John called it, "sideways," showing up for a plate as we sat on the front porch after dinner, watching the kids tumble around, or sitting in the kitchen with some leftovers, keeping me company while I cleaned up after the foofaraw of a big holiday meal.

"So." I reached down and scratched Socks behind the ears. "You really like Chicken Licken? I'm just getting it to keep them happy."

He winked. "Not my favorite, but she doesn't need to know that. I don't care what's on the menu." He handed me his empty mug. "Give me a holler when it's time to come over, dear," he said, then started down the path with Socks at his heels.

"Bill," I called softly. He half turned, hands in pockets, and lifted his eyebrows.

"Bill," I said, "I love you."

He ducked his head shyly. "Love you, too, dear." He took his hands out of his pockets and made a gentle fist, clasping it with his other hand close to his heart, and gave it a small firm shake. "Love you, too." Then he turned and ambled off.

Chapter 26

The Girl Who Came in from the Cold

THE WEATHER ON EASTER MONDAY WAS CAPRICIOUS BUT mild: The rain showers didn't pelt, and the sunny moments stretched out languorously before the clouds knit them over again. I got the sense that after our trip to the Elwha, we were spent, but not unpleasantly so. We'd arrived somewhere: the other side of the first holiday without John. It was an achievement and a relief. The hushed atmosphere outside seemed to reflect the calm indoors. The boys busied themselves quietly, and I did desk work in the kitchen. I balanced the checkbook and ascertained I'd need to go full time in about three months, so it was time to broach that with Terri. Then I reviewed the kids' midterm progress reports, after which I started browning the ground lamb for dinner. I was almost done by the time Bill's truck rolled up to the kitchen door. Grace came in, kicked off her shoes, and made a beeline for the stairs all before the "hello" had died on my lips.

Bill tapped gently on the open door. "How you doin' today, dear?" He set Grace's boots down on the mud tray. They, and he, looked less than fresh.

I lifted my arms in an emphatic shrug, which spattered grease from the spatula onto the floor. I bent to wipe it up.

"She's okay," he said. "She'll be fine. She'll talk about it in her own good time."

"About what?" I grabbed the audio remote to turn off Handel's *Jephtha*, my current oratorio fixation. "Talk about what?"

"Her day. No big deal. It was a good day." He leaned over the saucepan. "That smells good."

"It's moussaka. I'm trying to think if I've ever given you that before."

"Don't think so." He sat down and palmed his head. "Say, I could do with a cup of coffee."

I set up the single-cup maker Karen had given me for Christmas. "By the way, I guess I really am looking for a kitten. Jackie just mentioned it a second time."

"I'll keep my eyes peeled," Bill replied, chin in hand, watching the machine in action. It was still a novelty; for it, he made an exception to his "no fresh coffee" rule.

"So. Was it a good bonding experience?" I joked.

"Just about." He laughed. "She's tuckered. Fell asleep in the car." The machine beeped. "You done now?" he asked it, then removed the mug and took the first sip. "Pretty good for fresh coffee. Okay, so moussaka. Which kind of ethnic food is that?"

"Greek, Bill. It's Greek food. All food is ethnic food to someone, Bill."

"Not American food. America's too young. I mean, what kind of ethnic food do we have? Nothing! Ethnic food comes from some ancient culture. Like…tacos."

I threatened him with the spatula. He ducked, then stood and gulped down the last of his coffee. "Well, time for my weekly shower, I guess."

After he left, I layered the lamb mixture in the casserole dish and covered it with tinfoil. Then I went into the front hall to investigate. I could hear the shower running. I hadn't always been a helicopter parent, but since being widowed I had to constantly monitor everyone's anxiety level. It kept me very busy. So busy, it was often hard to monitor my own. I folded laundry and carried it up to the second floor, by which time the shower was off and Grace's door was ajar. I hovered, but no sound came from within, so I went into Jackie's room.

He was lying on his bed, communing with the tie-dyed stuffed iguana reposing on his chest. His train quilt was swathed about head and shoulders. I laid his short stack of clothes on the dresser, next to his Easter basket.

"You put these away, Jack-a-Dandy, got it?"

"Mmm. Hey, look." Using only his wrist, so as not to disturb the iguana, he lifted the Paddington book tucked against his thigh. "I finished my chapters."

I checked the fore-and-aft bookmarks. "Good deal."

"What's for supper?"

"Moussaka."

"I don't like that. It's squishy."

"I know. Don't worry. I'm making you a hamburger out of ground lamb. A *lamb*burger."

"I'm hungry now. Can I have some crackers?" He scrambled off the bed but braked himself with a hand on the doorframe. "Did you ask Uncle Bill about a kitten?"

"Yes. He's thinking about it."

"Remember, it has to be a kitten that will get along with Socks," he said, and barreled away.

Grace's door was now open a little wider, but I wasn't going to press my luck. I set the basket down with a thump and opened the linen closet next door. This was my favorite room in the house because it smelled so good. It was lined with deep shelves on three sides, the bottom one high enough that children could sit under it and curtain themselves off with unfolded pillowcases. When they grew too big for that, it became a magic elevator. They made a sign and asked me to tack it up over the door, where it had remained for the ages. I'd only taken it down last year, but even then I couldn't bear to throw it away; I'd simply switched it to the inside. I felt for the brass pushbutton switch, pressed it, and stepped in, then looked up. There it was: ELEVADOR in rainbow block letters. I took my time putting the towels away.

"Mom?"

The metal switch had probably done the trick. It was loud.

I stuck my head in her door. Grace was sitting on the edge of her bed, hunched over her phone. "Hey there!" I said nonchalantly. "Can I drop off your laundry?"

"Sure," she said, giving me a quick glance. Her face looked pale, but perhaps only because her burnished gold hair looked black when it was wet. She had Karen's hair, thick and wavy, so detangling was a two-handed affair. She gripped hanks close to her scalp and worked on them quickly and efficiently from the bottom up, stopping once in a while to tap on the phone in her lap.

T-shirts, tanks, underwear. I stacked little piles on her dresser top, which was ornamented with the usual detritus of the middle school years: rubber bracelets, raffle tickets, Mardi Gras beads, animal-shaped pencil erasers so tiny an adult would need tweezers to pick them up. In back were a couple of framed photos—the daddy-daughter portrait and last year's cabin photo from Camp Nemahbin.

The daddy-daughter picture was the one from John's office. I'd given it to her after determining the one we'd recovered from the blackberry thicket was too damaged to keep. She'd accepted it wordlessly and put it in a drawer. That was a few weeks ago. Now I saw she had it back on display. I started a new mental file folder:

Good Signs

Put picture back out.

Let me in her room.

I ran my finger across the top of the frame and observed the thick rime of dust. She caught me at this and noisily expelled air from her lips, then flipped her hair over her shoulder and began tugging on the other side. *Whoops.* I picked up the empty basket and made for the door.

"Mom?"

I turned.

She put her brush down and tucked her hands under her legs. "Can I invite someone to sleep over on Saturday?"

"Sure." I took a small step back in. "It's opera night, so I'm feeding everyone. But maybe we'll just do pizza?"

"Oh! Opera night. That means I get to go to the matinee next weekend, right?" Her phone buzzed like a fly trapped between windowpane and screen. She caught it up, jabbed at it, then put it face down on her bedside table.

"Yes," I affirmed. "Matinee next weekend."

"Good."

I shifted the basket to my other hip.

"Mom?" She smoothed her hair behind her ears. "I wanna tell you something." She pulled the towel away from the foot of her bed to clear a space. I sat down and ran my hand over the ivory chenille. We'd redecorated her room a few years ago in pale colors: not girlie, but soft and welcoming. Neither of us had ever been one for pink and ruffles. The bedspread looked like the one I'd had in my own room as a child but was much flimsier. I'd bought it online, so how could I have known?

She sat back cross-legged against the pyramid of stuffed animals in the corner and tucked her hands under her ankles. She was not forthcoming.

I waited tactfully, looking around the room with a smile and avoiding direct eye contact. Then I saw a Band-Aid on the wall. "What's that doing there?"

"I can't remember," she said impatiently. "It's been there for, like, years." She made as if to rip it off, but I stayed her hand.

"No. You might pull off the paint. I'll work on it."

She subsided again and wrapped her arms around a bright red pillow in the shape of a giant candy lozenge. She had two more, one in yellow, one in green. Her collection of stuffies was the only bright spot of color in the room. We heard a car, and she craned out the window.

"Nathan," she announced, stating the self-evident, and I suddenly remembered John, long ago: "It's good our driveway is unpaved. When they start driving, they'll never come home late because they'll know we'll always hear them."

Grace went on: "I want to tell you. I think he should keep that car."

"Yeah. I was thinking that too." We'd been planning on buying him a beater of his own, but now I had one more car than I needed. "I think that's what we'll do. Makes sense."

Her phone buzzed again. She snatched it up and this time turned it off.

Nathan bounded up the stairs and stuck his head in the door long enough to say, "Don't worry, I'm going to do it right now." It took me a minute to realize he'd come back to mow the lawn before dinner, which I'd asked him to do that morning.

"Don't forget to tie those shoes!" I called after him.

Grace shut her door, then got back on the bed and added another Life Saver to her stack. She propped her arms on it and hugged her elbows. "It's not about the car. It's something different. But I don't want you to think I'm stupid."

"I won't."

She lapsed into silence.

I could see she needed a little prompting. "So how was the trap run?"

"Different than I thought."

"Well, you know it wasn't going to be exactly like when Daddy did it. Nathan said the same thing—"

She interrupted me. "No, no. That's not what I meant. I saw the bear. I *did* see her. It was just different than I thought it would be."

I saw it written clearly on her face: the anxiety was due less to fear her mother wouldn't take her seriously than to fear she wouldn't be able to explain herself. "Okay." I nodded, then looked away, down into my lap, chin in hand, thoughtfully, just listening.

"She wasn't big until she stood up…and then she was big. And it was scary because she was angry. Because she was stuck, and it hurt. Bill said, 'Don't be afraid; she's not going anywhere,' and I said, 'I'm not.'" She was talking smoothly now, fast. "And *he* said, 'She's the one. It's time now, so get behind me,' and I said, 'Wait.' And he stopped and looked at me and he said, 'The best thing to do right now is put it out of its misery. You understand that, don't you? She's a peeling bear. She's stripping the bark and killing the trees. I have to do it now, quickly. Remember, we talked about this in the truck, if this would happen.' I said, 'I know.'"

She leaned forward, entreating me. "I didn't know what it was going to be like. And I couldn't get out of it. It was too late. It was scary, but not because of that—it was scary because it was *real*. You know what I mean?"

I nodded soberly.

"It was real. So the only thing I could do—" She slowed, her voice no longer fraught. "The only thing I could do was to know what was happening." She sat back. "I just wanted there to be that…space. I wanted to have time to breathe. Between. Between knowing what was about to happen and it happening."

She sat back. Wonderment appeared on her face as she realized she was finding the words. And then, suddenly, softly, she bloomed into tears. They seeped up like a spring percolating to the surface after a long drought, a spring that visibly refreshened her whole being, washing away the dust, mending the earthen cracks. Her brow smoothed and her visage brightened but not back into that of a child. The waters were the same, but deeper. She was transposed into a new key.

She swiped her eyes with the palm of her hand and went on. "When it was over...afterward...the air was dead. Before, there was a lot of energy all around. And it was gone. Like muffled. But it was a peaceful goneness. I said to Bill, 'I'm sorry I made you wait so long,' and he said, 'What do you mean? It wasn't but half a shake.' Half a shake is what he said. I don't know what that means. What does it mean?"

"A shake of a lamb's tail," I said. "He meant really quick. No more than a moment."

"But it was longer," she insisted. "Mom—it was like an *hour*. I know. There was a long time between. I got to look at everything and see all the details for so long. I was just standing there. Breathing. Things were happening. All the trees and bushes and sky and stuff but also the bear. The bear was there and he—she—was angry, and I looked in her eyes and there was so much power coming out of her. The air was so bright. You could see the bright, like separately. You could see it like the air was quivery, striped but kind of see-through, and it made everything shine. It was all moving, not just the bear but everything around in the woods. And I was just there. It was a long time. It was *real*. I got to feel that and see it and just be...there."

I put an arm around her. "Yes," I said. "It was real."

She looked straight into my eyes. "I'm glad Daddy got to see that," she said softly. In the baby face I knew so well and could still see, a new expression shone through, calm, dignified, mature. I caught glimpses of the twenty-year-old, the thirty-year-old, I saw that face, I saw the future of her. It hovered and clung in wisps that were the opposite of shadow because they were made of light.

Then she buried her face in my shoulder and gave out a low, deep moan that racked my bones and began to sob in pure, unadulterated grief, not for herself, I could tell, but for him. That she was alive and he wasn't, that here was a man who died suddenly;

here was a man who had no time to prepare, who didn't get to say goodbye, wouldn't get to see his children grow up. "It's nobody's fault," she cried into my shoulder. "It just happened."

We sat there with our arms around each other even after she'd quieted down, rocking silently, and the awareness began to grow on me that I myself was in that space before something was about to happen. Grace's experience had been slower than slow, but mine was faster than fast; the next thought came quickly, unbidden—*what is it?*—and then it hit me. The realization: This was what John had done for her. His death had ushered her over a painful threshold on a tide of beauty; she stood now on the other side, a woman. This was his parting gift, one she wouldn't recognize for many years to come, and then, just as suddenly, I knew with absolute certainty how to answer the question I'd been asking myself since my heart smashed to pieces on the floor of the hotel lobby. He'd given her his gift, and small though it might be in comparison, I could give her mine.

I took the tissue box from her bedside and held it out. "Honey, I just found something out recently. Something nice. That I want you to know."

She pulled a handful and wiped her face. "Yeah. Okay."

"Remember I told you how the police officer said Daddy had some client appointments that night…that night. She had to go research that a little…"

"Because, because, she had to talk to people 'cause of Dad's phone got stolen and stuff?"

"Right." I hadn't been able to keep that from them, because I'd had a loudmouthed baby hissy fit about it on the phone without realizing my children were within earshot.

"And you thought maybe the maintenance guy was trying to put the blame on someone else."

"Yes. It took a little detective work, but we finally found this other person."

"You found them!" She sat up. "The last person to see Daddy. The very last person. Was he okay? How was he? Did he say anything? What did they say?"

Never was I more grateful for the incipiently developing conflation of the singular and plural personal pronoun. "Well," I said carefully. "So they had a meeting, and they said he was fine, and when they were leaving, they said 'It's so late! You look tired. You should go home to your family.' And this is what Daddy said. I wrote it down. He said exactly: 'I'd love to go home to my family, but I've still got a lot left to do.'"

Her eyes widened. She took in a deep, satisfied breath, then let it out. "Say it again!"

"'I'd love to go home to my family, but I've still got a lot left to do.'"

Another happy sigh. "Those were his last words! *Family* was his last words. That's us. He said family. He said *us*. We were his last words! Right? That was what he said. *We* were."

"Had to be." I nodded solemnly. "That was his last conversation before he...got sick. The last person he saw."

"Who was it?"

What do I say? Tell me what to say, I prayed. "A client," I said.

"But I mean who? What was their *name*? I mean, who *was* it?" She collected her damp hair, threaded it through her fingers excitedly. "This is an important person!"

"It was a woman. It was a woman who worked downtown and Dad was helping her with something. I actually don't know her real name because she wanted to protect her identity because of her legal problem. It was kind of embarrassing. I think she got falsely accused of theft or something. So I said okay. I mean, I wanted to respect her privacy."

Grace nodded, smoothing the ponytail back over her shoulder.

"I really just wanted to talk to her about Dad. I talked to her, and she was very nice. She said Daddy was the best lawyer she'd ever met. And he was a real gentleman. She was very sorry about everything. She was glad she could help."

It was all true, or mostly.

Grace took this in, looking at the floor, nodding thoughtfully, for some time. Then she looked up at me, crossing her arms and hugging her elbows.

"Mom? Mom. I want to take voice lessons. Can I still do that?"

I doubled over, hand clapped to my mouth.

It was over, just like that. Just like that, it was over. Over in more ways than one. I came back up quickly. I took my hand away from my mouth, so she could see I was smiling, and her look of alarm evaporated. I rocked a little bit, with a knuckle against my lip, regarding her, and then we just sat there, smiling at each other in great good humor.

Two women exchanging glances.

Finally I mastered myself. "Of course, absolutely," I said, in the most casual tone I could muster.

"Oh, good. So, Mom." She opened her bedside drawer and pulled something out. "Hey, look." It was the little black stone from the river.

"I thought—I thought you threw that away?"

"I was just faking it. To make you mad." She hesitated. "You keep it for a while now. We can share it." She laid it in my palm. "It's your turn."

"Oh, Grace," I said. "Grace. You *are* my rainbow in the stone."

Chapter 27

The Bargain

THAT NIGHT I DREAMED A YOUNG MAN CAME DOWN OUT of the woods. Not along the angled footpath from the saddle of the ridge, but straight down from the steep, thick woods right behind the house. I didn't know him; he was much younger than me. I thought he might have been looking for someone else, someone his own age, but he came for me. I was standing in the kitchen. He walked right up and presented his arms for a dance. In the dream I didn't know how, but he taught me, and it was a wonderful dance that got better and better as we swirled around through every room in the house. The kitchen, where the children when they were little would clap their hands in delight when we sashayed around the island; the living room, where he'd tell stories as they sprawled in their pajamas in front of the fire; and the dining room, where he'd never miss catching them when they surreptitiously disposed of their vegetables under the table. Then the front hall, where he'd come in the door after work every day and call, *Where's my beautiful wife?* Then up the wide stairs and into the bedroom, where he'd turn to me under the covers, afterward falling asleep with his hand anchored on my hip. We danced in every room of the house.

Now it was over. We were standing still. We'd waltzed all the way outside and down the porch steps to the patch of woods near the creek where we'd made love one night beneath a crescent moon when the children were away. This time the moon was full, the time we always liked, when you could almost see colors in the dark. The grass was already wet with dew. John stood tall and strong like Two Leggings in his portrait, rooted to the ground. I looked into his eyes and they were the eyes of the old John.

He said, *I don't know why, either.* I said, *I'm sorry, I didn't see...I didn't help...I could have...maybe...What if I'd*—and he said lightly, *Let's not play the "what if" game,* which he always said, and that made me laugh, and I put my head against his chest. He said: *I always loved you. I never stopped.* I heard his voice, not just through my ears but through my bones. I was granted this, that I could feel and smell and see him and know, for sure, that this, *this* was the last time. The last moment of words.

And then I gave a little gasp as I saw what happened next: *I don't know how I feel anymore,* I said.

But this did not perturb him; being dead seemed to lend a calm detachment, perhaps signaling a variety of spiritual progress unknown to us, the living. He just held me closer. *The best thing I ever did was to marry you and give my children the mother they have. The biggest gift you gave me was those kids. All I can give you is the promise I will never interfere.*

What do you mean? I don't understand.

It doesn't matter. You may not understand this now or ever, but I swear to you I will never interfere. After everything that happened and how things turned out, I have nothing else to give to prove my love. I leave them in your capable hands. I can do no more. I can do no more than this. I will never interfere. This is my solemn vow.

Suddenly I was flooded with my marriage, the old one, the real one. The mists cleared; I stood on the curb in Springfield, Illinois, holding my cell phone as he asked me to marry him, and high up across the pale blue sky, over the Sangamon County Courthouse, the word came, flying past the gold-tipped dome shining in the sun, unfurling itself as it flew over the leafy crowns of trees and arrived before me, and inside me, and emerged from my throat: *Yes.*

I'd recovered the *Yes,* the beginning, and, having done that, I could now countenance the end. With my own two hands I could bend those points in an arc until they met and joined, the gap was bridged, and *hello* and *goodbye* became one.

John had been paying attention. And he'd waited for the right time. He'd waited to see what I'd do with the truth. He waited for that moment, the moment with Grace, when, with dignity and innocence, I'd said the right thing. He knew me well, but he'd had to make sure. And then he came down from the mountain. He came down from the hill, not just from beyond the evergreens but from whatever lay beyond that. His bargain, though, had not been with me; his real bargain lay elsewhere. From out of the mystery he'd walked down from the woods to complete that exchange, by making this vow, and not for his own benefit alone but for the benefit of his children, in so doing finally establishing his place in the world. He'd found his own lost music. He'd found his own voice, only to willingly silence it. Goodbye was hello—was goodbye.

Then I realized I'd given him something too: My gift to him was not abandoning him. We stood there together on the brink of a new and different future, in which this reciprocity possessed a potentially profound and far-reaching significance. We stood there, like Grace and the bear, in that space between something about to happen and it happening.

And then it did.

He released the embrace and moved away. It didn't hurt, because it had been a very long time that satisfied us both, a time that encompassed not just our marriage but our entire lives, even before we'd met. He retreated toward the wooded ridge while facing me the whole time. He wasn't turning his back on me because I hadn't turned my back on him. Though the distance increased, we were still together, looking into each other's eyes, as closely as if we were dancing, as closely as the moment of Grace's birth, when those perfect and living figures encircled and wove about us, and we stood in the harmonic, in the unity of time, and delivered her together. Then he was gone.

I stood now outside of the house of my marriage, alone. Peace crept in, followed by a slight sense of bewilderment: I was starting over again now for real, and without a compass. I'd have to forge a new one—forge myself into a new and stronger metal. Monroe had told me this would happen. And forgiveness was the order of the day if I wanted to get things done. I didn't need to be perfect; I just had to pay attention. I sat down beside the creek and trailed my fingers in running water I could not catch, but as it purled along, I heard its voice: *It's all right if you don't know the words. You may not always know the words, but you know the music well and sing it beautifully.*

A bubble appeared deep inside me. Something was born. It floated up my spine. I'd been hiding, inside my body, way down at my feet, but when this bubble appeared, I climbed atop and floated up. It was my mending heart, no longer smashed on the floor of the hotel lobby. When it reached my chest, it anchored there yet didn't stop, it kept going, welled up and out into the world, tremendous and shivering with light, transparent but with a rainbow sheen. And with this enormous, mended heart, I created a new world, in the way that mothers do, in the way that lovers do, by force of will I created it: a world where no one was alone, where all, not some, held hands, where laws of gravity could be reversed and downward falls arc upward into flights of butterflies, and in that world I changed the tune to this: Hello was goodbye was hello.

If everything that was, and is, and ever shall be is at this moment present, then that includes the rainbow in the stone. The rainbow in the stone was always there. This was the song my mother taught me, and my grandmother, indeed, all my grandmothers and grandfathers down to the very first note, the very first word. It braided me into the root of the earth. Time held no fear or sway; rather, I was crowned with it.

Hello was goodbye was hello. All the notes of the scale settled into place, and the air was bright and clean. I went back to my house, back to my children. I had all the time in the world.

Epilogue

The Rainbow in the Stone

"Mom!" a deep baritone voice called behind me.

I turned to see Jack standing at the top of the steps to Elmwood's dock with his hands in the pockets of his dress suit. He gave his head a little toss in the direction of the house.

"Mom! She wants you now."

She wants you. Music to my ears.

I made my way up the hill to the mobile bride's room on the old tennis court. Grace had heard the story and wanted the same, except that she called it a "pop-up," so her aunt Karen had obliged. Inside the trailer, the bride was standing very still, eyes closed, while my sister-in-law, Cassie, camera in hand, made a few adjustments to the veil.

"Is that you, Mom? Are you here?"

I reached out and gently captured her hand with both of mine, as Miss Lindgren had done all those years ago at Eastridge— helping her discover her voice and start on her own road, so different from mine. "I'm here," I said. "And I brought your 'something old.'" Grace opened her eyes and looked down at the tiny black stone in her palm.

"Oh, *Mom*. The rainbow stone. It's the rainbow in the stone." She closed her hand over it reverently. "I totally forgot about it!

From when we went to see the Elwha after the dam came down… Easter, that year. *That* year." She opened her hand. "And then…I gave it to you."

"I've had it a long time. It's your turn again."

I looked out the open door, down the hill to our little lake. My mother once told me: *The past is just the present of another day.* If that were true, then the same could be said of the future. That through all the seasons of my young life here at Elmwood, all the countless summer days of jumping off the dock, today— my daughter's wedding day—was present then: a tiny reflected gleam on those wavelets, a barely visible wisp like a bird on the wing, or the brightness limning a small, lone cloud on the western horizon. *The present is the future of the past.* And this was what I'd added to the songs my mother taught me, the songs I'd taught my children.

Karen was right: My mother had been hard on me because she saw herself in me. She, too, had a questioning mind, tried to understand the "why," longed for the universe of lost answers when bereft of her father, then her husband. Even as a young woman—singing arias in her beautiful mezzo, standing in the living room in her apron while we played quietly upstairs—she, too, had been striving for the harmonic. She knew it was the only way to return to lost time. *I prefer the poetic to the merely literal.* This is the song my mother taught me: Time is a river, and the river has music, sometimes harsh, sometimes plaintive, sometimes joyful. You can be haunted by waters, or buoyed by them. But if you listen closely, if you pay attention, you can dance to the music of time, and acquit yourself with grace.

We stepped out of the trailer. On the porch, our family milled quietly about in subdued but happy expectation. Behind my mother in her wheelchair stood Nathan with his wife, holding their baby daughter in the crook of her arm. Behind this little downy cornsilk head, and seemingly emanating from its aura, was another: my late grandmother's, with the same cornsilk hair in a braid wrapped around her head. She stepped out, in the powder-blue suit I'd imagined her in at my own wedding here, years ago, and laid a hand on my daughter-in-law's arm. As I watched, she raised her other in a curious gesture; at the same time, my mother sat forward and mirrored it exactly. Was it hail or farewell? Come or go? Hurry up, or slow down? I turned to look at the long winding drive that led through the woods to the road, then back. Impatiently, they motioned again, and I realized: *Go on!*

Grace turned. We stood there for a moment, beaming at each other, and I fingered the butterflies on the edge of her veil. My only daughter had, long ago, on her own, gone beyond the evergreens. Perhaps, unlike me at her age, she was fully equipped and needed nothing more. But I had my instructions.

"Let's take a little walk now," I said. "It's a tradition. Did I ever tell you the story about when your dad proposed to me on the road? After I moved from Tulsa with your brother, when he was two? I left Tulsa in a cloud of butterflies…"

I took her hand and led the way.